FOREST OF THE HANGED

FOREST OF THE HANGED

by
Liviu Rebreanu

CASEMATE | uk
Oxford & Philadelphia

Published in Great Britain and
the United States of America in 2017 by
CASEMATE PUBLISHERS
The Old Music Hall, 106–108 Cowley Road, Oxford OX4 1JE, UK
and

1950 Lawrence Road, Havertown, PA 19083, USA

© Casemate Publishers 2017

Series adviser: Elly Clark

Paperback Edition: ISBN 978-1-61200-468-6
Digital Edition: ISBN 978-1-61200-469-3 (epub)

A CIP record for this book is available from the British Library

Printed in the Czech Republic by FINIDR
Typeset in India by Lapiz Digital Services, Chennai

For a complete list of Casemate titles, please contact:

CASEMATE PUBLISHERS (UK)
Telephone (01865) 241249
Fax (01865) 794449
Email: casemate-uk@casematepublishers.co.uk
www.casematepublishers.co.uk

CASEMATE PUBLISHERS (US)
Telephone (610) 853-9131
Fax (610) 853-9146
Email: casemate@casematepublishing.com
www.casematepublishing.com

In remembrance of my brother Emil, who was hanged by the Hungarians on the Rumanian front in the year 1917.

L. R.

BOOK I

UNDER the ashen autumn sky, which resembled a giant bell of smoked glass, the brand-new gallows reared its head defiantly on the outskirts of the village and stretched its arm with the halter towards the dark plain, dotted here and there with copper-leaved trees. Superintended by a short, dark-skinned corporal and assisted by a peasant with a hairy, red face, two old soldiers were busy digging a grave. They spat frequently into the palms of their hands, and groaned with fatigue after each stroke with the pickaxe. From the wound in the earth the diggers threw out yellow, sticky clay.

The corporal twirled his moustaches and stared contemptuously around him. The scenery oppressed him, though he tried not to show his vexation. On the right stretched the military cemetery, ringed in by barbed wire, with its graves arranged as if on parade, the white crosses new and uniform. On the left, a few steps away, began the villagers' cemetery, overgrown with nettles, gateless, the crosses sparse, broken and rotten. It looked as if no dead had been buried there for years, and as if none would ever be buried there again.

The village Zirin, headquarters of the infantry division, hid itself under a pall of smoke and fog, through which the scattered, leafless trees, the few thatched roofs, and the church tower, split by a shell, poked their timid heads. On the north side the ruins of the station and of the railway line blocked the view like a dyke without beginning and without end. The highroad, marked out in a straight line on the dreary plain, came from the west, passed through the village and ran right out to the front.

"What an ugly country you have, Muscovite!" said the corporal, suddenly turning towards the diggers and casting a baleful glance at the peasant, who had stopped to breathe. "Do you hear? Country . . . places . . . *niet* pretty!" he added, pointing at the landscape and raising his voice to make himself better understood.

The peasant stared at him with perplexed eyes and, smiling humbly, muttered something in Russian.

"He doesn't understand our tongue, corporal," volunteered one of the soldiers, straightening his spine.

"Well, it isn't their fault, anyhow, that theirs is such a rotten country," said the other soldier, leaning on his spade.

All three soldiers now stared very contemptuously at the peasant, who, not understanding the foreign words, bent shamefacedly over the yellow hole, which had now a depth of about half a metre.

"Here, what do you mean by stopping, you lazy beggars!" exclaimed the corporal all of a sudden, remembering his duty. "Call this a grave? Aren't you ashamed of yourselves? The convoy will be here in a minute and the grave isn't ready. Or is it that you want me to get into trouble? Now then, you, put your back into it and stop gaping at me!"

"You're right, corporal," mumbled one of the soldiers, tackling a huge lump with his pickaxe. "But that's not army work, corporal. . . . To think that we should have come to be grave-diggers. . . . Well . . "

The men fell to work with a will, and the corporal, appeased, answered once more in quite a friendly tone:

"A soldier's duty in war-time is to do any job that comes to hand. That's why war is war. Here, or at the front, or in the hospital, it's all in the war. Why don't you say instead how lucky we were to be delayed. . . . What on earth should we have done with ourselves if we had arrived at four as the orders were? We should have been jolly fed up, all of us. . . . But I'll say one thing: I am an old soldier, but never till now have I heard of people being hanged like that, almost in the dark."

He broke off abruptly. His eyes had fallen on the gallows, whose arm seemed to threaten the men standing in the grave. And just then the halter began to-swing gently. The corporal, with a cold shudder, turned his head away quickly, but his eye fell on the straight line of white crosses in the military cemetery and, greatly agitated, he left-about-turned, only to face the graves in the village cemetery. Fear gripped him as if he had come face to face with ghosts. He recovered his self-control quickly, however, and, spitting to show his disgust, muttered:

"What a life this is! . . . Wherever you look, there is nothing but the dead and the graves of the dead."

An autumn wind, damp and dreary, began to blow from the direction of the village, swallowed in fog, carrying on its wings echoes of unending moans. The unutterable loneliness, which seemed to drop from the grey sky, oppressed the corporal so much that he stood there as if turned to stone, staring at the church tower and so lost to his surroundings that he did not notice that an officer was approaching on the road leading to the cemetery. He only roused himself when he heard the sound of footsteps. Startled, he turned to the grave-diggers and said, his voice still hoarse with uneasiness:

"Hurry up, boys, an officer is coming. . . . The convoy won't be long now. . . . Phew! If only we could finish and be done with it! . . . Say what one will, this is not work fit for soldiers. . . ."

The officer approached unsteadily. The wind fluttered the flaps of his top-coat and seemed to drive him towards an undesired goal. He was of middle height and had a little beard, which gave him the appearance of a militiaman, though he did not appear older than about thirty-five. Under the rather wide-brimmed steel helmet his round, fair face looked troubled, the large, brown, protruding eyes were fixed apprehensively, in an unblinking stare, on the gallows. He seemed to find a morbid, insatiable interest in it. His mouth, with its full lips, drooped tremulously. His hands hung limp.

Noisily clicking together the heels of his heavy boots, the corporal saluted and stood at attention. The officer stopped a few paces away, nodded slightly, and, with his eyes still on the halter, asked:

"For what time is the execution fixed?"

"It was fixed for four o'clock, sir, may you live long," answered the corporal in so loud a voice that the captain threw him a quick glance. "But I see it is five now and they haven't arrived yet."

"I see, I see . . ." muttered the captain, looking down on the diggers, who were digging away silently, their heads bent towards the earth. He then asked in a firmer tone: "And whom are you going to hang?"

"We couldn't say, sir," said the corporal, rather confused. "There are rumours that it is an officer, but we don't know for sure."

"And for what crime?" demanded the officer, staring at him almost angrily.

The corporal, more and 'more abashed, answered hesitatingly, with a smile of bitter compassion:

"Well, sir, how can we know? In war-time a man's life is like a flower, its petals fall off and leave us wondering why. The Lord has made us very sinful, and mortals are not forgiving."

The captain stared hard at him, as if he were surprised at his words, and asked no more questions. He looked up and, his eyes having caught sight of the gallows, he drew back a few paces as if from a threatening foe. At that moment from the road leading to the village a harsh, commanding voice called out:

"Corporal! Ready, corporal?"

"Ready, sir!" shouted the corporal, turning round smartly, his hand at the salute.

The lieutenant, with the grey fur collar of his trench-coat turned up, came along quickly, almost at a run, talking all the time.

"Is everything ready, corporal? The convoy is on the way and will be here in a few moments. Where is the sergeant-major? Why has he not come on first? If I, who am not directly concerned in this, could take the trouble to come along, surely . . ."

He broke off abruptly on catching sight of the unknown captain, who was looking at him uneasily. The lieutenant saluted and, advancing to the margin of the grave, exclaimed excitedly:

"The stool, corporal! Where is it? Why are you staring at me like a fool? What is the condemned man to stand on? What men! Such indifference I have never met! If need be, you'll have to dig me out a stool from the bowels of the earth! Now then, look alive! What are you gaping at?"

The corporal set off for the village at a run, and the lieutenant, with a side look at the captain, who was standing apart, went on more calmly:

"With men of that type, we'll certainly not beat Europe. Where there is no sense of duty . . ."

While he was speaking he crossed over to the fir-wood stake and stood under the now motionless halter. He examined the grave and, displeased, muttered something. Then, looking up, he caught hold of the rope above his head with both hands, as if he wished to test its strength, but, meeting the scared gaze

13

of the captain, he let go the halter, confused and abashed. He stood where he was for a few seconds undecided, then, making up his mind, he went up quickly to the stranger and introduced himself.

"Lieutenant Apostol Bologa."

"Klapka," put in the captain with hand outstretched, "Otto Klapka. I have just arrived from the Italian front. At the station I heard that you were having an execution, and, I don't quite know how, I found my way here."

The captain's voice was so obviously nervous that the lieutenant, much against his will, again felt ashamed and, to hide his embarrassment, said with forced heartiness:

"Then you have been transferred to our division?"

"Yes, to the 50th Field Artillery."

"Ah, our own regiment!" exclaimed Bologa, really pleased this time. "Welcome!"

The captain's face cleared. It seemed as if the lieutenant's open-heartedness had brought to light a new man. They exchanged a look of sympathy. A short silence, then Klapka shuddered and asked nervously:

"Whom are you hanging?"

In Apostol Bologa's blue and deep-set eyes there flashed an odd look of pride. He answered with barely restrained indignation:

"A Czech sub-lieutenant, Svoboda; all the more shame for the officer fraternity. He was caught just as he was about to go over to the enemy with maps and plans in his pocket. Shameful and revolting, isn't it?" he added after a short silence, as Klapka had said nothing.

"H'm . . . yes . . . perhaps"; the captain started and answered uncertainly.

This ambiguous answer made Bologa obstinately determined to convince him, and he began to talk with a volubility that one could see was not natural to him.

"I had the honour to be a member of the court martial which judged and condemned him. As a matter of fact, he did not even deny it. Not that it would have made any difference; in face of the undeniable proofs any sort of defence would have been useless. He did not open his mouth during the whole proceedings, and would not even answer the President's questions. He looked at each of us in turn defiantly, with a sort of superb contempt. Even the death sentence he received with a smile and a look in his eyes like. . . like . . . Of course, not even an infamous death terrifies that type of man. When a patrol led by an officer caught him, he tried to shoot himself. What clearer proof of guilt could there be than that attempt to commit suicide? The court condemned him unanimously, without discussion, so obvious was the crime. I myself, although I am usually inclined to waver, feel in this case that my conscience is perfectly satisfiedabsolutely satisfied."

Disconcerted more especially by the harshness of the young man's tone, Klapka muttered:

"Oh, my God . . . proofs . . . when it's a question of a man's life!"

The thin, colourless lips of the lieutenant curled with a mixture of irony and contempt.

"You forget, sir, that it is war-time and that we are at the front! One cannot consider a man's life when the life of one's country is in jeopardy. If we allowed sentimental considerations to influence us, we would have to capitulate all round. One can see that you are a reserve officer, otherwise you would not speak thus of a crime. . . .

"Yes, that's true enough," Klapka made haste to agree nervously. "I was a lawyer in time of peace. Now, however . . ."

"I also am a reserve officer," interrupted the lieutenant with pride. "The war snatched me from the midst of my studies at the University, where I had almost lost touch with real life, but it did not take me long to wake up, and now I realize that war is the real generator of energy."

The captain smiled as if he found the answer absurd, and said softly, with a tinge of quiet irony:

"Really? I had always thought that war was a destroyer of energy!"

Apostol Bologa blushed like a girl and avoided the captain's eye; he felt fearfully ill at ease and tried to find a harsh answer to put an end to the conversation. Just then the gasping corporal returned with the stool.

"Excuse me, sir!" exclaimed Bologa, relieved, turning to the perspiring corporal as if the latter were bringing him salvation. "It is too high, can't you see?" he shouted angrily. "How is the prisoner to climb on that? But really I don't see why I should worry about it, for I am not responsible for the execution. . . . You must listen to what the general will have to say to you, and mind you remember his words! What on earth are you waiting for now? Get a move on and try to put things straight. . . . Pull up that rope a bit. . . . What beings!"

He raised both hands, revolted, and turned his back on them. But he immediately calmed down at sight of a group of officers who, with very solemn demeanour, were approaching from the direction of the village. At their head walked the C.O. of the division, small and fat, with very short legs and a very red face. He kept on striking the leg of his boot with a riding-whip, while he listened to something that the military prosecutor—a captain with a big belly and grey moustaches—was explaining, while gesticulating widely with the right hand, in which he held a sheet of paper.

"The convoy is coming—look, and the general also!" whispered Bologa with a quick wink at the captain, who drew back as from an unexpected vision.

The lieutenant ran to meet the general and, saluting, reported importantly:

"I happened to get here earlier, Excellency, and I noticed that there was no stool."

"No stool?" repeated the general with a dissatisfied glance at the prosecutor, who was desperately trying to catch Bologa's eye.

"But I at once took measures to remedy this," added the lieutenant hastily to relieve the confused prosecutor.

Nevertheless, the prosecutor felt that the general was annoyed and, muttering an apology, he hastened his steps so as to arrive first at the place of execution and see how his orders had been carried out. One quick glance showed him that all seemed ready, and without taking the slightest notice of the corporal, who was still standing at the salute like a petrified figure, he was about to turn smilingly to the general, who had almost caught him up, when suddenly a thought struck him, and he asked in a worried voice:

"Where's the executioner, corporal?"

"We don't know, sir," answered the corporal. "We had orders to dig the grave and . . ."

"What do you mean by saying you don't know, you fool?" exclaimed the prosecutor, really disturbed. Then he shouted angrily: "Where's the sergeant-major? What has the sergeant-major done about it? Sergeant-major! . . . Imagine, Excellency, we have no executioner!" he added, now completely flurried, turning to the general, who had just come up to the grave. "In vain I take all the required measures; the men have no sense of duty. . . ."

A sergeant-major with an ashen face came running up at full speed and halted tremblingly at the side of the gallows.

"What have you been up to, you rascal? Where's the executioner?" the prosecutor shouted at him, and, grinding his teeth, added: "I'll . . . I'll . . ."

"Thirty days' confinement!" barked, the general, stroking his left moustache and cracking his whip. "A man, however, will be wanted at once . . ."

"Corporal, you'll act as executioner!" broke in the prosecutor quickly, somewhat relieved.

"Sir, I beg with all submission to be excused," mumbled the corporal, turning pale. "I beg you, sir, with all submission . . ."

The prosecutor did not even listen to what he was saying; he had again turned to the general and, as a kind of indirect excuse, began to complain of and to bemoan the lack of sense of duty amongst the men. The general, however, with restrained indignation, cut him short:

"We'll talk later. . . . Now to our duty!"

On the grey road in the rapidly descending twilight the body of the convoy swung slowly nearer. The condemned man, wrapped in a greenish cloak, with collar turned up, and wearing a civilian's hat on his bent head, walked mechanically, leaning on the arm of an old chaplain. Four soldiers with fixed bayonets surrounded the two. Groups of officers and soldiers followed. These had been brought back purposely from the front to witness the execution. All were dressed in dirty uniforms smelling strongly of the trenches, and were wearing their steel helmets. They came on in a thin, straggly line just as they pleased, and the tail end of the convoy almost touched the outskirts of the village.

Under the gallows, the corporal, anxious-eyed, stood stock-still waiting, while the sergeant-major told him in a whisper what he had to do.

The moist wind had gathered force and was now sweeping the ground, whirling round the graves of the cemeteries and buffeting the men who were approaching.

The priest with the condemned man halted at the margin of the grave. A slight shudder shook the latter at the sight of the sticky yellow clay.

"God is good and great," the scared priest mumbled into his ear, holding up the crucifix to the prisoner's lips.

"To the other side, Father, please!" came again from the prosecutor, whose voice sounded strained and hoarse. "These things must be done in accordance with the regulations. . . . Sergeant-major, attention! Don't you know your business?"

The pace of the convoy increased as at a word of command and in a few minutes the men had formed a circle round the gallows. They were all silent, as if afraid of disturbing the sleep of a sick man, worn out with suffering. The sound of impatient footsteps mingled with the moans of the insistent wind.

"Doctor, doctor, will it last long ?" whispered Apostol Bologa, seizing the arm of the doctor, who was endeavouring to make his way through the closely huddled circle of soldiers.

"You'll see. . . . There's no time now to . . ." the doctor replied in a worried voice. "Make way there! Good God! Now then, boys, let me through, will you?"

Bologa had managed to slip through in the wake of the doctor until he had reached the foot of the grave opposite the gallows. His throat was parched, a bitter taste filled his mouth, and the excitement within him was almost painful. He felt glad that he would be able to see it all, and in order to calm his impatience, he looked round, seeking acquaintances and friends amongst the many war-strained faces frowning under the weight of the steel helmets.

The general stood only a few paces away, dour and immovable. A little farther on, Lieutenant Gross, greatly agitated, followed with desperate attention every movement of the prisoner, who had been a good friend of his. Seeing Gross, Bologa remembered the foreign captain of a little while ago and discovered him standing not far behind the general, his chin resting in his hand and his figure as immovable as a statue.

"What a man!" thought Bologa with annoyance. "He comes here straight from the station and wants to teach me humanitarianism as if I were a savage beast or . . ."

At that moment a hand caught hold of his arm.

"Ah, Cervenco!" murmured Bologa, looking round. "You here? I am surprised. . . . I am sure you did not come of your own free will. Did you know that I was on the court martial?"

Captain Cervenco was prevented from answering by the voice of the prosecutor, which, sharper and harsher even than heretofore, barked:

"Everybody fall back three paces! Make room! Make room!"

The spectators, startled by the noise which dared to break the silence, hastened to fall back a few steps. Only the general remained in the cleared space round the margin of the grave. Standing by the stake, the condemned man, with a look of exaltation in his eyes, stared straight in front of him at the embankment, which cut off the view. Bologa, with a tight feeling at his heart, now looked straight into his large, burning, dark eyes. And he saw the man under the halter turn to the priest and heard him say very clearly:

"I want to die more quickly."

The general knitted his bushy eyebrows and said to the prosecutor:

"See what he wants."

But the prisoner now raised his eyes above the heads of the people and did not even seem to hear the prosecutor's question. The latter, vainly waiting for an answer, suddenly called out, with a nervous ring in his voice:

"Ready? Then . . . yes . . . then . . ."

And, looking uneasily at the general, he moved on to the heap of freshly dug clay at the side of the grave, smoothed out the sheet of paper, which had become crumpled in his hand, and read out the sentence of the court martial of that division, which condemned Lieutenant Svoboda to death by hanging for treason and desertion to the enemy. His voice sounded hollow and unnatural; he stumbled over the words, which drew each time a sharp glance from the general, and at the end his voice was as hoarse as if he had yelled with all his strength a whole day.

With flushed face, Apostol Bologa stared tensely at the prisoner. He could hear his own heart throb wildly, and the helmet on his head felt as tight as if it had been a few sizes too small for him and had been forced on. An unaccountable amazement filled his mind, for while the prosecutor was reading out the crimes from the sheet which trembled between his fingers, the face of the lieutenant under the halter had come to life, and the radiant and confident eyes seemed to look right into the next world. At first this look disconcerted and angered Bologa, but presently he felt distinctly the flame from the condemned man's eyes shoot into his heart like a painful

21

reproach. He tried to look away, but the eyes, which looked so contemptuously at death and were beautified by so great a love, fascinated him. And tensely he waited for the prisoner to open his mouth and utter one of those terrible cries of deliverance which the early Christian martyrs were wont to utter at the point of death, when the vision of Christ was vouchsafed to them.

The prosecutor folded the sheet quickly, slipped it into his pocket and muttered something inaudible. The sergeant- major approached the prisoner and whispered very humbly:

"Allow me . . . the cloak."

Svoboda, without looking at him, slipped off the cloak at once and remained in a civilian's suit with a turned-down collar which left bare his long, slim, white throat. Then he took off his hat, smoothed the hair on his forehead, and kissed passionately the crucifix in the hand of the priest, crossing himself the while quickly. Then he looked about, slightly dazed now, as if he had forgotten something. Then, with a flash of joy, he remembered, and mounted the stool near the fir stake. With his shining eyes and his white, radiant face, he looked as if he were about to announce to the world a great victory.

"Go on, man, don't be afraid," muttered the trembling sergeant-major to the little corporal, taking him by the shoulders and pushing him gently towards the prisoner.

The corporal approached hesitatingly, not knowing what to do. He looked back over his shoulder, and, at a sign from his superior, stretched up his arms towards the halter.

"Off with the tunic!" barked the general in a voice of thunder. "A soldier in uniform may not act as executioner!"

A minute later the corporal, now in his shirt-sleeves, and bare-headed like another prisoner, once more stretched out his hands towards the rope. Meanwhile, however, Svoboda had of his own accord slipped the noose over his head, as if he were merely trying on an unaccustomed collar.

"Pull the stool away!" whispered again the sergeant-major.

The corporal snatched the stool clumsily from under the prisoner's feet. The arm of the gallows creaked and the body began to twirl in trying to find a support. In the eyes the strange radiant light blazed in quick flashes, which seemed to grow brighter and brighter. Bologa could see the eyes swell and turn purple, but they kept their spiritual brightness, as if death itself could not put it out or destroy it.

The sergeant-major said something again to the corporal, who rushed forward desperately and with both hands seized the twitching feet of the hanging man.

"Let go!" shouted the horrified prosecutor. "Stand back! What are you doing?"

The doctor at Apostol Bologa's side stood, watch in hand, waiting. It was getting darker and darker. The wind had stopped abruptly, like a runner who comes suddenly upon a precipice. Then the silence which followed was pierced through and through by a long-drawn moan like a call. . . . Bologa was the only one who turned round to look, and he saw a soldier, whose face bore the scar of a bad wound, with the tears streaming down his cheeks, moaning with pity. He wished to sign to him to stop, but when he saw the flash of tears in the eyes of others around him, he became confused, and the roof of his mouth went dry.

"Why does that soldier moan?" he thought to himself, trying to think calmly. But even as the thought passed through his mind, his eyes again met the eyes of the man on the gallows, and he saw that the light which had shone in them a minute ago so bravely and confidently was now struggling desperately with the coming darkness.

A few minutes passed. The hanging body had long since stopped twitching. The twilight covered the whole earth with a black pall.

"What are we doing here, doctor?" suddenly burst out the general bearishly. "Can't you see it's dark?"

"Our duty, Excellency," answered the doctor quietly, his eyes on his watch.

"What duty! Make your declaration! That's *your* duty!" said the general roughly.

The doctor shrugged his shoulders, drew nearer the stake and felt the hanging man's pulse, then muttered:

"He died quicker than is usual, as if he had been tired of living."

"We don't want comments," stormed the general. "The result!"

"Excellency, the prisoner has expired," reported the doctor, saluting.

"Now? What?" asked the general, impatiently turning to the agitated prosecutor.

"Excellency, the sentence has been carried out!" answered the prosecutor hastily, clapping his heels together like a zealous recruit.

The general had come on purpose to make a speech on desertion to the enemy, and more especially on the punishment which would be mercilessly meted out to all those who forgot the duty of a soldier. But now he felt too tired and was no longer inclined for speeches.

"Then we had better go," he muttered, and turned so swiftly that the men had barely time to draw back and make way for him.

The prosecutor quickly gave the necessary orders to the sergeant-major and then ran after the general to explain to him that the hitches which had occurred were entirely due to the lack of sense of duty amongst the men. All the others followed in the wake of the general, and the plain re-echoed with the sound of many feet. Only Apostol Bologa seemed rooted to the spot, his eyes fixed on the hanging man, whose coat-tails flapped in the wind.

"Poor fellow!" suddenly said the tear-filled voice of Captain Cervenco, close to Bologa.

"What? What do you say?" asked Bologa, jumping, and added immediately, to hide his emotion: "Why 'poor fellow'? Why should . . .?"

But he did not finish, nor did he wait for the captain's answer. He set off on the road towards the village as if he were afraid that the night would catch him there. Thirty paces on he caught up Klapka.

"Well, did you like it, philosopher?" asked the captain with a gentle reproach in his voice.

"Sir, punishment—crime—the law . . ." stuttered Apostol Bologa, upset by the captain's question.

"Yes, yes, but still . . . a human being!" muttered Klapka darkly.

"Human being . . . human being . . . human being . . ." repeated Bologa, shivering.

The darkness around them had increased considerably. Bologa looked back over his shoulder. On the plain, as far as the eye could see, black silhouettes moved hither and thither like restless phantoms. Only the gallows shone white, indifferent, amongst the white crosses in the military cemetery.

Bologa shivered again. An icy feeling clutched at his heart. He whispered fearfully:

"What darkness, Oh God, what darkness covers the earth . . ."

His voice trailed like the song of a sick man and died away in the moans of the wind.

§ II

The darkness gripped the straggly village, in which there dwelt to-day more enemy soldiers than civilians. The dark houses kept an anxious watch over the wide unballasted road, full of holes and deeply rutted by the thousands of wagons which passed unceasingly on their way to the front, loaded with provisions for the men, and always returned loaded with the wreckage of battles. . . . Here and there shone an eye of yellow sickly light which meant headquarters, hospitals, and taverns.

Cursing and swearing, the men coming from the execution floundered into the large puddles.

Apostol Bologa walked silently at the side of the foreign captain. He continually tried to increase his pace in order to separate himself from this distrustful fellow, who seemed to reproach him even when he did not speak. But in some odd way he expected him every moment to make some momentous statement, and he was so annoyed that the other kept his lips tightly closed that he felt like screaming. . . . And the damp, overwhelming night tightened its iron grip more and more pitilessly round his heart.

Then, opposite a house with lighted windows, the sound of the general's voice reached their ears. Klapka started and said: "I stop here . . . to . . ."

Bologa did not answer, did not even salute, but went on more quickly, relieved and glad to be free of him and fearful lest he should call him back, just as if the captain were directly responsible for the burden which weighed down his soul. Soon he turned off into a narrow little street and entered the yard of the reed hut where he was quartered. From an outhouse at the back came the strains of a mournful song. It angered him that his orderly should be in a singing mood just then. Nevertheless, he listened awhile, thinking: "It's a Rumanian song. . . ." He opened his mouth to shout for Petre, but changed his mind and hastily walked into the passage. He could not find the door of the room and that infuriated him. "He sings instead of . . ." On a table in the room a lamp, with smoke-blackened chimney, was burning with a sickly flame. Bologa threw his helmet on the chest and flung himself on the bed, where he lay full length on his back, his hands on his breast, his eyes fixed on the cracked and blackened ceiling. He felt terribly done up, as if he had been engaged on some very exhausting work.

"I'll rest until mess-time and try to make my mind a blank," he said to himself, yawning and closing his eyes. But immediately, from all the hidden places in his brain, thoughts swooped down on him like birds of prey, and in his ears the orderly's song sounded as clear and loud as if he had been singing under his window. Dismayed, he reopened his eyes. The thought passed through his mind that he ought to call Petre after all, to tell him that to-morrow at dawn they were going back to the front, and that he was to be careful not to leave any of their things behind. . . . Simultaneously he realized that he was afraid to remain alone with his own thoughts, and he made answer to himself: "My conscience is quite clear. . . ." And immediately, as if they had been waiting for this, dozens of arguments sprang up in his mind, all tending to prove Svoboda's guilt. Undoubtedly the fellow had tried to desert and turn traitor, therefore he, who, by chance, had been called upon to try and condemn him, had nothing to reproach himself with, nothing at all. . . . Nevertheless, while he was listening to these soothing justifications, there appeared on the ceiling with the blackened rafters, at first only like indistinct circles of light and then more and more clearly, the eyes of the man under the halter, with their proud and disquieting look which had been like an appeal and in whose strange fire the string of arguments melted helplessly.

"Will that Petre never leave off? Why doesn't he leave off?" he thought presently, closing his eyes again and wearily giving up the struggle.

Now nothing but the song which the soldier was singing floated through his brain, sweet and soothing like a velvety caress, rousing whole strings of memories and wafting his soul on the wings of dreams, home to the little town of Parva on the banks of the Someş.

There stood the house he was born in, old and solid, right opposite the resplendent new church. From the flower-surrounded enclosure, through the branches of the walnut-trees planted on the day of his birth, one could see his father's tomb, ornamented with a cross of grey stone on which the name, carved in gilt letters, could be seen a long way off: Iosif Bologa.

The house had many rooms, filled with stiff old furniture in mixed styles, and there was a big courtyard, at the far end of which were outbuildings, and beyond this a garden which stretched right down to the Someş with its gurgling waters. This, with a few acres of fertile land, had been the dowry of Doctor Hogea's daughter. His grandfather had been the best doctor in Parva, and was also buried in the churchyard, where his tomb remained a lasting testimony to an honest life of hard work and to a worthy descendant of that prefect who had lived during the rebellion and the power of Avram Jancu. The happiest day in the old doctor's life had been the day on which his daughter had been married by the Protopop Groza to the lawyer, Iosif Bologa. He lived but a few months after the marriage of his only child.

Maria had well deserved her good fortune. She had been a good, steady, sensible girl with a great faith in God. Left motherless at an early age, she had been brought up in a boarding-school for young ladies in Sibiu. There, just when she was about to take the final sixth form examination, she met at the house of her head mistress Iosif Bologa, who, a week later, without saying a single word to her on the subject, wrote to Doctor Hogea, of Parva, and asked for her hand. A week after that her father appeared and informed her that the "great lawyer" loved her, and three days later they celebrated the betrothal at the very house of the head mistress, who bemoaned the fact that "Mariti" had not had the chance to finish her schooling. She was engaged for five months, until—after long and complicated negotiations with his future father-in-law—Iosif Bologa decided to move his lawyer's practice, which did not boast very many clients, from Sibiu to Parva. Thus Maria had had time to get used to the idea of marrying a man who, even after the betrothal, remained a stranger to her. Instead of love, she felt a scared respect for Bologa, partly due to the laudatory way in which her father always spoke of his future son-in-law.

Iosif Bologa was certainly not the type of man to satisfy the romantic dreams of a girl of seventeen. His hard, rugged face, with the deep-set eyes overshadowed by thick eyebrows, with the heavy chestnut moustache and square chin, blue from constant shaving, seemed to invite hate rather than love. Though he spoke little and was always serious, he had a deep, vibrant voice, proof of a kindly nature and of a soul that knew spiritual struggles. He was the eldest son of a poor priest in the Motzi district, in whose family the memory of their ancestor Grigore—a leader in Horia's[1] rebellion, who had eventually suffered death on the wheel at Alba-Iulia after the quelling of the peasants—remained as a trophy. In the soul of Iosif Bologa the remembrance of this heroic and martyred ancestor increased his zeal for hard work and set up an ideal. As soon as he had qualified as a lawyer he threw himself so wholeheartedly into politics that he succeeded in attaining the distinction of being the youngest person sentenced in the Memorandum[2] trial and of spending two years in the State prison.

Apostol was born just at the time when his father was awaiting his sentence at Cluj. Until his father's return from prison the child had known only a world surrounded by an idolizing maternal love. Deprived of love in early youth, Doamna[3] Bologa became entirely wrapped up in her child—so much so that her pious soul was at times filled with misgivings. Did she not perhaps love her child more than the Almighty? In order to appease her conscience, she took great pains to instil into little Apostol's heart a great love of God. Thus the child's first recollections were dominated by a kind, gentle, and forgiving Deity, who, in exchange for daily prayers, granted men pleasures on earth and everlasting happiness in Heaven. In his

---

[1] The Rumans of Transylvania and the Banat, having been deprived of their ancient privileges, rose under Horia, Closca and Crischanu in 1785. They were suppressed, but subsequently Joseph II declared the peasants free.

[2] At Hermannstadt, in July 1893, a Pan-Rumanian Congress drew up a memorandum of the grievances of the Rumanians in Transylvania. The Austrian Premier had twenty of the leaders tried and imprisoned on a charge of treason.

[3] Rumanian for "Mrs".

lively imagination the countenance of that Deity was somehow mixed up with that of Protopop Groza, who came to see them often, who always asked for news of "our martyr", and whose hand his mother always kissed.

His father's return effected a great change, a kind of revolution, in Apostol's life. The station platform was crowded with people, gentlefolk and peasants from the whole district. The child clung frantically to his mother's skirts, as if he were expecting some terrifying experience. Then the train came in and drew up with an ugly grinding noise. Bologa, dressed in black, bare-headed and with a long brown beard which he had grown in prison, descended from one of the carriages. For a moment or two he stared at the crowd on the platform, and then quickly made his way towards little Apostol. He picked the child up in his arms and kissed him noisily on both cheeks, while the people cheered. Terrified, the small boy began to cry and to struggle in the arms of the stranger, who was now listening to the speech of the Protopop and was trying to pacify his son by rocking him gently in his arms. Finally, as the little one's frightened sobs almost drowned the words of the speech of welcome, Bologa, enervated, felt obliged to hand him over to his mother, whose face had turned crimson from shame and emotion. In her arms Apostol became quiet, but he continued to stare fearfully at the gentleman with the brown beard.

That very evening Bologa had a solemn talk with his wife regarding the child's education. He enunciated in pompous phrases certain principles, quoted the names of several well-known educators, advising her to read their works, which he himself had read in prison with Apostol in mind, and, above all, begged her to bring energy, concentration, and firmness to her task.

"The child must understand right from the beginning that man's life is only of value if he follows an ideal!" added Bologa, rather touchingly. "Our parental responsibility is only just beginning. We must do our utmost to make a man of our boy."

Doamna Bologa wept and wrung her hands. . . . From her husband's speech she gathered that she was being asked to moderate her mother-love, to give up her petting and spoiling. Nevertheless, she gave in without a murmur. Bologa, fêted by everybody, a martyr with the halo of imprisonment and that impressive beard, seemed to her an unspeakably wise master, whose right it was to exact obedience and submission. So she resigned herself to loving her babe in secret and to keeping her caresses hidden from Bologa's eyes. On the other hand, she increased her religious instruction, and kept alight the faith in Apostol's heart. In this matter her husband left her a perfectly free hand; although he himself was not a believer, he included religion in education as a means for developing the imagination.

Apostol, subdued and timid, without playmates, felt deeply the stern atmosphere which his father imposed on the household. The fright of that first meeting remained imprinted on his heart, and he looked upon him as a stranger who had come to terrorize them. His only happy hours were those spent with his mother, when they were alone in the house or with Protopop Groza, who, being a childless widower, found pleasure in the company of the gentle and intelligent child. But over all the little boy's thoughts and fancies there hovered a mystic kind of love in which God was paramount.

When he was six years old another strange event made a deep impression on him. Doamna Bologa, thinking that the child would have to start school soon, talked the matter over at great length with the Protopop Groza, wondering what she could do to make this change less difficult for him. They both agreed that help from the Almighty would have to be asked. Finally, they decided to make Apostol say an "Our Father" on a certain day during Holy Mass. They made their preparations in great secrecy, in order that Bologa should not get wind of it and spoil their plan. At last, on the chosen day, the Bologas took their places as usual in the right-hand-side pew, and in front of them sat Apostol, dressed in new clothes, his eyes shining with excitement. Doamna Bologa, tearful and trembling, kept on crossing herself, and nervously fluttered the leaves of her prayer-book. Then, when the time for prayer had arrived, she bent over fearfully and whispered: "Now, my pet!" With head held high and firm tread, Apostol walked up to the altar, fell on his knees, and folded his hands. A moment later his thin voice floated like a white silken thread through the tense silence, rose upwards towards the star-sprinkled ceiling, and fell back among the hundreds assembled there. At first his eyes saw only Protopop Groza, who, from the altar, smiled at him kindly and encouragingly; afterwards he only saw the golden cross, which seemed to him to be floating in the air. Then, just as he was crossing himself at the end of the prayer, the sky seemed to open all of a sudden, and in the far distance, and yet so near that it seemed to be in his very soul, there appeared a curtain of white clouds in the midst of which shone the face of God like a golden light, dazzling, awe-inspiring and withal as full of tenderness as the face of a loving mother. And then from the midst of this divine radiance there emerged a living eye, infinitely kindly and magnanimous, which seemed to pierce all deep and hidden places. The vision lasted only a moment, but was so unutterably sweet that Apostol's heart stopped beating and his eyes filled with a strange, ecstatic light. He was so filled with happiness that he would have been glad to die there and then in the presence of the divine miracle. When he went back to his seat his face seemed changed and the blue eyes framed in the pale face were like two pools of light.

"Mummy, I have seen God!" murmured the child fervently, while Doamna Bologa vainly tried to stay her tears with her sopping handkerchief.

Apostol's vision gave rise to countless discussions in the Bologa household. The Protopop and Doamna Bologa were firmly convinced that God, as a special act of grace, had shown them by this means what path of life the boy was to follow. The lawyer, on the other hand, tried to prove to them that the whole "miracle" was merely the result of the child's religious exaltation. Finally, unable to convince them, Bologa lost his temper and accused them of endangering the well-being of his son by filling his impressionable mind with popish fantasies, and as he, the father, was responsible for Apostol's spiritual welfare, he forbade, once for all, such exhibitions in future.

Apostol did his elementary school work at home with his mother for teacher. Bologa cross-examined them both every Saturday with a severity that grew more and more rigorous, treating them as if they had been accomplices bent on deceiving him. Although Apostol was industrious, his father decreed that he was to go to the College at Nasaud, explaining that it was necessary for the child to come into contact with people and with the outside world. The truth was, however, that Bologa, displeased with the ultra-religious education which the child was receiving at home in spite of his instructions, wished to curb the evil while there was yet time.

They boarded him with the professor of mathematics, a good friend of Bologa's, in order that he might be well cared for and supervised as at home. After his parents had gone and he remained alone, Apostol was filled with a painful dread. He felt abandoned and exiled, strange and helpless. And he couldn't even weep for fear the children of the house should make fun of him. But at the very moment when he felt almost hopeless, he caught sight of a picture of Jesus Christ crucified, which hung on the wall, and his loneliness disappeared as if by magic. He was no longer alone. God had soothed his pain.

As Parva was not far from Nasaud, Doamna Bologa used to come over every month to see him and pet him. But now Apostol seemed cheerful and contented. He loved learning. At the end of the school year, when he came home for his holidays, he gleefully presented to his father a brilliant report.

"I congratulate you!" Bologa said to him after reading it carefully, shaking hands with him as with a friend of his own age.

That handshake made a curious impression on the boy. For the first time he felt that his father loved him. Until then he had thought that affection must needs be associated with tears and petting. Now he began to understand that affection could also be restrained and manly. So he also became more discreet in displaying his feelings. He liked to be considered a man. His best friends, Alexandru Palagiesu and Constantin Boteanu, were three or four years older than he.

When he had got through his fourth form and again brought his report home, his father thought it a fit opportunity to say a few serious words to him in the presence of his mother. After an introduction, peppered with Latin quotations, he reminded him of their heroic ancestor of Alba-Julia, and then went on speaking impressively :

"Henceforth, my son, you are a man. If it were necessary you are now in a position to earn your own living. In the

35

upper school your outlook will become wider. You will learn to understand many things as yet unknown to you, for life and the world are full of strange enigmas. You must ever try to win the respect of men, and more especially your own self-respect. Therefore spirit, thought, word, and deed in you should always be at one, for by this means only will you be able to obtain a stable equilibrium between your world and the outside world. Always do your duty like a man, whatever the cost, and never forget that you are a Rumanian!"

When Apostol was in the fifth form, about Christmas time, during a mathematics lesson, he was fetched out of class. In the passage he found their own coachman waiting for him, cap and whip in hand.

"What is it? What has happened?" asked Apostol agitatedly.

"It's all right, young master, everything is all right—but during the night the master died from heart failure, and the mistress has sent me along to fetch you home for the funeral. . . ."

Apostol wept unconsciously all the way to Parva. The funeral was imposing. Thousands of people followed the coffin to the grave, and many sorrowful speeches were made. Afterwards, for a few days, Apostol remained at his home. He no longer wept, but he would sit for hours staring at a photograph of his father in a stiff, truculent pose. (It had been taken at Cluj, just after the lawyer had been released from prison.) Up till now this photograph had always intimidated him. Now it filled him with remorse. All round him black-winged questions seemed to hover, and he did not dare to face them. He kept on telling himself that he had failed to appreciate his father, he recalled his severe admonishments, and he was haunted by a fear that something—he didn't know what or where—should crumble away. On the third day

Doamna Bologa, worried by his deep dejection, said to him gently and tenderly:

"You must not grieve so, darling. . . . It can't be helped. It was God's will."

"Why?" asked Apostol abruptly, staring at her vacantly.

His mother made some answer, but he gave no heed to her words, for even as he uttered that "Why?" something within his soul, some agelong structure with foundations strong as the roots of an oak, collapsed with a terrifying crash.

"I have lost God!" flashed through his mind. He closed his eyes as if by this means he would ward off the catastrophe. He felt clearly that he was slipping down into a bottomless pit and that he could not stop himself; there was nothing to which he could cling. All this took about a moment or even less and left him filled with a paralysing fear such as he might have experienced if he had found himself stranded alone at dead of night in an immense graveyard, without notion of direction.

He returned to Nasaud in a bewildered state of mind. His soul was torn by doubts, and he felt convinced that he had become an outcast. At first he had tried to build up a new house with the wreckage of the old, but he found that from under every stone a painful question would leap forth, a question for which he could find no answer. He soon wearied of these hopeless efforts with their continual torture. But presently there arose above everything else, like a victorious banner, the desire to find true answers to these perturbing questions.

As an undergraduate he spent his holidays arguing and disagreeing with his mother and Protopop Groza, who, remembering the vision he had had, wished to make him enter the Church. But Apostol turned a deaf ear at the bare mention of theology. He was nearly twenty now, tall, very slim, with a white,

LIVIU REBREANU

puckered brow, rather long chestnut-coloured hair brushed back from the face, and there was that in his appearance which brought to one's mind the young men of the beginning of the last century who had been ready to die for a dream. The more wildly his heart throbbed with eager desire to live, the more his mind tortured itself with unsolvable questions, and he actually suffered physically each time his search for a solution was arrested by the boundaries beyond which human knowledge has not yet penetrated. He became introspective, a dreamer with obstinate determinations. Doamna Bologa was wont to say, with a shade of regret, that he resembled his dead father, at which Apostol felt flattered, for the older he grew the more he admired his father's wisdom and tried with all his might to emulate him. When he saw that resistance without arguments would not convince his mother, and more especially Groza, he told them bluntly that he had ceased long ago to believe in God, and that consequently he could not possibly choose a profession which would be based on a lie.

The Protopop became very indignant and left the house without shaking hands with him. As for Doamna Bologa, she wept for a whole week, and prayed to the Almighty to turn her boy back again into the right path.

Apostol had determined long ago to take up philosophy. When the Protopop heard this his indignation increased, and in order to overcome the obstinacy of her erring son he advised Doamna Bologa to refuse him the financial means. The young undergraduate fumed. For several days running he had long consultations with his only friend in Parva, Alexandru Palagiesu, who had studied law and was now a full-blown lawyer waiting for the retirement of the old lawyer so that he should take his place. As a direct consequence of these confabulations,

Apostol ran over to Nasaud, consulted his quondam host and the head master of his college, with the result that he petitioned the Ministry of Education for a bursary from the State. Three weeks later the answer came; he had been granted a place in an endowed college in Budapest, which meant full board and lodging, and even a few crowns a month pocket-money.

At the University he met with expected and unexpected difficulties. He overcame them with enthusiastic courage. He learnt Hungarian and German in a few months, and so well that after his first examination he received congratulations and an invitation to dinner from his Professor of Philosophy, who was old, poor, and the scion of a noble family. The relations between master and pupil then became those of a father-confessor and a believer. A good judge of character, the professor soon understood Apostol's restlessness and took him to his heart. To him it seemed that this young man was typical of a generation which, losing its faith in God, strives to find something outside the human soul, a scientific God, free from mystery, an absolute truth beyond which there should be nothing and which should contain and explain all things.

The serenity and sympathy of the professor gradually calmed the exaltation of the student, and when he came home for his first vacation he brought with him a "conception of life" which he explained all the summer to Alexandru Palagiesu, who had now a lawyer's practice in Parva.

"Man alone is nothing but a worm," the student would assert with as much confidence as if he had discovered the philosopher's stone, "a mere spark of fleeting consciousness. Only organized collectivity becomes a constructive force, old man! As a single unit man is useless, whereas in a collectivity every effort finds its place and altogether contributes to the advancement of the individual, while the concerted activity of all collectivities brings humanity nearer to God. To-day, through lack of organization, at least 90 per cent. of the work done by the human brain is wasted. . . . Just imagine what would be the result if, by means of a perfect system of organization, the mental efforts of all human beings were directed to the same aim! How many men are there on the earth to-day? Let us say two thousand million. Very well, would the unknown still exist if two thousand kilograms of grey matter would in one common impulse storm the closed gates?"

"Which means in plain Rumanian that we are to do things in common," said the lawyer, "that we are to do our duty to the State—that's it, isn't it? Well, our laws enjoin us to do the same thing."

"No, not the laws. . . . Conscience must dictate your duty, not the laws. There's a great difference. . . ." Apostol would flare up and vehemently he would begin his explanations anew.

For two years in Budapest he tested his "conception of life" in all circumstances, and after each test he found it better and more satisfactory. But he hated living in the capital. The noise of the streets, the self-centredness of the people, the mechanizing of life, irritated him. He desired ardently the enlightenment of the soul, and that he believed was impossible to attain amongst large congregations of men. In the midst of nature he felt free and nearer the heart of the world. Whenever he had time he ran away from the town. He was as familiar with the hills round about Buda as he was with the country surrounding Parva. It was only when he came home that he noticed that he had shaped his life on a last which was not appreciated at all there. In Parva his "conception" rocked and efforts were needed to prevent it from collapsing. Here the State was looked upon as an enemy. It was during his third vacation, whilst arguing with the lawyer Domsa, who, after the death of old Bologa, had made a fortune in Parva, that he succeeded in finding a satisfactory reasoning.

"I don't affirm that our State is a good one," exclaimed Apostol with sudden inspiration. "I don't affirm that at all. Give me a better State and I'll take my hat off to it. But so long as this one exists we must do our duty by it. Otherwise we should fall into anarchy, sir. In life we must reckon with realities, not with longings."

The lawyer Domsa was very fond of him, and foresaw a brilliant future for him, an opinion shared as a matter of fact by all the gentlemen of Parva, and even those of Nasaud. It was common talk that Apostol was the darling of the Faculty and that he would most certainly become a professor at the University. For that reason Domsa paid court to him to a slight extent in the hope of attracting his attention to his daughter Marta, a little girl of about seventeen, sweeter and more ingenuous than any lass on the shores of the Someș, and who, in addition, had a substantial dowry, being Domsa's only child.

One fine day, wishing to continue the discussion, Apostol called at the lawyer's house. The latter was out, but Marta received him. He stayed half an hour chatting on indifferent topics, expecting Domsa to come in any minute. The next day he came again, and spent half an hour with Marta. Then for a whole week he went there every day at the same hour, and grew daily more pleased to find the lawyer out. During the following week he said to his mother joyously:

"Mother, I am going to marry Domsa's daughter!"

Doamna Bologa was aghast. Marta seemed to her too coquettish and too frivolous. A girl brought up without restrictions—Doamna Domsa had died four years ago—could not be a suitable wife for Apostol. She tried to make him change his mind, and once again called in the aid of Protopop Groza. All to no purpose. The betrothal was celebrated quietly, just a family affair, and it was arranged that the wedding should take place in a year or two, when Apostol would have completed his studies.

Soon after the betrothal there came to Parva a lieutenant of the Imperial Light Infantry, son of the Hungarian judge and very arrogant and conceited. Apostol looked on him disdainfully, whereas Marta thought him interesting and attractive. The Sunday following his arrival the "Charity Ball" took place. Although Apostol did not care for dancing, on that night he danced furiously so as not to run the risk of letting "that other fellow" outdo him. The lieutenant, however, danced very little and with only three girls, one of whom was Marta. And Apostol saw the ill-concealed pride and pleasure which this caused her.

In three days the young man's heart had become filled with bitterness. He was wretched, and thoughts of suicide floated through his mind. He compared himself with the lieutenant, and felt sure that Marta in her heart preferred the brilliant uniform . . . and he, being the son of a widow, had not even served in the Army. At one desperate moment he thought he would renounce this privilege in order to be able to come back in a year wearing an officer's uniform and to show that he also could look like "that other fellow". In any case, he was not going to be done out of Marta's love. Just because she was like that he loved her all the more. He'd fight and win her for good and all. If she was not able to rise to his level, he would go down to hers. But Marta would have to love no one but him!

Just about that time rumours of war began to spread, and one fine day the lieutenant was obliged to cut short his leave and rejoin his regiment in a great hurry. Next day a triumphant Apostol called on Marta. But when the talk veered round to the lieutenant Marta remarked with melancholy eyes:

"A nice man! Now he will become a hero!"

Apostol's face paled. He made up his mind to break off the engagement, to admit uncompromisingly to his mother that she had been right, and to go back to his books. But that would be cowardice. If at his first encounter with life he owned himself beaten, what would his future be?

And then on the top of his troubles came the war. And his "conception of life", which for three years he had been building out of and propping up with philosophical reflections, tottered on its foundations. The war had not been reckoned with in his "conception". And a decision had to be arrived at at once. He talked it over with Palagiesu, without result. Palagiesu declared emphatically that "we must all do our duty to our country". This, however, was an opinion of a representative of the State and therefore enforced and not the spontaneous outcome of free conviction. Apostol, in his heart, believed that the best thing would be to ignore the war as something abnormal. Yes, that was all very well, but suppose he were called up to-morrow?

"You see, darling," said his mother uneasily, "if you had but listened to us and gone into the Church you would be a priest to-day and there would be no need for you to worry about the war. . . . Whereas now, God only knows what . . ."

And Apostol, in order to convince himself more than for any other reason, made answer:

"One of these days I also shall go off to do my duty."

Doamna Bologa, frightened and indignant, asked:

43

"You'd endanger your life? For whom and for what?"

"For my country," muttered the student with an irresolute smile.

"We have no country!" exclaimed the mother indignantly. "This is not our country. It were far better for the horses of the Russians to trample over it!"

She sent immediately for Protopop Groza, and together they tried to evict from his mind these imprudent ideas. Apostol's irresolution grew. He left the house with his mind in a whirl, and found himself presently in Domsa's house.

"What, you? Our hope? You to fight for the Hungarians who fight us? When one has a country like ours one is not in any way obliged to worry one's head about one's duty to it—on the contrary!"

"And yet there's the principle . . ." put in Apostol without conviction.

"What principle? When a man's life is at stake all principles may go to the devil. We must wait, Apostol! Our watchword must be 'Reserve.'"

"Reserve means passivity, and passivity is worse than death. . . ."

"Passivity keeps our hopes unharmed, whereas activity just now is synonymous with annihilation."

Apostol was silent. In his heart he was now convinced that he need not go. But before he had time to answer Domsa, Marta, who had been out to see a friend, came in. The lawyer, as was his custom, left them alone.

"Everybody is joining up . . ." said Marta.

In her eyes, in her voice, Apostol caught a strange tremor. Marta was thinking of "that other fellow". They talked for about an hour, and all the time Apostol saw that his fiancée was like a stranger to him, yet he knew that by a single gesture it was in his power to win her whole heart. For an hour he hesitated and then, as he was going, he looked deep into her eyes and said firmly:

"The day after to-morrow I am joining up."

Marta smiled incredulously. But the next minute her cheeks flushed, her eyes flashed with pride, and with a passionate gesture she ran into his arms and kissed him on the lips. And in that kiss Apostol realized the fullness of his success.

Two days later he left for Cluj and presented himself at the recruiting station, where a lanky colonel congratulated him warmly. When he had put on his uniform, he stared at himself in the glass and hardly recognized himself, so soldierly had his appearance become. The town throbbed with an enthusiasm which was infectious. On the pavements, in the cafés, at the University, everywhere people were gay, as if the war had freed them from some terrible danger, or as if it promised them some heavenly bliss. In this atmosphere the remnants of his hesitation melted away like wax. He felt proud and happy in his spruce gunner's uniform, and he saluted smartly all the officers he met, deeply convinced that in doing this he was also doing his duty to his country.

He trained for two months at the artillery school, after which he was sent to the front. Then he was made an officer, and was twice wounded, the first time slightly, but the second time so badly that he had two months in hospital and one month's sick-leave at home; he was decorated three times and promoted lieutenant—all in two years. The war had taken front place in his "conception of life", from which, a little while ago, he had wished to eliminate it. Now he said to himself that was the true source of life and the most effective means of selection. Only in the face of death did man understand the true value of life, and only by danger was the soul properly disciplined. Then had come the court martial which had condemned Svoboda. And after that the gibbet and the eyes of the condemned man and the Rumanian song of the orderly—like a reproach . . .

§ III

"Sir, it is late; time for supper."

Apostol Bologa opened his eyes, his mind confused. By his bedside stood the orderly, mumbling these words softly, like a witch weaving a spell.

"What is it, Petre? Have I been asleep?" asked the lieutenant, jumping up and glancing quickly at his wrist-watch. "That's nice! I've missed the mess. . . . And it's your fault. I don't know where you're always stuck, instead of being here to help me."

While he was scolding Petre he knew perfectly well that he was trying to stifle memories which had caught him in their toils and which he dreaded like the pricks of an unforgiving conscience. Anxious to go, he could not find his helmet, and muttered:

"Turn up the lamp; this place is like a crypt."

From beside the lamp the orderly picked up a letter and held it out.

"It came midday, but with all this hullabaloo . . ."

Apostol took the letter, looked at the address, and then remained several minutes staring vacantly at Petre as if he did not dare to read it.

"Fine thing this; I am even afraid of Mother's letter," he thought bitterly. "To such a state of cowardice has the execution of a traitor reduced me!"

Thereupon he sat himself down angrily on the chest, drew the lamp nearer, tore open the envelope, and read without stopping:

MY LONGED-FOR DARLING,

I am terribly worried about you, for I have not had a word from you for a week. Here the earth groans under the number of troops and Austrian soldiers. We live in fear and trembling. I feel a little easier since I have been told that there has been no recent fighting in the part where you are. Oh, if only God would make it all end, for so much warring has embittered our souls and dried up our tears.

We are always hoping to see you arrive unexpectedly, even if it be only for a few days; other officers get leave frequently. We also have a major quartered on us: a very good fellow—a Pole. The poor man sighs all day for his family, for he is married and has six children. Do you know, my darling, they have taken Protopop Groza away and have interned him in Hungary because Palagiesu denounced him and said that he was a danger to the peace of the community. O Lord, great is Thy patience and Thy mercy! And Palagiesu boasts, even in my presence, that had he wished he could have had him hanged, for, he says, his hand is heavy on those who cannot keep quiet. But, he says, he pitied Groza's eighty years, otherwise he would not have been satisfied with mere internment. For, he says, the Protopop preached from the pulpit that we were not to give up the language of our ancestors nor our faith in God, but that we were to hold them sacred. And for this they arrested him and locked him up, and there is only the deacon left to take the services both at the big church and across the water, at the little church in Jerusalim. I pray fervently to God all the time, and I do hope that our prayers will find pity and compassion in Heaven.

I often think and shiver as to what would happen if your poor father were alive! My God, how brave he was! Perhaps you would not be where you are either, for nothing on earth would have made him allow you to go: But I, a poor widow, what am I to do? I weep, and pray the Almighty to care for you and protect you, and to enlighten your soul and your path in life.

If only peace would come, so that men might be freed from torture and terror! For since Rumania has entered the war we feel even more embittered and heartsick.

Marta says she has written to you constantly but that two letters of hers have remained unanswered, and that she thinks that perhaps you are offended about something or other. Write to her, my dear boy, for Domsa is very decent and cares for you like a father. She is a good girl, too, and soft-hearted, but she is young and inexperienced. She keeps on telling me that she misses you terribly, but she can't stay at home, and must needs talk and joke with all the little officers round here—that's how things are now. If you were at home we would also have someone to lean on. But it doesn't matter, the storm will pass and God will reward each one according to his deserts. Until the hour of our salvation comes I seek consolation in your letters. I wait for them and tremble when they don't come. For you are my consolation, my hope in this world, and my faith in God.

Good-bye. Write to me soon. God bless you and keep you.

YOUR MOTHER.

Apostol folded up the letter again, slipped it slowly into his pocket, sighed, and with a wry smile said:

"Poor mother! One can see she is the great-granddaughter of Avram Jancu's prefect."

The contents of the letter weighed heavily on his mind. Only the part concerning Marta seemed to have made no impression, although, as a rule, it would have been that very part which would have set him thinking.

Looking up, he met the gaze of the orderly, who was staring at him with curious, humble eyes. Apostol started as if he feared that he had read his thoughts.

"What's happening way down home, sir?" the soldier suddenly asked respectfully.

"What can happen, Petre? Trouble and bitterness," answered Apostol gently.

He put on his helmet, turned up the collar of his trench-coat, and went out into the courtyard, followed by the orderly. At the gate he looked back and said in the same gentle voice:

"Remember, Petre, that to-morrow at daybreak we go back to the front. Get everything together. . . . It's no use, Petre, one feels happier over there than here!"

§ IV

The officers messed in a one-time tavern, next door to the house where General Karg lodged. All the staff officers messed in the large front room, the windows of which were shuttered so as to prevent the light from showing outside. At the back, in the small room, messed those who were only passing through—that is to say, those on their way to or from the front who were compelled to stay there a while in connection with the numerous services of the division.

As he was late, Bologa did not want to go through the big room, so he went through the courtyard and into the lobby, where soldiers were busy washing up crockery, opening bottles and bringing in, through the passage from the distant kitchen, plates of food and bottles of wine. From here one door led directly into the big mess-room and another on the left into the "guests' room". A soldier rushed forward and opened the door for Bologa.

In the small room there were only two long tables and a broken-down couch on which were heaped, pell-mell, a pile of cloaks, helmets, revolvers, swords, bayonets.

There was no longer anyone sitting at the table on the right. A soldier with a long-shaped head and a forehead the width of a finger was leisurely clearing away and sweeping up the crumbs. The tobacco-smoke, the smell of food and drink, filled the room right up to the beamed ceiling, obscuring the light from the lamp with the rusty tin shade. The shutters of both windows were closed, and the holes in the shutters were stuffed up with dinner-napkins. There were no curtains to the windows, and on the walls there were a few corpses of overfed bugs.

At the upper end of the table on the left Captain Klapka was sitting, bare-headed, his round, clean-shaven face radiating kindness and gentleness in spite of the uneasy look in his eyes, which he tried to conceal under a formal and set smile.

As Bologa entered the room the sound of voices, which had been audible from the lobby, stopped abruptly, so that his "Good evening" fell into a startled silence. But by the time he had divested himself of his coat and helmet the wave of embarrassment had passed, and Lieutenant Gross, half in fun and half in earnest, called out:

"I believe you were ashamed to join us earlier, Bologa, weren't you? Come, own up!"

"Ashamed? I? Whatever for?" shot out Apostol, stopping short.

"Do you think that we don't know that you voted for death?" smiled Gross, making his voice less challenging because he saw Bologa was annoyed.

"Well, and what about it?" asked Apostol, his manner becoming stiffer. "In any case, I have to account to no one but my conscience, which found him guilty."

"Conscience!" came plaintively all of a sudden from Captain Cervenco, who was sitting on Klapka's left. "Who has a conscience left these days?"

That voice insinuated itself into Lieutenant Bologa's ear like a needle. He wanted to answer but could not think of what to say. He stood looking at the speaker and his heart softened. Cervenco was a fine, strapping fellow with broad shoulders and a brown beard which covered almost the whole of his chest, and in his eyes there always lurked a look of undefined suffering. Bologa had met him at a hospital in Trieste, and had discovered in him the heart of an angel. He was a Ruthenian, a professor in a college at Stanislav. The officers all considered him a sort of maniac because during his two years' soldiering he had never once touched a weapon of war. He always went into the fight armed merely with a reed wand and singing hymns. Cervenco, however, asserted loudly and unashamed that he would much rather chop off his hands than shoot at his fellow-creatures. And because he was extremely conscientious in his work and contemptuous of death, his superiors did not interfere with him, but merely said that he was a bit cracked.

"Everyone does his duty as he thinks is right," muttered Bologa in answer to Cervenco. He sat down at the table opposite Klapka, and, turning to the soldier, ordered: "Bring me something to eat!"

The soldier disappeared. Presently Gross said rather harshly:

"No duty in the world would induce me to murder a comrade. . . ."

"Comrade?" shouted suddenly Lieutenant Varga, revolted, and jumped to his feet. "Traitors and deserters are your comrades? Gentlemen, you go too far. I personally can no longer listen indifferently to words so—so—compromising for any soldier who has still within him a spark of love for his country."

The outburst of the lieutenant in the Hussars, the only regular officer present, fell like a cold shower, reminding them that they were at the front. All eyes turned on him, and in all of them gleamed a question. This flattered the vanity of the dark-haired hussar, who was young and good-looking, had a short, clipped moustache and a conceited air. He was the nephew of the Professor of Philosophy at the University of Budapest, and his great ambition was to be considered a connoisseur in horseflesh. Apostol had met him often at the professor's house, and although he had thought him rather silly and empty-headed, he had become friendly with him because he was straight and sincere.

"Would you believe it, my dear fellow," continued Varga, addressing himself to Bologa as to one who shared his beliefs and speaking quietly as if he wished to wipe out the impression caused by his indignant outburst, "we have only twice mentioned Svoboda's execution, and do you know whom these gentlemen have voted guilty each time?—those who condemned him!"

Varga ended with a mocking smile directed at Gross, and by his speech put an end to further protests.

"No one condemns with a light heart," said Apostol thoughtfully, "but when guilt is obvious one is compelled to do so, for the State is of far greater importance than the man and his individual interests."

"Nothing is of greater importance than man!" said Gross, jumping up quickly as if he feared someone would prevent him from speaking. "On the contrary, man ranks above everything, even above the universe! What use would the earth be without man to see it, love it, measure it, surround it? As the earth, so the universe, which has only become an interesting reality through man. Otherwise, I mean without the soul of man, it would be nothing but a sterile heaving of blind energies. All the suns of the universe can have no other mission than to warm the body of man, which shelters the divine spark of intellect. Man is the centre of the universe because man alone has succeeded in attaining the consciousness of his own ego and in knowing himself. Man is God!"

Lieutenant Gross, who was in charge of a company of pioneers, was lean and spare, with small black, flashing eyes and a little, closely clipped goatee. When he talked he quickly became excited and his usually harsh, unpleasant voice became eloquent. He was a Jew and an engineer, employed at works in Budapest.

He stopped speaking a moment and looked round as if expecting an interruption. Meeting the eyes of Bologa, who disliked him and considered him a *poseur*, Gross went on contemptuously:

"The State! The State which kills! Behind us our State, in front of us the enemy State, and we in the middle, condemned to die in order to secure a peaceful, comfortable life for those brigands who are responsible for the massacre of millions of unconscious slaves. I marvel that—"

"We protect our homeland, friend, the land of our forefathers!" broke in Varga quietly, with a proud superiority in his voice.

"Is your homeland here, in the heart of Russia?" asked Gross disdainfully.

"Where one's duty lies there is one's homeland!" threw in Apostol, but so diffidently that no one took any notice of his words.

"Our homeland is death . . . death everywhere and all the time," mumbled Cervenco with deep conviction.

"Because we are cowards!" shouted Gross excitedly. "One moment of united courage would put an end to all these infamies!"

"If everyone were like you!" said Varga, laughing so heartily that they all brightened up. "Luckily we others have not forgotten that first and foremost we are the sons and protectors of our country, my dear anarchist! Sir," he added, turning to Klapka, "I beg you not to judge us by our words but by our deeds! We are all friends here, and when we all get together we allow ourselves more licence than perhaps we should. In this way we let off steam for the hardships we have endured. But when facing the enemy all of us do our duty with a will, even Gross, in spite of the fact that he likes to appear a rebel. In the third year of the war, after we have given so many proofs of courage, these little weaknesses of ours may well be overlooked!"

Klapka nodded with an indulgent smile, which, however, was not in keeping with the strange light which shone in his protruding eyes.

Gross was about to protest, but just then the door opened and the soldier entered, carrying platefuls of food, which he set down in front of Bologa.

After a few minutes' silence, the conversation, chiefly carried on by Gross and Varga, again warmed up. Apostol Bologa forced himself to eat. Although he had had nothing since midday, he wasn't hungry. He felt as tired and done up as if he had been carrying heavy loads all day long. He would have liked to take part in the discussion as usual, but he did not dare for fear that the others should notice how false and insincere his words were. That dread tortured him unceasingly and agonized his soul. He felt as if he were standing on the brink of a precipice and dared not look into its depth, although the urge to do so became more and more insistent.

"Victory is bound to come!" averred Gross pathetically, gesticulating and blinking with emotion. "A monstrous crime must of necessity engender a gigantic movement of universal revolt. It must! And then across the blood-filled trenches, across the frontiers, furrowed with graves, all the downtrodden ones will join hands with the revolutionaries and in one annihilating swoop will turn on those who have exploited them for thousands of years, and into their blood, thick with sloth, they will dip their banners of peace and of the regenerated world."

Bologa could no longer keep silent, and asked quietly:

"A world of hate, comrade?"

"Hate—only hate will wipe out injustice!"

"Hate always engenders hate," said Apostol, shivering. "You cannot build on hate, just as you cannot build on a swamp. . . ."

Before Gross could answer, Varga jumped up and said with a smile:

"Wait! Allow me! Our anarchist would have an International, wouldn't you, comrade? Very well, behold the International!" he added with pride, raising his voice and indicating those present with a sweep of his arm. "Behold! You are a Jew, the captain is a Czech, the doctor over there is German, Cervenco is a Ruthenian, Bologa is Rumanian, I am a Hungarian. . . . Isn't that true? You, what are you, lad?" he asked, turning suddenly to the soldier, who seemed to find the task of clearing the table unending.

"A soldier!" answered the fellow, startled, springing to attention.

"Of course, we are all soldiers," Varga answered contentedly, "but what I am asking you is: what is your nationality?"

"A Croatian, may you live long!" muttered the soldier without blinking.

"You see, a Croatian!" continued the lieutenant addressing the officers. "And I am sure that in the big room over there or in the lobby we would find Poles, Serbs, and Italians, in fine all nationalities, that's so, isn't it? And all fight shoulder to shoulder for a common ideal against a common foe! That's the true International, comrades!" Varga resumed his seat exultant.

"The International of crime!" said Gross gravely, adding immediately and ironically: "It's no use, you'll never understand, Varga. It is time lost for us to try to make you. You are a decent chap and a brave one, but in other respects . . ."

"In other respects, meaning in respect to your ideas, I do not even wish to understand, for in that direction lies the court martial," answered Varga quickly, laughing contentedly.

There followed a silence, and then unexpectedly Cervenco's voice wailing like a belated reproach:

"We need to suffer much, tremendously . . . Only amidst suffering can love grow and thrive, that great, real, and victorious love. . . . Love, dear fellows, love!"

Apostol Bologa stared into the eyes of the Ruthenian, tearful eyes yet shining with a magnetic light. But as he stared deeper Bologa became scared and startled as if he had found himself staring into the depth of the abyss which he had avoided all the evening. He wanted to say something and found himself muttering unknowingly:

"Love . . . love . . ."

"Your love, however, feeds us with bullets and gibbets . . ." came from Gross with offensive harshness. "To-day Svoboda, to-morrow I or perhaps you others with your love. Svoboda anyway did try to lift himself out of the mire, whereas we go on floundering in it."

"I hope you do not intend to defend treason?" interrupted the Hussar lieutenant gravely.

"Suppose while you were suffering hardships and performing deeds of gallantry over here some miscreants hanged your father at home under some accusation or other, tell me, my hero, would you not imitate Svoboda?"

"Do you mean that the father of the man hanged . . .?" queried Bologa, his eyes like saucers, his neck stretched towards Gross. "But why did he not speak, why didn't he?"

"And if he had told," said Gross contemptuously, "at most an aggravating circumstance . . .?"

"Oh, oh, but it is . . . is . . ." stammered Bologa, and broke off suddenly confused, a curious feeling of dryness at the roof of his mouth, as if he had just awakened from a sleep haunted by nightmarish dreams.

"Nothing can excuse treason, and besides an officer who deserts is more criminal than . . . more criminal!" averred Varga, getting up. "And as we are on duty again to-morrow morning, I suggest that we should be off. . . . For no other reason than that, I am afraid that if I stay any longer you will end by convincing me that to desert to the enemy is a gallant action!"

He tried to laugh, but not very successfully, and, going over to the couch, he picked out his coat and arms. Gross looked at his watch and said to Cervenco:

"What are we thinking of? It is late. . . . We can barely get three hours' sleep. . . ."

The three went off together and left a heavy silence behind them. Presently Captain Klapka began to drum lightly on the table with his fingers, looking surreptitiously at Bologa, who was shaking in his chair, his face distorted with uncontrollable horror. At the table there was no one else left but a second-lieutenant of infantry, very young and very dour, who hadn't said a single word but who had drunk several bottles of wine with the nonchalance of the precocious drunkard, and Doctor Meyer, a taciturn bear who suffered from insomnia, had a special tenderness for his "clients", as he called those in the trenches, and who had all his meals in the small room of the "passers-through", without ever joining in their discussions. Because the silence was becoming oppressive, Klapka said to Doctor Meyer, endeavouring to make his tone light:

"I shall have to stay here till daybreak, for I have no quarters. My orderly is keeping an eye on my kit at the station."

The sound of the captain's voice roused Bologa, and speaking rapidly as if he wished to stifle some guilty feeling, he said:

"If you are tired you can rest at my place, sir. I will gladly give up my bed to you. Anyway, I . . . I intend to go to . . . to my duty earlier."

"Well, why should we not go together, friend? I don't know the district and shall need a guide. . . . I have been told that I shall be in charge of the second division."

"Then you are my commanding officer!" exclaimed Apostol, brightening up. "A still greater reason for me to repeat my invitation!"

"And I am going to accept it, for to tell you the truth, my friend, I feel rather done up, what with fatigue and emotions," answered the captain, speaking more frankly.

The doctor who suffered from insomnia passed into the big room, and the second-lieutenant asked the soldier, who was still busy fussing at the other table, to bring him another bottle of wine. In the street Klapka and Bologa stood still to listen to the noisy laughter from the mess-room, above which there arose a hoarse voice singing flat and with great passion a sentimental love-song. The darkness was writhing all round them, and above in the sky the winds were driving hither and thither shoals of tearful clouds.

"Which way do we go, comrade?" asked Klapka in a changed voice.

At that moment, however, there appeared in the sky towards the east a beam of white trembling light, darting hither and thither hurriedly, searchingly, like a cunning spy, now standing still, now sweeping the ground swiftly and cleaving the darkness. And a minute later, far away, hey heard repeated rumblings.

"What's this?" said the captain, surprised. "They told me there was no fighting down this way, whereas . . ."

"Yes . . . it's nothing . . . nothing!" answered Bologa, following with interest the light and the rumblings. "It's really farcical, more than farcical. Those Russians are mad. . . . Do you know, sir, that for the last week, nearly every night, they tease us with a search-light as if they wished to make fun of us! A searchlight, you understand, when it is a question of fixed positions where they are familiar with every little mushroom. Ridiculous! But even more ridiculous and upsetting is the fact that we are unable to put out their toy! We have already wasted so many shells that we are ashamed of the number, and all in vain! It almost seems as if their light were bewitched, as if . . ."

Bologa broke off abruptly, for the beam of light disappeared, leaving the darkness blacker than before. The sound of the guns continued for a little while and then died down in its turn. The two officers went on in the impenetrable darkness, their boots squelching in the mud. The village was asleep, its houses hidden behind their thorny hedges. Presently, without stopping, Klapka said in a low voice:

"What a strange effect to-day's execution had on those gentlemen! And they were brought over purposely so that they should go back into the trenches filled with dread, and that they should tell their men that it is better to face the bullets of the enemy than the gibbet of their own country. . . . Very, very strange! But if the father of the condemned man had really been hanged, then . . ."

Apostol looked back quickly over his shoulder as if he had heard a voice speaking to him from behind, then he muttered beseechingly:

"He was guilty, sir; he was guilty!"

They reached the corner of the lane in which the lieutenant lived. At that very minute the white light sprang up again in the sky, nearer, clearer, followed immediately by more furious rumblings.

"The light!" groaned Bologa. "It challenges one, that light . . . challenges one. . . . It seems as if no shot in the world could put it out."

The white streak, however, again melted away, and the darkness gripped them once more like cold steel. Only within their mangled souls a few multi-coloured, comforting sparks lingered. They turned into the lane. The mud here was clayey. Bologa felt his knees trembling. He seemed to be carrying a millstone round his neck; and his lacerated heart was so full that he was tortured by a need to speak, to explain.

"Sir, consider the circumstances," he said feverishly. "It was the first time I had sat on a court martial . . . And my conscience bade me do it. . . . He was guilty, sir. . . ."

Klapka was silent, as if he had not heard him speak.

§ V

Apostol Bologa took over the command of his battery, chatted a while with the other officers of his sector, and then retired to his dug-out to rest. He stretched himself on his plank bed. He was worn out with fatigue and insomnia, for all the previous night he had tossed in torment, but now his heart felt lighter, as if he had escaped from a torture-chamber and as if all his anguish had remained behind in the village with the gibbet. A hazy light trickled down from outside and outlined vaguely the entrance to the dug-out, the improvised table with maps and compasses, books and a few empty plates, the telephone on the wall, the two stools put out of the way. He heard the monotonous, depressing, lulling rain, and he was glad, for now his mind was held, as always when he was in the trenches. No other thought than searchlights, guns, Russians, maps, decorations . . .

Towards evening, Captain Klapka came to inspect. At sight of him Bologa's spirits sank, especially when the captain informed him that he had already inspected all the other batteries and that he intended to tarry here a while as if he were in his own dug-out. Apostol made his report coldly and succinctly, as if he hoped by this means to avoid any further contact but that necessitated by the service. Klapka listened thoughtfully, staring compellingly at him all the while with a persistence which confused Bologa and reminded him of their meeting of yesterday in front of the gibbet. When he had finished, the captain said suddenly, speaking with great warmth and sincerity:

"You have a heart of gold, Bologa; yes, a heart of gold. . . . That is why you are as dear to me as one of my own kinsmen!"

The lieutenant started nervously. He could not understand what Klapka was driving at, and the thought crossed his mind that he was being drawn. In his ears, however, echoed the kindly, perturbing words which, despite their kindness, filled him with dread and made him feel as if he were being dragged towards some danger.

"I saw how you were torturing yourself the whole night long," continued the captain, "and I understood. Perhaps I was the only one who did understand, because I . . . Yes, yes, don't stare so because I have stopped short. We must ever refrain from speaking out! We must keep silent! Otherwise . . ."

"Sir, I think you are making a mistake. I think that . . ." said Bologa harshly, almost viciously. "And I really do not know what makes you attribute to me such . . ."

Klapka smiled so kindly that Apostol became quite confused and broke off in the middle of his sentence.

"Since the first minute we met I understood that you looked upon me as an enemy," proceeded the captain. "I would not have minded your enmity in the least if, later on, I had not happened to see—whilst my kinsman was dangling from the rope—that your eyes were full of tears. . . . Don't protest! You didn't know it, but you were weeping. . . . And those tears revealed your whole heart. . . ."

Bologa made another attempt to defend himself. In vain. The captain seemed to feel an invincible need to create for himself a friend with whom he could share some spiritual burden. The lieutenant's mistrust made him hesitate a little, but then fear of loneliness emboldened him to try again. So he told him that he had learnt last night from a Hungarian captain that Bologa was a Rumanian, but for all that a model officer and an incomparable patriot. That information had saddened him, for it had made him think that those tears had been misleading. He had met many Rumanian officers since the outbreak of war, and he had always got on as well with them as if he had been their kinsman. He would not believe that he had now come across a renegade. Then later on, at mess, he had understood everything, for he also had been acting a part for two years, and like a veteran actor had concealed his strong feelings under a perpetual mask. As a matter of fact, the danger for him was far greater than for Bologa, firstly because he was a Czech, and all Czechs were suspects, and secondly . . . He did not, however, state what the second reason was, but went on telling him that he was a native of Znaim, a charming little town, Czech to the core, and that his parents had sent him to the military school in order that he might be able to earn his own living as soon as possible, for they had had a large family and no money. He had left the military college at eighteen, but life in the Army did not appeal to him. In the summer after he had been promoted second-lieutenant he had gone home on leave and had fallen madly in love with the daughter of a professor in Znaim. He had wanted to marry her, but his beloved had not had the dowry which was obligatory for the wives of officers—in fact, she had had no dowry at all. So, as he absolutely could not give up the girl, they had become engaged. He had made up his mind to take up a new career, and she had promised to wait for him. That autumn he had entered his name for the Bar and had begun to grind at his books. It had been hard work. The service had continually retarded his progress, and his superiors had not viewed his civilian efforts with kindly eyes. Nevertheless, he had finished in seven years. He was then a lieutenant. Upon his resignation he became a captain in the Reserves and a candidate for the Bar. A year later he had started a practice and had been able to get married. His marriage had been fruitful; every year had brought its child. To-day there were four, two boys and two girls. The war had interrupted the series. The fifth was only now on its way. From a letter-case he extracted some photographs and showed them to Apostol with much pride and emotion: first the little ones in proper order, giving the name and habits of each one, then the wife.

"But, mind you," he added passionately, "these are abominable photographs, especially my wife's! She is a thousand times lovelier . . . dainty, sweet, and pretty. That's why her photographs can never do her justice. To know her is to adore her!"

He kissed the photographs, put them away, and murmured softly, his eyes full of tears:

"Because of them and for their sake I am as I am, Bologa! Otherwise, God knows, perhaps I, also . . . As it is I can't . . . I am capable of any act of cowardice or meanness if it but keep me from dying before I have embraced them . . . What would you? I am an unfortunate wretch. . . . And for all that, in two years I have been home only once—for five days! Do you understand? Oh, the devils, the devils!"

He ground his teeth while the tears ran down his plump cheeks, now flushed with passion. Steps were heard coming down into the dug-out, and Klapka shut up abruptly and looked fearfully towards the entrance. It was a second-lieutenant who had come to arrange with Bologa about the night duty.

"The search-light may visit us again to-night and it would be good to prepare a warm reception for it . . ." suggested the subaltern.

They sat at the table, spread out the maps, consulted together, found the place where the search-light had last appeared and deliberated as to where it was likely to appear that night. They lit a candle-end, made calculations and drew up range-tables.

His mind full of the enemy search-light, Apostol Bologa completely forgot Klapka. All that night he was on the look-out, running from the command post to the guns, from the guns to the various observation posts of the battery, going even as far as the observing station of the infantry line, as agitated as if his whole happiness and the fate of the whole world were at stake. The hours slipped by, daybreak came, but the search-light did not appear.

And the next night the same thing happened, and the next. Not until the fifth night, when they no longer believed it would come, did it actually shine again, more defiantly and mockingly than ever. Dozens of shells were spent, but the light flashed on unconcernedly over the fields furrowed with trenches.

The next day, about midday, Bologa again came face to face with Klapka in the battery plotting-room. He was very pale and his eyes looked more troubled and protruding than usual. He told Bologa that the colonel had just ordered him point-blank to put an end to the searchlight scandal because their section had become the laughing-stock of the Army, and he had added that the divisional commander had promised a decoration to whoever should put a stop to the Russian mockery.

"Last night I marked it down and it eluded us all the same!" exclaimed Bologa furiously, ending with a Hungarian oath. "In the whole of my two years' service I have never received a reprimand, and now, because of a bally . . ."

"Don't lose your temper, friend, and don't swear," answered Klapka dejectedly. "The reprimand was not intended for you but for me!"

"It's intended for us all, sir, and that's just . . ."

"Perhaps, before I took charge, but to-day all the guilt is mine! I felt that very clearly from the colonel's words and tone, from . . . He asked me why I had been transferred to this front, do you understand?"

The captain sat down on the chair near the table with the maps and looked at Bologa questioningly and afraid. The latter answered uneasily:

"In the interest of the service, of course. In war-time nothing else counts."

"Well, the colonel knows, he must know, and still he asked me," said Klapka in a lower tone with a shade of mystery in his voice. "And when I funked and told him a lie he did not move an eyelid, and I felt ashamed of my cowardice!"

He fell silent, awaiting an answer or question. But the attitude and tone of the captain perturbed Bologa and aroused anew in his soul all the disquiet which he had thought allayed for good. He would have liked to protest and be done with this fellow who pursued him with his confidence and forced him to share ideas fraught with so much danger, but he was aghast to find that at the bottom of his heart these ideas were dear to him, and that he kept them stored there like precious jewels.

"Sir," murmured Apostol, staring into the other man's eyes beseechingly.

In that look and tone Klapka seemed to find a stimulant which lifted the anxiety from his face. He sighed deeply, as if he were about to make a clean breast of it, and said:

"This cowardice stifles me, Bologa! I can't stand it! I thought that if I concealed it I could get rid of it, but now it is strangling me. You saw the look in Svoboda's eyes under the gibbet? You must have noticed it—everybody saw the contempt, the pride, the hope. That death is the heroic one for us! On the Italian front a Rumanian was hanged for the same crime. I was quite close and he had that same look when facing the halter. But then I did not understand. Only a few months later did I grasp with fear and dread the meaning of that look. Three officers from my own regiment, one out of my own division—all Czechs— were caught one night between the lines with plans and maps and secret papers. I was to have been the fourth, but on the day fixed for our desertion I received a letter from home and I hid like a thief. The letter reminded me of my home, my children, my wife; in the letter I found hope of a future and of happiness, I found much love, all the love of my life. How could I risk all this for something . . . for something . . . for a dream? I, too, was had up with them before the court martial as an accomplice. And there I shook them off as I would leprosy, and I denied everything, clinging desperately to a shameful life. And they kept silent and did not even look upon me with contempt. The scythe of death flashed before their eyes, but they did not flinch. And then, when the sentence of death by hanging was read out they all three shouted with one voice, in front of the court: 'Long live Bohemia!' while I shook like a wretched beggar asking for alms. And to prove to all that I was innocent I went to see them executed. You see to what lengths cowardice can drive one? Near the village there is a forest through which the army has cut special roads for the requirements of the front. These roads are hidden from Italian aeroplanes. I accompanied the convoy of execution and we reached a large clearing. The convoy halted in the centre of the clearing and I looked round for the gibbets. There were no gibbets, but on each tree men were hanging, strung up on the branches. All were bareheaded, and from the neck of each man dangled a label bearing the words 'A TRAITOR TO HIS COUNTRY',

inscribed in three languages. My heart froze within me, but still
I did not dare to tremble. To enable me to hide more easily my
terror I had the idea of counting them, to see how many there
were. . . .You see how base man is! But how could I count them
when the whole forest was full of hanged men? Perhaps fear
made them seem more numerous than they really were! Then
I closed my eyes, thinking with stupid amazement: 'This is the
Forest of the Hanged.' A Hungarian major, a tall fellow with the
profile of a bird, whispered into my ear, perhaps to challenge
me: 'They are all Czechs, both officers and men, only Czechs!'
I made no rejoinder, as if I had thought his remark had been
meant for a reproach. Then all three were hanged simultaneously
on the same tree, an old beech with hollow trunk. When the
noose was put round their necks I looked at their eyes. They
were shining brightly, like stars which announce the coming of
the sun, with so much nobility and hope that their faces seemed
bathed in a radiance of glory. Then I felt proud of being the
kinsman of the radiant three and I longed thirstily for death!
But only for a moment, a single moment! Then I became aware
of the struggling bodies. I heard the creaking of the branches
and my heart trembled silently, timorously, thievishly, so that no
one near me should hear it. A few days later I was transferred
as a suspect. Now you know why I was transferred. And do you
think that I had at least the decency to shed tears on my return
from the Forest of the Hanged? Or even in the train on my way
here? Or since I am here? I rejoiced, Bologa, do you hear?—I
rejoiced that I was alive, that I had escaped from the Forest of
the Hanged! Until just now I rejoiced, until the colonel asked me
why I had been transferred! Just now I wept for the first time,
with my head buried in my cloak so that not even my orderly
should hear me. Only just now—because I am terrified of the

Forest of the Hanged! Because the Forest of the Hanged has followed me here!"

Klapka stopped speaking, his eyes so wide and terrified that Bologa's heart was filled with compassion. In the silence of the dug-out their hearts beat with the same tremulousness. The lieutenant wished to say something comforting and found himself whispering:

"Sir, the Forest of the Hanged . . ."

He realized what he had said, and dropped his eyes helplessly, humbly.

"Now you see what the colonel meant, don't you?" said the captain, shaking himself as if he wished to shake off a weight. "And his remark about the search-light? You see how the two are connected? The remark is a threat for me—either the search-light or . . ."

He shook himself again and continued in a strangled voice: "We must destroy that search-light, Bologa, my brother in anguish! Otherwise . . ."

"The Forest of the Hanged!" breathed Apostol, his eyes flashing with a new hatred which had sprung up in his heart unnoticed.

Klapka, as if the telling of it had lightened his heart, now spoke of nothing but the Russian search-light and began to point out places on the map, to take measurements, to combine figures and formulae. Bologa listened to him more and more morosely without uttering a word. The captain's voice, tremulous with fear, began to arouse his indignation. He controlled himself, but a feeling of hatred seemed to infuse itself into his blood and spread through his veins like a poison. He stared at the map and saw only the captain's fingers which held the compass and moved hither and thither, casting a strange shadow shaped like a gibbet.

Presently Klapka went off, relieved and full of trust, with a smile on his face, leaving Bologa alone in the damp dug-out.

§ VI

His heart throbbed within him and his brain seethed. He stood still a minute, staring after Klapka, then he threw himself into the chair facing the map, clinging to the compass as if his salvation depended on it. But even his fingers obeyed him no longer. Within his soul and all around him there was an anguish in which his whole life was being engulfed.

He rested his head on his hands and stared at the lines, dots and angles marked on the map. They seemed to him cabalistic signs, and he wondered how he had managed to understand them up till to-day. And simultaneously a question sprang up in his mind: what was he doing here? Then round this question answers grouped themselves, explanations, more questions and more answers, which in proportion as they became more numerous became more unsatisfactory because none of them opened out a way to salvation.

"How ridiculous I was with my conception of life!" he thought all at once. "How was it that I did not realize that a stupid formula could never cope with life."

Now, looking back, it seemed to him that all his life had been as empty as a paper bag. He was ashamed of his past way of living, and he recalled with sad regret the times when Life had tried to draw him into her current and he had stupidly resisted, anxiously stifling his instinctive inclinations. Even his present struggles with their desperate attempts to overcome his heart's bidding . . .

"Sir, I have brought your dinner," said the orderly suddenly, speaking from behind Bologa's chair, where he had halted with his tray. Apostol, hearing the Rumanian tongue, sprang to his feet as if he had received a heavy blow on the head.

"All right, all right, Petre," he stuttered, startled, shaking on his feet, and he threw himself on his bed so that the orderly should not notice his perturbation.

The orderly set the table, watching Bologa out of the comer of his eye. He saw that he was depressed and, wishing to sympathize with him, he asked humbly:

"Have you had bad news from home, sir?"

"What news, you ass?" vociferated Bologa furiously, sitting up. "What business is it of yours? You think of nothing but home, you damned fool—home!"

The soldier stiffened where he stood, facing the lieutenant red with fury. He was a man of over thirty, tall, broad-shouldered, with hands like spades, bony cheeks, and wonderfully gentle eyes in which burnt piety and resignation. Apostol had had him as orderly for about seven months, and Petre looked after him with a canine devotion, happy that Apostol had taken him from the firing line. Besides, he had been specially recommended in a letter from Doamna Bologa, for he also came from Parva, had known the "young gentleman" in his cradle, and had five children waiting for him at home.

Meeting the orderly's eyes, the lieutenant's fury melted in a wave of shame. He understood that it had been a sudden hearing of Rumanian which had driven him beside himself because it had come as a rebuke to his reproach-laden thoughts. He was sorry that he had lost his temper, and this regret gave him a feeling of self-satisfaction and nobility. He got up, took three steps towards the entrance of the dug-out, turned back, and said sadly and frankly, as if he were speaking to an old friend:

71

"I am depressed, Petre, and I don't know what is the matter with me. . . . O God, this war!"

He shivered with apprehension. It was the first time he had ever complained of the war. Until now even the sufferings of war had seemed natural to him, and he had looked upon those who complained as cowards.

The soldier, calm with the sombre light of resignation in his eyes, answered gravely:

"God's punishment, sir, for the sins of men."

"But what if it be not the sinners but the sinned against who suffer the punishment?" persisted Bologa.

"God holds the scales evenly," answered Petre with profound faith. "Death is no punishment. Life is a punishment. And it is only by means of the body's pain and anguish that the soul's salvation is attained."

Apostol sat down to eat. He had long been aware of his orderly's deep faith and he had heard him utter these very words dozens of times before. Petre, who even at home was famed for his piety, had, as a result of war conditions, become a religious fatalist. Besides, as he was the only Rumanian in the regiment, he was the only one with whom Bologa spoke his native tongue. The soldier went on babbling about suffering and about God, and Bologa, while he ate, listened to him and thought to himself that never before had he listened to the fellow with so much affection. Presently he interrupted him and turned the conversation to Parva and to the folk at home. Petre sighed and filled the dug-out with all sorts of remembrances which moved them both equally. Apostol felt his heart swell, felt its passionate throbbing, and felt the throbbing turn into a song of victory. An immense tenderness filled his soul. Greatly moved, he turned his eyes on Petre, seeing embodied in him all Parva and all those who spoke the Rumanian tongue. He felt inclined to embrace him and to kneel at his feet and ask his pardon. Finally, unable to control himself any longer, he breathed happily:

"Petre, Petre, my brother, my hope. . . ."

The soldier was silent for a while, perplexed. Then he shook his head and said calmly and resignedly:

"O Lord, help us . . .

§ VII

For several nights the search-light did not appear. Apostol Bologa, on the look-out at the observation post in the infantry trenches, waited for it with strained expectancy, bent on satisfying Klapka. In the stillness of the nights, broken only at rare intervals by stray rifle shots, he had plenty of leisure to weigh, as was his custom, his new creed, for he was convinced that nothing but that which could endure keen scrutiny of the mind was worthy to dwell eternally in the soul of man. And he rejoiced, feeling his spiritual regeneration, no matter how he viewed it, send a warm glow through his heart, whereas his old "conception", for which he had risked his life for twenty-seven months, had always been as unkind to him as a stepmother. He now told himself that life acted only through the heart, and that without the heart the brain would be nothing but a mass of dead cells. But he was ashamed to think that it had required two years of war for him to reach the point from which he had started, against the advice of Doamna Bologa, of the Protopop, and of everyone else except Marta. Round his neck he wore a locket which contained a mesh of blond hair and the picture of a charming little head. She had given him these when he had been home on leave and had whispered to him: "My hero!" She also called him that in her letters.

"It's all Marta's fault," he tried to tell himself secretly as an excuse in face of his rebuking conscience. But he pulled himself up and put away such cowardice. "Marta never urged me by a single word to enlist. It was only my wretched jealousy which counted on the uniform and the glamour to win over her frivolousness. So that I alone am to blame, and I must face my conscience."

The past seemed dead to him, and he took care not to dig it up again. He was more preoccupied with the future, which dawned for him like a dazzling morn after a stormy night. He did not yet perceive it clearly, but the fog which veiled it from his sight had rosy tints. His heart was full of comfort.

"From to-day a new life begins!" he kept on thinking joyfully. "At last I have found the right road. Gone are hesitations and doubts! Henceforth, forward!"

A wild desire to live filled his breast. In the morning, when he came away from the observation post, he stretched himself on his plank bed and quickly fell asleep and dreamt of happiness.

Late one afternoon he again met Klapka by the battery. Bologa, remembering how worried the captain had been that last night, was surprised to see him serene and smiling, with a look of almost challenging equanimity in his eyes. After they had inspected together guns and men, they went down into the command post, where a candle-end was burning.

"I've had no luck, sir," said Apostol hesitatingly. "It didn't appear . . ."

"What?" asked Klapka. "Oh, yes . . . the . . . oh, well, let that search-light go to the devil, Bologa!" he added indifferently.

74

The lieutenant kept a worried silence, staring into the captain's eyes, in which, only a few days ago, he had seen reflected the Forest of the Hanged. But Klapka proceeded serenely:

"A man with a troubled conscience takes fright at every shadow. That's what I did, too, with regard to our colonel. I took him for a man-eater, whereas he is a very decent fellow. Ah! of course, I haven't told you! He has been to my dug-out every day, about four times a day. You can imagine in what a blue funk I was. I felt sure he wanted to make an end of me. Finally, yesterday, out of sheer fright, I told him straight out why I had been transferred over here, vowing, of course, that I was innocent, that . . . He listened to me and at last, without the least hint of censure, you understand, he said: 'Yes, I know, that's the way misfortunes befall mankind.' And that was all! Then we talked about Vienna, about musical comedies, about Americans—in short, chatted like comrades! In fact, I even think that he has taken rather a liking to me, for this morning he came again to inspect—a so-called inspection. Instead, he gave me a definite proof of trust. A decided proof! In absolute confidence he told me a great official secret. So that henceforth I have no fear, my mind is at rest . . ."

The captain's high spirits and serenity annoyed Bologa. Censoriously he interrupted him.

"Of what importance is an official secret to us? Trust and suspicion are equally troublesome!"

"No, no!" exclaimed the captain with warmth. "Do not let us exaggerate. There are decent people everywhere, in every race. Why exaggerate? Well, the colonel is a man who cares nothing for his rank, we must acknowledge that! Besides, the secret does affect us also, because there is some talk of changing the division. There is a tired-out division on its way from Italy to take our place."

75

"And are we to go back to the Italian front?" asked Bologa.

"No, not to the Italian front," answered Klapka quickly, with some pride. "To the Rumanian front."

As he was uttering the last word he remembered that the lieutenant was a Rumanian, but it was too late to do anything but utter the word in a lower key. Bologa paled, and as if he had not caught the words, repeated mechanically:

"To the Rum . . ." Something seemed to clutch at his throat and he could get no further. He remained with his mouth open, staring idiotically at the captain, who, realizing how imprudent he had been, was murmuring inanely:

"Forgive me, friend. I had forgotten that you . . . I am a . . ."

But Apostol's brain was only just beginning to grasp the meaning of the words which had given him so sharp and poignant a shock, as if he had received a dagger-thrust. He leapt to his feet and walked backwards and forwards, wringing his hands and whispering desperately:

"Impossible, impossible, impossible! . . ."

Klapka, nonplussed, tried to console him by saying, without conviction:

"Calm yourself, Bologa; what the hell . . . When all is said and done one cannot live without compromise, without sacrifices and . . ."

Suddenly Apostol Bologa stopped in front of him, his face white, his eyes dull, and the captain's words dried in his throat.

"Anything else, anything else, but this—this cannot be," burst from Bologa in burning tones. "That would be . . . a . . . a . . ."

The walls of the dug-out turned his efforts to find a word into a long-drawn-out echo, which made Klapka seize him by the arm and bid him speak lower. And Apostol, as if he had understood, became embarrassed, dropped his eyes, and ended in a mutter:

"A . . . a . . . crime . . ."

"So it is, but what are we to do?" said the captain in a smothered voice, his eyes fixed on the entrance. "I understand and share your perturbation, but you others have at least the consolation of knowing that there are kinsmen in the other camp fighting for your salvation, whereas we can hope for nothing from anywhere! For us, the only means of proving our patriotism is to die on the gallows!"

Bologa, overcome, had dropped into a chair. Klapka, thinking that he had calmed down, went on speaking with more confidence.

"War is, in any circumstances, a colossal crime, but a still greater crime is the Austrian war. When people of the same blood take up arms, whether they are in the right or not, they all know that success will be for the good of the race and consequently each man can die with the conviction that he has sacrificed himself for the good cause of all. But in our case cruel masters have sent their slaves to die whilst strengthening their chains! Well then? In the midst of this turmoil of crime what can the small crime like the one that is crushing your soul matter? Who cares here about our souls?"

"Which means that . . .?" Bologa, who had begun to listen, queried impatiently.

"That you are to go where we shall all go," said Klapka gravely, with painful resignation. "That you are to go and do what we shall all do, and that you are to seal hermetically all the inlets to your soul until peace comes or until the world will be destroyed, or until your turn to die will come and put an end to all your torment!"

Apostol started and answered protestingly:

"But if I don't want to die? I don't want to, I no longer want to! Now I want to live, I no longer want to die!"

Klapka was silent for a moment, and then said with a smile that tried to hide his embarrassment:

"I know I am hardly the person to talk to you of death. Through fear of death or love of life—perhaps it is the same thing—I am a coward. . . . Yes, yes, I acknowledge and confess that I am capable of swallowing any shame, any humiliation. Nevertheless, I have told myself many a time, yes, even as I am I have said to myself that the dead are happiest, because they at least have finished with suffering. I like you, Bologa, and had I not found you here I should not have had so much confidence in myself. But you see, even we, whose souls have been drawn so close together by our common suffering, even we must share our anguish in a foreign tongue! How, then, can we help envying those that are dead, Bologa?"

The lieutenant was no longer listening to his words. Klapka's calm increased his agitation. And all of a sudden he asked with a glimmer of hope in his eyes:

"Do you think that it is a certainty?"

The captain, after a slight hesitation, answered resolutely, as if he wished to cure him by drastic means:

"Unfortunately there is no doubt about it, my dear fellow. The other division has already left Italy. To-morrow or after to-morrow it will arrive. In a week's time it will have taken our place, and a few days later we shall be in Ardeal, on the Ru . . ."

Bologa's eyes scorched him. He broke off abruptly and lowered his eyes, staring at his muddy boots and nervously jerking his knees, while Apostol walked up and down like a caged wolf, breathing heavily, his temples burning. Two minutes later, with a new determination, the lieutenant again halted in front of Klapka.

"Sir, I beg of you . . . I implore you, save me . . . You can save me. . . . I cannot go to that front. . . ."

Klapka raised his eyes and looked at him. He did not understand what Bologa wanted him to do. The latter continued frenziedly:

"A means of salvation must be found! Transfer me to a regiment which is staying here; or send me back to Italy, wherever you like, only not there! I'll fight as I have fought until to-day, I swear I will! I'll . . . I have three medals for bravery; all three won with . . . But there I cannot go! There I feel sure that I shall die. . . . And I don't want to die! I must live!"

He fell on the bed, his face in his hands, convulsed by sobs. The captain was deeply moved and felt that if he tried to speak he, too, would weep. In the dark dug-out Apostol's sobs made the air heavy, and the smoky light on the table threw uneasy shadows on the walls. Presently, when the lieutenant's sobs had ceased, Klapka said:

"Do you feel better now? Well, then, we can talk as man to man and soldier to soldier! The truth is that in war-time one must not think, one must just fight. . . , Anyway, that's what a general said in a speech at headquarters the other day. But this thing we must consider very carefully and without hurry, otherwise . . . If you stop to think you will see that I am powerless. I cannot propose anything because I am stigmatized: a Czech— that is to say, a traitor. . . . It was for people like us that the idea of putting machine-guns behind the lines was invented, so that they should sharpen our desire for glory in case there should be any hesitation. If I dared to suggest your name for transfer we should both be suspected immediately—immediately! A Czech with a record like mine to take the part of a Rumanian? You can imagine the to-do there would be, the . . . Only the general could save you, if he were human and had a heart. But do you really think that out here there are people that are human? Do you really believe that . . .?"

Bologa, who had sat up and was listening surlily, clung to one word and exclaimed:

"I'll go and see the general!"

Klapka became cold with fear, as if the general himself had caught him plotting, and said in a whisper:

"Calm yourself, Bologa! Please! Don't you know General Karg? Why, he has been your C.O. for nearly a year—Karg! A dog, a . . . He would be quite capable of court-martialling you straight away instead of giving you any answer at all . . ."

"Consequently I am to leave without even trying to protect myself or to prevent a crime?" burst out Apostol again, but this time furiously and grinding his teeth.

"Listen to my advice, friend," answered the captain quietly. "I am older than you and have suffered much during my life. War has no other philosophy but luck. Trust to luck! Death has whistled in your ears in all keys during the last two years, and yet luck has protected you. Perhaps Fate loves you! Don't rub her up the wrong way, don't tempt her. . . . Leave her alone."

"How certain I am that a terrible danger is awaiting me over there!" murmured Bologa, shuddering and feeling all at once fearfully depressed. "Never have I had so strong a presentiment."

"To-day there are dangers everywhere," said Klapka, keeping a tight hold on himself. "In the air, at the front, at home, in the whole world. The earth itself, it seems to me, is passing through a danger zone. What can we do? Luck is every man's shield, that's a fact! Take my advice. . . . You'll see, before long you'll tell me I was right. But without passion, without haste! Calmly, calmly!"

He rose slowly, put on his helmet, ready to go.

"Rather than go there, I'll desert to the Russians!" then came in a whisper from Bologa, as he looked straightly at the captain.

"That's easily said," answered Klapka calmly, as if he had been waiting for these very words from the lieutenant. "But if you don't succeed you know what awaits you! Only the other day I told you the tale of those three. They also spoke as you are doing—even more boldly. And yet, to-day they are probably still in the Forest of the Hanged to terrify others!"

"I don't worry about that," said Bologa confidently. "If I am caught I'll shoot myself and finish quickly! No matter what happens, I won't die by the rope, I promise you!"

"They also promised me that, friend, but circumstances proved stronger than their resolution. That's why I bid you take care, don't play with Fate! There are thousands, nay, tens of thousands in your position, and Fate looks after them as she thinks fit."

Klapka pressed his hand warmly, and the next minute Apostol Bologa found himself alone, rooted to the spot, with eyes staring into vacancy, haunted by apparitions. When he came out of his trance he felt so weak that he threw himself on the bed. On the table, in the improvised candlestick, the light began to flicker quickly, grew less bright, and suddenly went out. The darkness startled Bologa, but his feverish lips whispered bravely:

"It is impossible! It must not happen!"

§ VIII

"Have you heard the news, Petre?" said Apostol the next day to his orderly, who was squatting in a corner, reading with ardour and religious fervour *The Dream of the Mother of God.* "In a week's time, or at the most in two weeks' time, we are going home, to Ardeal."

"The Lord be praised!" answered the soldier, his face shining with joy, and he began to cross himself. "At last the Lord and the Blessed Mother have granted it! Most of them have had a week now and again, some even more; only we seem to be treated as if we had the plague."

Bologa's smile on seeing the man's joy was almost malignant, and he continued mockingly:

"What! Did you think we were going there to amuse ourselves? Put that out of your mind, my lad! We are going there to fight, to fight the Rumanians. . . ."

"My God, sir!" exclaimed Petre, starting up. "God forbid that such a thing should happen!" he added, crossing himself several times. "O Lord, protect us and do not abandon us! What sinfulness, sir! And shall not God strike them dead?"

The orderly's consternation was balm to his wound.

"If a simple man like that revolts, then what must I do?" Bologa said to himself, looking gratefully at Petre. And then immediately came the thought: "Surely, then, the general will also understand?"

Since the night before the thought of the general had pursued him, and he tried continually to strengthen his resolution. He told himself that he had thought it all out carefully, that he had seen all the probabilities and that—Klapka was wrong. Besides, Klapka was a coward who saw executioners and hangmen everywhere. Whereas he, Apostol Bologa, with three proofs of bravery on his breast . . . Advice had always annoyed him, but now Klapka's advice infuriated him. Resignation seemed to him a brute-like attitude, unworthy of a man. He felt that to make no attempt to-day would be as great a crime as had been his joining the Army.

The thought that he might have to go there stuck in his mind like an enemy bayonet. He would have to tear it out or life for him would be impossible. The more so because in the light of to-day's fears the memories of the past besieged him like sinister threats.

His hope in the general of the division dispersed his fears. That also proved Klapka wrong. He made up his mind to go to headquarters and explain the situation to him, to petition him and to assure him most solemnly that he would do his duty anywhere else but there. He wanted to go at once, to get it over more quickly and set his mind at rest. He put up his hand to take down the receiver in order to phone through and ask when the C.O. could see him. At the last minute, however, he refrained. How could he ask the general to transfer him when no one as yet was supposed to know of the intended change? He would be asked how he knew, who had told him. It would be a dirty trick to betray Klapka; it would be . . .

"Well, I'll have to wait for the present," he said to himself, "at least until the news of the proposed change has become known unofficially. I must act with care and dignity!"

He grew calmer. Three days went by. There was no whisper of a rumour that the division was being transferred. Nor did Klapka come again. It seemed as if he dreaded meeting Bologa, who, growing more and more hopeful, had begun to think that perhaps the order had been countermanded. His heart throbbed with a pleasant emotion. And because he felt happy he wrote a long and hopeful letter to his mother, two whole pages of which were devoted to the condemnation of Palagiesu's action with regard to Protopop Groza. He also wrote a passionate letter to Marta, telling her that his love was as strong as ever, in spite of all his suffering, and that he could hardly wait for the hour when he would be able to take her in his arms.

Another serene day passed. Then the second-lieutenant of the battery told him that he had heard from an infantryman that in four days at latest the whole division was being sent to the Rumanian front. Bologa turned pale, but he asked for particulars. The second-lieutenant then said, further, that the infantry officers had been told the news in confidence three days ago and the advance troops of the exchange division had actually arrived in Zirin.

That night the search-light reappeared in the next sector. Bologa, at the command post, with the telephone receiver at his ear, listened to the indications from the observation post. The guns boomed harshly, hoarsely, the earth shook, and from the roof of the dug-out, from between the heavy beams, thin trickles of sand oozed.

"Suppose someone else puts it out," he thought with odd regret.

When the booming ceased and he heard that the light had disappeared, Bologa felt pleased. He remembered that Klapka had spoken of a decoration for whoever destroyed the search-light.

"In any case, the lucky man who hits it is sure to be mentioned in dispatches," he thought, turning his back on the telephone. "I wonder who it will be."

Within him a voice answered that it must be he. He tried to stifle it, but the voice became commanding. Then there flashed through his mind the thought that if he should have the good luck to destroy the Russian search-light, and if, as a reward, he should be mentioned in dispatches or decorated, how easily and with what good chances of success would he then be able to go to General Karg!

This idea seemed to him so wonderful that he was amazed that it had not occurred to him immediately he had made up his mind to go to the general. All thoughts of sleep left him; he rushed to the map and began to calculate and to mark until daylight with untiring energy and with a sure confidence that his life depended on what he would do in this connection.

He spent the whole day looking through his field-glasses, examining the sector with attention and comparing in his mind the points marked on the map. Towards evening he began to worry in case the search-light, which was to be his means of salvation, should not appear that night. Nevertheless, he was quite prepared to watch for it for a whole week if need be in order to destroy it. If only the order for exchanging did not come before! No, that could not happen; it must appear, it simply must . . .

That evening at ten o'clock he gave his orders, and made his way to the observation post in the front line. A cold, slow, monotonous rain was falling. Arrows of water, glinting like steel, spurted through the dark sky. The clay, moistened by the autumn rains, clung to the lieutenant's boots and squelched at each step. The canopy of clouds seemed as if about to fall on the earth, dizzied by the endless darkness. Apostol Bologa, with his steel helmet pulled right over his eyes, wrapped in his fur-lined trench-coat with collar turned up, went forward cautiously, avoiding puddles, his chin sunk on his breast. His heart throbbed so violently that he did not even feel the beating rain.

He knew the way and the ground well. During the last three months, since this front had become fixed, he had covered this ground hundreds of times. He entered the labyrinth of communication trenches, where the water had gathered as in irrigation canals. His high Hessian boots sank up to the ankles in the clayey mud.

He was wet with perspiration by the time he reached the observation post, hidden in the front line of the trenches. He exchanged a few words with the wizened sergeant-major, and then sent him back to the battery.

Bologa felt his way gropingly and perched himself behind the theodolite. He could see nothing. The instrument was sheltered from the rain, but, on the other hand, the rain poured in through the holes in the roof at the back of the observation post. He tried to get his bearings, but the darkness was so thick that his eyes could make out no variation in the pitchy blackness. And in his ears the exasperatingly uniform patter of the rain which successfully drowned all sounds of life. He could feel the beating of his heart, but his brain seemed numb from too much thinking.

An hour later the patter died down a little and simultaneously Bologa realized that his mind had begun again to make plans and calculations. Then he found himself thinking:

"In weather like this I can cross over to the enemy without fear."

As soon as he took in the import of his thoughts he curbed them with disgust. From the moment when he had become convinced that by destroying the worrying search-light he would win his salvation from General Karg, he had regretted and been ashamed that he had even contemplated deserting to the enemy. In two years of war he had become so deeply imbued with the military spirit that desertion, from whatever motive, seemed to him an unpardonable crime.

"All the same, if you want to get away more safely, you'll have to go either at nightfall or at dawn," came again into his mind, the same thought pursuing him persistently, like a fly which one attempts in vain to chase away.

Gradually the rain stopped and a strong wind began to blow with sinister howlings, unravelling the darkness a little and rushing violently through Bologa's observation post. Before long he felt on his back a damp and icy patch. He cowered down, trying to protect his back, but the wind got through his clothes, through his skin, and clutched at his heart.

"And that search-light isn't coming!" he murmured trembling.

His eyes darted with impatient fury through the thinning darkness. Humble signs of life began to be visible in the dead stillness. To the right and left stretched the infantry trenches, crooked and capricious, like coarse lines on a crumpled sheet of paper. Here and there, in front of the trenches, like mushrooms grown rigid or frozen, he saw or divined the listening posts. About thirty metres to the right Captain Cervenco's sector began. "I wonder what Cervenco is doing? Dear old Cervenco!" Before him the plain stretched flat, lost in the darkness and whipped by the wind which now and again shook big drops of water out of the sky.

Apostol Bologa knew that exactly five hundred and eighty-three metres away lay the first line of the Russian trenches, and it seemed to him that he could distinguish the zigzags which meant the earthworks. His imagination travelled farther, and groping through the darkness found the second line, the third, the enemy's batteries, the place where the search-light had last appeared.

Bologa did not dare to look at his watch for fear he should lose his hope of the search-light appearing. He was sure, however, that it was past midnight. "There is still time," he said, more and more worried. His loneliness oppressed him. He felt a painful need of exchanging a word with someone, no matter whom, so long as he were not left alone to wait. The search-light had never shown itself before midnight. As a rule, it came at about two o'clock, so there was plenty of time; he could still hope. But suppose it did not come at all, then . . .

"It would be entirely their fault if I should ruin myself!" he thought with fury, shaking his fist at the invisible Russian lines.

And then suddenly, when he least expected it, right in front of him, in the battery's own sector, as if brought to life by his defiance, flashed a blinding, arrogant light, throwing first its rays towards the sky lined with clouds and then dropping to earth quickly, with feverish tremors. Apostol closed his eyes, as startled as if he were face to face with a ghost, forgetting his guns and his anger, forgetting everything, as if he were in a dream.

"Hi! Are you asleep over there? The guns! Can't you see the search-light?" growled a deep, mocking voice suddenly a few steps away in the infantry trench.

Bologa came to with a start. He knew that voice; it belonged to a very tall and thin infantry lieutenant, who ostensibly looked down on all gunners. He surveyed with the theodolite the source of the light and then barked a curt order into the mouthpiece of the telephone. A few seconds later the boomings began, slow and deliberate. But still the white rays glided on slowly, indifferent to the angry shells, cleaving the darkness and, as if defiantly, drawing nearer to Bologa. Then, as if they had not actually discovered him cowering in his damp observation post, they strayed over him, enveloping him in their cold magic, penetrating through his stricken eyes into all the hidden places of his heart, upsetting and confusing his thoughts like an unexpected sunrise. At first Apostol felt nothing but an immense hatred for the light which took him into its embrace without his leave. But when he tried to utter two words into the telephone to correct the aim of the guns, he found he could not tear his gaze away from it. The blandishments of the tremulous rays began to appear to him as sweet as the kisses of a maiden in love. Their spell was so strong that he no longer even heard the booming of the guns. Unconsciously, like a passionate child, he stretched out both hands towards the light, murmuring with parched throat:

"The light! The light!"

But at that very second, as if chopped off by the sword of an executioner, the rays went out and Bologa's eyes were filled with darkness. He didn't know what had happened. The guns continued to shoot at slow intervals as he had ordered.

"I think I've smashed that search-light," he thought, wondering how he could have brought himself to do such a blackguardly action and rejoicing that he had done it.

He remained dazed for a while, feeling that there was something he still had to do, and unable to remember what it was. Then suddenly, dismayed, he felt for the receiver and shouted:

"The rockets! The rockets!"

On the sullen sky there rose, hissing angrily, a globe of light like a spying eye. At the spot where the search-light had been Bologa, through his field-glasses, saw a quantity of little black worms rolling about helplessly. The light in the sky soon went out and simultaneously the guns became dumb of their own accord, without order from him, as if they had become satiated and were now satisfied. The darkness enwrapped Apostol like a rough shroud, and his eyes, with enlarged pupils, strained in aimless expectancy. In his innermost being, however, he yearned for the light—the kind, caressing light.

Then he heard again, this time just behind him, the voice of the infantry lieutenant:

"At last! Well, it's a good job you've finished with that search-light, for it had become a real disgrace! As likely as not you'll be presented with a medal for bravery, because that's how decorations are given in our Army. . . . In any case, I congratulate you. . . . Good night!"

Without waiting for an answer, the lieutenant, muttering to himself, went off through the puddles of the communication trench.

"God! What has happened?" Bologa asked himself apprehensively, trying to rouse himself from the numbness which had paralysed his thoughts.

The wind blew colder now, scattering again the thin, enervating drizzle. The drops rolled down his back like a thin trickle of sand. "That's how the thoughts in my brain are—weak, undecided, groping." Little by little, however, he managed to straighten them out. So he had attained his aim and he would now be able to go to the general. There would be no need now for him to go with his division to the Rumanian front, that was almost certain. Then, why did he not rejoice as he had rejoiced when the idea had come to him to destroy the search-light? Instead of an answer the white light which he had strangled just now flashed up in his soul, shining like a distant beacon. And the radiance resembled now Svoboda's countenance under the halter, now the vision which he had had as a child in the church before the altar, after his special prayer to God. The light put an end to his doubts and set his heart at rest as if it had opened out a straight, smooth road for him in a wild untrodden jungle. An hour ago all his hopes had been centred in others, and he had had no confidence in himself. Now he knew that he would sooner cross Fate than pollute his soul—for in his soul, in the light, lay his salvation.

The darkness thinned gradually. The wind blew unceasingly, and sometimes it sent out a call, long drawn out, troubled, with a note of shame and warning in it. Then, like a temptation, the thought that this was the hour for deserters slipped again into Bologa's mind. And the thought no longer seemed to him repulsive, just as if all his former convictions had been wiped off his brain.

A sergeant came to take his place, although Apostol had forgotten to give the order. He felt sorry to leave the loneliness, which now seemed precious to him. He made his way along the zigzagged trenches, behind the sentries standing rigid with their rifles at their side. As he was making his way towards the communication trench, he ran into Captain Cervenco.

"I haven't been able to close my eyes all night," murmured the captain dejectedly. "I am sorry that you have destroyed the search-light, I don't know why . . . You've killed the light, Bologa!"

"The light is here!" answered Bologa triumphantly, beating his breast with his hand.

"Yes, yes, you are right! The light is there, and the suffering, too! The whole world is there!" added Cervenco with a glint in his eyes.

Apostol went on through the twisting trenches, his back bent, his eyes shining, his soul full of confidence, reconciled and contented as if he had been purified in a bath of virtue.

§ IX

Towards midday, whilst Bologa was still asleep, a shrill buzzing at the head of his bed startled him and made him jump to his feet, under the impression that the dug-out was being blown up. The adjutant was roaring into the telephone:

"Lieutenant Bologa? Hallo! Himself speaking? Oh, is it you, old chap? Colonel's orders you are to leave immediately and report yourself to his Excellency. His Excellency wishes to see you. Very urgent! Of course, you'll call on us on your way, for the colonel also wants to speak to you. At the same time I want to congratulate you! You've saved the honour of the whole division. The colonel phoned to headquarters right away during the night. The fourth one is on the way, Bologa, bravo!"

An hour later Apostol was in a motor-car, sitting next to a staff captain whom he had met at the command post of the regiment and who had offered to take him to headquarters, as he himself was just due to leave. On the way the captain told him that the destruction of the search-light deserved a special reward—all his comrades, including the colonel, had told him so. Bologa listened thoughtfully and silently. Several times his eyes travelled down to his breast, where the three medals for bravery shone, and he remembered his emotion when the first one had been pinned on. How he had longed for it, and how small he had felt until he had received it! It had seemed to him as if he were the only one who had none, and he had felt unhappy and dishonoured. He had hurled himself where lurked the greatest danger, where death reaped oftenest, without fear, with no other thought in his mind but that medal! And when the colonel had pinned it on his breast in the presence of the troops, his heart had wept tears of joy. Not until then had he thought himself worthy to live.

In the courtyard of the divisional headquarters he met Lieutenant Gross, who, being a sapper, constantly had work to do at headquarters. Gross greeted him with an ironical grimace.

"Bravo, philosopher! You've killed a few more people for a bit of tin."

"Listen, Gross," answered Bologa, suddenly annoyed, "when you cease to carry out orders, then you may make imputations against others! Until then, be a little more modest, please!"

"I execute orders, it is true," said the sapper, still in a bantering tone. "I commit or help barbarities, but with nausea, friend! Not with enthusiasm, like others! I do not seek to distinguish myself!"

"It would be better if you practised what you preached," murmured Bologa, looking him straight in the eye. "To talk is easy, but . . ."

"Well, we'll see what you'll do to-morrow or the day after on the Rumanian front," interrupted Gross with a sour smile. "We'll see what you'll do there. . . ."

"I'll never go there!" said Bologa with a start and flushing deeply.

Gross was about to say something else, but just then there appeared on the doorstep a smart sergeant, who called importantly:

"Lieutenant Bologa! Please to come in, his Excellency is expecting you, sir."

A few seconds later Apostol Bologa was standing stiffly before General Karg, who was short and squat, with an ugly, harsh face, darkened by a bristling moustache and pierced by round eyes whose gaze, darting from under very thick, frowning eyebrows, made one think of two venomous daggers.

The lieutenant's heart contracted when he saw him rise heavily from the table laden with bundles of paper and maps. The recollection flashed through him that each time he had set eyes on the general he had felt a strange fear, as if he were in face of a merciless enemy or of a terrible and unexpected danger which he could not avoid.

The general, with chin uplifted, held out his hand and said heartily:

"Well done, Bologa! Your action has been reported to me, and I wished particularly to congratulate you in person. Yes, I wished . . . absolutely . . ."

His voice was rasping and penetrating, and he seemed to be scolding even when he joked.

Apostol bowed slightly, pressing the general's hand. Then he gave him a detailed account, using short, dry, military sentences, of how he had destroyed the search-light. While he was speaking, however, he noticed that the general's nostrils had hair growing out of them, and he thought that very probably he snored horribly at night; also he remembered that he had not seen him since the execution of the Czech. Karg listened to his account attentively, now and again nodding and darting pleased looks at him. Then, when Bologa had finished, he slapped him amicably on the back, murmuring:

"I have proposed you for the Gold Medal. You may be sure you will get it. We need soldiers like you, and they deserve all distinctions. Well done, Bologa! I am proud to have the honour of commanding brave officers such as you."

The general stopped, racking his mind to find one or two more suitable words to say. But he could not think of anything else, and, after a short pause, repeated more mildly:

"I am proud . . . very proud . . ." and again he stretched out his hand, ready to dismiss him. Then Bologa, completely self-possessed, his voice clear, and looking straight into the general's grey eyes, said:

"Excellency, I beg you to give me leave to make a request!"

General Karg, unpleasantly surprised that the lieutenant, especially after he had shown him such marked favour, should dare to speak without being addressed and to ask a favour without first having put his name down at orderly hour in the hierarchical manner required by the regulations, took two steps backward with knitted brow. Nevertheless, wishing to show every indulgence to a good soldier, he answered in a friendly tone:

"Yes, yes, I am listening. A good soldier . . . naturally . . . willingly . . ."

At that moment Bologa felt clearly that his audacity was vain and useless, and he hesitated. Beads of perspiration broke out on his forehead. To gain time and to regain his composure he coughed and bent his head. Then, his self-confidence reasserting itself, he fixed his eyes resolutely on the general's face and said, speaking rapidly and jerkily:

"Excellency, I know—I have heard—that in a few days' time our division is leaving here to go somewhere else, to another front. . . ."

"Quite correct," answered the general wonderingly as he saw that Bologa faltered.

"Then, Excellency," continued the lieutenant abruptly, as if the interruption had given him renewed courage, "then I would ask you to allow me to stay behind here. . . . Or, if this is not possible, to send me to the Italian front. . . ."

The general stared at him perplexedly and twirled his moustache nervously. Then he said:

"Very well. Although I am sorry to lose you. An excellent officer, brave . . . But as you are so keen on this . . . However, I think that here would be better than in Italy. . . ."

"I don't mind going there, Excellency. I was at Doberdo for a few months, and on the whole I should prefer it. . . ."

Bologa's face was now lit up with joy and hope. He could no longer control his emotion. He sighed deeply with relief.

"Very well, very well," repeated the general thoughtfully. "Though I don't understand why you should not want to come with us. My division has a holy mission in Ardeal! A great mission. Yes! The enemy has stolen our country's soil. There the Wallachians . . ."

Suddenly General Karg stopped short as if a ray of light had entered his brain. He again took a few steps backwards and glued his gaze on Bologa, trying to read his innermost thoughts. For several seconds there reigned a grave-like silence in the room, while outside could be heard the grinding of cart wheels and the noisy chirping of the sparrows in a tree under the office window. Apostol unconsciously closed his eyes to protect himself from the general's scrutiny.

"You are a Rumanian?" the latter jerked out abruptly, his voice almost hoarse.

"Yes, Excellency," answered the lieutenant quickly.

"Rumanian!" repeated the general, surprised and irritated, in a tone as if expecting a denial.

"Rumanian!" repeated Bologa more firmly, drawing himself up and puffing out his chest slightly.

"Yes, very well, of course . . ." stammered Karg presently, suspicious and scrutinizing. "Yes, certainly. . . . But then your request surprises me . . . very much. . . . It would seem to me that you differentiate between the enemies of your country?"

Apostol Bologa met the flashing eyes of the general with a calmness which made him marvel at himself. He felt determined and unshaken, as he always did when violently attacked. Now he wished obstinately to convince the enemy, though he realized very well that his efforts would be fruitless. He found himself talking calmly, without the slightest trace of emotion or hesitation; he might have been arguing with a friendly comrade.

"Excellency, for twenty-seven months I have fought in such a way that I can look anyone in the face unashamed. I have never shirked my duty. My whole heart and soul was in my work. To-day, however, I find myself in a morally impossible situation."

The general shuddered as if a sword had been thrust into his breast. His eyes flashed and glinted like steel. He rushed at Bologa with raised and bent arm, ready to knock him down, roaring:

"What is that? Morally impossible situation? What sort of talk is that? How dare you? I know nothing of such nonsense, which is intended purely and simply to conceal the cowardliness of men without patriotic feelings. I know nothing about it, do you understand? I don't want to know anything about it!"

Apostol tried to protest, but the general cut him short, purple with fury.

"I don't allow you to speak, do you understand? Each word of yours deserves a shot! The thoughts concealed behind your

words are criminal! Do you understand? Criminal! Oh . . . oh . . . !
So that's what your bravery amounts to? Behold what sort of
a person I've recommended for the Gold Medal! A fine thing!
Gold Medal! Shots—not medals!"

He glared at him with dislike and contempt and then
abruptly turned his back on him, smothering an oath between
his teeth and tugging at his moustache with his right hand, a
small, plump hand, laden with rings, like the hand of a woman.

Bologa remained serene, unmoved, persisting in the idea
that he must convince him. The fury of the general did him
good and gave him courage. When he thought that the latter
had calmed down a little, he said again, in the same clear voice:

"I asked a favour of your Excellency in the belief that you
would kindly try to understand my spiritual state. That is why I
have taken the liberty of speaking to you as man to man."

The general, who had paused by the window, cursing and
muttering, turned sharply on the lieutenant and answered with
more restraint:

"I do not listen to such requests, nor do I hold conversation
with such people! Do you understand ? As it is, I have talked too
much with you! You ingrate!"

He did not hold out his hand this time, but looked him
up and down with disgust, and then sat down at the table and
began turning over some of the papers on it. Bologa saluted and
went out quietly, confidently, as if after an intensely pleasant
interview. The general stared after him, shook his head, surveyed
attentively the closed door, and suddenly, again filled with rage,
banged his fist violently on the spread-out map. Just then the
adjutant sidled into the office, alarmed and filled with curiosity.

"Note down Lieutenant Bologa," mumbled General Karg,
addressing the amazed adjutant. "He is dangerous and . . . It

wouldn't surprise me to hear some fine day that he had deserted to the enemy. What men! What an army!"

The adjutant bowed, put some documents on the table and made haste to disappear on tiptoe, without noise, for fear the general should unload his fury on his own head.

In the middle of the courtyard Apostol Bologa gazed around him as if this were the first time he had been there in his life. The enclosure was large, with a wooden paling on the street side. The new plank door which had been let into it was now open. There were a few carts in a file at the back, near the stables, and the motor-car in which he had come stood there abandoned, its doors gaping. The stone house, roofed with old tiles and as immense as a barracks, was pitted with shrapnel dating from the period when the war had passed over the village and when a shell had actually exploded in the little front garden, tearing from its roots the twin of the tree in which a pair of noisy sparrows were now quarrelling. The sky had cleared and filled the atmosphere with a blue more tender than usual. The sun smiled in the west, yellow and frail as the face of a gay old man, and the light of it kissed the earth like a beneficent dew, diffusing joy and awakening hope everywhere.

Apostol stood a while with his eyes turned towards the sun, drinking in thirstily the smiling light. He felt relieved, as if he had just eased by a spell of passionate weeping a long-standing ache. His thoughts no longer oppressed him but bent docilely to his will, and had he wished he could have strung them nicely, like glass beads, on a thread.

He left the courtyard. In the street, opposite the mess-room, he saw a lorry loaded with equipment, ready to leave for the front. He jumped on. He wanted to get back as soon as possible to his battery. He was in a hurry. . . .

§ X

He reached the division in the evening and went to report that he was back. He found Klapka alone in the large dug-out. He was writing home. The captain gave him a long look, then shook both his hands and said warmly:

"Now I can congratulate you too, old fellow, with my whole heart!"

"It's true, you are the only one who has not congratulated me so far," answered Bologa with a bitter smile. "For my bravery!"

"For your bravery in telling the general what you told him!" interrupted Klapka with a shudder.

"What! You've been told the news already?" Apostol asked wonderingly. "Officially?"

"Your bearing, your pride, your calm told me!" exclaimed the captain with a curious exultance. "There is no need for you to tell me what has happened! Your eyes tell me everything, everything! Oh, if only I could be a man like you! If we were all like that in one hour the chains would be broken!"

As with all cowards, the courage and energy of others excited Klapka. He asked Bologa to give him an account from beginning to end of the scene with the general, interrupting him often with boisterous applause. Then, when Apostol had finished, he asked him with excited curiosity:

"Well, and now what do you think of doing?"

Bologa's eyes gleamed bright. He did not answer immediately, and then said quietly, as if he were merely mentioning an everyday occurrence:

"Now?—To-night I am deserting to the Russians!"

Klapka, not expecting such an answer, gaped at him for a minute, then he looked round, terrified lest someone had heard the lieutenant's words and so might possibly get him into trouble for not reporting what he knew to the authorities.

"Have you gone mad, man?" he whispered, his voice shaking with fear. "Don't say such childish things or we shall both find ourselves hanging from some tree like two rotten stumps!"

Apostol Bologa smiled, his white teeth glinting between his thin lips.

"A month ago, nay, even three days ago, I wouldn't have dared to think of desertion. I would have been the first to look down on myself with contempt. Because until to-day I was a different person. When I look back, it seems to me as if I had carried in me the life of a stranger. I have always imagined the soul as a treasure-house with many chambers, some full of treasures, others empty. Many men—most, in fact—live all their life in the little empty chambers, which are always open, because the others are locked with great padlocks and the keys thereof are hidden in the fire of suffering. The emptiness and darkness scared me. That was why I strove to find the keys of my treasure-house. But even treasures are deceptive. As soon as you have discovered one you begin to crave for the ones that are hidden away more deeply. It may be that death alone can reveal to your eyes the most valuable one, nevertheless you hanker after it with a miser's greed. As likely as not that longing will prove empty. But without it life would be valueless and would not differ in the very slightest from the life of an insect. To-day I feel that I have discovered a new treasure, and that I must protect it no matter what sacrifice it entails!"

"What treasures? What treasures?" interrupted Klapka impatiently. "This is just hysterical nonsense, friend! Words, Bologa, and neurotic dreams! What is real is the war with death on its arm! Put away these figments of the brain, my dear fellow; they only complicate and embitter life, which is already sufficiently damnable!"

"Sir, if you are really my friend, I beg you do not give me another word of advice!" said Apostol nervily; then he added more quietly: "Please don't! Do you think I found it easy to shed my past like a dirty garment and to stand naked, exposed to the storm? Do you think that I did not try to make myself believe that I was dressed, even after I had felt the lashing of the cold wind and rain? Now no one in the world can make me throw away my new and warm garments and make me go back to shiver in my discarded rags. You see, don't you? . . . Please . . . and . . . Perhaps the exchanging of troops may begin to-morrow night, which means there is no more time to be lost. I would run the risk of being compelled to accompany you to Ardeal! And that is impossible!"

"I hear what you say and yet I cannot believe that you are speaking seriously," murmured Klapka, now uneasy. "It is obvious that you are either out of your mind or else that you are anxious to die by the halter. But don't you understand, man, that especially after your interview with the general you'll be shadowed at every step, and that you'll be caught in the very act of . . ."

"That is just why I must go to-night!" put in Bologa firmly.

"Then the halter is calling you," whispered the captain desperately, fingering his throat as if he were trying to put away an imaginary rope. Then, after a pause, he added with a shudder of fear: "In any case, I don't wish to know anything about it, nothing at all. I wash my hands of it."

Apostol Bologa rose quietly and made for the entrance. Klapka barred the way and said commandingly:

"You are to remain here! I'll prevent you! I am your superior officer and I'll stop you by force!"

"Perhaps you'd like to denounce me?" Bologa asked bitterly, looking hard at him. "Mind you, I'll shoot myself if . . ."

Filled with powerless fury, Klapka began to pummel his own head with his fists, stuttering: "He is mad! He has gone mad! What am I to do with the madman? O Lord, O Lord, what shall I do?"

Apostol drew nearer to him and said, much moved:

"Perhaps I do not even deserve that you should worry over me, sir. I am ungrateful not to listen to you, but now say good-bye to me and embrace me!"

The captain, who had abruptly quietened down, looked long at him, his fat face distorted with grief. Then he kissed him on both cheeks, sobbing aloud and mumbling fearfully, yet with rapturous emotion:

"Good-bye, dear friend, good-bye!" And he embraced him again until, having calmed his emotion somewhat, he managed to say pleadingly:

"Perhaps you'll still change your mind? Promise me at least to think it over again; I beg you to, I implore you! It would be terrible for you to fall into their hands . . . to . . . to . . . ghastly!"

"Good-bye!" answered Bologa, as if he had not heard what he said, going out quickly.

Outside it was darkening. In the west the trail of the setting sun still brightened the pale sky. Bologa set off rapidly towards his battery, when all at once he heard the voice of Klapka, sharp and angry:

"Telephone operator! Telephone operator! Where is the telephone operator!"

Bologa understood and smiled. The captain wished to protect himself in case of any suspicion of complicity.

§ XI

The battlefield, deserted and silent, wavered in the evening mist. The steppe stretched limitless, flat as a sheet of packing-paper, dotted with stumps of trees set wide apart, leafless and mutilated by shells. The positions stood out like sombre lines, crooked and capricious, without beginning or end.

Close to the battery Bologa paused, seeking in the zigzag of trenches the foremost observation post where he had been the night before. When he believed he had found it, his thoughts wandered farther; they slipped under the barbed wire, along the five hundred and eighty-three metres to the border of the Russian trenches, where they remained without guide.

"A new life begins there, and a new world," he said to himself with clutching neart.

In the dug-out he found waiting for him the second-lieutenant who had taken his place and who was eager to know what had happened to him and how the general had congratulated him. To escape his questions Bologa, with assumed gaiety, pitched him a tale and quickly changed the conversation. He said, uneasily, that they would have to keep their eyes open so as not to be caught by a sudden attack in view of the change of division. The second-lieutenant, to show that he was well up in strategical previsions, declared gravely that, as a matter of fact, he quite expected a surprise attack if the enemy had got wind of the intended change. In the end it was arranged that the second-lieutenant should keep a look-out at the chief observation post until two o'clock, when Bologa would go to relieve him.

Left alone, Bologa sat down to write a few words to his mother and to Marta, to let them know somehow, by covert words, that he could no longer stay here and that soon he would send them better news. But before he had put down a single syllable on the paper he thought better of it—any knowledge they had might be the cause of unpleasantness for them. Better they should know nothing. So instead of writing he fell to studying the map of the front with feverish attention, to tracing lines with his finger in order to discover a short, safe road. Petre found him thus occupied when he brought him his supper.

"Do you know, I am so hungry to-night that I could almost eat you!" Bologa cried laughingly, and thought to himself he must, in truth, make a good meal, because who knew what awaited him over there.

Immediately after he had eaten he lay down to rest, after having ordered Petre to awaken him without fail at one o'clock in the morning. He wanted to get a few hours' rest because who knew when and where he would get his next rest?

Petre awoke him at the fixed time, and Apostol arose, spry and cheerful. In a few minutes he was ready to start. He looked round the silent dug-out, wondering which of his belongings he should take with him. He hesitated a little, and finally took nothing. The only thing he might need was his revolver, to save him from the Forest of the Hanged. As he went towards the exit he heard Petre's usual good-bye: "May the Lord help you, sir!" He half thought of shaking hands with him, but decided to go on without stopping or answering.

The night felt damp. There was promise of rain and wind in the air. Bologa was glad, and turned a friendly eye on the cloudy sky. If it rained, he thought, it would, of course, be all the better.

Passing near Captain Cervenco's dug-out and having another half-hour to spare, he stepped in to ask him how he was getting on. The captain was reading the Bible with tears streaming from his eyes as if he were trying to live down a great sorrow.

"What is it? What has happened?" Apostol asked in amazement. "What are you grieving for? Are you in trouble? Have you had bad news from home?"

"I am a tree without roots," Cervenco said bitterly, with a despairing look. "Bologa, do you hear, to-night the Russians will attack us!"

Bologa turned pale as if he had received a slap in the face. A little while ago he, too, had talked of a possible attack, but merely to avoid embarrassing questions and to have a pretext for going to the observation post. An attack would upset all his plans.

"Impossible. . . . We've had no information," he mumbled confusedly. "Whyever should they especially pitch on to-night?"

"Bologa, it is a certainty," began the captain plaintively. "Believe me, a patrol brought me news last evening that over there they are making hasty preparations. You'll see, Bologa. It's always like that."

For another ten minutes Cervenco kept on his lamentations, so that Apostol left him thoroughly upset, cursing the impulse that had caused him to call on the Ruthenian maniac. Outside, however, in the silence broken only by the wind and in the enveloping darkness, he became himself again and thought Cervenco must really be beginning to show signs of insanity if he dreamt of nothing but hand-to-hand fights and attacks.

The second-lieutenant was shivering at the observation post, and he saluted Bologa as he would a saviour.

"The infantry will have it that the Russians intend to attack us this very night," whispered Bologa. "Did you notice anything?"

"Not a thing! Just silence and cold," scoffed the second-lieutenant. "That's always the infantry way, they are scared by every shadow. The Russians are not fools to attack us to-night like that, without preparations, when the change begins only the day after to-morrow!"

Bologa pressed his hand, well pleased, and wished him a good rest. He had never liked that second-lieutenant better than to-night. He seemed to have taken the very words out of his own mouth: "The Russians are no fools . . ."

When his eyes had become accustomed to the darkness, he looked uneasily across at the lines over there. Was there any movement to be seen or heard? A few minutes later a rifle shot rang out deafeningly somewhere near by. Though he knew by the sound of it that it was no Russian shot, his heart jumped. Other startled shots broke out immediately, then others on the right and left, but always farther away. Bologa grew calmer. They had probably come from startled sentinels.

Towards three o'clock, in order to reassure himself entirely, he ordered a rocket to be sent up so that he should see and convince himself. In the greenish light the ground between the trenches showed no signs of life. On the right, between the barbed wire, lay the body of a dead man. He had been killed two days ago on his way back from patrol, as likely as not by his own comrades—by mistake or through fright. Apostol's eyes travelled over him as if he had been a mushroom, eager only to see the road which he had chosen on the map—a disused trench which began about twenty yards away and almost reached the Russian trenches. The observation post was surrounded by bushes, left there on purpose as camouflage. If he crawled from there through the two shell-holes he might manage to reach the disused trench unobserved, for the listening posts were a good way off. At the other end of the trench he would call out. He knew enough Russian for that. . . . Then . . .

The light of the rocket went out and Bologa was satisfied. At five o'clock exactly, when the darkness began to lift, he would start. Which meant he had another two hours to wait. His mind was so thoroughly made up that he felt neither emotion nor impatience. He waited with his eyes fixed ahead on his goal, his thoughts free. Time flowed over him as a cool and soothing water.

Presently the thought flashed through his mind that perhaps the Russians would receive him with contempt for being a deserter—he, an officer. At that very moment a prolonged and hoarse detonation rent the air. Apostol became rigid and remained tensely waiting. After a few seconds, which seemed to him unending, there came a terrible crash, as if the earth had been split asunder. This was followed by furious and more rapid firing. The seething darkness was furrowed by luminous trails.

"What can this be?" thought Bologa, looking at his watch and seeing that it was barely four o'clock. "The attack? So they were right after all! Which means that I . . ."

Apostol recognized that the Russian guns had concentrated a converging fire on their artillery, which now began to answer, but rather timidly, obviously dazed by the suddenness and fury of the attack.

"What shall I do now?" he asked himself with the telephone receiver at his ear, listening to the duel of the two artilleries.

All at once he heard on his right, about ten metres or so away, a whizz which ended in a quick bang. He turned his eyes in that direction, and it seemed to him that he saw an earth funnel being flung up into the darkness.

"They've started to blow up the infantry," he mumbled desperately, his brain feeling like a dry sponge.

Some time passed. All around the shells fell more and more thickly. Then a long, sinister whizzing almost deafened him. His heart clutched, and the thought flashed through his mind: "That's for me!"

In front of him, a few paces away, the sky opened and a shell carried off the roof of the observation post. Apostol felt a sharp stabbing pain in his breast and a blow on the helmet. He seized the theodolite with both hands to prevent himself from falling. Then it seemed to him he was lifted right up into the air and almost immediately he found himself again on the hard ground with a sharp pain in the thigh.

"Am I wounded, or . . . ?"

His thought snapped like a thread.

BOOK II

A MISTY patch of light lay at the foot of the two iron bedsteads on the white-tiled floor of the little spare ward.

Through the only window the dark branches of an old pear-tree, now shivering in the frost of the last days of February, peered in. The walls, imbued with groans and pains, mingled their exhalation with the sickly smell of a hospital ward and with the heat of the terra-cotta stove behind the door.

On the clean beds the two officers, in the regulation grey dressing-gowns, lay stretched, their eyes fixed on the high ceiling. On the wall at the head of each bed, on two little black plates, their names stood out in white lettering: "Lieutenant Bologa", "Lieutenant Varga". On the little night-tables the temperature charts, almost hidden by the medicine bottles, bore witness to the great physical sufferings they had endured.

In the air, laden with the memories of pain endured, floated an oppressive silence which Varga broke suddenly, raising himself up in bed and speaking with a voice as scared as if he had seen a ghost:

"Why are you silent, comrade? Say something, for God's sake! This silence is harder to bear than a shrapnel wound!"

Bologa turned his white face, drawn with suffering, towards him but did not open his lips. Varga hung a minute expectantly, then fell back on the bed, speaking more to himself:

"Four months now that we've been sick, sent on from hospital to hospital, each time nearer to the front. I am sick to death of doctors, bandages, and sisters of charity! If only they would hurry up with that sick-leave!"

Apostol remained silent. For three months he had been forbidden to talk because he had had his right lung pierced by a piece of shrapnel, and now he had come to love silence. During that interval his thoughts had got into the habit of falling into line quietly, without violent struggles, and especially without anguish. Besides, at the beginning his mind had been serene, as if some unseen master-hand had wiped all memories off his brain. When he came to, that first time, at the dressing-station of the division, his eyes had alighted on Doctor Meyer and on Petre. He did not know them, but his joy had been so violent that he had immediately lost consciousness again. The second time he opened his eyes in a Red Cross train, with the same gladness in his heart, and again for only a few minutes. Finally, the third time, he came back to life to find himself in a white ward in the hospital. His bed was surrounded by doctors.

"Well done, dead one!" one of them, who had white side-whiskers and a black moustache, had said, smiling. "About time you were resuscitated! Six days you've been like this!"

A wave of inexpressible joy at being alive had swept over Apostol's whole being, and with fever-cracked lips he had whispered, scarcely audibly:

"I've no pain, no pain at all!"

For another seven weeks after that he remained more dead than alive. Besides the wound in his chest, he had a broken bone in the left foot and a deep gash in the thigh.

"Your recovery is a miracle," the doctor with the white whiskers and the black moustache had told him at a later date. "Your vitality is extraordinary, otherwise you would long since be promenading in the world of the righteous!"

When his foot and thigh were healed, they sent him farther on—nearer to his own unit—to the hospital in which he was now, because over there they had begun to bring in daily large numbers of wounded from the new encounters. For nearly a month he had lain alone in the little spare ward at the end of the corridor on the first floor. Petre had sat by his bed all day, trying to guess his thoughts and anticipate his wants. In the mornings, and also after the doctor's visit, he had read to him *The Dream of the Mother of God* in a voice shaky with religious fervour, and Bologa listened without understanding the words but with a warm contented feeling in his heart.

Then one day the orderly had told him what was supposed to have happened on that night. From his tale Apostol did not gather much information; all he could make out was that he had been buried on the edge of a shell-hole, under the débris of the observation post, and that Petre had found him towards noon after they had, with the help of the division that had come to relieve them, driven back the Russians to their original position. But the soldier's tale recalled the hopes of that night and started again all the thoughts he had had then. He experienced a few moments of uneasiness, as at the sight of a rebuking apparition. Then for three days his thoughts, roused from their long torpor, tortured him and rent his soul. He said to himself that all his efforts to avoid his fate had been frustrated, and that henceforth nothing but death could save him. But now death seemed more terrifying even than the prospect of having to go to the Rumanian front. He tried in vain to whip up his ambition and accused himself of cowardice, but the new love of life, growing daily more and more intense, prevented him from making any headway, and whispered continually in his heart:

"First myself and then the others!"

At last, one night when he couldn't sleep, he found peace. After all, Fate had done the right thing. Why should he desert to the Russians just when the chance was being offered to him to cross over to the Rumanians? For the Russians he would simply have been a contemptible deserter, whereas the Rumanians would receive him as a brother. Over there desertion would have meant a dishonouring crime followed by a shameful captivity, here he would go in the guise of a real hero, with head erect, and he would be able to start fighting at once against the real enemies. How stupid had been his dread of the Rumanian front! It was lucky that Fate had intervened. His obvious duty was to live and to triumph. To want to die when one had an ideal was a sign of cowardice.

The next day his mind was less perturbed, and his thoughts became more settled and again obedient to his will. But he found that the hatred in his heart for all the foreigners that surrounded him had grown in intensity. He now hated the doctors who tended him, the sisters of charity, the convalescent officers, and was glad that on account of his wounded lung he was not allowed to talk. On the day when an old general, accompanied by a drove of very dapper boy-officers, had come to pin on his breast the gold medal awarded for the destruction of the searchlight, Bologa had pretended to feel ill so that he need not have to seem enchanted.

Later, one day, about a month ago now, Varga was brought into the ward. He had been badly wounded in the left hip on that same night and had been sent on from one hospital to another until he had finally reached the one in which Bologa was. At first Bologa had been glad to see him, and, as he had just been given permission to talk, they swapped adventures. Varga explained to him in detail what had happened during the Russian attack, how the Austrians had advanced almost to the artillery lines and had then been driven back by a swift counter-attack. Nevertheless,

116

in that encounter two infantry regiments had been almost entirely wiped out and his own Hussars had suffered severely, particularly during the counterattack; that was when he had received this wound of his, which had almost been the cause of making a cripple of him, for he had fallen into the hands of a maniac doctor, who had fought tooth and nail to have his leg off. The Hussar officer was fearfully indignant that this battle, in which nearly two thousand men had perished and in which he himself had so nearly gone west, had not even been officially recorded. The only thing that cheered him was the hope of a long sick-leave.

While Varga talked and exploded, Bologa brooded. Both Varga's eyes and words seemed to him hostile, and he wondered how he could ever have felt friendly towards this man.

In order to avoid talking, Bologa got in a number of books and began to hunt in them for explanations and proofs. He searched for a fortnight and exhausted himself. Nowhere could he find a logical explanation why right was not right everywhere and always. From all his books he received the impression that man was cut off from real life, was solitary and abstruse as a mathematical formula. Some person sits himself down at a table, full of faith in his own knowledge and experience of life, and decrees that men should be so and so, that to do this and this is right, but to do that and the other is wrong. And that somebody would do his best to force living souls into his scheme, to chain them to it, as if life could be moulded in accordance with the desires and conclusions of any one person. Life flowed on indifferently, destroying not only learned men's systems but even men's minds, inventing new situations at every moment, new ideas which the Lilliputian imagination of human beings would never be able to understand and much less to foresee. A caprice of life had set face to face millions of men branded with the mark of death on their forehead, forcing them by this means to discover in their souls unsuspected mysteries and to make unexpected decisions. In the vortex of life books became a conglomeration of words without sense. All a man had to do was to take care not to go against his conscience.

About that time he received a very friendly letter from Klapka, telling him a lot of unimportant things, all the gossip about life at the front, etc. He added right at the last, quite casually: "Over here I have so far come across Russians only, all Russians . . ." Bologa immediately said to himself, without anxiety or hesitation:

"It doesn't matter, I'll wait."

Varga had done his best to loosen Bologa's tongue, and could not make out why he had become such a bear. Silence weighed on him and depressed him. So he had been overjoyed when the doctors had allowed him to go farther than his own ward. He had now become friendly with men in other wards and spent more time with them than with Bologa.

Now, whilst awaiting the doctor's afternoon visit, the hussar was squirming like a fish out of water, more especially as he had been unable, in spite of all his efforts, to drag a single word out of Bologa.

"What's the matter with you, Bologa?" he burst out at last, annoyed. "You exasperate me with your dumbness! Don't you want to talk to me because you hate me? We were friends and . . ."

"Nothing, nothing," murmured Apostol without moving his eyes.

Varga had to stay his further questioning, for the doctor arrived, accompanied by a quaint little sister of charity.

"This is the ward of divine miracles!" exclaimed the doctor, who was short and fair, rubbing his hands and speaking brightly and cheerily. "From what I see I'll be giving you your passports very soon, gentlemen! At all events, it would be well if you began to take a little more exercise, anyway in the conservatory, if it is not possible in the park. It is true the weather is still wintry, but you will have to stretch your bones a little, gentlemen! It would be a very good thing, a very good thing indeed!"

"We'll stretch them well enough again at the front!" answered Varga, cheering up. "I hope you're going to give us sick-leave, doctor? You can't possibly send us back to the trenches with our wounds barely healed?"

"Surely . . . of course . . ." answered the doctor, his smile less bright. "So far as it depends on me, of course! All I can do is to propose, the decision lies in other hands; and to tell you the truth, for you are men, the authorities all keep on telling us that officers are wanted very, very badly everywhere."

"I understand," concluded Varga gloomily. "You intend to send us back direct to the front."

The doctor growled a few more words and hastened off with the ever serene and smiling sister of charity.

In a few minutes the room was quite dark. Only the windows remained grey, like sick and lifeless eyes. Varga, with hands behind his back, walked nervously backwards and forwards, but the sound of his footsteps was not so loud as the metallic ticking of the alarm-clock on the night-table. Presently Apostol, sitting on his bed with eyes fixed on the frozen branches outside, which were describing black arabesques on the misty windows, began to hum a gay tune.

"Bologa! What the hell! You feel like humming?" Varga stopped and stared at him helplessly. "Perhaps you are rejoicing that our chances of sick-leave have been knocked on the head?"

"I am rejoicing with my whole heart, old fellow!" Apostol answered, singing and gesticulating like an actor in Italian opera. "War, war, war, forward to the war!"

The Hussar lieutenant was speechless, and, convinced that Apostol was making fun of him, he left the room, banging the door violently behind him. Bologa stopped his singing abruptly, as if he only just realized what he had been doing. He felt sorry he had provoked Varga, and stretched himself on his bed, feeling strangely sad. A few minutes later Petre came in, made a light, and held out a letter, asking:

"Is it from home, sir?"

Bologa snatched the letter quickly, but, seeing it was from Klapka, did not hasten to open it. He guessed what it contained, and indeed, when he read it, he came across what he had expected in three elaborately obscured lines, from which he gathered that about a week ago the Rumanians had taken the place of the Russians. He stared thoughtfully at Petre for a while, and then said:

"It is not from home. It is from the front, from the captain. It's from there, not from home."

While he was speaking his thoughts wandered far away from his surroundings, and he saw in one bright, vivid flash the whole of Parva and those he held dear: his mother and Marta, towards whom he felt guilty, firstly, because he had only written to them twice all the time he had been in hospital, and secondly, because on that night he had intended to separate himself from them without even saying good-bye.

"My heart has softened now that I know that the day of departure is in sight!" he said to himself, his eyes still fixed unseeingly on Petre.

"One is sure to come from home soon, sir," said the soldier confidently.

"Yes, yes, I expect so . . ." assented Bologa, turning over slowly, wearily.

Varga came back later, unappeased. Apostol roused himself and said gently:

"Varga, I don't know what's the matter with me. Forgive me!"

The lieutenant's face cleared immediately, and he came up to him with outstretched hand.

"I am awfully sorry, old fellow. But you have changed terribly. A little while back you liked me, and we got on so well together . . ."

"A little while back!" sighed Bologa, his eyes full of tears.

They were kept at the hospital another ten days.

§ II

The train panted and sweated, climbing up between mountains the peaks of which were still capped with snow. The spring sunshine bespattered the air with powdered silver. The woods and meadows trembled under the caresses of the fiery rays. New life, young and passionate, reanimated the whole face of the earth. Only the train, laden with men and material of war, huge, grinding, puffing, seemed a monster from another world, come to defy nature's youth. The locomotive crawled along cautiously, as if it expected some enemy to appear in its path; it wriggled along under the stolid slopes and crags like a huge snake on the look-out for imaginary dangers at each twist and turn.

In a coach reserved for officers Apostol Bologa stop'd in the corridor by an open window, drinking in thirstily the mountain view, which reminded him of the valley of the Someş and made him forget his present destination.

Suddenly the door of the compartment behind him was opened and closed noisily, and in his ear Varga's voice said gleefully:

"Do you know, Bologa, who is on our train? You'll never guess! General Karg! Look round, there's Gross. He has just been telling us."

Apostol turned round. Through the glass door of the compartment could be seen, through a haze of cigar smoke, a few officers. Gross was banteringly explaining something with violent gestures.

"He said the general talked to him about us," continued Varga. "In fact, he swears that the general said he wanted to see us, and especially you. When one comes to think of it, it would only be the natural thing to do, for we've shed enough of our blood for our country. Gross has been travelling on a job with the general, so perhaps it's true what he says."

Bologa felt a loathing for them all, beginning with Gross. That was why he had kept away from them, and so far he had only exchanged two or three casual words with the sapper.

"Does he? That's fine!" he said, wishing to seem interested, but his eyes were disdainful.

"I'll tell you what I thought we'd do," the Hussar lieutenant began again, laying an arm across Bologa's shoulder. "If we do manage to get a word with the general, we must try to convince him that we really do deserve some sick-leave after nearly five months of hospitals and suffering. Isn't it true? I have great faith in Karg, in spite of his being severe and pig-headed, and, the Lord be praised, we *have* done our duty."

"Yes, of course, it wouldn't be a bad idea," agreed Bologa, convinced that Varga's hopes were childish, and longing to be alone again.

Varga cast a quick glance into the compartment, then, with a look of disgust, turned his back on it.

"I'm fed up with that sheeny and his anarchist theories. I really am, old chap. One can't talk to him two minutes without his beginning to mock and scoff at all we hold sacred—our country, our faith, our past. I really was beginning to feel downright sick and afraid, Bologa!" And after a minute's silence, he added: "You know, if I had to spend much time in his company I might discover some fine day that I had lost all my patriotic sentiments."

"Sentiments that are genuine should resist any onslaught!" said Apostol dejectedly.

"That's what they say, but in point of fact nothing resists for ever," smiled Varga. "You yourself told me that once, when we were arguing in Budapest at my uncle's, and I have never forgotten it. A drop of water can wear down a rock. And what about you: do you suppose you haven't changed? Perhaps you yourself don't realize it, but I, who shared the same room with you for nearly two months and had to put up with your weird behaviour—just you ask me, old chap! If my uncle, who was as fond of you as if you had been his son, met you to-day, he would not recognize you, Bologa, really and truly! I repeat, perhaps you are not conscious of it, perhaps . . ."

Apostol Bologa seemed to read a hidden challenge in the hussar's words. He answered with hostility, but also with a gravity in which struggled the desire to bare his soul, to lay it in the palm of his hand and to bear it aloft, proudly and confidently like a chalice, in the sight of all.

"I know perfectly well that I have changed. How can I help knowing it when the change was achieved in anguish, as if I had been born again? But it is as a result of that very change that I have acquired the real natural sentiments, as you called them just now. Only as a result of that change, Varga."

The hussar was disconcerted. Bologa's tone left no doubt as to his hostility, so he said in a low, dry voice, leaning his back against the door of the compartment and looking at Bologa intently:

"Bologa, it seems to me that your sentiments are unnatural. . . . Be careful!"

"Are you threatening me ?" asked Apostol ironically.

"Your sentiments are leading you straight into the arms of the enemy."

"Which enemy?" repeated Bologa mockingly.

"The enemy of our country, no matter who he is!" retorted Varga a little more sharply. "At this minute you, my friend, are a deserter in thought and feeling!"

Apostol gave a slight start, then he said quickly, almost passionately, taking hold of Varga's sleeve and staring intently into his eyes:

"Listen, Varga. Not long ago you boasted that you'd always keep a heart under that military uniform of yours. Put aside your casuistic reasoning and tell me what would you do if, for example, you happened to belong to the Russian Army and they sent you to fight the Hungarians, who had come to free you?"

"Stop, stop . . . you've got it wrong, old fellow!" stammered the lieutenant, reddening. "First comes our country . . ."

"Don't beg the question," insisted Bologa triumphantly. "Answer honestly! In such cases there cannot be two answers."

Varga was silent. The question, and especially Bologa's courage, embarrassed him. At last he said hesitatingly:

"There is one law for all and one duty to which we are bound by oath. If anyone attempts to judge these through the prism of sentimental selfishness, then . . ."

"Law, duty, oath, are of value only until you impose upon yourself a crime against your conscience!" interrupted Apostol quickly. "No duty on earth has the right to trample on a man's soul, but if it tries to all the same, then . . ."

Bologa broke off abruptly with a vague gesture which might mean everything or nothing. Varga, taken aback, stammered with wide eyes:

"Then my suspicions . . . So you have thoughts of desertion?"

"Thoughts?" murmured Apostol with a strange smile. "Thoughts are changeable, Varga! But in my innermost being I have a deep conviction, and if it bids me go over to the enemy, that is to say your enemy, I shan't hesitate a minute to do my real duty. And I am sure you others, if you judged honestly and without prejudice, would say I was right and would approve what I had done. I am sure that you, yourself, deep down in your heart . . ."

"No, no, Bologa, you are quite mistaken!" Varga, now having recovered himself, said dryly. "I'd never approve! I deprecate crime!"

"You would not?" queried Apostol with real surprise, adding immediately in a jesting tone: "You may rest assured that I won't ask for your approval. At most, if I happened to have to pass through your sector, and if I had the bad luck to meet you . . . perhaps then there might be a question of it. . . . But suppose it did happen, who knows what turn the conversation might take!"

"God grant you do no such thing, Bologa, for your sake!" replied the lieutenant gravely and threateningly. "I would arrest you, I would even shoot you if you tried to resist—in spite of your having been my friend!"

"Don't excite yourself!" came from Bologa, now again derisive. "I'll avoid your sector as I would the plague. . . . Now are you satisfied?"

"You may be joking, Bologa, but I mean . . ."

"I am not joking at all," retorted Apostol, becoming suddenly defiant.

Lieutenant Varga felt personally much irritated at the things he had been compelled to listen to, and Bologa's serenity and positiveness infuriated him. The thought of denouncing him actually crossed his mind—he would get the punishment he deserved that way. But police work was repugnant to him. Also, he reflected, they had been too intimate friends not so very long ago for them to fall out on things which, after all, were Bologa's own private business. Probably, if one could see into the minds of all officers, one would be pretty horrified at what one discovered. Most of them, of course, hid their thoughts, whereas Bologa at least was sincere.

"That's all nonsense, old chap!" Varga resumed, after a pause, in a changed voice and with assumed cheeriness. "We'd far better get along to General Karg and see if we can wangle some sick-leave!"

"That's just what it is, nonsense!" smiled Apostol, softened. "All human words are mere nonsense in the crises of life."

Varga led the way down the dirty corridor flooded with young sunshine. The train had just left a curve and the coach rocked as if it meant to topple over. The Hussar lieutenant clung to the wall with his hands, cursing furiously, but Bologa, only a few steps behind, walked boldly and easily as on a footpath.

§ III

They passed through a coach crammed full of soldiers and civilians all mixed up together. Peasants with scared faces congested the narrow corridor, so that they might keep an eye on their bags and bundles. They spoke little and in low voices, as if they were afraid of someone overhearing them. In the comer nearest to the officers' coach a Rumanian priest, tall, thin, with a scanty little goatee beard, and poorly clad, was talking dejectedly with three peasants who, to judge from their appearance, were Hungarians.

Apostol, pushing his way through the crowd, heard the Rumanian language as he was passing behind the priest, and, looking back for a second but without stopping, seemed to glimpse a face he knew. Because of the congestion he had no time to look round again, but the face of the priest lingered in his mind, and he kept on asking himself:

"Who can he be and where have I met him?"

In the next coach travelled General Karg. Here the corridor was encumbered with officers of all ranks, gossiping together and each one waiting for a lucky chance to exchange a word unofficially with the general. The coffee-coloured curtains of His Excellency's compartment were drawn and the adjutant had just come out, on his own initiative, to ask the gentlemen in the corridor to be quieter and avoid the danger of ruffling His Excellency's temper. Just at that moment Varga arrived. He took the adjutant aside and whispered:

"Gross told us that the old man wanted to see us—me and Bologa. . . . Do remind him, like a good chap!"

The adjutant shook hands with Bologa, whom he had not met since that stormy interview with the general, and then entered the general's compartment sighing despondently:

"We'll try."

Five minutes later the door was half pushed back, the adjutant half leant out and called out pleasantly:

"Bologa, come along, please, His Excellency wishes . . ."

He met Varga's questioning eyes and shrugged slightly, his face apologetic, as who would say: "Them's my orders!"

General Karg was in high spirits and excellent temper. He had at last succeeded, with great trouble, in getting himself recommended for the Order of Maria Theresa. He was sitting near the window with his short legs comfortably stretched out, his swarthy face turned towards Apostol Bologa, who had entered and saluted.

"Well, are you all right again?" asked the general carelessly, holding out his beringed hand and giving him a long look.

Bologa answered with a hesitating smile. His face was yellow, drawn, his lips colourless, only his eyes burnt, fed by an inward fire. The general again looked him up and down and then offered him a seat at his side. On the seat opposite His Excellency sat a colonel with angular features, who was a stranger, and a thin-faced major, whose eyes sparkled with intelligence. The adjutant, again hearing too much noise in the corridor, slipped out to warn the gentlemen out there anew that the noise might possibly anger His Excellency.

The general asked Bologa all sorts of questions: about his wound, about the hospitals at which he had been, about his recovery, etc.; but while Bologa answered he saw all the time an unspoken question in the general's eyes, which roused his defiance just as Varga's had done a little while before. Otherwise Karg, by the tone of his voice and the kindness which softened his harsh face, showed a real interest in him, an almost natural interest. At last the expected question came, but put in a joking, friendly form:

"Well, you see, the world has not turned to dust because you are here with us?"

Apostol saw clearly in the eyes of the general that he expected him to answer with a brief "No". That was why he could not help one second's hesitation, which, however, almost immediately died of its own accord. Then he spoke with a temerity heightened by the clearness of his voice:

"I have never been a coward, Excellency, that is why I will confess to you now that in my soul a world has turned to dust!"

The fat, beringed fingers tugged nervously at the straggly moustache, and the broad eyebrows were tightly drawn together as the general asked, rather bewildered:

"What do you mean? What world has turned to dust?"

Bologa smiled so serenely that the general's frown was transformed into an impatient curiosity and his hand dropped again quietly on to the arm-rest.

"I once read somewhere, Excellency," explained Apostol in the same clear voice, "that the heart of the human embryo in the first few weeks of gestation is situated not in the body but in the head, in the middle of the brain, and that not till a later stage does it move down lower, separating itself from the brain for ever. How wonderful it would be, Excellency, if the heart and brain had remained one, entwined, so that the heart would never do what the brain forbade, and, more especially, the brain would never act against the advice of the heart!"

The general stared at him a few minutes and then looked at the others and burst into a hearty laugh, opening his mouth wide, his moustache bristling and his whole face wrinkling up and looking for all the world like the shell of a bad walnut.

"Damned interesting!" he mumbled, laughing.

Then, mastering his laughter with difficulty and with a visible embarrassment at having given way so freely to his mirth, he resumed his ordinary gravity, and then related to the colonel that Bologa had begged him not to send him to the Rumanian front and that, in spite of this, he, the general, had forgiven him because he knew him to be a very capable and conscientious officer, although now he saw that he was an obstinate one as well. The colonel listened respectfully until the general stopped speaking, and then as respectfully remarked:

"Of course, I don't approve, Excellency, the law does not allow me to, but I can put myself into the lieutenant's place and I understand his bitterness. It is, indeed, regrettable that those in power should not have taken general precautions in this respect, so as to avoid such delicate situations, in the interest of the combative quality of the Army."

Apostol shuddered as if the colonel's words were needles being stuck into his heart, because to-day he no longer wanted to be understood; on the contrary, he wanted motives for hatred and defiance to fan and feed the flame of his conviction.

The general seemed surprised for a moment, but presently answered, convinced and with some pride in his voice:

"Obviously, obviously, it is so! From a humane point of view, of course. But if 'the powers that be' did not think of such a possibility? I can't take all the responsibilities. At best I can only make things easier in certain cases, as in the case of this lieutenant, for example. Yes! Without doubt we must make things easier. As he is still weak from sickness, I want to protect him from the hardships of the front, and we'll use him in a service which does not entail great fatigue. Look here, we'll transfer him to the ammunitions! There you are, that's what we'll do. For we are humane—we, in our Army! Where else would a commander worry his head to pander to such scruples? . . . What do you think, major? Have you ever come across examples of such humaneness in any Army since the beginning of history? And it is us that our enemies accuse of barbarity! What a world! What injustice!"

Just then the adjutant slipped in again. The general cut short his reflections and ordered:

"Note that Lieutenant Bologa is being transferred to the ammunition column!"

While the adjutant was getting out his note-book, Apostol Bologa looked at them all in turn beseechingly. On all faces he saw compassion veiled by different kinds of smiles. He felt humble and small, though hatred seethed in his soul. He had wanted to provoke indignation and lo! he had found pity and understanding. He watched the adjutant's pencil travel swiftly along the paper and suddenly exclaimed:

"Excellency, I would much rather take charge of my battery again."

"Never mind," murmured the general protectingly and gaily. "You must recuperate and get back your strength in an easier service where the dangers are not so great. I am glad you are still keen on the front, but for the time being I am compelled, in your interest, to oppose your wish and to spare you."

The incomprehensible and unexpected kindness of the general exasperated Bologa. He wanted to say that service with the ammunition column was more fatiguing than with the battery, when all at once the thought of the Rumanian priest in the corridor flashed into his mind, and he felt a sudden overpowering longing to speak to him. Neither the general nor the front interested him any longer. He stood up, mumbled awkward words of thanks, pressed a fat, flabby hand, bowed and went out with a luminous look on his face.

He rapidly made his way to the soldiers' coach and pushed past the peasants in the corridor. The priest was still at the same place. He saw him from afar, and the perspiration broke out on his forehead. Now he recognized him and felt overcome with joy.

"Don't you know me, father?" he called out eagerly, holding out both hands.

The priest paled as if he had been caught committing a crime. When Bologa mentioned his name a spark of eagerness showed in his eyes, but it died out at once, and he looked round fearfully to see if no one were spying on him. The priest was Constantin Boteanu, who had been one of Apostol's best chums at college.

"And where is your parish, Constantin?" asked Bologa eagerly, happily.

"Quite near Faget, where the High Command is—I don't know what its name is in the Army," answered the priest, embarrassed and nervous because he was talking Rumanian with an officer.

"Is it a Rumanian village?" insisted Apostol.

"Half and half; we call it Lunca, but in Hungarian it is called . . ."

"Lunca?" interrupted Bologa, as if he wished to stop him from uttering the Hungarian word. "Down our way there is also a village called Lunca. Do you remember?"

"Of course, I remember very well," answered the priest. "But over here all the Rumanians talk Hungarian, that's the custom when we are among Hungarians. And it is quite right that it should be so."

"Why right, father?" exclaimed Apostol seriously. "Can't you see that looking at it like that means that, sooner or later, you'll be left without a parish?"

"Well, yes, that's true enough," murmured Boteanu, confused and smiling humbly. "What can I do, though? We have no power and can't even interfere. Life lays such heavy burdens on us that I marvel how we can live at all."

"When man has an ideal he faces all hardships," said Bologa dejectedly and understandingly.

"Our ideal is God," answered the priest with a diffidence which concealed bitter fear. "When one has suffered as we have one no longer trusts or hopes in anything but God."

Then he told Apostol that, when the Rumanians had come into the war, the authorities had seized him and three of the peasant headmen and transported them to Hungary, near Dobritzin. His wife and his two babes had been left to the care of the Lord. For three months he had had no news of them, and he had felt sure that they must be dead. Only after the wheel of fortune had taken a turn in the opposite direction did he hear that they were well and were longing for his return. But many weeks had gone by and there had been no hint of his being allowed to go home. He had begged everybody in turn, he had humbled himself, he had kotowed, all in vain. Once they'd tell him his village was in the forbidden zone, then they'd say all Rumanians were suspects, then again that and the other, then something else. At last he begged to be allowed to bring over his family to Dobritzin until God should grant peace again. And then, unexpectedly, they set him free and allowed him to go home, bidding him look to his behaviour.

Apostol Bologa listened with a smile on his lips, but displeasure and disappointment gnawed at his soul. The priest's nervousness and the diffidence which marked all his words and looks hurt him, although he tried to avoid seeing them. In his turn he told Constantin how he had fared in the war, and then, shaking hands with him, said:

"Well, Constantin, I'll be sure to come over to your house soon, so that we can have a good old talk!"

The priest answered, panic-stricken:

"Please . . . My wife writes to say that there are always soldiers in and out of our house, for that's how things are to-day."

Bologa tried to smile, but his mouth set in a painful grin.

§ IV

The office of the ammunition column was in Lunca, in a little side-street, in the house of the grave-digger, Paul Vidor. The house faced the street and had in the middle a narrow lobby with a door which was always open. On the right there was a biggish room which had been turned into the office, and on the left two smaller rooms. The grave-digger had retired into the one at the back, and in the front one lodged the commander of the column.

Apostol Bologa took over, from the lieutenant whose place he was taking, the office with the registers and documents. He had not been able to sleep in the train, and as soon as he reached Lunca he made straight for the office. He felt dead-tired. He listened uninterestedly to all his predecessor's explanations until the latter unrolled a sketch plan of the front, showing the positions of all the units belonging to the division. Then he sat down at the table, feeling revived, as if he had drunk some magic draught, and devouring with his eyes the map with the red and blue marks, tried to follow the capricious lines with trembling fingers. But his head was so confused that he could not understand, so he stood up and said uncertainly:

"I don't understand anything . . . my brain is seething. I'll find out all about it later on."

"Of course you will," answered the other man quickly. "Besides, this sketch is out of date and you'll have to complete it. Look, for example, there at the edge, on the south, that sector is now occupied by dismounted hussars. There is a rumour that the Rumanians are getting ready to attack. You'll soon know all about it and become familiar with the situation. Naturally the sketch is merely to guide you and to give you an idea of the position of things, for really the only thing that is of interest to you here is our artillery."

To get rid of him more quickly, Bologa held out his hand with a not very successful smile.

"You are very pale and thin, comrade," said the lieutenant, taking his leave. "I don't believe you have quite recovered—anyway, by the look of you. You'll have to take great care of yourself."

Apostol lowered his eyes, hardly able to master a strange feeling of revolt and humility. He remained on his feet, leaning against the edge of the table. At the other long table a sergeant and a corporal were busy writing. Out of the corners of their eyes they looked at their new chief while zealously scratching away with their pens. He would have liked to say a word or two to them, but he found himself utterly unable to do so, and he was afraid to find pity there also. Just then, to his relief, Petre appeared on the threshold, saying:

"Sir, I have a meal ready for you; you must be very hungry. Please step over into the other room."

Hearing the Rumanian language, both non-coms, looked up quickly and stared at the orderly in astonishment. Bologa noticed their movement and answered with a childish pride, as if he were trying to defy their astonishment:

"All right, Petre. . . . I am hungry, for in the train I tightened my belt more than I ate!"

From the lobby, through the half-open door, he heard the voice of one of the non-coms.:

"I do believe the lieutenant is a Wallach, too!"

These words, almost contemptuous in tone, which at another time would have annoyed him, now soothed him as if they had been praise, and he crossed over into the other room feeling much calmer.

His room was clean, the bed comfortable. There were pots of geranium in the window, and on the walls hung flower-patterned wooden bowls and dishes. The table in the middle of the room was laid, and in the brick stove a fine fire glowed. Apostol looked round, pleased, but stopped short when his gaze fell on the figure of a young girl of eighteen or so squatting close to the stove. She had a scarlet kerchief tied round her head, big black, laughing eyes, and full, fresh lips. Now he came to think of it, he remembered that he had seen her just now, when he had entered the enclosure, and though he had not consciously taken any notice of her, it had struck him that her eyes had appraised him with unusual boldness.

"Who is it?" asked Apostol of the orderly, jerking his head in her direction.

"She is the landlord's daughter, sir."

Bologa's face brightened; he held out his hand and said in Hungarian:

"Is it you who have made this room look so nice?"

"With your soldier's help," answered the girl with a saucy smile, looking right into his eyes.

Apostol felt the rough, very warm hand in his own and asked again, for fun:

"And what's your name?"

"Ilona."

"Ilona. . . . H'm. . . . Yes. . . . And aren't you afraid with so many soldiers about?"

"Why should I be afraid?" answered the girl simply, adding quickly, with pride: "I am only afraid of God!"

While he was settling down to his meal Ilona, leaning against the stove, didn't take her eyes off him; she seemed under a spell. As a matter of fact, Apostol, too, while he was eating, looked at her out of the corner of his eye, at first with an impatient curiosity and then with a puzzled feeling of tenderness. He had always been bashful with women, diffident and ill at ease. He had always felt ashamed before them because he didn't know what to say to them. With Marta at first, and even after they had become engaged, he had often felt embarrassed and had blushed like a girl. The uniform and the war had woken him up and done away with his bashfulness. Three days after he had put on military clothes he had conquered a sentimental little cashier-girl, had sworn to be faithful to her for ever, and then had forgotten her in the arms of another. Wherever Fate led him ephemeral love affairs were thrust on him. And he accepted them as they came, without choosing, almost hurriedly, as if he wished to make up for lost time. Nevertheless, in a little separate chamber of his heart he kept his love for Marta untouched and pure, and took care that nothing should come near to defile it. When the image in his heart reproached him, he quietened the reproaches with solemn promises for the future. But the eyes of the little Hungarian peasant-girl seemed to have found their way right into that secret chamber without his being able to oppose it, because, for the first time since the war had started, he was again feeling bashful and confused. When he realized this he felt furious and made up his mind not to look at her again.

"I expect the little girl has done her best to keep all those who had this room before me from being bored with life," thought he, looking up again and staring at Ilona defiantly.

Her gay glance shamed him. He was sorry he had insulted her, even though it had been in thought.

Petre went out to see to his work, and he signed to the girl to go also, so that the lieutenant might have a little rest. Ilona did not budge; she seemed not to have understood the orderly's signs. Apostol, with his nose in his plate, was trying to break the silence and felt wild because he could think of nothing to say. Finally, he asked her abruptly, without looking at her:

"You don't know Rumanian, little girl?"

"I know a little, but round about here nearly everybody speaks Hungarian, for that's the custom here," answered Ilona quickly, almost uneasily. Then, because Apostol remained silent, she went on more quietly: "As a matter of fact, our church here is Rumanian, and the popa always takes the service in Rumanian; he only preaches in Hungarian so that we should understand better."

Apostol was just chiding himself for asking such a silly question, and her answer increased his embarrassment. Not her words but her voice, harsh and yet sweet and caressing as a silken ribbon, with little affectations like those of a spoilt child. All he longed for now was to hear that voice again, and he racked his brain trying to find some question which would make her speak. All his efforts were in vain. About three minutes passed in complete silence, during which he gazed desperately into her eyes, which seemed to fill the room with a soft, enticing light. Then suddenly he had a bright idea: he'd ask her how old she was—of course jokingly, so that she should not start imagining things. He was afraid that his voice would tremble and that Ilona would wrongly interpret his question. Before he could make up his mind to open his lips there was a loud knocking at the door. The girl straightened herself and whispered:

"It's father."

Without waiting any further for an invitation to enter, a peasant walked into the room. Bologa, furious, started up ready to knock him down. But Paul Vidor approached, jovially, with outstretched hand, and welcomed him into his house. His face was bony, with many wrinkles under the brown eyes, which were bright with intelligence and shrewdness. He had a thick, greying moustache with the ends pointed, as have all Hungarian peasants. The landlord's appearance soon put an end to the lieutenant's rage. He answered him quietly, and even invited him to be seated. The grave-digger looked round to see if everything was in order and noticed Ilona, who was now poking the fire with great energy.

"Ilona, come now, make yourself scarce!" he ordered, frowning. "What are you doing here? Have you nothing better to do than to stay here bothering this gentleman?"

"You don't think it's for love of him that I'm here?" mumbled the girl sulkily, without looking round.

"Come, come, not so much chatter!" said the grave-digger until the door had closed, and then added gently to Bologa: "We've got to be severe with her, otherwise we'd never manage to live in peace in the midst of so many soldiers. She is young and silly, sir, and doesn't understand that you have work to do and that you haven't come over here to waste your time in conversations."

Paul Vidor was extraordinarily talkative, and more than anything he loved to chat with gentlemen, believing himself to be more intelligent and more capable than the other villagers. He drew up a chair to the table, sat down deliberately, and immediately plunged into talk, although Apostol's brow had darkened. He was racked with the desire to hear the girl's voice again. His curt answers did not discourage the grave-digger at all; on the contrary, they seemed to encourage him. From one thing to another, he came to telling Bologa that he was a man of means, though he was a grave-digger. He had plenty of land, and good at that, if only he were able to work it better in these difficult times. He had only turned grave-digger since his wife's death—may her sins be forgiven—that was to say, about eleven years ago, when she had left him alone, heart-broken, with two small children on his hands. His original trade had been joinery, and he had learnt it as a child in the town, for his father had wished to put into his hands a means of livelihood, which was better than any amount of property. Besides, didn't the joiner go hand-in-hand with the grave-digger—one made the coffin and the other dug the grave—so that he had not been ashamed to dig the grave for the dead while he learnt to make their coffins. For in a village it is better to be a grave-digger than a joiner. A man can manage somehow to rig up a table and chairs for himself, but to dig his grave he requires someone else. He didn't mind hard work—he hated idling. When you're left a widower with a boy of eleven and a girl of seven on your hands you have to work hard if you don't want to be eaten up by poverty. Well, things went on somehow, really better than worse, until the war calamity befell the poor world. His boy had just reached the serving age and he had joined up, for he could not do otherwise, and he was dead within a year. They didn't even know where he had died— somewhere in Russia. God, how they had wept, he and the girl! But did tears and lamentations ever bring the dead back to life? May God rest his bones in peace and forgive his sins! Round about here it had been quiet until the Rumanians had joined the fray. Since then what trouble and bitterness! Many, from sheer terror, had run away inland. He had remained at home, come what might, for he could not bring himself to leave his property to take care of itself. Well, as a matter of fact, the Rumanians had not done much damage, it was only fair to say so. Just food they had taken, like all soldiers, especially when they had retired into their country. Much more pitiless had our own people been, if the truth be told, for no sooner had they arrived than they, without much ado, hanged three villagers, saying that they had signalled to the enemy. He'd almost got into trouble himself because the Rumanians had made him burgomaster instead of the one who had run away. As if it were wrong to do one's duty! Well, over in Faget, the next village, who was burgomaster? Why, his own brother-in-law! Well, then, why should the fact that he had been burgomaster for a few weeks have been held up against him? Well, he'd got over everything, so now if only God would send peace quickly . . .

Bologa let him ramble on. When the grave-digger had finished the tale of his life, he waited to be told some news in his turn, and because the lieutenant did not bother to speak, he asked him pointedly, lowering his voice mysteriously:

"What about the peace, sir? Is there no news at all in the town? Last night I was over in Faget, at my brother-in-law's, and I heard some rumour that the Russian had had enough and wanted to make peace. The great general is actually lodging at my brother-in-law's house, and next door are officers of the division. Perhaps you don't know it, as you are newly arrived. Yes, that's what the officers say over there about the Russians!

Whether it's true or not the Lord alone knows, but a good thing it would be if it were true!"

"I've come straight from the hospital and don't know what's happening in the world," explained Bologa, "but that things are far from right, friend, that much I can tell you!"

"Yes, that's true, very true," agreed the peasant, nodding his head gravely. "There is much trouble and pain; yes, there is! If only the Lord would make the authorities sufficiently merciful and intelligent to sheathe their swords and save us from being completely destroyed! It's all very well for them; they are safe over there and give orders, while over here men suffer, are being tortured, and die."

As the grave-digger gave no hint of ceasing, but, on the contrary, seemed to have just got into his stride, Bologa got up, cutting short the conversation by inviting him to continue their talk some other time, for now he had to see to his work. Paul Vidor heartily agreed "that that was true", but waited for the lieutenant to lead the way out.

Apostol Bologa, irritated by the peasant's insistence, crossed over into his office, took the plan of the front, ordered the non-coms. to keep on with their work as he himself had some official work to see to to-day, and walked out into the enclosure and into the young spring sunshine. The light and heat enticed him to look round against his will, as if he were looking for someone. On the high step inside the stable door sat Ilona, with her elbows leaning on her knees and her face resting between the palms of her hands. When their eyes met, Apostol understood what he had been looking for, and all the blood rushed to his face. He smiled at Ilona without meaning to do so, telling himself the while that he must take no notice of her and that she had the most fascinating voice he had ever heard.

Out in the street it seemed to him as if he were awakening from some accursed spell. Turning into the main street, towards the centre of the village, he thought: "If a little peasant girl is able to damp my faith and imperil my resolution, then I think it were better I shot myself." And he felt for his revolver, as if he wished to prove to himself that he would not falter.

He stopped short before the church and asked himself where he was going? Oh yes, he remembered now, he was taking his bearings under the pretext that he wished to call on his superiors and on his friends. Then he'd go this very night. He must not lose a single day, not a single minute. Not until he was safely on the other side could he find peace and happiness.

The priest's house across the way, opposite the church, seemed clad in sunshine. Apostol remembered that Ilona had told him that the priest preached in Hungarian, and he recalled Boteanu's shame in the train and his abject cowardice. He turned his head away.

He did not know which way to go. There was nothing in the village he wanted to see; only the front was of interest to him. So it would be better for him to go off there immediately, report himself to the colonel, examine the ground, and choose his place. Perhaps he'd see Klapka; in fact, he must tell him. All at once, from a house near the church, Meyer emerged, muffled in a heavy coat with collar turned up in spite of the fact that the sun filled the earth with an intoxicating warmth.

"Doctor! Doctor!" shouted Apostol, seeing that Meyer was going on and had not seen him.

The doctor turned round, and the grim face relaxed a little when he saw that it was Bologa who had hailed him and was hastening after him. They went on together towards the improvised hospital, located in the village school. On the way

143

Apostol told him how he had got over his wounds. The doctor, a reserved man, did not question him as to his present destination, but when the hospital door was reached, Bologa told him that he wished to go to the front to get his bearings but had no horse. Meyer offered him his own, but in the same breath said in a friendly tone:

"You are very thin, Bologa, be careful! Leave heroic deeds for a little while and look after yourself, otherwise I expect you'll be coming to me again in a day or so—as a patient! I think you have a touch of fever as it is, your eyes are too glassy. I think they might have given you some sick-leave to enable you to get your strength back. Anyway, take my advice and go slow!"

"I feel as strong as a dragon, doctor!" answered Bologa with unnatural gaiety.

The doctor muttered something into the collar of his greatcoat, but Apostol didn't even attempt to catch what he said, his soul was so full of hope.

§ V

Apostol Bologa rode off with the map of the front in his hand. Lunca was a long village on the left bank of a little noisy stream, caught closely between two rows of hills, covered with pine- and beech-trees. The highroad ran through the centre of the village, and the railway ran behind the houses through gardens and meadows which rose on the sloping hill-side. Round the station the valley widened out like the bottom of a cauldron, but beyond the village it narrowed again right up to the mouth of the torrent which ran down from the mountains on the left. Both the railway and the highroad crossed the river on a common bridge which had recently been repaired. Bologa went on for about thirty paces and then discovered on the bank of the river the road leading to the front. Here there was less traffic and the houses were few, some perched like nests in far-off clearings. The road ascended continually, and the river narrowed but became more buoyant, like an exuberant and turbulent child. In the bluish background were the crests of the mountains, crenelated in places like gigantic ramparts.

Then, at a spot which widened out a little, the road, together with the rivulet, now a mere thread of silver, disappeared into the brushwood of the valley. And then a new road began the ascent towards the north, a war-road made by soldiers. Here Bologa met soldiers more frequently, some coming down, others going up, and he also met a few carts drawn by sorry nags.

"At last I have arrived!" muttered Apostol, filled with excitement, stopping his horse and comparing the ground with his map. "The artillery lines must be quite near here."

He was standing on the fairly wide ridge of a hill sparsely covered with trees. The road here branched out fan-wise. Bologa first looked back. The rivulet was no longer visible, and the woody hills and slopes through which he had come now took on a different aspect.

"If the batteries are here, then the infantry will be on the hills over there," he thought, turning round quickly and looking with more attention at the row of ridges which cut off the horizon in front. "And a little more that way, perhaps even on the very next ridge, are the . . ."

All around reigned a serene silence over which floated the sun's smile like powdered gold. Not a pine-needle stirred in the wonder-struck trees, drinking in the gladness of the new spring. Apostol could hear the quick, hot beats of his heart, dominating by their passionate throbbing all the world around him.

"It's taken me three hours and a bit. It's noon now!" he said suddenly, looking at his watch. Then he continued straight on, trusting to luck, for he could make out nothing from his sketch.

A gunner led him to Klapka's command post, which was only a few yards off the road by which Bologa had come. The captain was just sitting down to a meal in the little wooden hut, which was quite cosy and roomy, considering the circumstances. When Apostol appeared in the doorway, saluting with a slightly embarrassed smile, Klapka dropped the knife out of his hand and murmured some startled words in Czech. But, recovering himself quickly, he came to meet Bologa, embracing him and kissing him with tears of joy running down his cheeks.

"Welcome back! Are you quite well again? Truly? Let me have a look at you! Why are you so pale? You'll have your battery back, won't you? In a day or two we are beginning serious work! But wait, sit down over there and let us eat together while you tell me everything from beginning to end. Begin from that night— you remember? Eh, eh! How I worried over you that night! Was it lucky, was it unlucky for you? God knows. One thing is certain, you have paid for the attempt with terrible suffering, dear Bologa. Do please sit down over there. That's it. You can't think how glad I am to see you again, safe and sound. Doctor Meyer assured us, of course very regretfully, that out of a mass of mutilated flesh rolled in the mud, such as you were when he had seen you last, immediately after the attack had been repulsed, it was impossible to reconstruct an artillery lieutenant, even if the whole medical faculty of the world were to put their heads together, and that nothing but the mercy of God could make you into a human being again. Then later, when we heard that you were on the way to recovery, Meyer said that you must have had a marvellously strong hold on life."

The captain chattered as if he had had no one to speak to for a century and now meant to pour out his whole soul. Apostol Bologa gladly accepted his invitation to eat. He was tired out by his journey and lack of sleep, and at his own place that morning, obsessed by the Hungarian girl's strange glances, he had eaten as if with another man's mouth. He hesitated just a second at the thought that he would probably again have to tell Klapka what he had already told him so often before. He was right. For the good part of an hour the captain examined him and cross-examined him like a judge, asking him minute details with regard to his wounds, to the meeting with the general in the train, etc.

"I'm awfully sorry you are not staying with me, but for you it is far, far better to be in the village with the ammunition column," said Klapka. "Besides, I'm sure you've had enough of dreams, haven't you?" he added gently, as if he were afraid of reopening an old wound. "Fate gave you a warning that time."

"Yes, Fate was against me that time because, to tell you the truth, my soul was not sufficiently prepared," answered Bologa simply but with obvious satisfaction at being able to talk freely to someone about it. "Then I was convinced, right to the marrow of my bones, that my conviction was perfect, and yet the thought of death terrified me. The pain I have undergone has taken that conceit out of me, and to-day I know very well that only convictions for which you are ready to sacrifice, without hesitation, even life itself, can save you. And to-day I realize that the love of life is far stronger in my heart than my convictions. I have come to feel afraid of myself. Convictions and resolutions have a habit of crumbling away if you weigh and examine them too much, and I cannot help weighing and examining mine! That's why I must go quickly before I can look into them too closely, otherwise who knows, perhaps . . . Only when man is alone with his soul, only then is there an equilibrium between his little inner world and the rest of the universe. As soon as reality from outside intervenes man becomes a helpless toy without a will of his own, going whither influences and decisions, strange to his real nature, lead him."

"Why, you talk even more than I do!" interrupted Klapka, smiling impatiently. "Suppose it is as you say, dear Bologa, although your views seem to me somewhat . . . childish, to say the least of it. The ideal remains here in my heart, and reality is reality, Bologa. Reality is revolution over there among the Russians, do you understand? Last night the news trickled through on the telephone; to-day it has been officially confirmed. Revolution has broken out in Russia—which means our hopes have vanished, like this, into thin air! Well, let us bow to the inevitable and carry on, Bologa!"

Apostol remembered that the grave-digger had also mentioned the Russian revolution, but neither then nor now did the news startle him in the least. He answered rather more irritably:

"What do I care what's happening over there? I don't want to know. It is the unknown that entices me, the unknown which is full of possibilities. All I seek in the world, either here or over there, is the salvation of my soul."

"You are as great a visionary as ever, Bologa."

"To you they may seem empty dreams, but all the purpose of my being palpitates in those dreams," said Bologa with eyes which seemed to dart fire and made Klapka draw back. "You don't suppose that I would not much rather just live on contentedly without worrying over anything? Sometimes I tell myself I am absurd, and yet I can't stop myself. . . . That's the unfortunate part!"

Klapka was very comfortable where he was. He had got pally with the colonel. There had been no fighting all the winter, so no danger had threatened him. He still quite often had patriotic paroxysms and he secretly prided himself on them, but he took great care to conceal them and to reserve them for some more suitable occasion. And now also with Bologa—after the first outburst of gladness at seeing him had subsided, and especially since he understood that Bologa had not given up his thoughts of desertion, he reckoned it would be wiser not to get mixed up in such dangerous plans. So he took advantage of a short silence and changed the conversation, asking him if he had reported himself to the colonel and telling him that the commanding officer's station was close by, not four hundred metres away. Soon after they went out, and Klapka hastened to show him which was the colonel's hut.

Naturally the colonel also wanted to hear Bologa's adventures, so he had to go through them all over again. Nevertheless, half an hour later he returned to Klapka, rather annoyed that he had wasted his time instead of reconnoitring the front and planning his great adventure. How could he cross mountains which he had not even seen as yet?

Behind the command post he saw that something unusual was going on: a group of Rumanian prisoners, surrounded by dismounted hussars, by divisional officers, and officers from the neighbouring batteries, gunners, etc. Apostol felt his knees give under him, and yet he could not stop himself from drawing near, although the only distinct thought in his mind was that he might not be able to find his horse at once, and get back quickly enough to the village.

When he drew nearer, Klapka saw him and signed to him with his hand to hurry. In the midst of the gunners there stood a Rumanian officer, dark, with a little black, clipped moustache, bare-headed, his uniform bespattered with mud; farther away, guarded by four armed hussars, stood about seven soldiers, their faces distorted with terror, staring wildly at the group which contained their officer.

"Bravo, that's fine, you'll be able to get us out of this fix!" called out Klapka, pointing to the prisoner second-lieutenant, his face reflecting a feminine curiosity. "Look here, for the last ten minutes we have been trying to understand one another, but it's no go. That gentleman either doesn't know or won't know anything but Rumanian, and there's no one else here who can interpret."

While Apostol Bologa was gazing agitatedly, now at the officer, now at the soldier prisoners, a Hussar lieutenant, pitted with small-pox and with a huge nose, began to relate for at least the tenth time how he had run across the Rumanian patrol behind the lines. They had obviously lost their way through not knowing the ground: it would seem they had intended to slip in amongst the infantry and cavalry which occupied the left wing of the division front. Apostol heard the hussar's words as in a dream, for his eyes and heart were with the prisoners, reading their thoughts in Rumanian, embracing them and telling them he was one of them and that that very night he would be where they had come from. Then, shivering as with cold, he approached the captive second-lieutenant and said, with the glimmer of a smile in the corner of his thin lips:

"Now that you are a prisoner you must . . ."

The prisoner was not in the least surprised to hear him speak Rumanian. He turned furious eyes on Bologa and stopped him short with a voice full of hatred:

"You over here behave like savages with your prisoners. A brute of an officer hit me across the loins with a stake because

I could not and would not betray my Army and my country! That's sheer barbarity, that's what it is . . ."

The prisoner's indignation re-echoed more mightily in Apostol's heart than it would have done in a microphone. His cheeks flushed and his glance softened. He felt an irresistible longing to get into spiritual touch with the prisoner. He wanted to hold out his hand and raised his arm slightly, hesitatingly, saying, in a voice shaking with emotion:

"Yes, yes, that's quite true, quite true—I am also a Rumanian."

"If you were a real Rumanian you would not shoot your brothers," answered the young officer quickly, with such contempt that his whole face was changed by it. "Your place, sir, would be on the other side, not here. But Rumanians such as you . . ."

Bologa turned white. His arm stiffened and his fists clenched. The whole world seemed to be rolling down madly into an abyss. The thought of hurling himself at the lieutenant and dragging the contempt out of his heart shot through his mind. But simultaneously he realized that the prisoner would make him the laughing-stock of the officers. Bewildered, he turned his back on the Rumanian and looked at the others with a wavering smile, now expecting them to save him from this awful situation. Captain Klapka's voice ended his torture with a question burning with curiosity:

"What does he say? What's he say?"

"Nothing; he won't speak," muttered Apostol, relieved, as if he had awakened from a nightmare. After a moment or two he added, with a horrified glance towards the prisoner, who, still muttering indignantly, had turned his head away: "I've . . . I've done my duty and I've tried to . . ."

The prisoners were escorted farther on to another command, and the group of onlookers melted away in a few minutes. Klapka waited, somewhat embarrassed, feeling that Bologa wanted to say something to him.

"Do you know what the prisoner said to me?" suddenly burst out Apostol, his face set grimly. "He insulted me and treated me with contempt, captain, do you hear? He spat on me! You see now that I must go at once, that I haven't another minute to lose . . . that to-night . . . Oh, how kindly I felt towards him, and how he humiliated me!"

Klapka was staring at him and understood that he expected an answer, or at least some word of consolation, but he was afraid to speak. Bologa stood waiting with eyes staring into the captain's silence, then he whispered:

"Good-bye!"

Klapka's orderly brought his horse, and Apostol mounted and rode off without looking round again.

"Au revoir, Bologa!" the captain called after him.

To Apostol it seemed as if Klapka were mocking him. He touched the horse with the spurs. He must get back to the village as quickly as possible, to make his preparations and be done with it. In his soul writhed a hell with tongues of fire so consuming that every moment they threatened to exhaust all the sources of his will. He again felt that he was running along the brink of the abyss, and the temptation to go over was lying in wait for him in a cloud of fog, in which the mind could no longer make any decision. . . . So he must hurry . . . hurry . . .

Half-way home he remembered that he had come to reconnoitre the front and to choose his route, and all he had done was to lose his time. He half thought of returning, then he said to himself that the plan with the positions would be sufficient guide and would show him the unoccupied places, which was what he needed to know. He could get as far as the first lines, and after that he'd trust to luck.

He arrived in Lunca almost at sunset, his horse covered with foam. He wanted to thank the doctor, but could find him neither at the hospital nor at home. On going past the church he saw, over the way, ensconced in an arm-chair on the *cerdac*,[1] the priest Boteanu, who was sunning himself happily and gazing down at the village as if he were viewing his own domain. From inside the house could be heard the furious, sharp voice of the priest's wife scolding the servant, and in the courtyard a troop of children were playing at "war", adorned with caps abandoned by soldiers quartered in the neighbouring houses. As soon as Bologa's eyes had sighted the parochial house he forgot all about Doctor Meyer, and felt an irrepressible longing to speak with the priest. He hurried across to the little gate and rushed in as if a man's fate were at stake for every minute's delay.

Popa Constantin, plunged as he was in vague and soothing bliss, suddenly saw an officer come up the five steps which led to the *cerdac*. A shudder of fear made him start up. He recognized Apostol, but the fear remained in his heart, and it made him utter his greeting in Hungarian:

"Welcome to our house, lieutenant!"

Bologa was so much moved that he did not at first notice that Boteanu was speaking Hungarian. His face seemed on fire and his blue lips trembled in a restless smile. When he spoke his teeth chattered and his voice had a harsh hoarseness:

"Father Constantin, I have come to you for confession."

---

[1] In peasant houses the *cerdac* is a sort of covered verandah, usually built over the entrance to the cellar.

When he heard his own voice the sound of it seemed unknown to him, and instinctively he looked to see if it hadn't been someone else who had spoken.

"Please come in, come in," said Boteanu, wondering and wavering.

They entered into a white room, and Apostol noticed that on the wall between two holy ikons there was an empty place, caused by the removal of some picture. Then only he remembered that the priest's greeting had been in Hungarian. He turned and looked at Constantin and became as confused as if he had inadvertently come across someone else's secret. The priest asked him to sit down on the divan, in front of which stood an oval table covered with an embroidered cloth. Bologa sat down hesitatingly, ill at ease. His mind could not remember what he had wanted to say or how to start, although his soul felt crystal clear. The popa remained standing a few moments, waiting doubtfully, then he sat down on a rush-bottomed chair at a fair distance and murmured:

"Here we can speak in peace, Apostol."

"And without danger!" added Bologa, glad to be able to ease the pressure on his soul by uttering these few words.

The priest felt ashamed of his own suspicions, and said with real bitterness:

"The man who has suffered as I have has a right to be on his guard even with his own shadow, Apostol!"

"Then I who have been brought here to kill them from the distance, what must I be suffering? Can you imagine it, Constantin?" broke out Bologa suddenly, as if his heart had burst.

Then he spoke for a quarter of an hour without stopping, with an alarming passion. He raved and stormed, converting his

anguish and torment into a torrent of words. The priest listened
with downcast eyes. As a matter of fact, Apostol did not look at
him at all, and would have been infuriated had Boteanu dared
to stop him or even to interrupt him. He talked to relieve his
overburdened soul, just as one weeps to alleviate too great a
sorrow. Only after he had regained some of his composure did
he address himself directly to the priest, but with a changed
voice and a new light in his eyes:

"And now the cup is full, Father! I can stand no more! A
deadly hatred gnaws at my heart. I loathe everything here,
everybody—friends, comrades, superiors, inferiors, everything,
everything, Constantin! The air here is unbearable and chokes
me. If I stay among these people any longer I feel that hatred
will be my undoing—it must, for it is bound to burst through
sometime, even against my will. . . . And then . . ."

Boteanu made an involuntary gesture: he put both hands
crossed on the table. Apostol stopped a minute inquiringly. But
because the priest had again turned to stone he went on more
hurriedly, as if he had remembered that time was precious:

"Listen carefully, Father! To-night I leave here. I am going
across. You know where, for your heart, too, must . . . Yes! I
am ready. Only I cannot let my mother know. I cannot write
to her, my letter would be censored, and who knows what
trouble it might get her into. That's why I want to entrust you
with the task of letting her know, Constantin—later on, when
it will be possible. I'll leave you mother's address, and you'll
find a way to let her know that I have gone over. Perhaps
through some trustworthy person later—when there might
be a chance."

The priest's face blanched with terror, and for a few minutes
he was totally unable to speak, moving his lips helplessly. Then,

as with a mighty effort, he burst out with tears in his voice, raising his right arm in timid protest:

"Why do you wish to ruin me, Apostol? I returned only this morning from internment—you know very well—I told you in the train. I was innocent, and all the same I had to suffer. How can I now listen to your plans and even become an accomplice? I have a family and great worries as it is . . . and must you choose me of all people to . . ."

"But you are a Rumanian, Father, my kinsman!" answered Bologa aghast.

"To-day I am just a human being, Apostol," answered the priest a little more calmly. "A wretched human being eaten up with want, with a never-dying fear in my heart and faith in the Divine Mercy. That's all we can be—just human beings—and all we can do is to hope that God will look after us, since Fate has flung us here and has exiled us."

Apostol Bologa had risen to his feet, stunned, and had bent his head so that the priest's words should not hit him in the face. His ears were buzzing, and the meaning of the priest's answer drilled itself slowly into his brain.

"You must do as God directs you, but you must not mix us up in it!" resumed Boteanu firmly. "We have enough dangers and difficulties of our own."

Bologa looked up quickly, so changed did the priest's voice sound, and in his face he read an inflexibility which startled him. He had put his steel helmet on the table; he now stretched out his hand mechanically and pulled it towards him by the strap. Then he put it on, slowly, carefully, muttering vaguely:

"You are right, Constantin . . . quite right . . . quite."

And he left the room with slow, dragging footsteps, leaving the door open; he went down the *cerdac* steps and passed through the courtyard where the children, gay and noisy, were still playing. Boteanu, seeing him go, took two steps forward, whether to stop Apostol or whether to accompany him to the gate he did not know himself. On the threshold he thought better of it, and he crossed himself and thanked the Almighty that He had given him strength to resist temptation.

In the street Apostol no longer knew which way to go, he seemed to have forgotten where he was. But his feet walked on without guidance, and presently he found himself in his little back street.

He felt so utterly weak that all he longed for now was one hour's rest. In the courtyard the office sergeant stiffened to attention. Bologa tried to say something to him, but he was too tired. In the doorway, leaning against the framework, he saw Ilona, who seemed to be waiting for someone. He looked at her as at a stranger, with dark, vacant eyes.

"Sir, you are ill!" exclaimed the girl, changing colour.

Bologa, without knowing he did so, stopped and looked at her inquiringly.

"You look ghastly and you are dead-tired. You must rest," added Ilona firmly.

The voice seemed to him so soothing that he thrilled with pleasure. But simultaneously a strange fear stabbed at his heart which made him answer angrily:

"Look here, my girl, haven't you anything better to do than to worry about me?"

§ VI

Apostol had intended to go into the office to see what work the men had done all day, but instead he found himself opening the door of his room. The grey twilight filtered in through the windows adorned with geraniums. In the dim light the walls seemed to curve and the things in the room rocked strangely. Bologa closed his eyes and sank into a chair, an inert lump of flesh. The buzzing and ringing in his ears made him so dizzy that he grabbed the table with both hands and held on lest he should fall over.

"Long may you live, sir. I have had your dinner ready all day," said Petre from the stove, thinking that his master was waiting for him to speak.

Bologa shuddered as if his orderly's voice had stabbed his wounded nerves. He stared at him as if he didn't know him, surprised that someone was in the room and that he hadn't known it. He tried to ask him something, but before the question was born in his brain a new, peremptory thought forced him to mutter:

"Make up my bed, Petre, and draw off my boots. I want to rest for an hour, only an hour, because in an hour I must . . ."

While he was drawing off the boots the soldier said something more to him. Apostol could not grasp what he was saying. He was thinking he'd like to tell Petre how frightfully tired he was, but he couldn't find the necessary words, and he no longer seemed to have the strength to express any thought. He got up from his chair, dragged himself to the bed and lay down. As soon as his head touched the pillow he felt his body go numb. At the same time his brain began to race wildly. Thousands of thought-fragments flashed into being in the same second, hurtling against one another, mixing, becoming entangled. And through them all, like a red drone, buzzed backwards and forwards—now loudly, now more softly, and continually assuming different shapes—the obsession that to-night it should end, end without fail. He was sleepy, he longed to sleep, but the more he strove to quieten the ferment in his soul the more tempestuous became his thoughts. Then, tired of trying, he let them go their own way, and it seemed to him that they all raced on, trying frenziedly to get ahead of one another, towards a luminous, shining goal, as towards a haven of real peace. He noticed that in this mighty race time remained behind, unrolling itself like a coloured canvas, and he was filled with an immeasurable satisfaction, as if little by little his whole being were melting into an immense revelation.

Then abruptly, without transition, the red thought that he must go that night reappeared and continued to dodge in and out among thousands of senseless thought-fragments. But now they all seemed encompassed by a burning feeling of regret. He felt he was still awake. It seemed to him that time had stood still like a watch out of order, and that because of this he could not go to sleep, and never again would he be able to go to sleep. Then he heard Ilona's voice near the bed saying, in a mixture of Rumanian and Hungarian:

"Ill, can't you see? Go for the doctor. I'll stay with him so you need not worry."

He couldn't catch what the orderly answered, but soon he heard the door creak and a gentle rustling. He thought: "A fine thing if I am ill and can't . . ." His thought trailed, unfinished, and on his forehead he felt a light hand, cool and rather rough-skinned. Under that touch the ferment in his mind quickly subsided as under the influence of a spell, and sleep came like a soothing balm. When he awoke he heard a strange voice near him. He felt terribly tired, so tired that he could not even lift his eyelids, and he tried hard to recognize the voice that was mumbling near his ear.

"It is Doctor Meyer!" he gasped presently. "So I am ill."

He opened his eyes to convince himself. His eyes rested on Ilona, who was standing at the foot of the bed, and who, on seeing him move, cried out joyfully:

"Look, doctor, he is awake!"

Doctor Meyer bent over the sick man, gave him a friendly tap on the cheek, and asked with kindly reproach:

"Well, what's the matter with you? What has happened to you? Is that what you call being strong? After I had warned you yesterday to take care of yourself and to . . ."

"What's the time, doctor?" whispered Bologa with a sad foreboding.

"It is morning, friend. What does it matter to you? Just keep quiet. It's nothing serious—nothing. You are just overtired and overwrought, that's all! But you'll have to keep very, very quiet."

Apostol's lids drooped as if they had been weighted with lead. He felt something give way in his soul and he longed vaguely for death. After a while he murmured, scarcely moving his lips:

"Doctor, I want to die."

"What, what?" shouted Meyer with unusual energy. "To die? Better say you want some sick-leave, to which you are certainly entitled."

Then, busying himself at the table, he added lower, in a natural voice and to himself:

"What a wicked thing to do, to send sick people to the front! Sometimes one really feels inclined to run away and let them all go to hell!"

Bologa's heart was filled with despair. The value of life lies in the future, and his future seemed to him to be padlocked like an iron gate on which he had bruised his fists by hammering in vain. One's powerlessness in face of life frightened him now more than it revolted him. The consciousness that all his endeavours and efforts were as powerless and aimless as the writhings of an earth-worm sank more and more deeply into his soul, together with the bitter certainty that a man's life was unbearable unless he had a solid prop to keep straight the balance between the inner world and the outer.

When he reopened his eyes some time later he again saw, sitting at the foot of his bed, the grave-digger's daughter, her head bent in thought. As if she had felt his glance resting on her, Ilona started up and came nearer, bright and cheerful, asking:

"Are you better? You do feel easier, don't you?"

"Yes, I am quite all right," said Apostol in a whisper.

The childish, dreamy joy in her eyes drove away the thoughts that tortured his sick brain. It seemed to him that there was a new witchery in that strange voice of hers, as if something, faith or passion, had changed it since yesterday and made it deeper and mellower. Seeing her standing there, confused by his luminous gaze, her face shining with pleasure, Bologa felt a warm thrill in his heart and wanted to encourage her to speak.

And Ilona, as if she had guessed his longing, began to talk quickly, breaking off occasionally in the middle of a word, apprehensively, as if she feared some unknown danger. She told him that the doctor had wanted to have him moved to the hospital but that she had opposed it, for he would surely be better looked after here, where he was the only one, than at the hospital, where there were so many. She had sworn she wouldn't leave his bedside, and, in fact, she hadn't budged. She hadn't any too much to do in the house, for her father didn't make her work hard. Her father was awfully kind, though he liked to make out he was severe with her. But she did not mind about his severity, for she knew how to behave and take care of herself.

"I saw you were ill as soon as you set foot in the enclosure the day before yesterday, and I told the orderly to look out. But now that you are in my care you don't need the help of the orderly any more. He is a good fellow, there's no doubt about that, and he is attached to his master, but men are no good with sick people, no matter how hard they try. From to-day onwards you've got to understand that I am master and that you must obey me absolutely until I tell you that you are well again, otherwise . . ."

Here she broke off abruptly, took up a medicine bottle and a teaspoon, came up close to his bed and said:

"Now you've got to take this; it's quite sweet, I've tasted it."

"Leave that, Ilona. Go on talking!" begged Apostol.

The girl's face turned as red as the geranium in the window, and for a moment she hesitated. But then almost immediately she repeated, with sweet severity:

"If you don't take your medicine you may as well know that I'll never tell you another thing, so there!"

Bologa closed his eyes a minute as if he would lock up her sweetness in his soul. Ilona filled the teaspoon and held it to his mouth. Her fingers trembled slightly, and Apostol put his hand on hers. The girl's cheeks crimsoned again, and to hide her emotion she said:

"My goodness, how hot your hand is!"

Apostol tasted nothing. He again closed his eyelids, filled with a happiness in which all his thoughts were drowned. He heard Ilona put down the bottle, wipe the spoon, walk about on tiptoe, and finally sit down on her chair at the foot of the bed. He felt her caressing gaze on his cheeks, his forehead, his lips. He did not dare to move for fear of scattering this joy that was in his heart.

From then onwards Apostol lost count of the time. Doctor Meyer came twice a day, always told him there was nothing wrong with him, but that he was to stay in bed until he'd bring him a miraculous medicine which would immediately cure him. Then one morning the doctor arrived in high spirits and called out from the threshold:

"Come on, out of bed! I think after to-morrow I'll bring you what I promised. But until then, mind you, you are not to leave this room! Not even to go across the passage into the office—not leave the room at all. You understand? Have patience! You've waited ten days, so you can wait another two. And because then, you know, you whispered some nonsense, let me tell you now, my young friend, that life is never a burden, but that death is the greatest burden of all. There! Remember what a morose and embittered doctor has told you. In point of fact, the most wretched life is of greater value than the most heroic death."

On the third day, at midday, an unusual hour for him to come, Doctor Meyer arrived, triumphantly waving a sheet of paper in his hand.

"Look at the little miracle, my friend!" he said, with an exuberance so little in keeping with his nature that it seemed forced. "A month's sick-leave! Do you think it was easy to get? I assure you it wasn't! But I wouldn't stop trying until His Excellency had to capitulate. At last here it is! I think there is a train which leaves here at four; which means there's plenty of time for you to pack and clear out! What! You are not even glad? That's military gratitude! Here am I, a grumpy fellow, rejoicing and he puts on airs! Bravo! Oh, by the way, don't forget that when you get home you'll have to feed up and rest with a vengeance! Now hurry so as not to miss that train!"

"Will he come back here, doctor?" then asked Ilona, her face white and an ill-concealed anxiety in her eyes.

"Surely, girlie!" answered the doctor cheerily, taking hold of her chin. "Don't you worry, he won't run away!"

"I didn't mean that, but I just wanted to know!" stammered Ilona, her face and ears pink.

Petre grasped that the talk concerned an *Urlaub*,[1] and to the doctor's satisfaction immediately set about happily getting the lieutenant's things together. Ilona retired behind the door and did not move from there until Meyer had wished Bologa "a pleasant journey and a good time over there."

A wave of sadness had crept into the little white room where the white rays of the young sun laughed in through the crimson geraniums at every window. Apostol stood by the table with the permit in his hand, looking now at Petre, who, in his joy, muttered prayer after prayer while busily putting things together, now at the grave-digger's daughter, who, standing stiffly behind the door, was gazing out into the distance with a tense expression of anxious fear. Bologa thought it his duty to say something to her, but an obscure fear tightened round his throat like a rope. At last he managed to utter, in an almost peremptory tone:

"Ilona . . ."

The girl, as if she had expected this, answered with a darkened glance. Then she rushed out of the room, banging the door after her, and ran away somewhere to hide her heart.

"I can manage alone, sir," said Petre, thinking the lieutenant had wanted the girl to give him a hand. "What a mercy that the Lord has at last helped us also to get away for a little while from foreign parts and set eyes on our home again."

---

[1] German for "leave".

And then it was that Bologa realized that he wasn't at all glad of this leave.

"My heart does not beat any faster because I am going home, nor do I seem to mind in the least that my plans have failed," he thought sadly. "And I am losing my head for the sake of a little peasant girl."

He threw the permit on the table and began to walk to and fro with his hands behind his back, unconsciously gripping his fingers. All at once he felt the betrothal ring on the third finger of his left hand and stopped aghast. How long was it since he had given Marta, his fiancée, a thought? And he had not even noticed the ring all this time; the cause of this was most certainly the grave-digger's daughter.

He left early for the station. The grave-digger and Ilona accompanied him as if he had been a favoured guest. When the train arrived he shook hands, first, with Vidor, then with the girl. Her hand was burning hot, and in her eyes flamed a question. Then he got in and stood at the window until the train began to move. The grave-digger at once turned towards the exit, but Ilona remained on the platform immovable, her gaze glued on the window in which Apostol, smiling dreamily, stood framed. And then the head of an old cherry-tree in flower hid, first, the window, then the compartment, and finally the train from view.

§ VII

Parva's beech avenue, straight and neat, from the station to the centre of the little town, seemed an unending tunnel at night when it was dark. Apostol's footsteps crunched noisily on the damp gravel. Petre, weighed down by two portmanteaux, could hardly keep pace with him and panted heavily behind.

The square market-place was deserted, all the houses were asleep. They went up the main street, but met no one here either.

"Here we are at Lawyer Domsa's, so there's not much farther to go," gasped Petre from the back, snorting like a bull and jerking his head in the direction of an imposing-looking house on the right.

Apostol made no answer, as if he had not heard, though the orderly's words sounded in his ears like a reproach, for he himself had just been staring at the house where Marta, his beloved, was mistress. He felt so guilty towards his fiancée that he could hardly wait till the morrow to run over to her, fall at her feet, and beg her to forgive him.

Soon the spires of the church towers became visible in the darkness and Apostol increased his pace. His home was plunged in darkness. When he opened the little gate an old mastiff bounded into his path, barking furiously. Apostol quietened him with a whispered word and the dog lay down at his feet, beating the earth with his bushy tail, rather shamefaced that he had not recognized his young master sooner.

The noise of the little gate and the dog's barking recalled the house to life. A yellow light sprang up at one window, disappeared, reappeared in the hall and was coming nearer the front-door. Apostol went up the steps and knocked. The candle stopped and wavered. From another room Doamna Bologa's voice could be heard, and then the key was turned twice in the lock from inside. Apostol's hand turned the handle and the trembling light flashed straight into his face. The servant began to yell as if she had seen a ghost.

"Help, mum, help! And goodness gracious me, if it isn't the young master!"

Apostol walked in, laughing, and Petre shut the door. In the doorway of the room at the far end Doamna Bologa appeared, bareheaded, her face as white as paper, looking as if she could not believe her eyes. Then she burst out through her tears:

"Oh, my darling! my precious!"

They clung together in a long embrace, muttering broken words and disconnected sentences in which their joy and tenderness found the needed relief. When she had grown calmer, Doamna Bologa turned to the servant, who, with the candle in her hand, seemed to have been turned into stone, and said:

"Rodovica, what are you standing there for like an idiot? Put the candlestick on the table and run and light the fire; we must get the young master something to eat. Run, Rodovica! And you, Petre, put the bags over there near the door and rest a while; you also must have something to eat before you go on home."

"I would much rather go on at once, please, mum, for fear I might be overcome with fatigue," said the orderly, wiping away the sweat that was running from his forehead down his cheeks; "I have a goodish step still to do to get across the water!"

"Yes, so you have! Of course, you come from Jerusalim, on the other side of the Someş—I had forgotten that, Petre. Very well, go then, and God be with you!"

Doamna Bologa led Apostol into her bedroom at the back of the hall. It had only one window, and that was shuttered. A lamp with a china shade hung from the ceiling. The bed was turned down for the night. Here Apostol had spent his childhood until he had gone to Nasaud. His little bed had stood there, where that sofa was now, and here he had repeated aloud fervent prayers, mornings and evenings, on his knees, his eyes fixed on the old ikon hung on the wall above the bed, gazing passionately at the Good God who sat in the white clouds on a throne of gold.

Everything was as it had always been, only his little mother had shrunk a bit and now showed innumerable little fine lines at the corners of her eyes, which still, however, burnt with the fire of faith. But Apostol seemed an alien, or he seemed to have fallen into an alien world.

Doamna Bologa asked him to tell her at once everything that had happened to him day by day since he had been home last. But before Apostol could make up his mind to begin, the childish memories conjured up by the little room having plunged him into a kind of torpor, Doamna Bologa, firstly to empty her heart, and secondly because the older she grew the more talkative she became, began to relate, one after another, all sorts of small incidents of her daily life and of the life of the small town.

"God had told me that you would come, darling! If you only knew what a state I was in when I heard all that you had been through! I waited and waited for letters from you and nothing came—even Marta wondered what could have happened. Then I talked things over with Domsa, who is a sensible, wise man, and we came to the conclusion that you had gone over to our people, for we heard that the regiment had been sent over here to fight the Rumanians—the Lord protect us and have mercy on us! Lucky that the Lord enlightened you and you stayed where you were, for if they had laid hands on you, my precious, O God! you might have fared like our poor protopop—even worse . . . What luck that we were not in bed yet! Usually about this time we are all asleep, but to-day it seemed as if God had whispered to us to stay up a little while longer. I had been talking to and keeping an eye on that fool of a Rodovica, for it so happens that the Polish major quartered here left this morning, and we have been hard at work all day cleaning the room he has had for nearly seven months—your room—and your father's before you, may his sins be forgiven him. I must say the major was a man of the world, but he had to go, for he said that heavy fighting was about to begin again. It's no use, there's no sign of peace. There were rumours that peace was coming, that the Russians are doing this and the other, but alas! it was nothing but talk! All the soldiers who were round here have gone; just a few have been left on account of the magazines—perhaps you noticed them coming along— wooden sheds, a whole townful, near the Feleac road."

She was interrupted by Rodovica, her cheeks red through bustling round, coming in with food for the young master. While she was laying the cloth she said:

"You see, mum, how true signs are? The whole blessed day long my right eye kept blinking, and there you are, God has sent us joy in the house!"

"Hold your tongue; Rodovica, signs come from the devil," stated Doamna Bologa, displeased that the maid had taken the conversation upon herself. "Better run and make up the young master's bed."

While Apostol was eating with good appetite, Doamna Bologa, after a few questions which she answered herself, began again to talk of Palagiesu, of household troubles, of Protopop Groza. When he had finished eating, Apostol asked one single question:

"And how's Marta, mother?"

"She's all right, darling, for she's healthy and young," said Doamna Bologa rather embarrassed, as if she had expected the question but had forgotten the answer she had got ready. "It's no use my telling you about her because you'll be seeing her yourself and . . . Is everything ready, Rodovica?" she added quickly to the servant, who had just appeared in the doorway. "That's right, for the young master is tired and needs a good rest!"

She accompanied him into his room and kissed him on the forehead as she used to do when he slept in the room with the picture of God on the wall. Then Apostol was left alone. On the little night-table wavered the orange flame of a candle ensconced in a tall brass candlestick. Soft shadows danced on the floor, on the walls, on the ceiling, like the dreams of a harassed man.

"Good night!" Apostol said to himself, throwing off his clothes quickly, slipping into bed and tossing hither and thither until he had settled himself comfortably.

He blew out the light. He wanted to sleep at once, for in truth the journey had tired him. "Why was mother ill at ease when I asked her about Marta?" flashed through his mind. Of course, his mother wasn't so very fond of her and had opposed the match until the betrothal, but afterwards she had become reconciled. Well, it was no good, he *was* guilty towards Marta, and he'd go without fail to-morrow. He loved her and must love her only. In her stead, however, Ilona kept on appearing before him, Ilona with the red kerchief on her head, with her eyes in which danced strange laughter, with her voice which caressed and hurt. And against his will he felt an immense pleasure in knowing with certainty that far away in a village there was someone who even in her dreams carried no one but him in her heart. But this must not be! Marta! Where was Marta? To-morrow, without fail, he'd go to her.

The next day he awoke under the kisses of the bright April sun. It seemed as if spring had re-entered that room with white waves of light and promise of gladness. On the table, on a tray with a flowered cloth, he found waiting for him, as of yore, a cup of coffee and a good chunk of *cozonac*.[1] A great content filled his heart. He loved all the world.

"If I had succeeded, who knows where I should be now?" he thought with a stab of fear.

But the thought died as if it could not withstand the joy of life which flamed in his heart.

From this room a double door led on to the front balcony, which was surrounded by a little flower garden. There, in an arm-chair covered with an old rug, Bologa sprawled restfully at full length, like a citizen without cares after a copious meal. He intended to rest a little and then go and see Marta.

The scarcely formed shadows of the walnut-trees in the little garden, trees that had been planted on the day he had been born, danced on his cheeks soothed by the warm rays. From the sky, very blue and clear, peace descended, and from the scattered houses, from the trees in bloom, from the fields furrowed by ploughs, from the yellowy hills, from the black-green forest, rose unseen waves of the great life, all-powerful, implacable and yet unendingly alluring. Love of life floated in the air on silver wings, singing hymns of praise which distilled true happiness and a thousand hopes into human hearts.

Apostol's soul drank in greedily the magic of spring. His eyes gazed but saw nothing, and his ears only heard the heavenly sounds. People passed along the street and called out greetings to him, but he took no notice. His surroundings had brought back memories of his childhood and had wafted him back into the past. And time flowed over him, measureless and impenetrable, as it flows over those who are no longer tempted to pursue happiness.

---

[1] A kind of brioche.

And then all of a sudden there burst on his ears a well-known voice, blithe, a little shrill, with glints of roguish laughter in it. Apostol had the impression that he had fallen from a pinnacle, and he jumped to his feet as if stung by an adder. In the street by the gate Marta, who had not seen him, had halted and was talking in Hungarian to an officer of the Home Defence Corps, pointing out the house to him. When she entered the courtyard and saw him, she called out "Good morning!" still speaking Hungarian, while the officer behind her raised his hand to the peak of his cap, smiling constrainedly. In a few moments Marta was standing before Apostol. She was wearing a white, lace-trimmed blouse and a small hat, from under which the brown curls escaped. Her cheeks were on fire and her squirrel's eyes sparkled with intense mirth.

"Rodovica has trumpeted all over the town that you arrived last night," she chirped, drawing near. "I was waiting for you to come over, but I couldn't wait any longer, and here I am!"

She was still speaking Hungarian, and with such pleasure that her full lips trembled. Apostol was nonplussed to hear her. He tried to smile, but made no attempt to take the hand which was being held out to him. After a moment, however, he took her fingers mechanically and answered, also in Hungarian:

"Oh, mademoiselle, I did not expect that . . . Forgive me, I don't know what I am saying!"

Because he did not kiss her hand as he usually did, and because he had called her "mademoiselle", Marta wavered, and her smile faded for a second. But she quickly regained her composure, and, turning to her escort, spoke to him with even noisier gaiety, as if she wished by this means to dispel her slight feeling of discomfort.

"This is my fiancé, whom you almost know because I have talked so much about him to you! You know," she said, turning again to Apostol, "this gentleman kept me company all the winter, otherwise I should have died of boredom!"

The officer of the Home Defence Corps, smart, spick-and-span, with powdered face, came forward more boldly. On his left arm he carried Marta's coat. He saluted ceremoniously, clicking his heels:

"Lieutenant Tohaty . . ."

There followed a silence, each one waiting for the other to speak. Marta again cut short the silence with such exaggerated heartiness that both men dropped their eyes.

"I went to shop in the market and there I met the lieutenant . . ."

She broke off giggling, then continued:

"So then what did I say to myself? I'll take him along and introduce him to Apostol, so that there should be no fear of him being jealous! That's how I happened to bring him. Also he's engaged, so that . . ."

She laughed again. The two embarrassed men, however, now, smilingly, exchanged a slight bow. Marta, encouraged, became more natural, stopped her forced laughter and said softly:

"You weren't very assiduous with regard to letter-writing. I did not mind, but I cried a lot because . . . because . . . of you, especially when I heard how you had suffered. Five wounds, and five terrible months in hospital! This gentleman kept on telling me that you would be sure to come home on sick-leave, but I didn't believe him at all. Now he has been proved right. Luckily I did not bet, but I very nearly . . ."

She met Bologa's eyes and stopped short, filled with a fear she could not master. Through Apostol's mind passed the thought that he had actually intended to ask her forgiveness. That thought was reflected in his eyes in a phosphorescence of hatred and crystallized into a gaze so hostile that it scorched. When Marta stopped speaking, he shuddered as if he had awakened and found himself clutching a dagger in his hand, ready to strike. He felt ashamed and looked at the lieutenant questioningly. Then he looked at Marta and smiled, a little frightened himself at her terror.

"Sit down, M . . . In the arm-chair!" he muttered, not daring to call her by her name, and drawing the armchair nearer to her.

Then the officer came to the rescue with hurried questions about the battle in which Apostol had been wounded, about the news at the front, and about the hopes of peace. . . . And Bologa, to prove to himself his self-control, answered him with technical details and with a certain superciliousness that was in rather bad taste. Marta, who had sat down in the arm-chair, soon recovered herself and mixed herself in their conversation, now jokingly, now plaintively. They went on talking lest the icy atmosphere should return. And when, in spite of their efforts, there was a pause, Marta jumped up with her former forced gaiety, ready to go. All three sighed with relief.

"And when do you intend to come over to us, old bear?" she asked in Rumanian as she was going, arranging the folds of her blouse on her bosom so as to avoid looking into his eyes. "Daddy is expecting you . . . if you are not keen on coming to see *me*," she added more saucily, after an imperceptible break.

"Of course I'll come," murmured Bologa, controlling a sudden feeling of revolt. "But in a day or two. Don't you see in what a condition I am?"

"From here to our house there are about thirty steps," answered Marta, genuinely gay again and raising her eyes to his in sweet defiance. "And you're not so thin that you can't go about! You have become colder and more grumpy, otherwise you haven't changed."

Her self-assurance amazed him so much that he answered almost humbly:

"I have become a savage."

But Marta, now rather nervous again, quickly crossed the little garden with Tohaty following at her heels like a faithful shadow. Once in the street, curiosity overcame her and she turned her head to see what Apostol was doing. He was leaning against the pillar of the balcony, his face terribly distorted. Nevertheless, she smiled at him and sent him a kiss with unconscious coquetry.

Apostol Bologa gripped the pillar with both arms as if he had been stabbed in the heart. He followed them with his eyes and saw them both laugh—she especially was swinging her hips gaily as she kept pace with him. Then, when they were out of sight, he began to shake the pillar of the balcony with all his strength and with a horrible despair, like a madman, grinding for some moments between his teeth without knowing it:

"Get out! . . . Get out! . . . Get out! . . ."

And just as suddenly his fury abated and he felt ashamed of his outburst. Hatred still filled his breast, but his mind began to judge more clearly. He dropped into the armchair and kept repeating to himself that he must judge fairly and without haste what had happened, otherwise the consequences might be fatal for him. She was really rather proud of her guilt, whereas he had wanted to go to her and beg her to forgive him. He had been storing her image in the sanctum of his heart and had worshipped her as though she had been an ikon, while she had been busy killing her boredom with that puppy.

"Horrible . . . horrible!" his lips went on muttering.

Now he felt convinced that it was her fault that he had enlisted; simply to gratify a caprice of hers he had imperilled his life. To gratify a mere caprice! That showed him how he must have loved her!

Over the road the cross on the church-tower glittered like gold. Apostol's eyes stubbornly persisted in staring at the rays which issued from the body of the cross, as if their dazzling and triumphant light were trying to defy him or to rebuke him, just when his brain was harassed by the fickleness of the woman who had spoilt his life. Then all at once his glance fell from the cross to the graveyard round the church and found the stone with the gilt inscription which marked the grave and the memory of his father. It seemed to him that the letters had become somewhat faded, and he determined to get the old stonecutter to renew them. And then, clearly as on the day when his father had first uttered them in Nasaud, he heard in his mind the elder man's words: "Do your duty always, and never forget that you are a Rumanian!" He heard perfectly, not only the voice but the intonation, the emphasis on "never" and "Rumanian" and the way he had rolled the "r" in "Rumanian".

"Why should they come into my mind just now?" wondered Apostol, finding no connection between them and the matter that preoccupied him just then.

He sat there another half-hour or so seeking a solution. Then he went back into his room, depressed, irresolute, his thoughts disconnected. He began to hunt for something, then, hastening to his desk, drew out a sheet of writing-paper and wrote down hurriedly a few lines addressed to Domsa, telling him that he now felt that the betrothal with Marta had been a piece of childish folly, and so he was returning the ring.

"How simple it is; fancy my not thinking of it before!" he thought whilst addressing the note.

He hunted through his drawers and at length discovered what he was looking for—a little case lined with blue velvet. He slipped the ring off, put it into the box, wrapped up the box neatly and sealed it with red sealing-wax.

Then he called Rodovica and sent her with the letter and the parcel to Domsa, ordering her to hand it to him in person.

After that he went out again on to the balcony, again read the inscription on the grave, and once more recalled his father's words: ". . . never forget that you are a Rumanian!"

§ VIII

Doamna Bologa had prepared a royal feast in honour of Apostol. When they had reached the roast, Lawyer Domsa burst into the house, his face red and perspiring and his round eyes bulging with excitement. He called out from the hall:

"I beg of you to excuse me, dear lady, for intruding upon you in this manner."

Startled by his appearance, Doamna Bologa sprang to her feet, certain that something dreadful had happened to Marta— either she had run away with the Hungarian, or . . . something even worse. Domsa, however, went on hurriedly, throwing his hat on a chair and wiping the perspiration from his face:

"Nothing on earth would ever have made me believe that Apostol could play me such a trick! I swear it, Doamna Bologa! I had such confidence in him—in his common sense and decency—that this hit me like a blow from a hammer, full in the face! I assure you, dear lady!"

The more he talked the more worked up he became, and the more the perspiration oozed from his face—for God had made him stout. He tried to calm himself, lowering his voice, but he could not succeed in banishing the look of anxiety from his eyes, more especially as Apostol had remained undisturbed in his seat and had continued to battle with the chicken leg on his plate as if nothing had happened.

Doamna Bologa became still more bewildered when she heard that Apostol was the cause of the lawyer's excitement, for Apostol had said nothing to her about having had any misunderstanding with his future father-in-law. True, Rodovica had hastened to whisper to her in the kitchen that the young master had sent her to Lawyer Domsa's, but Doamna Bologa had thought that the parcel had probably contained some war souvenir for Marta. So she didn't know what to say, and to get over her embarrassment she invited Domsa to sit down and to honour her by tasting a small piece of the roast. Her invitation and Apostol's coldness brought forth new showers of perspiration from the lawyer. He thanked Doamna Bologa with a despairing smile and turned to Apostol.

"You know very well what a lot I think of you, my dear boy," he said rather hesitatingly, as if he were talking to a stranger, "otherwise I should not have troubled to come here at all after your letter . . . in fact . . . after your gesture, which hurt me, Apostol, very, very much."

"It was my duty to make that gesture, Domnu[1] Domsa," answered Apostol, raising his eyes and looking at the lawyer with unruffled calm.

"But what is it? What has happened?" then asked Doamna Bologa, recovering herself a little and adding: "Do sit down, do sit down, sit here! Oh, my goodness! You gave me such a fright, and I don't even know what it is all about!"

---

[1] Rumanian for "Mr."

"How is this? You know nothing? Hasn't Apostol told you?" asked Domsa, astonished, a little ray of hope illuminating his features. "You really don't know? Well, you shall hear, dear lady, and I'll warrant you'll cross yourself when you've heard!"

He explained to her in great detail—for Domsa had the gift of the gab—that while they had been waiting for Apostol this forenoon, after Marta had had the nice thought of running round here to bid him welcome—without worrying about etiquette and conventions—Rodovica had suddenly appeared. Wondering what the letter could possibly be, he had broken the seal, had read it, and had almost collapsed. Marta, as a matter of fact, had actually fainted, and it was no wonder, for such a smack in the face could blight a girl's reputation and compromise her future. They did not even open the box, they forgot it. His first impulse had been to make Marta return immediately her ring and cut Apostol entirely out of their lives. Then he had reflected that the boy was young, and youth was rash. Who knew what had come over him, and it would indeed be a pity if through some childish folly a couple so suited to one another should become separated. So he had come over to find out the cause of that "gesture" and to draw his attention to the seriousness of so unjustified a decision when a young lady's honour was in question. "My decision is irrevocable, Domnu Domsa," broke in Apostol with the same imperturbable calm. All the time the lawyer had been speaking he had gone on eating steadily, scraping clean with marked attention each bone on his plate. "It is irrevocable, because I no longer love Domnisoara[1] Marta."

"How do you mean, you don't love her any more ? Why not?" asked Domsa, opening his eyes wide.

---

[1] Miss.

"Why? Because I don't love her!" said Bologa, wiping his mouth on his napkin and looking smilingly at Doamna Bologa, who was sitting on her chair, struck dumb, unable to believe her ears.

"That's impossible!" exclaimed the lawyer. "That's impossible! That's no reason! Because of some childish foolishness you cannot be allowed to spoil a girl's happiness! Tell him, dear lady, you tell him also, for you are a sensible woman and know the world, tell him that that sort of thing isn't done."

The appeal found Doamna Bologa unprepared. In her inmost heart she was pleased that Apostal had come to see that she had been right. Marta's "goings-on" had scandalized her, who had never known what flirting meant. Not that she suspected her of any serious misbehaviour, but for her son she wanted an entirely self-sacrificing wife as she herself had been. And she had not been able to forgive Marta for leading a life of pleasure and irresponsibility while her fiancé was risking his life every minute of the day and night at the war. She had not written to tell the boy because she had not wished to embitter him, but she had determined she would tell him everything when he came home. Now, however, she felt sorry for "poor Domsa, such a decent fellow", and even a little sorry for Marta, thinking how ashamed she would be when people knew. So she told Apostol immediately to reflect well on what he was doing, for a broken engagement was no joke, no child's play.

For a whole hour they both talked at Apostol. Rodovica came in several times and signed to her mistress in dumb show that the remainder of her dinner was getting quite spoilt. Doamna Bologa, however, had by now warmed to her task, and much to the lawyer's joy waved her aside. The lawyer, becoming more eloquent, kept on asking Apostol to give him his "reasons and motives" for so inexplicable an action. Apostol remained unshaken, refusing curtly to give any further explanation, simply repeating that he no longer loved Marta. So that in the end Domsa, perplexed and depressed, was forced to go home as he had come, empty-handed, without the slightest hope of a reconciliation.

As a matter of fact, Domsa had also noticed and condemned in his own heart Marta's flightiness, but he had never been able to stop it or even curb it. He loved his only child more than the light of his eyes, with a love sinful in its indulgence and which had only one aim in view, namely that Marta should be happy. And now, was her whole happiness to be destroyed ?

At home he discussed with Marta what they should do to protect themselves, for it was obvious that in a few days the whole town would know and discuss the extraordinary event. It was important, very important, that the blame for the broken engagement should fall on Apostol, who would suffer no disadvantage, whereas the girl . . . Looking at it this way and that, Marta arrived at the conclusion that her fiancé's annoyance had been caused, without a manner of doubt, by the conversation in Hungarian.

"I am certain of it, daddy," she exclaimed triumphantly. "I also noticed a strange hardness in his eyes which frightened me. And look here, daddy, how could we two speak a language which the other person present could not understand? It would have been fearfully ill-bred, wouldn't it?"

"Perhaps he has become Chauvinistic, like his father, who was a real fanatic," said Domsa, agreeing. "He spent two years in prison in connection with the Memorandum."

"Chauvinism is horrid, isn't it, daddy?" said Marta, after a pause. "One should love one's own people, of course, but not feel hatred for other races, should one?"

This reflection seemed to the lawyer so "deep" that he could not conceal his admiration, and, embracing Marta warmly, he exclaimed:

"What a clever little girl it is! And to think that a girl like you should be thrown over by a . . ."

He was on the point of saying a "scoundrel", but fore-bore to do so, either because he felt ashamed or because he nursed a hope that Apostol would come to his senses and all would be well. To be on the safe side, and so that the news should not reach them from another quarter, Domsa told the doctor in the afternoon and the Hungarian judge in the evening at the club, what had befallen him in connection with young Bologa, ending thus:

"And for what reason do you think, my dear fellow? You'll never believe it, it is so utterly absurd—merely because the child spoke Hungarian! Isn't it queer? Is it such a terrible crime to speak Hungarian? Especially if there is a Hungarian present who speaks no other language? No, no, I am also Rumanian, and I even pride myself on being ultra-Rumanian, but such exaggerations are abnormal, absolutely abnormal, not to say dangerous."

The next day all Parva knew that Apostol Bologa had broken off his engagement with the lawyer's daughter because he had heard her speak Hungarian. And everybody pitied "poor Marta", predicting that Apostol would put a rope round his neck if, while war was in full swing, he began to do as his dead father had done. In the evening at the Rumanian Club, where nowadays all the gentlemen met because the officers' mess had been installed in the Hungarian Club, they talked of nothing but Apostol with the same passionate interest as they had shown two or three weeks ago concerning the Russian revolution.

And when Lawyer Domsa, as a rule not very popular, arrived at about seven o'clock, they bombarded him with questions, which he answered with great modesty and much indulgence for the youth and thoughtlessness of "the boy". But the great sensation was the appearance of Apostol himself. Everybody expected something sensational to happen, even a scandal seemed possible. To the general regret nothing happened. Apostol shook hands, first with Domsa, who gave him a friendly smile, then all round with everybody. Naturally no one dared to mention the subject that filled everybody's mind. They all talked rather constrainedly about the topics of the day, the food difficulties, etc., some complaining of the flour rations and the unfortunate rise in prices, which was very discouraging.

Apostol left after about ten minutes, saying that he had only looked in to shake hands with them. After he had gone, the manager of the Parvana Bank remarked that the lieutenant had worn no decorations, and the accountant, that he hadn't breathed a word about the war.

The following days the excitement in the little town increased, more especially owing to strange rumours that seemed to have got about. Some said that things would soon be straightened out, because someone had seen Apostol talking to Marta right in the middle of the market-place; others again said that the affair might take an unexpected turn if the notary Palagiesu interfered, and he was supposed to have declared at the club, before several gentlemen, in a very significant tone, that he had no intention of allowing anyone, not even his own father, to disturb the harmony of the place.

In truth, Palagiesu, worried at the scandal, thought it his duty to report it to the sheriff, who, as a matter of fact, knew all about it and also felt somewhat anxious. They consulted

LIVIU REBREANU

together as to what steps to take to ensure that "the peace should be kept". They had to own that it was a very delicate business: firstly, because it was a private quarrel in which the State had no call whatever to interfere; secondly, because an officer was involved, over whom civil authorities had no power. At the same time the quarrel affected public opinion by reason of its initial cause, which put into the people's mind the pernicious thought that he who made use of the official language of the State was not an honourable Rumanian. The guilt was all the greater because the author and spreader of this idea was a soldier, who for that very reason was under the sacred obligation of raising the *morale* of the citizens, more especially just now, when the country was carrying on a life-and-death struggle for the good and happiness of all. The notary in a burst of indignation gave it as his opinion that this business was even more serious than the preachings which had made necessary the internment of Protopop Groza. They differed with regard to the steps to be taken. Palagiesu would have liked to apply to Bologa's superiors and get him recalled to the front in the interest of peace and quietness. The sheriff had thought of that himself; he had even talked about it to the commander of the battalion which was still stationed in Parva. The captain, however, who was a drunkard and despised civilians, had told him that he had no time to worry about foolish things. These soldiers thought everything foolish that was not armed with rifle or gun! It would be better, he thought, if one tried, for the time being at any rate, to smooth things over by a friendly intervention.

"You are the lieutenant's friend," the sheriff concluded, "you were children together. Why don't you try to have a word with him?"

§ IX

On the day that he broke off his engagement to Marta, Apostol Bologa felt very happy. In his happiness there was a touch of pride for his firmness in sticking to his resolutions and satisfaction that he had got over so trying a situation. After Domsa's departure he had a long explanation with his mother, who, convinced by the lawyer's arguments, and thinking more especially of Marta's disappointment, did her best to save the engagement, exactly as only a short while back she had done her best to prevent it, and she felt sorry that the poor protopop was not at home to give her a hand.

But Apostol's peace of mind did not last long. That night he had retired to his room immediately after supper in order to avoid any further discussions with Doamna Bologa, and as soon as he was alone he was beset by all kinds of doubts. He now became conscious that all day long his most secret thoughts had wandered far away, over there, as if in search of support. He wondered whether, if Ilona had not been in his heart, he would have been in so great a hurry to return Marta her ring. He had not been indignant, because Marta had come accompanied by a strange man, but because she had come with a Hungarian and had spoken Hungarian. So it was not because he was jealous that he had given her up, but because he loved the other one. If this were so his indignation against the Hungarian and the Hungarian language had been a farce. What was more, the farce had begun before that—it had begun when he had not regretted in the least that his illness had for the second time prevented him from going over to the Rumanians. He had felt far more upset at leaving there to come home, as if the axis of his life had been left behind there, in Lunca. And even the future no longer interested him, except vaguely. Although in a month's time he would have to go back there to the Rumanian front, he no longer seemed to be horrified at the idea, as if he no longer cared. Did this mean, then, that love was the cause of all the agitations and joys of mankind? And yet the love for woman could not satisfy the soul; it was only transitory and spasmodic. Not so long since he had believed that all heaven and earth and all the secrets of the universe were hidden in a glance of Marta's. For love of her he would have committed any folly, made any sacrifice. He would have died happy if she had asked him to, and it had been the wish in her eyes that had been the deciding factor, in overcoming his reluctance to joining the war. His love for her was still a living thing when the eyes of the man hanged in Zirin—in whose death he had had a hand by uttering that very decided "Yes"—had bored through into his heart, and yet it had not been able to soothe his agitations until he had discovered a new belief.

"The soul needs constant food," Apostol said to himself, walking up and down his bedroom, still dressed, not daring to go to bed for fear of his thoughts. "But it is vain to seek that food outside in the world of the senses. Only the heart can find it, either in some secret place of its own or else in some new world beyond the reach of mortal eyes and ears."

Doubts gnawed at his brain all night. When he put out the lamp, the dawn was breaking between the white curtains. He again felt guilty with regard to Marta and fell asleep planning how to repair the wrong he had done her.

But the scandalmongering of the little town made him change his mind. It began the very next day. At each meal Doamna Bologa served up all the things she had heard: that So-and-so had said that and that, that everybody blamed him, and rightly, she was bound to say, for a man had no business to make a fool of a poor, silly little girl; that the Hungarian lieutenant intended to demand an explanation. . . . Apostol listened to all this news quietly, and even smilingly, appearing indifferent and firm. But in his soul he revolted. How dared all these strangers mix themselves in a business which concerned only the two of them, Marta and him?

A few days later, Doamna Bologa sat down to dinner with eyes red with weeping and looking so anxious that Apostol felt upset, and, feeling instinctively that it meant something serious, he omitted to ask her why she had been crying, so that Doamna Bologa was compelled to tell him unasked that she had heard from several sources that danger threatened him, that the whole of Parva was saying that he had shamed Marta simply because she had spoken Hungarian, and that such a thing was bound to have serious consequences—the Lord alone knew how serious! Merely from imagining the consequences, Doamna Bologa burst into loud weeping. To quieten her, Apostol said:

"Do you mean to say, mother, that you think I haven't the right to ask my fiancé to speak Rumanian with me? You really work yourself up for nothing! With regard to my heart and my thoughts, I am, and mean to remain, my own master as long as I live!"

Doamna Bologa, without even wiping away her tears, answered:

"My goodness, how can you talk like that, boy! Don't forget that there is a war on and that no one is master of anything any longer. Death and fear are masters to-day over all men, my darling. You are cleverer than I and must understand this better. Now is not the time to show our hearts to our enemies or we shall fare like the poor protopop. For Palagiesu is always on the look-out to do someone an ill turn or get people into trouble. You, like your father—may his sins be forgiven him—always look straight ahead, but in war-time people must just get along as best they can. Until the danger is past, we must howl with the wolves, otherwise they'll eat us. Everybody does this, and we must do as others do, my darling. Don't get angry because I teach you and advise you, for I am your mother, and only my heart knows what it suffers from anxiety on your account. All the men say that what you are doing is not right because you are an officer, and it is possible you may have great unpleasantness on account of such thoughtless daring. Even the manager of the Parvana, and he has always been a staunch Rumanian, told me to my face to tell you to keep quiet. He was a good friend of your poor father, but to-day he just looks to his bank and keeps mum, just as all the others do, here and everywhere else."

Listening to his mother's words, Apostol's thoughts travelled back over the ten days he had now spent at home, discovering suddenly many things that he had passed over without noticing. He had walked about the town every day for an hour or two, and he had met almost everyone he knew. All had seemed to him changed and frightened, although he had merely exchanged banalities with them. Now he understood the constraint and panic in their manner, now he realized that they had all fought shy of him because he had objected to Marta speaking Hungarian. He looked down at his empty plate as if he could not endure his mother's gaze. From that moment all her words fixed themselves in his heart like thorns and stayed there embedded in bitter anguish. Then when his mother's voice fell silent, he whispered, so low that it seemed as if he were afraid of awakening someone:

"I'm sorry, mother, that I came home at all!"

That whisper fell on Doamna Bologa like a blow from a cudgel. For a long while now, even going back to the time when Apostol, instead of going in for the Church, had gone to Budapest, she had suspected that the light of her eyes, the prop of her old age, no longer loved her as he had once done. He seemed cold to her, reserved, and his unbelief especially had frightened her. And now he had actually told her that he was sorry that he had come home, so estranged had he become! She burst into such endless sobs that Apostol only succeeded with the greatest difficulty in quietening her.

Nevertheless, after this Apostol felt a stranger in Parva. He sat whole hours on the *cerdac* in the sun, drinking in the blue ether in which his thoughts wandered. Sometimes his eyes tried to rest by gazing at the cross on the church-tower, made dazzling by the sun's rays. But immediately his soul felt caught in the grip of a strange remorse, and longing only for peace, he hastened to turn his gaze away, panic-stricken. It lingered longer round the stone monument on his father's grave. He knew the inscription off by heart, and yet every time he looked at it he tried to spell it out, for while he did this he always remembered the straight, unswerving path that the older man had followed. He also had longed passionately to follow a straight path. But in vain. Between his heart and his mind there was a wall against which all his efforts broke helplessly. When he thought he had knocked it down, he discovered with anguish that it was still there, no matter how hard he tried to deceive himself.

Then one afternoon, just as he was about to settle down on the balcony, in walked Palagiesu, whom he had met only once, on the first day of his return, and with whom he had barely exchanged a few words in the marketplace. A grey film had grown over their pre-war friendship. As a matter of fact, since he had become a notary, Palagiesu had by degrees taken up a challenging attitude even towards the older inhabitants of the place. Son of a peasant in Nasaud, poor and humble while at school, he had kotowed and cringed until he had succeeded in his aim and had become the right hand of the Hungarian *szolgabiro*,[1] who at the outbreak of war had used his influence to keep him there, although the notary was perfectly fit, except that when he walked he turned his feet out too much and threw out his legs from the knees downwards, like a horse on parade. His heavily jawed face seemed to glory in the huge moustache which hid a very large mouth with loose lips and wide teeth showing gaps between them. His long, black hair, always uncombed, hung over his deeply furrowed forehead and almost covered his ears. The most striking thing about him was his amazing self-confidence.

For a fortnight Palagiesu had postponed the interview with Bologa. He would have preferred to meet him somewhere accidentally to acquit himself of the task he had undertaken at the suggestion of the *szolgabiro*. Although he was some three years older than Bologa, he still felt for him an instinctive respect which dated from the time when they had discussed philosophical problems together, which he, poor attorney's clerk, did not understand any too well and which therefore impressed him deeply.

"As you don't seem to worry any longer about your friends, you see, the friends come to you!" said Palagiesu, entering the room with a smile that laid bare his gums.

Apostol looked at him open-mouthed. The visit was so unexpected that it deprived him of his composure and he forgot

[1] Sheriff.

to ask Palagiesu to take a seat. The notary, however, took hold of both his hands, shook them heartily, and then sat down, unbidden, quite as if he were at home.

"How . . . What brings you to our house?" stammered Apostol, still standing and continuing to look at him in surprise.

"Does it seem so strange to you that the friend of your childhood and boyhood should call on you?" asked Palagiesu, with a cunning look which lit in Apostol's heart a spark of hate. "My word! But you have changed a mighty lot, brother. In the last three years you have changed so much that I can hardly recognize you!"

The notary's self-confidence transformed Apostol's surprise into a sharp impatience.

"What is it you want, Alexandru? Out with it, what do you want?" he burst out, his eyes glassy.

"I?" answered Palagiesu, running his hand through his hair and pushing it off his forehead. "What do I want? Nothing—well, practically nothing! Firstly, I want to see you, and, secondly, to have a chat with you! I must say I expected a better reception!"

"Forgive me, Alexandru, please!" murmured Bologa, suddenly softened. "If you only knew the torments which I have gone through since I have been home!"

"Whose fault is it, Apostol?" asked the notary in a different voice. "Do you think I don't know? I? Do you think the slightest thing takes place here without my knowledge? That is why you must make amends, Apostol! Without doubt you must make amends in the interest of all."

The change of tone and the notary's words again confused Bologa, who stopped expectantly to listen.

"By my devotion, by my work, I have created here, in this town, an atmosphere of patriotism which is absolutely necessary, both in time of war and in peace-time," continued Palagiesu, staring at him scrutinizingly as if he challenged him to contradict what he was saying. "Then you fall into our midst like a lump of rock into a peaceful lake and disturb us. You've given them an excuse for arguing, for approving and disapproving—in short, for disorder, and again disorder. An officer coming from the front cannot take up the attitude you have without demoralizing some and egging on others— you understand, don't you, what this means? Not the things you say, but the things you leave unsaid are the harmful and mischievous ones!"

"Is that what you said when you caused Protopop Groza to be interned?" broke in Apostol, speaking with barely moving lips and without unclenching his teeth.

"The punishing of crime has no need of justification, because punishment is the natural consequence of crime," retorted the lawyer more sharply. "In any case, I never justify my actions, because before I act I always consider carefully. I, for instance, would never break my engagement with a girl simply because she talked Hungarian, Apostol!"

"Really, you wouldn't?" quoth Bologa with white lips and feverish eyes.

"Really, I wouldn't!" repeated Palagiesu energetically, rising to his feet in order to dominate him more completely. "That is why it is your duty to repair what you have spoilt through your thoughtlessness. We are friends, and I advise you as a friend to . . ."

The notary had walked round his chair and was resting his right hand on the back of it. His hair had again fallen over his forehead and a lock hung over his left eyebrow, ready to cover up his eye at any moment. When he talked the skin on his jaws stretched and the bristles of two days' growth rose and fell. Apostol Bologa, however, could only see his mouth, and especially his lower lip, slightly swollen so that its looseness was not so apparent. The notary's voice sounded triumphant and self-confident and seemed to distribute in turns slaps, reprimands, and praise.

Apostol, his face as pale as a corpse and his eyes like pin-points, skirted the table and approached Palagiesu. He was biting his lips and muttering in a choked voice as if he were trying to keep in his hot breath:

"You . . . you . . ."

He stopped within two steps of the notary and then, with lightning speed, he shot out his fist and caught him a terrific blow on the mouth, whispering like one demented:

"You . . . you . . . you scoundrel, scoundrel . . ."

The notary swayed as if struck by a thunderbolt. The blow was so unexpected that it dazed him completely. Blood ran down his chin from the broken lip. For a second he stood gaping at Bologa with his mouth open.

"Get out, scoundrel, get out!" panted Bologa, looking round in search of something.

The hollow voice roused Palagiesu from his dazed condition and made him understand what Bologa was searching for. On a small table he saw a revolver from which dangled a yellow strap. He turned quickly, opened the door and went out, muttering unconsciously:

"All right, all right, all right . . "

In the hall he took his hat off the peg and saw Rodovica cowering there. The door behind him was banged to with such violence that the walls of the house shook.

§ X

Doamna Bologa, who had been out, learnt towards evening from Rodovica that something had happened and that the notary had left the house with blood running down his chin. Although she was eaten up with curiosity, she did not dare to question Apostol, but nursed her anxiety in secret, and she and the maid shed many secret tears, convinced that "the thick-lipped one"—for so had Palagiesu been nicknamed long ago—would not rest until he had harmed the young master. Apostol had gone out for a walk, but had avoided the market-place and had walked right up to the far end of the town. He came back in time for supper, feeling cheerful, and joked with Rodovica, reminding her of the fight they had once had when they were children on the banks of the Someş. The girl lost her head, laughed, tried to move more quickly and dropped the dirty plates on the floor near Doamna Bologa, smashing them to smithereens. Not to spoil Apostol's good humour, the mistress controlled herself and held back the scolding words which hovered on her lips, hoping secretly that Apostol would tell her all about his interview with the notary. Apostol was very gentle to her all the evening and stayed up gossiping till late, but he talked only of the past, dwelling especially on the "vision" he had had in the church, to his mother's great joy. She told him all over again all the details of that "divine miracle", finding also the opportunity of saying casually that "the more people learnt, the farther away from God they seemed to go", to which Apostol retorted jokingly:

"But, mother dear, God also goes out of fashion, like everything else!"

The words so horrified Doamna Bologa that she crossed herself three times before answering gravely, in a voice trembling with wounded religious fervour:

"God is ever new in the soul of man, my darling. Only when one has lost the true faith can one talk like that of things sacred. But to lose God means to lose the peace of one's soul, and then the soul tortures itself and perishes without prop in the vicissitudes of life—it gropes about in the dark exactly like a small child that would go out alone into the great world at dead of night."

Even as Apostol had uttered his joke he realized that it would hurt his mother's feelings and he had regretted it, but it was too late, the words had been uttered. Her answer sounded to him like a smothered voice from his own soul and terrified him. He quickly caught hold of her hand across the table, caressed and kissed it, murmuring shamefacedly:

"Forgive me!"

Doamna Bologa, surprised at his repentance, also felt abashed, stammered a few indistinct words until she had regained her composure, and then went on telling stories of his childhood. But the spell was broken; she could not re-establish contact and avoided his questioning eyes, which agitated her and seemed to reproach her. At last she broke off in the middle of a sentence and said abruptly, very tenderly, with a strange smile in her soft eyes:

"That is why you are restless and wear yourself out, my darling, that is the reason."

He, who seemed to have been waiting for these words, as if he had known what they would be, answered with great relief in his voice, smiling also:

"When I think how much I have suffered and endured in my short life, it seems to me that I have lived long enough and that to-morrow I could die without a qualm! Some people live years and years and yet when they close their eyes they can say that they have not lived at all, for they have been mere birds of passage through life or lookers-on who did not understand the meaning of life. On the other hand, Fate drives others into the most terrible maelstroms and forces them to endure all the tortures of life, every one of them, and they never find true rest and peace down here."

Three rainy days followed, horrid days, spreading sadness in the world. From morning till night Apostol sat on the *cerdac* surrounded by his old books in which all his hopes had centred in the old days, and which each time that he had needed help in life had let him down like powerless and timorous friends. He ran hastily through the proud systems of wisdom, knocked at all the doors more and more anxiously, but as soon as he stopped and raised his eyes from the book to the rain-swept, mud- covered street, to the green and clean-washed meadows and hills, to the sky covered with dark clouds, he felt immediately that all the monumental structures in his soul tumbled down with a clatter of meaningless words, squeezed dry of real wisdom, not leaving even ruins in their wake but just a barren, unending, and engulfing emptiness. And a strange sensation would come over him that the earth was slipping away from under his feet and he was left floating in nothingness, clinging desperately to the cross on the church spire.

Often with his book on his knee his thoughts would turn back into the past, scrutinizing his former life, seeking out motives. And then all his actions, gestures, longings, seemed paltry, selfish, and even ridiculous. How indignant he used to get in hospital and afterwards over words and things which did not conform to his expectations! He had divided the whole world into two halves, one of love and one of hatred. Now he realized that he had never known love at all, the true, deep love

FOREST OF THE HANGED

that saves—he had known hatred only in different forms. He had thought that all those who were of his own race were dear to him, but as soon as he had discovered that his hatred found no echo in their hearts, his love was scattered like dust by the breath of the wind. True love never died in the soul of man, but accompanied it right through the portals of death into eternity. But love could not take root in a heart tainted with hatred, and in his own heart hatred had ever dwelt, like a rusty nail embedded in living flesh.

The rain rapped on the roof of the *cerdac,* loudly, peremptorily, like hurried knocks on a bolted gate. Listening vaguely, Apostol Bologa was suddenly confronted with an alarming question which he knew with certainty that he had carried about in his soul all his life without ever facing it, as if he were ashamed of it and dreaded it. But the strange thing was that the question contained the answer that Apostol had longed for with passion and which he constantly avoided like an obstinate child who has transgressed again and again and no longer dares to approach its parents, possibly because it knows that all its transgressions would be forgiven. He tried to avoid it now also. He closed his eyes, but this time the question lit in his soul a white flame, round which all the thoughts of his life formed a chain; they were all there, beginning with the tiny fragments which had died in his brain before they had crystallized and ending with those heavy, logical, proud reflections which he had chosen with confidence as the right guides for his life, and all were equally colourless and submissive, like slaves round an all-powerful master.

Strange, indistinct feelings awoke and melted in his heart, filling his being with a warm content. In his mind a thought tried to raise its head and remind him of the rusty nail of hate, but the mysterious flame smothered it at its birth.

Then it seemed to him as if the pattering of the raindrops died down gradually, changing into a sweet, alluring sound like the flutter of doves' wings, growing sweeter and sweeter and diffusing in his heart a magic enchantment so exquisite that it hurt. And then suddenly he began to sway and rise as if borne on the wings of song. He felt no surprise, although the *cerdac* and the fields and the whole earth had disappeared and there was only the cross of the church spire, shining softly and so near that by stretching out his hand he could have touched it. The white flame in his soul burnt more brightly, like a glowing funeral pile which consumed his past and brought forth his future. The stillness and the mysteries of heaven and earth mingled and pulsated in his heart and distilled into it the dew of eternal joy. He could feel his soul, linked to the infinite by thousands of tiny threads, palpitate enchanted, in the rhythm of the great unseverable mysteries, as in a sea of light. Then a rapturous happiness filled his whole being, more potent than the joy of life and more poignant than the anguish of death. And he knew that one moment of such bliss is sustenance for all eternity.

Apostol Bologa started as if he had awakened from a spell. But his eyes were open, large and misty, and on his smiling lips the touch of that ecstasy still lingered. The book had slipped from his knees and was lying at his feet like a worthless rag. The rain still drummed on the roof of the *cerdac* with a lingering, soft, watery sound. Up on high behind the cross, between slate-coloured clouds, laughed a strip of luminous blue, announcing a new sun.

For a while Apostol sat there with aching eyes. Fragments of thoughts sprang up in his brain and died at once, useless. A new feeling lay heavy on him, an obscure yet withal urging desire. He wanted to embrace the whole world, to weep with joy and to share his tears with all mankind. He stood up, stretched out his arms, and all at once the pent-up tears ran down his parched cheeks, while his eyes and lips smiled with joy. His heart, overburdened with love and thirsting to love, thrilled. Every moment he could feel more clearly the roots of the white flame in his soul, penetrating into all his fibres, blending with the source of life and dominating his being for the rest of his life and for all eternity.

And then all his feelings, clear and obscure, crystallized into one solid whole, and into his brain there flashed the tremendous thought:

"My soul has found God again!"

A nimbus of white rays scintillated from the rain-bespattered cross. The flame in Apostol's soul united with the scintillating rays, with the sound of the rain, with the green of the fields, with the patch of blue sky which seemed an eye of the infinite, with the infinite itself, into one thrilling harmony. He was conscious of God in his soul as his soul was conscious in God.

§ XI

Towards the evening the rain stopped; all the clouds were swept away and at night all the stars flamed in the sky as if it were the eve of a great holiday. Next day the whole town awoke clad in a garment of white flowers and roses which embalmed the whole earth. When Apostol went out on the *cerdac* and saw all this riotous wealth of beauty, he started as at the sight of a miracle. He wondered how he could have wasted so much time brooding in that arm-chair on the *cerdac* instead of going out into the world, mixing with human beings or communing with nature and rejoicing in each moment of life. Now he was anxious to carry his happiness into the sight of all and humbly to make known that he had found the great mystery. He wanted to share his brotherly love with others, for all men needed love and were eager to get it. He was fearless now and no longer dreaded loneliness. In everything his soul found the living God, in all the miracles and in all the small things of life. He felt a constant desire to humble himself and to beg forgiveness of all those whom he had wronged in thought or deed.

Every minute he discovered new reasons for joy and love, like a small child for whom the mysteries of the world and of life begin to unfold.

About four days later, Doamna Bologa indignantly brought him the news that that cursed creature, Palagiesu, had called him a "traitor," a "jail-bird," and "an agitator" in the presence of all the men at the club, and that he had boasted that he would teach him a lesson in good manners which he would remember all his life. Apostol, without saying a word, caught up his cap and rushed off quickly in the direction of the market-place, leaving his mother trembling and in mortal fear—for now he would surely kill that godless, loose-lipped brute—and regretting that she had repeated to him what, as a matter of fact, she had heard from poor Marta herself. Doamna Bologa spent an anxious hour wringing her hands aiid scolding Rodovica, who "had become so insolent and so lazy that there was no doing anything with her."

Then Apostol returned, serene and happy.

"What have you done, my darling?" Doamna Bologa asked in fear and trembling.

"I apologized to him, mother," answered Bologa with gladness in his voice and a flame of happiness in his eyes.

Three days before the month was up, Lieutenant Apostol Bologa received a wire ordering him to report himself immediately.

"Evidently things are getting pretty hot or they would not be cutting down leaves," Apostol had remarked quietly and confidently to his mother when he communicated the news to her.

"Well, I would not be surprised if this were the doing of the 'loose-lipped one,' " exclaimed Doamna Bologa, still indignant at the thought that Apostol had humbled himself before that cursed creature.

All along Apostol had felt that he still had a duty to perform, but he had not been able as yet to summon up enough courage to do it. Now he realized that the time for hesitation was over. That afternoon he knocked at the door of Domsa's house and found Marta at home. He took her hand and kissed it, looking deeply into her eyes, and begged her to forgive him with so much passion that the girl became confused, smiled shyly, and then burst into tears, stammering that it had been all her own fault.

The next morning, soon after dawn, Doamna Bologa accompanied him to the station, for the train left very early. Pctre, with the kit on his back, panted even more loudly than he had done on the night of their arrival. Apostol was almost gay. He was very gentle with his mother and kept on repeating:

"Everywhere there are men who seek love, mother dear, and God accompanies one everywhere! Now I know, mother, and now my path in life is straight and clear."

When the whistle blew, Doamna Bologa, near the steps of the compartment, whispered to him anxiously :

"Don't forget, my darling, that to-morrow Holy Week begins. Be sure to go to church, and don't forget God!" Apostol smiled tenderly and answered her with a look of fervent faith. The train began to move out slowly. And for Doamna Bologa, left alone on the platform, that look in his eyes was a divine consolation. Then the crown of an apple-tree in bloom veiled her as with a bridal garment. At that instant a wave of bitterness welled up in Apostol's heart like a black foreboding in the midst of great rejoicing.

BOOK III

WHEN, round the bend of the hill, he saw the first house of Lunca, that wave of gloom swept once again over Apostol Bologa, but almost instantaneously died away, leaving in its stead a joyous anticipation. He thrust his head out of the carriage window, feeling certain that someone would be waiting for him. From a long way off he could see the old cherry-tree, which, in honour of his arrival, had decked itself out with a marvellous crown of white flowers in the place of the delicate buds of a month ago.

In the station bands of soldiers hurled themselves at the train, which puffed and snorted furiously before coming to a standstill. But Apostol's eyes ran impatiently over the crowd, darting hither and thither almost with fear in their depth, until with a flash of unrestrained gladness they alighted on what they sought. On the platform, in the same place where he had left her and looking as if she had not moved from there these last four weeks, stood Ilona, scanning, with ever-increasing anxiety, one carriage after another. A tense look of expectancy made her face look more rugged and thinner. Then suddenly she caught sight of Bologa and a wild light flamed in her eyes and her lips relaxed into a frightened smile.

Apostol Bologa jumped off the train, deeply moved and excited. His heart bade him rush over to Ilona and take her in his arms in front of everybody, but an overpowering feeling of constraint made him wait near the railway carriage until Petre came up with his luggage.

"Come on, man, hurry up!" he muttered to the orderly, who was fighting his way down the carriage steps through the crowd of soldiers eagerly clambering up.

Out of the corner of his eye Apostol watched the gravedigger's daughter, thinking with anxiety how disappointing it would be if she should leave the station before he had had time to hear her voice. Nevertheless, when he reached the spot where she was, he stopped and looked surprised, pretending that he had only just seen her, and he said rather coldly:

"What are you doing here, Ilona?"

The girl also pretended that she had not seen him till then and exclaimed in assumed amazement:

"Fancy! If it isn't Lieutenant Bologa! Did you come by this train? Father was saying you had another three days or so. As a matter of fact, I was waiting for him; he has gone up to town to . . . But perhaps he won't be coming till the next train, after all."

They stared a moment into one another's eyes. Apostol shook her hand and saw Ilona's lids droop and her smiling lips tremble, but her hand was cold.

Then Bologa passed on quickly for fear he should do something foolish if he did not hurry away. Once in the lane he looked back. The girl was wrangling with the orderly; she wanted to carry one of the bags, but Petre proudly refused, explaining to her that he needed nobody's help and that, anyhow, the kit was now much lighter than when they went, because his master had left at home lots of things which were not needed in war-time. Apostol could not keep himself from chiming in:

"Don't, Ilona; why should you tire youself? A soldier can carry much more than that."

The grave-digger's daughter smiled as if she had expected this; then as Bologa went on she began to pump Petre in Hungarian, trying to find out what sort of a time they had had at home. But Petre did not understand her questions very well, and Apostol, a few steps in advance, heard very well what she said and knew that it was really from him that she wanted answers to her questions, and his heart ached with joy.

From all the gardens on the way to the house trees in bloom greeted them and scattered on their path light petals as at a fairy wedding. In his room the scent of flowers was so strong that it confused him. He sighed and looked gratefully at Ilona, who, suddenly embarrassed, said, as if in answer to a question:

"Since you left I have been sleeping here. The officer who took your place wanted this room, but father thought it would be better for me to sleep in here, as you would be coming back, and why should a stranger have the room and mess it up when you were coming . . ."

She broke off, her face fiery red as if she had given away some great secret. Bologa had the same impression and wished to thank her, but he knew that if he tried to utter a single word he would be unable to restrain his tears of joy and would make a fool of himself in front of the soldier, who had begun to unpack his kit and to put things back as they had been a month ago. Then, as a means of escape, he remembered his work and hastily crossed into the office. The two non-coms, stood up and he, in order to get rid of some of the kindliness with which he was overflowing, smilingly shook them by the hand and inquired how things had been going on during his absence. The sergeant began to explain, but Apostol, running his eye over unimportant documents, was not listening at all, for his thoughts were back in the other room where he had left Ilona and where Petre seemed stuck, as if he did not want to leave them alone on purpose. Then, before the sergeant had finished his say, Apostol was back in the other room, and, without glancing at Ilona, said impatiently to the zealous orderly:

"All right, Petre, that'll do. You'll do the remainder another day. That's enough for just now."

"I've finished, sir, anyway," answered Petre in a relieved voice, leaving the room immediately in order to make up his own bed in the lobby.

When he was alone with the girl, Bologa flushed deeper than the girl had done just now. He was thinking that probably both Petre and the girl had guessed his thoughts, and he was as ashamed as if he had planned a crime. At the same time he felt an urgent need to tell her that he loved her, and yet he was conscious of the absurdity of making a declaration of love to a little peasant girl who would probably not understand what he meant and as likely as not would laugh in his face. Ilona seemed even more disturbed. While Petre had been present she had moved about too, setting things to rights, but now she stood quite still near the bed, not knowing what to do with her hands, gazing at Apostol with timid curiosity and waiting from moment to moment for something wonderful to happen.

At last, after a heavy silence, Apostol Bologa sat down on the little chest that stood between the windows which looked out on to the street, and said suddenly, in a cold, aloof voice, as if he were talking to some soldier:

"And what has your father been doing all the time I have been away?"

Ilona threw herself on the question as if it were really the wonderful thing she had been expecting, and answered with hasty and almost offensive pride:

"What's father been doing, you ask? Why, do you think work and worry isn't enough to keep one occupied? Even though we have some property, like all decent folk, yet we've got to work all we can if we want to live. Only God knows . . ."

Apostol was looking at her and listening to her with great attention and yet understood nothing. But her voice, with its thrilling cadence of a primitive song, sank into his being and soothed his nerves. And his eyes rested on her rather full, dark-red and moist lips, which moved convulsively, obstinately, and with a sort of secret reproach.

When Ilona stopped speaking, Bologa shook himself as if something had snapped in his heart. Their eyes met, and he saw in hers the timidity that had settled in his own soul, too. Then into the silence that lay between them there fell like a deliverance a loud shout from the courtyard outside and at once they both came to life, and the girl, her voice sweeter and her eyes laughing, asked:

"Did you have a good time at home? Is it nice over there in your home ?"

"It's the same as over here, Ilona; the only difference is that the war is farther off, a little farther off."

"You didn't miss us, I can see. Naturally, why should you miss us, for of course when one is at home . . ." continued Ilona, hiding her question in a smile.

"I missed *you,* Ilona," answered Bologa, also smiling but in a deeper voice than usual, a voice which tried to sink into her heart.

The girl's eyes gleamed feverishly, while her lips said quickly:

"Goodness! I don't know why, but I had a strong presentiment that you would be coming back before the month was up, and for the last three days I have been meeting all the trains, I don't know why—all, all the trains, all day long . . ."

The setting sun shone full on the window which looked out on the garden. A band of gold quivered slantingly across the table and on the yellow floor right up to the door, separating

Ilona from Apostol like an enchanted bridge. The happiness in his heart hurt him, and just one thought filled his brain: if Ilona only knew what she was saying she would feel ashamed and would run away. He stood up in order to beg her not to leave him, although the girl was still speaking with those strange flashes in her eyes. The pool of light between them laughed and seemed to mirror its laughter in Ilona's cheeks. Then Apostol forgot why he had got up and wondered how to go across to her without disturbing the patch of sunshine. While he wondered he found himself right in the track of the rays and stopped, disconcerted, for the girl was also coming towards him, as if pushed forward by some secret force. Her lips were still moving, but he no longer heard her voice. He whispered hoarsely:

"Thank you, Ilona . . . for . . ."

He looked into her eyes and he could see himself as in a mirror. He raised his arm a little as if to take her hand and suddenly caught her round the waist. The girl relaxed in his arms with a weak protest:

"My goodness! You . . . you really should not . . ."

Their burning lips met and clung together for some minutes with furious passion. Then Ilona came to her senses, slithered out of his arms and straightened the kerchief on her head with one and the same movement, and disappeared through the door.

Simultaneously the magic of the room seemed to vanish like a dream. Apostol looked round apprehensively. He felt suddenly as if he were in a strange house. The strip of sunlight was still there, but now the melancholy of twilight was in its tremulous gleams. Then the whole room seemed to fill with his thoughts, as if they were a flight of birds escaped from a cage.

"What's the meaning of all these ridiculous romantics of a schoolboy in love?" he said to himself with a disgust which he knew very well was not genuine, but which he hoped nevertheless would help to quieten the regret which was piling up in his heart. "Such a fuss, such excitement, for . . ."

And at the same time, in another part of his brain, surged the tantalizing question: "Where has Ilona gone?"

He ran his hands through his brown hair as if he were trying to calm his thoughts. Then he approached the window on the left to distract himself by looking out. The courtyard was surrounded by a paling, and in the garden over the road the white trees in bloom brightened the gathering twilight. Near the gate, leaning against the fence, was an infantry soldier, very dirty and ragged, with his helmet pushed back on his neck, his face hairy like that of an ape. He was talking gently and happily to someone who was in the lobby and he was constantly showing his white, glinting teeth. Apostol's eyes tried to ignore him, but his heart asked: "To whom is the fellow talking?" He felt sure he was gossiping with Ilona, and at the thought his face unconsciously contracted with pain. The soldier caught sight of him at the window and immediately his laughter stopped and the white teeth were hidden behind a look of nervous gravity. He sprang to attention, pulled up his helmet, saluted and then slowly, keeping the comer of his eye on the dangerous window, he shuffled farther along in the courtyard until he was out of the lieutenant's sight.

"What does it matter to me with whom that lout was talking, even if it was with her!" said Bologa in answer to the question which still filled his mind. "I'll become the laughing-stock of the place if I start doing that sort of thing," he added irritably, and sat down again on the little chest where he had been sitting just now when Ilona had been in the room.

He tried to think of something else, but he felt he couldn't. In his heart he heard a clear voice say: "I love Ilona." Then he gave in to that voice and his soul grew serene and was filled with a new alluring joy. He gave himself to this joy, shyly and selflessly as a girl gives herself to her first love. The grey twilight filtered in through the window-panes, in between the somnolent geraniums, enveloping him in a net of happiness.

Presently he tore himself away from his dreams, put on his cap and went out. In the lobby doorway the dirty infantryman was still gossiping with an artilleryman, and Bologa, seeing him, was glad. He avoided looking round for Ilona, both in the lobby and in the courtyard. The coolness of the twilight seemed to sober him.

He reached the street but did not turn towards the centre of the village, but in the opposite direction, as if he were running away from a danger. He walked along for some five minutes, then the lane forked abruptly on the banks of the noisy river. In the sky, on the very summit of the hills whose feet bathed in the waters of the river, the white moon rose, cold as an eye from another world. Bologa, as if he had recovered a forgotten treasure, drank in with passion the heavenly light.

§ II

Next day Apostol Bologa took charge again, and remembering the regulations, rang up the adjutant of the regiment and informed him that he had arrived in Lunca yesterday afternoon in consequence of the telegraphic orders received.

"There will be no need for me to report in person now, will there, because the work has accumulated over here?" concluded Apostol, and he was just about to hang up the receiver when he remembered something, and added in a slightly reproachful tone: "I say, I was forgetting. Just a minute! Tell me, old chap, why have you people chewed three days off my leave? Don't you think I might be told the reason?"

"I've no idea," answered the adjutant hastily. "Ask at headquarters if you want to know."

Bologa winced. In his mind he relived the moment when he had shown his mother the contents of the telegram and she had felt sure that the order to return had been the result of Palagiesu's denouncement. Why had he gone just then to Palagiesu to apologize, and why had he felt so happy because the notary had held back and made him beg before he had kindly consented to give him his hand? Now he felt slightly ashamed at the thought of his abasement, but still he did not regret it; on the contrary, he felt it had been a decent action, by means of which he had lightened and cleansed his heart. At that time he had not worried about the effect Palagiesu's denouncement might have, so little had he cared just then about the world, or anything that was outside his own soul. To-day the figure of Palagiesu had abruptly come to the fore. Suppose the notary's denouncement were really at the back of this? The general's adjutant was a coward with a pliable back and would probably not tell him anything. . . . Still it would not hurt to try to pump him; the direct method always proved best in the end.

"His Excellency's orders—His Excellency's *personal* orders. I don't know the reason," buzzed General Karg's adjutant into the phone.

"Then am I to report to His Excellency?" inquired Apostol.

"Why? You do your work and keep quiet! If it is necessary we'll send for you, you needn't worry. Just now important events are looming large—very important events! Everyone must be at his post!"

Apostol Bologa smiled derisively as he hung up the receiver, for the adjutant, who had never set foot in a trench, and who would have been capable of betraying any day all the generals in the Army to save himself from the firing-line, had, while he uttered "very important events", hollowed his voice like a coffee-house hero.

Presently Apostol found himself studying intently the new plan of the front which had arrived during his absence and gave the exact positions. This was no approximate and out-of-date sketch, but an accurate map on which the position of each and all units, even the most insignificant ones, could be seen at a glance. So to-day he could get his bearings far better than that other time. Then he had been so excited, so nervous owing to his determination to cross over without fail. Or perhaps his excitement had been due to his sickness—or, who knew? it might have been caused by a cowardly fear that each moment would weaken his confidence in his own will and destroy his conviction that what he intended to do was right. He followed with his pencil the road that had taken him to Captain Klapka's dug-out. Yes, but from there the infantry line was a goodish step; he saw that now, and yet when he had been on the spot it had seemed to him so near! Of course that was because he had forgotten the winding roads which led to the front lines. If one kept to the main road one came upon the dismounted hussars. And Varga's squadron—where was that? Ah, there it was—the third one! How curious the front was here—one lot on this ridge, those others on another ridge, and in between nothing— nothing—a thousand metres perfectly empty. He wondered why the line had been fixed that way. Why had not the hussars or the others been moved nearer? "I could have gone that way if I had known. . . . But suppose I had met Varga? He told me once that he would arrest me and . . .

"Well, I am wasting my time now anyway, because the Lord alone knows what will happen!" Bologa said suddenly to himself, as if he were feeling uneasy about something unknown.

He looked up. Opposite him at the other table, among the piled-up registers and documents, he saw the sergeant, on whose bent head the dust-covered window at the back shed a light as of old silver. Outside in the courtyard and beyond, right away to the foot of the hills which cut off the view, the stillness and peace was so complete that Bologa's soul was again filled with hope and confidence. But he regretted that not the tiniest bit of sky came within his view.

Just when his heart was completely at peace Ilona appeared from somewhere in the courtyard, her face red and tired and her eyes flashing with anger. And as if he had fallen from a dizzy height, Apostol felt all the peace and content ooze out of his soul and in its stead surged a strange anxiety and an obstinate desire. He felt he wanted to leap out of his chair, run to Ilona, take her into his arms and keep her at his side for ever. He had not see her at all since she had run out of his arms and out of his room. Where had she been since, and why had she not come to him?

Nevertheless, he remained at his desk and lowered his eyes again on to the map. On his lips he felt again the scorching touch of last night's kiss. In his soul remnants of the peace of a moment ago still lingered, but in his brain stormy thoughts and doubts seethed. He vaguely felt that between God and his love there yawned an abyss, and he could not understand the purpose of this abyss. If God was love, why was not, then, Ilona comprised in Him?

215

§ III

In the afternoon Apostol Bologa went off to the General Ammunition Depot to have a talk with the commander, who lived beyond the railway station in a tumble-down hut so as to be near the depot, which had been excavated in the side of a hill. There he ran into Lieutenant Gross.

"What are you doing here, old fellow?" asked Apostol, crossing himself[1] and pressing his hand warmly.

"I have been working here with a small detachment for the last four days," answered the sapper, also delighted to meet him.

The commander was out and Bologa decided to wait for him, especially as Gross was there to keep him company. After a few questions and answers the lieutenant said all at once:

"Don't think, Bologa, that I have forgotten that reproach of yours—you remember, in the general's courtyard at Zirin!"

"What reproach?" asked Apostol, puzzled.

"What! You don't remember?" continued Gross almost mockingly. "Oh, well, of course, at that time all you could think of and fear was the Rumanian front, so perhaps you didn't even realize what you were saying! But I haven't forgotten, my friend! And look you, that reproach of yours is still stuck here in my soul like a nail! And you were wrong! For seven months I have ruminated over your words and I have been waiting to give you the answer. You practically told me that I was a coward because I said one thing and acted another."

"Oh yes . . ." murmured Bologa, ashamed. "Yes . . . that is to say, not exactly a coward. . . . In fine, at that time I felt such bitterness in my heart, my dear chap, that . . ."

---

[1] Rumanians always cross themselves to indicate surprise at some unexpected event.

"I am a coward and a hypocrite, I acknowledge!" hissed Gross, seemingly infuriated by his comrade's diffidence. "Because the time hasn't come yet! But when the time comes I shall be thorough, Bologa, don't worry! Now I receive the orders, grind my teeth, and execute them. I don't complain and I pity no one, but I collect the drops of hatred for the day which will come without fail, which *is* coming nearer! Here frankness in any form meets with bullets. So that my cowardice is a weapon of war and of defence. We must carry on until our sun shall rise, we must carry on and live if we want that sun to rise!"

Bologa was taken aback at the hatred which flamed in the lieutenant's eyes and said sadly:

"You'll never be happy, Gross, because your heart is full of hatred!"

"I don't need happiness—but I need revenge! Happiness is the shield of cowardice, whereas revenge . . ."

"Is also a form of happiness," smiled Bologa, interrupting him.

"Of course, if that's what you mean by happiness," said Gross angrily. "I suppose when you are thirsty happiness is a glass of water!"

"Happiness is always love," said Apostol Bologa in a changed voice, looking at him a little reproachfully.

"And love is God," added Gross, laughing ironically. "Yes, yes, we know all about it! The beginning and the end is God, because we have no idea whence we came or whither we go, so we substitute for the darkness a big, empty word."

"Once you feel God in your soul you no longer ask to have either the past or the future explained," Bologa went on quietly. "When you really believe you have risen above life!"

"What's the matter, Bologa? Have you gone crazy?" abruptly asked the other man, looking at him very seriously.

"No past or future knowledge will ever be able to stifle the voice of God in the soul of man!" continued Apostol with humble fervour. "Everywhere doubts assail one; only in God can one find conciliation without doubts! If God is not in one's soul one is for ever puzzling over the purpose of life and never can one be certain what is right or what is wrong, for what was right to-day will be wrong to-morrow. The minute that God would abandon man definitely, without hope, the world would become an immense machine without controller, condemned to go on creaking endlessly to no purpose. In such a world life would be such cruel torture that no living creature could endure. It would, indeed, mean the end of the world."

Gross stared at him, at first with smiling contempt, then with amazement, and, finally, he exclaimed, deeply indignant:

"For thousands of years man has been beating his breast and imploring the bounty of the God of Love, and every year more and more so! Because love is the dowry of the timorous and the helpless. The Christian martyrs died praising rather too loudly that God of Love. The victory of Christianity has been won by meekness, humility, and cowardice, that is why it has installed upon earth the reign of untruth, of hypocrisy, and of unfairness. The God of Love has murdered more men than all the other gods put together!"

"Love has never murdered, Gross," put in Apostol serenely. "It is only mankind who kills in the name of love. But when the true domination of love will be here . . ."

"My dear fellow," interrupted Gross excitedly, "the domination of true love can never come, because it would be an absurdity. Once man became convinced that beyond this, our earthly life, there awaited him after death a new happy life, then yes, in truth, our purpose of life would be at an end. Why should I go on living here if, with the help of a bullet, I can reach in one second the Kingdom of Happiness? He who honestly believes in an after-life and still tarries here is an imbecile, my dear chap!"

"He who really believes is one with God, both here and over there," answered Bologa. "If God is everywhere there is no need for one to rush to Him by forcing the bolts of death!"

"Yes, yes, that's how you all talk for the last two thousand years!" muttered the sapper, again contemptuous. "Always love in your mouth and the sword in your hand! Always hypocrisy. But not the occasional and temporal hypocrisy of the fighter, but dogmatized hypocrisy, which has become instinctive and unconscious."

Walking to and fro in the little narrow room, Gross cast a furtive glance at Bologa now and again, as if he were wondering whether to unveil to him all his thoughts. Finally, he stopped, his mind made up. His small eyes flashed and his voice had a new, passionate ring and strange inflections.

"Love has gone bankrupt, so has meekness and humbleness. Man now wants to be proud and masterful and selfish, to fight and to overcome his enemies, whoever and wherever they be. That is why we must sweep away the ruins from the soul of man and make ready for the coming of the new God, who asks for neither adoration nor abasement! Until to-day we were ashamed of the hatred in our soul, although hatred is own sister to love. Until to-day we have kept it hidden and squashed as if it were some poor little Cinderella or some remnant of animalism. From to-day onward we ought to give it the place of honour in human life, because men no longer want to die but to live. When you die fighting, death is redeemed, and if you win through fighting, victory is all the sweeter. Frankness, even if it be brutal, must take the place of hypocrisy! Nothing but hatred can destroy the falseness that poisons the world!"

Apostol Bologa, bewildered, almost frightened by the lieutenant' outburst, stammered:

"Well, Gross, I thought you were a socialist and that . . ."

"And that under my label there was concealed another kind of hypocrisy?" said Gross, taking the words out of his mouth and speaking in a harsh, unpleasant voice. "The great merit of Socialism in the history of mankind is just that it has the audacity to preach hatred frankly, to divide men into two camps which shall hate one another for ever and aye! While the various forms of Christianity butcher mankind in the name of love, we declare without hypocrisy that we hate those who are in power and those who lie, that we mean to fight against them without mercy until we exterminate them. You others talk of love and God, but only so that behind this shield you may follow more easily other unconfessed aims! You, yourself, are a living example, that is why I have studied you closely ever since I have known you. For me you are an interesting case, Bologa. Don't get angry, please! You, at the bottom of your heart, are a great Rumanian Chauvinist—now don't protest, for it is as I say! Circumstances have thrown you into the war as they did others and your Chauvinism has been compelled to put on in turn various masks in order to escape from peril. You became a hero and distinguished yourself by words and deeds until the war or Fate, or the devil, wishing to make sport of you, sent you suddenly to face your Rumanians. I shall never forget your despair when I met you in the general's courtyard on the Russian front. Your poor Chauvinism was torturing you, was clawing at your heart and searching for something! You would have murdered joyfully a thousand Russians or Italians to save yourself from shooting at your own people. To kill here would seem a crime to you, whereas elsewhere— anywhere else—you wouldn't mind, or you'd consider it a deed of bravery. And now you have unearthed Love and God, behind which your Chauvinism can go on thriving quietly until a good opportunity will arise for you to run away! And all this in the name of Love, Bologa! Can't you see that it is . . . it is horrible? Not your Chauvinism, but the hypocrisy, probably unconscious, in which it hides."

Apostol swayed as if he had received a slap on the face. An ungovernable anger sent the blood into his cheeks and then died away in a wave of disgust. His thin lips trembled as he answered:

"Hatred blinds you, Gross, and gives you these delusions!"

"Now you hate me, Bologa," replied the lieutenant with a satisfied smile. "But if you were sincere with yourself it would be meet for you to thank me for understanding your great secret. I don't know if others will be as understanding as I am, Bologa! *I* don't get angry that you speak to me here of Love and God and that at home you egg on the poor wretches there to revolt—not against war itself, but against the Hungarians. At most I shall be sorry for you when the general . . ."

"Did the general tell you that I had . . . ?" asked Apostol incredulously.

"The general has no conversation with me except with regard to the service. But he did say this one day at mess to the adjutant—your friend . . ."

"The adjutant told me this morning on the telephone that he knew nothing!" objected Bologa rather anxiously.

Gross shrugged contemptuously, turning his back on Bologa, who, more and more perturbed, would have liked details but did not dare to ask him for them. After a while the sapper faced him again and went on quietly, stroking his clipped goatee:

"Besides, my dear fellow, I should insult you if I were to take your religious metamorphosis seriously, because I consider real believers either fools or charlatans! As you are neither a fool nor a charlatan, I should have to take it that you are crazy, like Cervenco. And, as a matter of fact, Cervenco, through this love for love's sake, is nearer to me than any of the others. He loves mankind so much that in reality he hates everybody, convinced that he, only, is a true man. I saw him yesterday and I was touched. He is here in hospital with a bullet in his lungs. You should see with what passion he suffers! As if he were the saviour who wished to redeem the sins of all mankind for a second time. And Doctor Meyer believes that in ten days at most the poor saviour must die!"

Apostol Bologa felt very tired all at once. He made no answer and, rising, looked about him as if he did not see Gross at all, and wondered how he had come to be there. Then he said low, in a whisper, as if to himself:

"The captain is evidently not coming yet. I can wait no longer—I must go."

He walked to the open door. On the threshold he remembered Gross, who was staring after him disdainfully. He turned back, held out his hand without a word, and went out into the spring sunshine. From behind came the mocking voice of the other man:

"Good luck, Bologa, and a pleasant journey!"

"Why is he wishing me a pleasant journey?" Bologa asked himself while he was threading his way in and out among the railway trucks in the station, as if Gross's words had only just penetrated to his brain. And without attempting to find an answer to this question, a new question flashed into his mind: "Suppose he is right?"

Now he knew that this question in another form, and more especially that which lay behind it, had been lurking in his mind yesterday, when he had first caught sight of Ilona waiting for him at the station. His soul swayed as if driven by contrary winds, and more doubts and yet more surged and battled in his mind. He came out into the station lane and suddenly found himself face to face with Ilona. The moment his eyes rested on her all his thoughts were scattered as if driven away by an irresistible force and there was only gladness left in his heart.

"Where are you going to along here, Ilona?" he asked tenderly, as if he wished to pour out his whole soul in words which otherwise meant nothing. "Where have you been hiding that I haven't had a glimpse of you since last night?"

"I am afraid of you," murmured the girl, lowering her eyes and avoiding him.

"Artful one! Artful one!" reproved Apostol, delighted at her answer. "However, I did see you a little while ago, through the office window. You were coming back from somewhere and you were angry and it made you look very pretty."

Ilona had gone past him without saying another word, and accelerating her pace, was soon out of sight. Bologa stood still and watched her go with flaming eyes. He was just about to continue his way when from the same bend round which Ilona had disappeared a great wagon, heavily laden with ammunition cases, lumbered into sight. Sitting next to the driver Apostol recognized Lieutenant Varga. When the wagon had caught him up Varga stopped it, but did not get down. They exchanged a few words and questions, scrutinizing one another curiously the while. Finally, Varga said jestingly but nevertheless with a searching look:

"I have been waiting for you, Bologa, to arrest you! But obviously you've changed your mind?"

Apostol felt the other's eyes bore into his heart. He smiled uneasily and answered in a similar jesting tone, but unable to conceal a slight trembling of the lips:

"Oh! So you haven't forgotten that conversation? Well, but do you think that it's too late now?"

"I don't know. That's for you to know!" answered Varga, immediately becoming serious.

"Is that so? But hang it all, old chap, the front is large, why should I just choose your way?" continued Bologa with the same set smile.

"Of course, undoubtedly. . . . Still, I expected you. I don't quite know why. . . . I just thought you would . . ." averred the Hussar lieutenant with a strange flicker in his eyes. "All right, let them go!" he added, turning to the driver. Then, holding out his hand to Bologa, he said: "Au revoir! I'll go on waiting for you, Bologa; you may be sure I'll be waiting for you."

The wagon started off with a grinding noise in which Varga's last words were swallowed up. Apostol Bologa followed in the wake of the wagon, the set smile still on his face as if there was still something he wanted to say to the hussar.

When he reached the hospital he felt he must see Cervenco, that Cervenco was the only one who could divulge to him the secret of real peace and give him a remedy against all the tortures of the soul. The improvised hospital in the school building had two wards with about thirty beds. In a corner of the ward facing the street lay Captain Cervenco.

A boy doctor with ashen cheeks explained to Bologa, before taking him to Cervenco, that the latter had been there a fortnight with a ricochetted bullet in the chest. The bullet had broken two ribs, and losing its velocity had become lodged in the left lung, near the heart, so that it was impossible for them to reach it.

"The patient finds it terribly painful, and unless some unexpected happy change takes place it will almost certainly provoke a fatal haemorrhage. Of course we hope . . . with the help of God . . . but you understand, the sick man must be treated with great gentleness, and especially is he forbidden to speak. He suffers intense pain and . . ."

Apostol Bologa approached Cervenco's bed on tiptoe. The captain, very pale, lay on his back with his eyes fixed on the raftered ceiling. His cheeks were dry, the shiny skin, stretched tight on the bones, was so white that the brown beard resting on the stone-coloured coverlet seemed black. In his eyes burnt a light with flickers of pain, exaltation, and humility which seemed like secre breathings of his soul.

Bologa stopped about three paces from the bed, but the sick man did not turn his gaze towards him; he seemed to hear nothing that was going on in this world. Not until Bologa uttered his name did Cervenco's eyes answer with a glimmer of joy.

Then Apostol sat down at the foot of the bed and made a few remarks that needed no reply. The sick man's eyes and lips smiled at him so gently and with such kindness that Apostol's heart began to tremble violently, fearfully, like a frightened bird experiencing at the same time a poignant remorse and a deep trust. Bologa sat there by the sick man for nearly an hour without uttering a word, drinking in the messages in his eyes more and more thirstily, as if he were trying to gather to himself a huge reserve of strength. He could not have explained what he

225

felt during those moments, but his soul rejoiced, as if permeated by an infinite mystery.

When he got up to go he could see Cervenco's lips move soundlessly. Nevertheless, he understood what he had said, and in answer bent down and kissed him on both cheeks. The sick man's eyes accompanied him to the door and beyond, through the walls of the ward right into the street.

§ IV

Towards evening the grave-digger, Vidor, returned home from the town where he had been with his brother-in-law, and immediately wanted to know from Bologa what prospects of peace there were, for over here there were again rumours of pending battles.

"We shall be the last to hear of peace," Apostol told him, "because peace is arranged by those who have not known war!"

That same evening on leaving the office and going into his room he found Ilona there, who, without shyness and almost defiantly, said to him:

"I have been waiting for you to tell you that I am not angry but I am ashamed."

Apostol took her in his arms and she hid her face on his breast.

"Ilona, Ilona!" murmured Apostol, straining her madly to him and seeking her mouth.

But the girl freed herself abruptly and ran out as if she were afraid of something. A few minutes later Petre came in to light the lamp.

The next two days Apostol Bologa spent in a fearful state of agitation. His work in the office was torture to him. His mind was empty of any thoughts but those that referred to Ilona, and his heart and the whole of his being longed for her all the time with desperate passion. Every five minutes he crossed over into the other room, hoping to catch at least a glimpse of her. Several times he tried to think of Cervenco, of God, of the love of mankind. But he simply could not; besides, he felt that by trying to do this he was insulting her. He would have liked to speak of nothing but Ilona all day long, and it was all he could do to refrain from asking even the non-coms. in his office what they thought of the "landlord's daughter". With Petre, however, he could talk more freely. He pumped him as to what "the little lassie" was doing now, where did she sleep, how did she spend her time? The most commonplace details seemed to him enchanting. The grave-digger no longer bored him; he invited him to chat with him, and found special delight in hearing tales of "my lassie's" childhood.

On the other hand, Ilona no longer hid herself, and saw to it that there should be plenty of work for her to do about the house so that he should constantly see her or come across her. However, she avoided entering the "officer's room", not so much because she was afraid of her father catching her there, but rather because she feared that if Apostol found her there again it might well happen that she would not be able to escape so easily from his arms. In these two days she only crossed his threshold twice, and both times Apostol felt that she was there, rushed across to his room and did not let her go until he had kissed her with such passion that she almost lost her head. In fact, the second time the orderly caught them.

On the third day, after sunset, the grave-digger told the lieutenant that he was going to Faget, where he would stay until Saturday afternoon, for he had a bit of maize ground over there and wanted to plough it with his brother-in-law's plough and oxen, and so be done with the working of his land and feel easy over the Easter holidays. Bologa had forgotten that it was Holy Week, although his mother had reminded him of it even as his train was leaving. He asked the grave-digger one or two questions about the holidays, but all the time he was thinking that Ilona would be left at home alone. After the grave-digger had disappeared, Apostol, happy, set out to look for Ilona, but he could not find her. Then he waited for her. In vain. A tormenting sadness filled him at the sudden thought that the girl would probably sleep at some neighbour's or some relative's house. At supper, however, Petre told him casually that the "lassie" had locked herself in the little room at the back and she hadn't even stirred from it, as if she were frozen stiff with fear of "the Lord knew what!"

The next day seemed to him all wrong. He didn't catch a single glimpse of Ilona. In the evening he met her in the lobby. She was all dressed up. On her head she had tied a grass-green kerchief, her bosom was caught tightly in a red velvet bodice. There was no one in the office, but in the other room Petre was moving about, muttering prayers. Apostol, who was just coming out of the office, caught her trying to slip out quietly. He could have shouted with joy, and yet he seemed turned to stone and stood looking at her with eyes at once passionate and frightened. She also stopped, terrified, and swayed slightly as she stood. A few moments passed thus, the silence broken only by the orderly's prayers issuing from the officer's room.

Then Bologa whispered with a new light in his eyes:

"Why are you hiding from me, Ilona?"

The girl, as if she had not understood the question, turned white and answered immediately the other question which trembled in his eyes.

"Let me be. . . . I have to go to church. . . . It's Good Friday. . . . And after to-morrow it's Easter Sunday."

Apostol saw only her lips, he did not hear her voice. Then his eyes fell on her breasts, which seemed ready to burst the velvet bodice which oppressed them. The blood flew to his face. He caught her hand and whispered with such ardour that the girl shielded her face:

"Ilona! I shall wait for you after church."

Because she was silent Apostol went on still more passionately, looking down with burning eyes into her frightened ones:

"You must come, Ilona, you must. . . . After church without fail. . . . I shall wait for you. . . ."

Ilona shuddered and tried to pass. He barred the way, waiting for her answer before he allowed her to go. Their breasts touched and Apostol gathered her into his arms and kissed her long, as if he wished to absorb her whole soul. The girl, her arms limp, kept murmuring almost desperately:

"Lord . . . Lord . . . forgive me!"

"You must come, Ilona. . . . Ilona!" stammered Bologa as he freed her, and watched her leave the dark lobby with faltering footsteps.

Apostol Bologa remained a few minutes in the lobby, dazed, uncertain whether it had really been Ilona, or whether his hungry imagination had played him a trick. Her kiss burnt his lips, and so riotous was the happiness in his heart that he began to shout unknowingly, as if he were trying to shout down an inner voice that was perturbing him:

"Petre! Petre!"

The orderly appeared in the doorway thinking that something had happened. Apostol, recovering himself, looked gaily at Petre for a moment and then said—for something to say:

"What are you doing, Petre? Is supper ready? I am hungry, Petre, and I feel so happy, so . . ."

The soldier answered gravely, as if his master's gaiety shocked him:

"I have prepared everything, sir, so that I can go to church afterwards."

"All right, all right, Petre. Go wherever you like!" shouted Apostol, barely preventing himself from embracing him, so delirious was the joy in his heart.

He did not go into his room, but hurried out of doors, as if he wished to announce his happiness to the earth and sky. The coolness of the evening calmed him. He turned back. When he had reached the house again an idea occurred to him: Why shouldn't he go to church also? He decided he would go, but the next minute he thought he had better not, as the crowd there would prevent him from finding Ilona; he might also miss her at the end of the service, and by the time he got back she might . . .

In the street one or two people passed from time to time on their way to church. In his room the lamp was lit, and through the window, the little white curtains of which were not drawn, he could see the bed with the bedclothes turned down.

"But suppose she doesn't come?" whispered his mind suddenly. And immediately all the joy departed from him.

A cold shudder shook him. He entered the courtyard feeling miserable—a live coal in his heart. Petre had gone. He was all alone in the house. On the table a cold supper was laid out. He did not go near it. He took a book from the shelf above his bed and sat down with it to pass away the time and distract his thoughts. But the letters were all blurred, seemed to run away, and became all jumbled together. And his heart was full of obscure admonitions.

"If she doesn't come it will mean that she doesn't love me, and then . . ."

The last word remained suspended in his brain. . . . Then . . . then . . . He knew that this love drew him away from all his creeds and aspirations, and yet he felt that without it his heart would perish and life itself would lose its purpose and the world be turned into a wilderness. Not for one moment did he wonder where his love for Ilona would lead him, as he used to wonder about the future a little while ago, when he had loved Marta and he had thought she would be his wife. Now he could think of nothing but that he wanted Ilona with all his heart and soul. The fear that Ilona might not come penetrated right to the marrow of his bones. The book shook in his hands, and the light of the lamp began to get on his nerves. He threw down the volume on the little chest and started to walk backwards and forwards more and more rapidly, as if he wished to hasten the passage of time and bring nearer the decisive moment.

At last he could not bear the light any longer and put out the lamp. He walked up and down a little while longer, but his restlessness would not leave him. Dressed as he was, he lay down on his bed. The darkness and the stillness soothed him. The throbs of his heart sounded to him like stifled gasps. To beguile the time he began to count, but before he had even reached ten he lost count.

An eternity passed. Then suddenly he heard voices in the street. He started to get up, but on second thoughts stayed as he was. "I ought to have waited for her outside," he said to himself with frantic despair in his soul. Just then footsteps sounded in the courtyard. He recognized them as being hers, although he had never realized that he knew her footsteps. They entered the lobby, slowed down, and finally stopped hesitatingly. Apostol could hear the hesitation, and again he heard clearly the throbbing of his own heart. Then the handle of the door turned noiselessly, the door was opened just as noiselessly, and only wide enough to allow her to slip in. Again Apostol felt like leaping off the bed and again he remained as if glued to the spot, trying to quieten the beating of his heart and trembling lest he should frighten the girl. "Why does she not close the door?" he thought, filled with a new despair. But even as the thought flashed through his mind he heard the bolt being shot home, and joy flooded his being.

Ilona stood stock still for about two minutes near the door. In the lobby other footsteps now sounded, heavy, dragging. Bologa and Ilona both shuddered as if they had expected a castigatory foe to appear. Soon the noise in the lobby ceased. "It must have been Petre," thought Apostol, relieved, and he heard immediately the rustle of a skirt drawing nearer. The girl stopped by the bed, uncertain and tremulous. Apostol could hear her breath coming in gasps. He could no longer control himself. He stretched out his arm, and his fingers touched her breasts straining against the velvet bodice. Ilona gave a smothered cry.

"Ilona, my little wild dove!" whispered Bologa hoarsely, taking her cold hand and trying to rise.

"I am afraid. . . . I am afraid. . . . Forgive me!" murmured the girl, trying to push him away with a sudden new power of resistance. But even as she spoke she felt her strength ooze away, and, bending over him, she murmured passionately:

"I don't care . . . let him kill me!"

Her foot slipped on the floor, and with a moan she fell limply on the bed at Apostol's side.

§ V

The next day Apostol Bologa felt as after a shameful drinking-bout. He was as disgusted with himself as if he had committed a crime. He went into the office very early, found pretexts to scold the two men, and even Petre, but work he could not. He went out of doors, trying to run away from his remorse.

"I came into her life like a whirlwind, I turned it upside-down, and I thought only of myself!" he kept repeating disgustedly to himself, striding from one place to another.

And then he came face to face with Ilona's smile, happy, submissive, radiant with love and trust.

"You are not sorry, Ilona?" he asked her uncertainly.

"No!" answered the girl firmly.

"You trust me, Ilona?" he continued, trembling.

"Yes!" she answered passionately.

In her face there was pure happiness, unperturbed by thoughts, careless of the world, triumphant and alluring. Looking deeply into her eyes Bologa could see the whole of her warm, simple, wild heart, and in this warmth his anxiety melted slowly away. He understood that Ilona was worth all the mysteries of the world, and for the space of a second or less it seemed to him that the universe had been converted into nothingness and he was left alone with her standing before the face of God.

"But I must go now," said the girl, "for I have a lot to do. I must dye[1] the eggs, make *cozonac*[2] and the *pascal*.[3] It's the Resurrection to-morrow, don't forget!"

---

[1] A big dish of red and other coloured hard-boiled eggs is a special feature of the Easter festivities.

[2] Plaited brioche.

[3] A special cake made at Easter.

She lingered a minute or two longer, as if her heart were reluctant to leave Apostol. Then she ran off into the house, laughing.

And through the open office window Bologa heard distinctly the voice of the sergeant saying:

"It seems to me that our lieutenant has cast his eyes on the grave-digger's daughter."

"Well, one must own that he has good taste," replied the corporal, chuckling.

Apostol scowled at the window, but almost immediately his face cleared as if he had found the key of wisdom, and he muttered:

"It's rather early, still . . . it must be done!"

He went on without casting another backward glance and did not stop until he had reached Popa Boteanu's gate. At the far end of the courtyard, by the stable door, the popa, hatless, his back to the street, was talking to someone. Apostol opened the gate. The creaking of the hinges made Boteanu look round at once. The sun flooded his face with light. He called out something towards the stable and made rapidly for the gate. When he recognized Bologa, he began to smile cheerfully, as if he had not met him since they had sat on the same bench together at school, "as he should have smiled a month ago", thought Apostol instinctively.

"Apostol! Apostol! So you've come to see us again? What kind wind blows you hither?" said the priest delightedly.

Bologa pressed his hand, encouraged by his cheerfulness, and mumbling some indistinct words.

"How cold he was then, and how friendly he is now," he was thinking, amazed at the change in the priest.

"Come along, Apostol, into our peasant verandah!" proceeded Boteanu, putting an arm round his shoulders and leading him towards the little front garden.

Now the whole aspect of the parochial house seemed more friendly. On the *cerdac* there was a table covered with a white cloth and three chairs were set round it. Round the pillars and the railings a wild vine twined its green leaves.

"Sit down, Apostol, please!" exclaimed the popa, rubbing his hands with pleasure. "Sit here. . . . It is very pleasant out here. And the good wife will bring us coffee and milk such as you have never tasted, even in Pest! Excuse me just a second, Apostol, only a second!"

Apostol sat down while Constantin Boteanu hurried towards the house to tell his good lady that a guest had arrived. The *cerdac* basked in the gentle warmth of the morning sun. On the table two or three flies surrounded a brown coffee spot.

"Last time I was angry with you, Father," said Apostol to the priest, who was returning cheerily. "I was so depressed and embittered that day, and you would not understand me, nor even say a kindly word!"

The reproach in Bologa's voice brought a momentary shadow to the priest's face, as if he had reminded him of something painful. He answered gently with lowered eyes:

"You were very much overwrought, Apostol, and I had only just got back. When man suffers he is more selfish and is deaf to the sufferings of his fellow-creatures. Only death reconciles us really with the world and with God!"

"Does not love?" asked Apostol quickly, almost dreadingly.

"The great, true love is in God only."

Suddenly from the house came the sound of children wailing and crying. In the street a detachment of soldiers was passing on its way to the front, the men tired, depressed, with heads bent down like cattle being led to the slaughter. But on the *cerdac* the brightness of the sun glowed like the smile of a pretty girl.

"These little children can never keep still," murmured Boteanu in a different voice. "And the poor wife must needs scold them all the blessed day."

Apostol smiled. The priest, now cheerful again, continued: "I heard you had gone home on leave, Apostol. That was why I had caught no glimpse of you. O God! At least the war did not touch that spot!"

"I remember how studious you were of yore in Nasaud, Constantin," said Bologa, as if he were afraid of forgetting something, "and I wonder how you have managed to get used to this place, away from the world, without books, without people of your own class? You must find life very difficult?"

Popa Boteanu flushed, but into his eyes came a radiant humility which diffused all round him waves of trust and sympathy. He answered without hesitation and with a serene smile:

"It was a stiff, arduous fight, Apostol. But God helped me and opened my heart and gave me consolation. For there is life everywhere, in a grain of sand as in the soul of man. And everywhere men need pity—to give and to receive. Books are good things, too, but only life can bring you near to God! As long as you live amongst books and on them it seems to you that all wisdom is contained therein. Then when you go out into the world you feel your soul is sad and has nothing to uphold it, even though you may have digested the contents of all the libraries in the world. That's what happened to me, and I endured terrible torment and thought I would never find peace anywhere. Then, gradually, in the midst of nature the torrent of life caught me up and carried me along through suffering and bitterness, without my knowing whither. And so the hour came when I awoke to find my soul full of understanding! I felt the power and glory and goodness of God in my heart, and in this feeling all mysteries were revealed to me, Apostol! Since then I no longer need books, but only God. Also God is nearer the ordinary man who lives in the world, amidst the hurly-burly of life—much nearer! Faith runs away from books and can only dwell in the hearts of those who long for it passionately!"

Apostol Bologa stammered with burning cheeks:

"Father, I feel your words in my heart! I feel them, Father!"

The priest shook his head and said, still smiling:

"Philosophers of all men find it hardest to realize the truth of God because they seek God with their weak, mortal mind and not with a trusting and all-comprehending heart! When man forgets his divine origin and rummages in the mire in order to discover the purpose of God's mysteries, how can the soul rise and gather wisdom and contentment?"

The priest's question floated a little while in the sun's rays, then trailed off into a long silence. Apostol stared at the ground, weighed down by a terrible depression. Popa Constantin stood a short distance away from him, his face in the path of the light. All at once Apostol Bologa looked up at him with eyes full of pain and longing.

"Constantin," murmured Apostol in a voice so hollow that it seemed to come from the depth of his soul, "all my life I have battled with God! Do you hear? I have struggled every minute of my life, seeking Him, adoring Him, and cursing Him! I have always felt I needed God, and God has tortured me terribly! I have had moments when I have felt God in my heart and I have not been able to keep Him there! Why was I not able to keep Him, Father? Why did He not drive away all doubts so that they should never return? And because these moments have been inexpressibly blissful and peaceful I have gone on without resting—cursing, and seeking everywhere. That struggle shackles me and I am terrified lest it should never end, not even in the world to come."

Apostol's stricken eyes, swimming in tears, waited as if they were expecting supreme salvation from the man standing there.

"Believe, Apostol, and God will descend into your heart when the hour will strike and will abide with you through all eternity," said the priest in a voice full of hope and encouragement.

Bologa, as if in truth the voice had dropped a wonderful balm into his soul, continued more quickly, his eyes still fixed on the priest's face:

"I want to believe. And sometimes I feel as pure and receptive as a chalice. But I implore in vain, I hammer in vain at all the doors, no one answers me! I believe, I believe, Father! All the fibres of my being long for faith even when uncertainties and doubts rend me! I have fought with the temptations of hate and I have driven them from my soul. I am ready to humble and debase myself, to put ashes on my head in order to win one atom of implicit faith."

He was silent for a while, and then went on in a different voice:

"I am always walking between two abysses, Constantin! Always, always! An abyss outside and an abyss within my soul. And at every false step I find myself looking down into the chasms—at every false step. More than once I have realized that man cannot travel on the road of life without a trusty guide, and yet I have continually tried to do so! But the path of life is full of cross-roads, and at every cross-road I was forced to stop and reflect, and never once did I hit on the right road, and I had to go back, and then I did not even manage to find the road on which I had come."

"I also have carried your cross, Apostol, and when my despair was at its bitterest God sent me enduring faith to lean on and saved me!" The priest uttered the words like an annunciation. He moved to Apostol's side. "Only perfect faith can save man, either here or in the world to come. Faith is the living bridge over the chasms between the tormented soul and the world full of enigmas, and more especially between man and God. And you, too, can only find the trusty guide you seek in perfect faith, for only faith can encourage at every step and tell you at every moment how to reconcile your soul!"

Apostol Bologa, with head bowed down, listened to the priest's words as to a benediction. And when Constantin was silent he also said nothing more, as if a perfect guide had in truth descended into his soul.

Just then the priest's wife came out on the *cerdac* carrying a little basket of rusks, and behind her followed an old maidservant, walking very carefully in order not to spill any of the contents of the full cups set on a flower-painted tray.

"Put it down there gently!" whispered the priest's wife after she had given Bologa a timid smile.

"I don't think you have met my wife before, have you, Apostol?" the priest asked with pride. "Here you are; look at her, and tell me if you have ever seen such a sweet little doe!"

"My goodness, Constantin, aren't you ashamed to talk like that?" said the wife, blushing to the tip of her nose and signing to the servant to go.

The priest's wife was plump, glowing with health, with chubby cheeks and very kind, light-green eyes. Apostol kissed her hand, mumbling a few words.

"You must excuse us and our primitive ways," added the lady, still blushing and arranging the table, "for this is the country, and we are at war. Time was when we were better off, but while the popa was interned the Austrian soldiers reduced us to poverty."

"Don't worry, it's all very nice, little doe," said Boteanu, caressing her affectionately. "And Apostol is not a stranger. Eh, eh, you were in the cradle when he and I were making things hum in Nasaud!"

The lady waited until they had settled down, taking care to tell them that she herself had mixed the coffee but that they were to be sure to help themselves to more sugar or black coffee if it wasn't to their taste. Then she excused herself, blushing anew, for a thin wailing had again broken out in the house, and went away, smiling very bashfully.

"A woman in a thousand, Apostol!" the priest began immediately in a voice warm with affection. "She has been the joy of my life. I met her at a church dance in Gherla, blessed be that dance! As a matter of fact, she is the daughter of my predecessor here. He died the year we were married. My mother-in-law lives here with us. You cannot imagine what it means to have a wife who loves you really, even to sacrificing herself endlessly. My wife is such a woman, Apostol! Some day, when I shall tell you all our sufferings, you'll understand why I love her with my whole heart and soul. And, mind you, she is a well-educated girl; she studied four years in Blaj. . . ."

Apostol interrupted him abruptly and, holding his eyes with his own, said:

"You love her much—as much as you love God?"

Boteanu was taken aback for a moment, his coffee spoon arrested in its stirring. Then he answered firmly, almost solemnly:

"Yes, much—as much as I love God! Love is one and indivisible, exactly like faith. My heart embraces in the same love both God and the companion of my life and the mother of my children! By means of true love the coalescent souls approach nearer to the throne of the Almighty."

The light which flamed in Apostol's eyes was so bright that Popa Constantin could hardly restrain his wonder.

§ VI

Apostol Bologa went back to his office, his heart at ease, and settled down to his work with the deliberation of a man who had arranged his life in every detail; only from time to time he glanced out of the window as if he were waiting for someone, but without anxiety, as if he knew for certain that the one he was waiting for would turn up in time.

Towards eleven o'clock the grave-digger Vidor, carrying a bundle in his hand, came in at the gate, looking very downcast. Then Apostol stood up, and with fingers which trembled slightly laid down his pen on the ink-stand. The office door was open, and soon the grave-digger was standing in the doorway. He wished Bologa good day, as was his wont. Bologa answered his greeting and then, without waiting for the old man's usual questions about peace, he added:

"I would like to speak to you about something—something very important. . . . Now, at once."

The grave-digger, wondering, made as if to enter the office, but Apostol stopped him.

"Over there . . . in my room . . . I'll be over in a minute."

"Yes? Very well," answered Vidor, looking perplexedly at the two non-coms. as if he were trying to find a clue on their faces. "Very well, I'll just go and hand my bundle to the lassie and I'll come back."

Apostol stood waiting by his desk until he saw the old man enter the room opposite, then he walked across firmly, clearing his throat a little on the way. On the grave-digger's face he saw a kind of fear mingled with cunning.

"Bade,"[1] said Bologa resolutely, "I love Ilona, and I want to marry her if she will have me and if you will give her to me."

The grave-digger Vidor gave him a long look and made no answer, either as if he had not understood what had been said to him or as if he were waiting for further explanations.

"I must have your answer now, at once!" went on Apostol, slightly irritated by the peasant's suspicious silence. "Don't think that it is just a sudden whim. I have thought the matter over carefully."

Vidor gazed through the window into the courtyard, sighed, scratched the top of his head, shook his head, and then said slowly, looking rather askance at the officer:

"Well, sir, you've said something big, I own, for we know the world and what is becoming, though we are simple folk as God has made us. I don't say that you don't really love the girl, but I am an old man, and I have lived through a lot and I have swallowed whole ladlefuls of trouble, and that is why I think that our little lass is not for you. She is poor, she has neither wealth nor learning and is not suited for you, sir!"

"Because I love her we are suited," murmured Apostol, upset, for he had not expected any objections.

The grave-digger scratched his head again, then scrutinized the lieutenant once more for a few minutes, uncertain and suspicious. Finally, he went to the door and from the threshold called:

---

[1] A mode of address used by the peasants when speaking to an elder brother or to an older man.

"Ilona! Ilona! Come here a minute, quickly!"

The girl came at once wonderingly, her fingers wet with the red dye of the eggs. When her father told her that the officer had asked her to be his wife she was startled, then she looked at Bologa and burst into tears. The grave-digger bade her give the gentleman an answer, but all in vain; Ilona went on weeping, and nothing would induce her to utter a word.

"We are wasting our time, sir," said Vidor finally, in a tone of contempt. "Women are all the same; once they start crying you can't stop them. Besides, there's no object in wasting words, the girl has to do what I tell her!"

He scrutinized Apostol yet a little while, then he went up to him with hand outstretched, saying heavily:

"You have done us a great honour, sir. May you live long, and the best of luck be yours henceforth!"

Apostol, his face shining with joy, approached Ilona, who had hidden her face in her apron and was still weeping with stifled sobs.

"Ilona!" he whispered, deeply moved. "Will you be my bride, Ilona?"

She uncovered her face and answered him with a passionate look, born of tears and beautified by a smile of happiness. And Apostol kissed her without shyness on both cheeks, damp with tears.

"Then let us hurry to the village priest that he may betroth us!" said Bologa, the taste of her tears on his lips. "I'll wait for you both in the office."

He went back to the office calmer than he had left it. In half an hour the grave-digger knocked at the door, announcing that they were ready to go. Both Vidor and Ilona were dressed in their Sunday best. Apostol noticed the girl was wearing the green kerchief of yesterday, and more especially the bodice of red velvet which showed the roundness of her breasts.

Popa Boteanu crossed himself when Bologa reappeared accompanied by Vidor and the girl. He asked, with a little anxiety in his voice:

"What is it, Apostol? What has happened? It is not three hours since . . ."

"It was you who showed me what to do, Father, and we made haste to come and ask for your blessing!" answered Apostol, smiling.

Boteanu, perplexed, asked them into the room where a little while ago he had received Apostol and begged them to explain. When he heard what Apostol wanted he looked at all three in turn, unable to conceal his astonishment. Then he excused himself for a moment and went out, of a certainty to tell his wife the wonderful thing that was happening. He returned with the stole, the cross, and the prayer-book.

"Let us pray that the Lord may bless your union," murmured the priest in kindly tones, opening the book.

He read the usual prayers, trying to invest them with more than usual fervour and solemnity. Then they all kissed the cross and the young people embraced. The priest added a few more words, bidding Ilona especially to guard preciously the happiness which God had sent her and to endeavour to deserve the joy granted to her through the mercy of Heaven. The girl wept and the grave-digger was touched.

"And now do please sit down and let us drink a glass of wine to this happy hour, as is the traditional custom of our people!" said Boteanu, taking off and folding up the stole.

As if it had all been arranged beforehand, the maidservant entered at that very minute with a bottle and glasses, and a few minutes later the priest's wife came in herself, burning with curiosity.

"Look, little doe, our friend has chosen Ilona for his bride!" called out the priest gaily, filling all the glasses.

The good lady congratulated Apostol and praised Ilona, saying she was a good girl, etc. But there was so much amazement in her voice that Apostol did not dare to answer, and was glad when "the little doe" went over to Ilona to pump her and satisfy her curiosity by asking all sorts of questions.

After the priest's wife had settled down Boteanu told them a piece of news which a soldier, who was quartered somewhere in the neighbourhood, had brought him just now after Apostol had left. The soldier had just returned from Faget, and there he had heard that during last night they had caught—no one knew where—three wretched peasants who were supposed to be spies and to have given away important information to the enemy on the front. The grave-digger hastened to interrupt with more detailed information. He had seen with his own eyes the arrested men. The great general was quartered in the house of his own brother-in-law in Faget, and as his brother-in-law was burgomaster he knew everything that went on. The truth was that a fortnight ago an order had been issued to the village forbidding anyone to go anywhere near the front, either with grazing cattle or to fetch wood, but there were lots of stupid, clumsy fools who did not understand when one spoke nicely to them, and they had kept on going into the forbidden area as if they had verily done it on purpose. The military authorities closed their eyes to this and just chased them away. But for the last few days the division had been making great preparations— why and for what purpose was not known. And since, they had noticed that whatever order was given over here and whatever movement took place over here was known to the enemy a day or two later. In fact, they had come to the conclusion that there must be spies here, and that the spies must be those peasants who, in face of the drastic orders issued, had still persisted in hanging round the forbidden area. Hence they seized three last night and brought them between bayonets to Faget. The general was so infuriated that he had ordered all three to be hanged, to make an example of them. To-morrow the court martial would try them, and, as the great general had said they would be hanged, there was no doubt but that they would be hanged.

"My sister-in-law, poor thing, has been crying her eyes out, she feels so sorry for them," concluded the grave-digger. "Two are from Faget, well-known men, Rumanians, and one is from here, from our own village. Poor Horvat, Father, you must know him; he lives in the lane leading to the station. God help him! I thought I would tell his wife, but I don't know. . . . I dare not. . . . That's how it was! I was just on the point of telling the lieutenant all about it when he started to talk about the girl, and it went clean out of my head, fool that I am!"

"O Lord, forgive us our sins and protect us from dangers!" murmured the priest, crossing himself fervently. "Death holds great sway these days. O Lord, Thy decisions are too deep for our poor understanding; have mercy on our weakness and do not leave us without consolation, now and for ever and ever, Amen!"

Apostol Bologa crossed himself three times, his eyes wet with tears, his heart bleeding with a great pity.

When they left, the priest pressed his hand warmly and said:

"Be sure and come to the Resurrection service, Apostol, to strengthen your heart and faith in God, for you see what terrible times these are and what need the soul of man has of strength and help."

"I'll come without fail!" answered Apostol fervently.

In the afternoon he went as usual into the office to work. In the evening, at supper-time, he told Petre he was going to marry Ilona. The orderly wished him joy rather half-heartedly. He had heard the news from Ilona herself, and he could not understand why on earth the "young master" should take for wife a poor and stupid little peasant girl when he could have had so many young ladies by merely stretching out one finger.

Before going to bed he ordered his soldier to waken him in time for the Resurrection service. Towards midnight he was awakened by Ilona's caressing hands.

"Get up, lazy one. Hurry, or you'll miss the Resurrection!"

By the time he had shaken off sleep the girl had disappeared noiselessly. He dressed quickly. The coolness of the night made him quicken his steps. The sky was serene, greyish-blue, and the stars twinkled like tiny lights in the dome of an immense cathedral.

The churchyard was full of people, and yet more and more kept on coming, some singly and others in parties. The little wooden church—old, giving way on one side and propped up with beams to prevent it from collapsing, with its slightly crooked little tower, with its door so low that one had to stoop in order to enter—could hardly be distinguished in the darkness from the old trees which stretched out their branches like protecting arms right over the roof. Issuing from the inside of the church as from a cavern could be heard a tortured voice mumbling, now dolefully and painfully, now harshly and shrilly.

"It is too early," whispered someone near Bologa, "the priest arranges the service so that Communion is over just as day breaks."

"Better to be too early than not to have room even in the churchyard," answered another reprovingly.

The people were crowding in, whispering. Here and there smothered laughter could be heard. The darkness began to thin.

At last the door of the church became illuminated, and a few minutes after the priest, with the Bible in the crook of his arm and a lighted candle in his other hand, appeared on the threshold. Dozens of candles were stretched out eagerly towards the priest[1] in the splendid vestments, and soon the whole churchyard was full of tiny yellow, twinkling lights, like a company of timid souls waiting tremblingly at the gates of heaven for the call of deliverance.

Amongst the peasants who crowded round the priest Apostol Bologa also saw many soldiers, their faces transfigured with fervour, eagerly muttering prayers. He was surprised to see, not far off from where he stood, the Hungarian sergeant who worked in his office.

Then the service began. Popa Boteanu chanted softly in his thin voice, with eyes either closed or raised towards heaven. The light played on his emaciated face, making him look like a saint in an old ikon. All round Apostol the dry lips of the people moved quickly, hungrily. The incense spread in bluish waves and the worshippers inhaled it with gladness as a perfume from another world.

"We must obey the Holy Word!" chanted the priest, looking over the heads of the crowd with a look that seemed to announce a new mystery. The congregation fell on their knees. Apostol listened transported, his eyes fixed on the lips of the priest. The sentences wavered, floated, and united into a wonderful melody which diffused into his soul implicit faith. Slowly, unconsciously, he bowed his head to the ground. Then suddenly he heard again

---

[1] The people all light their candles from the priest's.

the voice of the priest, triumphant, strong, and now blithe as a silver bell:

"Christ has risen from the dead!"

Apostol sprang to his feet. All were singing, their faces luminous with joy. And the voices fluttered like little flags of truce, and rising into the clear air climbed higher and higher until they reached the throne of Divine Consolations.

§ VII

On Easter Sunday there was rather a lot to do in the office, nevertheless Bologa knocked off at midday and had his meal with Vidor and Ilona. For the second time, but this time with more details, the grave-digger told him the tale of the three arrested peasants, and after dinner the old man, eaten up with curiosity, hastened over to his brother-in-law's to hear if there was anything new. He could now go off with his mind easy, for he needed no longer to worry about his girl.

"From now onwards you'll guard her more jealously than I!" he told Bologa, winkingly slyly.

Towards the evening, before the grave-digger had returned from Faget, the rumour spread in the village that the three prisoners had been condemned to death by the court martial and that they would be hanged the very next morning. The news filled the villagers with horror, and entered like a sinister messenger into all the houses, casting a gloom over the Easter festivities.

And the grave-digger brought further news. Firstly, that the condemned men were in truth to be executed the next day before sunrise. The wives, children, and friends of the men had knelt and wept at the general's feet, begging him to pardon them, to have mercy. In vain! The general had been furious and had had them driven away by the police. Secondly, that on the night before, four more men had been arrested, also Faget men, and also in the forbidden area, and that to-morrow these, too, would be tried.

"In fact, it is obvious that the general intends to hang us all in turn!" sighed the grave-digger gloomily.

He went out to tell some of the neighbours the misfortune which had fallen upon their fellow-creatures like a bolt from the blue, but he soon returned, changed his clothes, and went off again to Faget.

"My trade may be of some use to the poor fellows," he said as he wished Apostol and Ilona good-bye, and then, crossing himself, added: "O Lord, what a misfortune! O Lord, protect us!"

The next day Vidor returned home at midday in order to tell them that the three had been hanged in a private wood on the margin of the highroad, half-way between Lunca and Faget.

"They did not even trouble to set up a gallows," said the grave-digger, weeping like an old woman. "They strung them up like dogs, each on the branch of a tree. We wanted to bury them, as is meet for Christians, but they would not take the bodies down. They said the orders were that they were to hang there three days and three nights so that all may see and take the lesson to heart. Lord, Lord, protect us! Right up to the moment when the rope was put round their necks the poor fellows swore they were innocent. Do you think anyone took the slightest notice of their protests? Orders and again orders! And look, all that on Easter Monday! O Lord, great is Thy power and great Thy mercy, Lord! And there are four more prisoners!"

He went back at once to Faget without putting a single morsel into his mouth, his eyes red with weeping, his back bent as if this one day had aged him by ten years.

About two hours later, just when Apostol was busiest, Captain Klapka blew into the office, shouting:

"Bologa! You lucky fellow! You are back from leave? Have you been back long? Oh, you lucky, lucky fellow! Anyway, I hope you have quite recovered now?"

He embraced Apostol noisily, overwhelming him with questions. He was a little thinner in the face, and his little militiaman's beard seemed fairer, scantier, and less well cared for. After a few minutes Bologa asked him to come over into the other room so that they could talk in peace. There they found Ilona, who now scarcely allowed Petre to set foot in the room, jealously wishing to look after and do everything for her betrothed herself. Klapka, seeing her, went up to her and without much ado chucked her cheekily under the chin and was rewarded with a smart slap.

"Aah? Lively lassie!" murmured the astonished captain. "She strikes hard, there's no denying it! Who is the pretty one, Bologa? Well, well, you seem to be having a good time here! That's why you don't worry your head about us!"

"She is my betrothed," said Apostol, smiling.

"What? Your . . . betrothed?" repeated Klapka quite nonplussed. "But . . . but . . . this is madness, Bologa! Excuse me, perhaps I am a clumsy, mannerless lout, but all the same, I don't understand! I don't understand at all!"

"Oh well, if man understood everything he now doesn't understand, where would the charm of life be?" Bologa answered gaily. "You'd better sit down here and rest a while and we'll crack[2] Easter eggs, for don't forget it is Easter Monday to-day."

---

[1] It is the custom to crack red eggs with guests at Easter.

And while Klapka, rather at a loss, settled himself at the table, Apostol went out into the lobby and came back with Ilona, who was carrying one plateful of red eggs and another of *cozonac* and *pasca*. The captain stood up very politely, and somewhat embarrassed said to Ilona:

"I was very rude just now . . . but I didn't know . . . I thought that. . . . Please forgive me!"

Though she didn't know a word of German, Ilona understood what Klapka was trying to say. She gave him a long look and then burst into such a merry laugh that both men had to join in her laughter.

"The lassie . . . I mean your fiancée . . . is very saucy!" said Klapka, after Ilona had run out of the room to laugh at her ease. "But," he added seriously, "this engagement is a mystery to me, of course . . ."

"And for me!" whispered Apostol exuberantly. "But not only the engagement but life as a whole, beginning with my soul and ending with the starry infinite!"

The captain looked at him wonderingly, and proceeded uncertainly:

"Yes . . . that's so. . . . These are some of the big things we all feel and no one really understands, but the engagement is something material—an actual fact. What I don't understand in this engagement are the motives that induced you to tie your future to a little girl who is very sweet, there is no doubt about it, but totally uncivilized. What can a man like you see in a little peasant girl, and Hungarian at that? That's what I can't make out, my dear fellow!"

"The soul is the same in the peasant girl as in the countess," answered Bologa with warmth, "at all events in its essentials. Only the shape has been changed by civilization. And are you sure that the change has increased man's happiness? No, no, I think that civilization has corrupted man and demoralized him. Primitive man is kind and just and believes—that's why he is happier than civilized man. All that civilization has bestowed on mankind up till to-day is war, which puts millions and millions of people face to face, and which kills thousands and thousands of souls in one second! The benefits of civilization are reflected only in a few favoured ones who suffer from boredom and spleen. For one thousand five hundred million people civilization is a calamity, if it isn't in truth a refined system of slavery."

"But without the benefits of civilization, would you yourself be able to rail against them?" asked Klapka with a smile.

"Then I would not feel the need to scorn them, and I should most certainly be happier!" shouted Apostol obstinately. "Your civilization raises nothing but doubts in the poor human soul, but is incapable of giving a single answer! Every 'conquest' of civilization has knocked off a bit of man's happiness until there is nothing left in the soul but a mass of ruins. Instead of faith it has substituted formulæ. It would like to define even God Himself by a formula, and then it would rub its hands and say gleefully: 'Here you are, I have conquered God also!' It has taken to pieces and explained the divine music which is life, so that to-day the poor 'civilized' man no longer knows whither to turn, disgusted with his own being. I am sick of civilization, captain! Ten thousand years of civilization are not so precious as one single moment of spiritual contentment!"

Klapka listened to him more and more perplexed. He stroked his little beard impatiently, thinking to interrupt him and to tell him that he had come over here for something else.

"Dear Bologa, I . . ." tried Klapka.

But Apostol, hurriedly, as if he were afraid of losing the thread or as if what he wanted to say weighed on his soul and he wished to ease it with all possible haste, continued:

"Just a moment, captain! Let me bury civilization in my heart for good! It has spoilt my life and has tortured me unceasingly for twenty years. It was civilization which made me guide my life by 'conceptions' and formulæ and principles. As, soon as life wiped out my foolish constructions I built up new ones more foolish still, and I prided myself that I—with a capital 'I'—had succeeded in arranging my fate and had got the better of life and God! I have had to touch the very depths before I succeeded in escaping from the claws of fallacies, before I succeeded in finding my own self again, my soul athirst for God and happiness!"

"Yes, yes, man needs a spiritual prop," murmured the captain.

"That's it," Bologa said insistently, as if the other's assent had fortified him. "It's true, isn't it? A prop, captain! Faith—great, implicit, blind faith. Faith is God, captain!"

And then, as if he were suddenly ashamed of his exuberance, he stared a minute at Klapka and in a totally different voice said:

"I go on talking, talking, and . . . Don't mind me! My heart is full. Do please help yourself!" he added, smiling and pointing to the plates on the table. "My fiancée made them. Her name is Ilona. Sit down! Why do you stand?"

Both sat down. Klapka took a bite of *pasca* and munching said:

"I remember the time you came over to see me at the front. Do you remember, when there was the Rumanian officer incident? How upset you were. I thought you were angry with me because I did not wax enthusiastic over your plans of desertion. Do you remember? You left in a rage."

"Yes . . . in a rage," said Apostol, nodding.

FOREST OF THE HANGED

"You were lucky to fall ill," continued the captain, swallowing the yolk of a hard-boiled egg. "I don't know why I had and still have a presentiment that they would catch you if you tried to go over to the other side. . . . I don't know why. For this reason I am always worrying about you. Perhaps it is mere superstition. Anyway, you must have been born under a lucky star, Bologa! Firstly, because you have escaped from the front—here one would not even guess there was a war on. . . ."

"It's true, it does seem as if there were no war on," assented Bologa with a contented smile. "I feel like an old Civil Servant or like a tramway horse! All day long with the same registers and the same ammunition sheets. I note, control, add. A real office machine! It's true! I no longer think about the war or about anything. In reality happiness narrows one's outlook dreadfully, don't you think so?"

"Perhaps. In any case, at the front you don't get a chance of forgetting where you are," said Klapka, sighing and lowering his eyes, in which a very worried look had appeared. "For the last ten days we've been in a state of excitement and great preparations, and we get orders upon orders, enough to give you cold shivers. What is about to happen God knows—whether we are about to attack or to be attacked. I went to headquarters to-day, in fact, that's where I come from now. They are all dumb and grave and shrug their shoulders, curse them! And everywhere an extraordinary watchfulness, the more so because within the last few days men have begun to desert to the enemy at the further ends—the Rumanians especially. I heard that last night about five infantrymen did a bunk, so you can imagine the state of things out there!"

Klapka looked at Apostol searchingly, as if he would like to discover what impression the news made on him. Apostol, however, listened quietly, and in his eyes there was nothing but pity and sadness. The captain continued with more confidence:

"And here with the civilians. You'd think the general had gone mad. I saw, going through Faget, three men hanging in a little wood by the road-side. It reminded me of the Forest of the Hanged. Even my horse took fright and broke into a mad gallop. Now, on the way back, I did not come by the highroad but came along the railway line, so as not to see that horrible sight. And the court martial has only begun its activities! Just as I left I heard that four more peasants had been condemned. The trial lasted one hour, and in one hour four men are condemned to be hanged!"

The captain was silent, as if he were waiting for something. Bologa's eyes, drowned in tears, stared at him long, fixedly, tensely.

"But I also heard at headquarters," said Klapka after a pause, his face somewhat brighter, "that they were going to take away all Rumanian soldiers from the front and were sending them somewhere else. I don't know if this applies to officers also. If it is so, you will be able to breathe more quietly! That's why you must keep quiet, Bologa," he added with sudden warmth. "Be thankful that you are here, and trust to your luck. I told you once before that luck is our saviour."

"Yes, luck and God," stammered Apostol, perturbed, closing his eyes and allowing two thin trickles of tears to roll down his pallid cheeks and to drop on to his chest, making two salt stains on the pockets of his tunic. "Now I no longer desire anything; now God looks after me and guides me. As God wills so will I do, for all my hopes are centred in God . . . only in God."

Klapka stood up gaily in a burst of joy and embraced him, exclaiming:

"Well, then, I can confess that that was the only reason I blew in, Bologa! I knew you were mad, and I was mortally afraid that you would fall into the trap. If you knew how glad I am you would embrace me! The Lord be praised! Henceforth I need not trouble each time I see men arrested on the front."

Apostol Bologa, deeply moved, kissed him on both cheeks.

That same evening the order arrived that Petre was to report to regimental headquarters within twenty-four hours; in his place the regiment would put another soldier at Lieutenant Bologa's service. When Petre heard this he begged Apostol not to let him go, and all night long he spent reading *The Dream of Our Lord's Mother* and reciting prayers. But the next day he had to go. Because Apostol was very much cut up, Ilona assured him that he no longer needed an orderly now that he had her to look after him and that she was ready to follow him anywhere, even to the front.

In the afternoon the grave-digger returned, heartbroken, and instead of telling them what he had seen, he kept mumbling tearfully:

"Now there are seven . . . seven . . . seven . . ."

§ VIII

Apostol Bologa kept on telling himself that the greatest misfortune that could now befall him would be separation from Ilona. It seemed to him that his life had begun somewhere a long way back, but only since he had known Ilona had it become bright like a little room full of sun and joy. A simple, delirious, childish happiness had settled down in his heart. He worked hard and conscientiously in the office, and the time passed quickly because at the end of his day's work Ilona was waiting for him. They loved one another and made plans for the future. Apostol would describe to her how he would teach her lots of things, how he would dress her more finely than any lady, and how she would be the most beautiful woman in the world. Ilona, naturally, listened spellbound, agreed to everything, but kept on asking him to swear to her that he loved her and that never would he, even out of the corner of his eye, look at any other woman.

Thursday afternoon, exactly at four, Apostol stopped working in the office and went across to Ilona to tell her that he had decided that they should be married at Parva in great style, with musicians and all, and that Popa Boteanu should officiate. He hadn't quite finished speaking when they heard in the bumpy lane the sound of a motorcar approaching at great speed. Bologa, surprised, went to the window and saw the car stop abruptly before the house. He looked at Ilona questioningly. In her eyes, over the joy of a minute ago, there was a look of fear.

"Go quickly, it's you they want!" she whispered, hanging on his arm.

Apostol, perplexed, went out to the door leading into the house. A sergeant-major, tall, lanky, with a thin ashen face, no moustache, and dark whiskers, was just entering the gate. His face seemed familiar to Apostol, but he could not remember where he had seen him before.

"Urgent orders from His Excellency!" reported the sergeant-major, saluting respectfully. He spoke softly, yet his tone was peremptory and almost impertinent.

He held out an envelope. Bologa looked first at the envelope, then at the sergeant-major, and still wondering where he had seen the man before asked:

"You are waiting for an answer?"

"Yes, sir, the answer is very urgent!" said the sergeant- major, even more peremptorily but saluting again.

While he slit open the envelope Apostol could not help asking:

"I have seen you before, sergeant-major. Where are you on duty?"

"At the court room of the division," answered the sergeant-major with an ugly smile.

"Oh?" murmured the lieutenant, still perplexed, feeling sure that he had seen him elsewhere . . . somewhere . . . and it annoyed him that he could not remember just now where.

He glanced at the official letter signed by the adjutant. He was invited to report himself immediately to the divisional commanding officer to receive orders.

"Very well," said Bologa quietly, "I'll come to-morrow morning, for to-day it is already late, and by the time I reached there His Excellency . . ."

"The car is at your disposal, sir," interrupted the sergeant-major insistently. "In fact, I was ordered to . . ."

"Oh well, if that's the case, all right! Just wait a little," answered Apostol, put out merely because he would have to leave Ilona.

He went into the office, told them that he was going to headquarters, then he went across to his room, where Ilona was waiting for him trembling, her eyes wet and an ugly fear at her heart.

"Why do they want you?" she whispered very low, as if the whole room had been full of spying enemies.

"Oh, goodness knows for what piffle!" mumbled Apostol indifferently, getting ready to go.

Then when he had put on his helmet he went up to her, now also feeling upset and weighed down by a sudden dark foreboding. But he tried to hide his uneasiness and muttered:

259

"Ilona . . . au revoir! Don't worry. And tell your father . . . I mean . . . why, of course, he is in Faget . . . of course, I'll tell him myself. Don't worry, little one, don't worry!"

"Have a care over there!" murmured Ilona pleadingly and afraid, her cheeks wet with tears. "May God help you!"

"Amen!" whispered Apostol, crossing himself.

Then he gathered her into his arms and kissed her, whispering in her ear as if it had been an endearment:

"Don't worry, my bride . . ."

The sergeant-major was standing in the middle of the courtyard, resting on one leg with hand on hip, his eyes closed as if he were afraid of the sunlight. Seeing him thus, Apostol Bologa remembered abruptly that he had seen him in Zirin at Svoboda's execution, giving instructions behind the gallows to the short, dark corporal who had been compelled to act as executioner. Apostol shook himself as if he were shaking off a loathsome beetle, and entered the car without another glance at the man. Only when the car started did he look back. Ilona was standing at the gate—her mouth was smiling but her eyes were weeping.

On the level highroad the car flew. Bologa stared straight ahead, seeing in one and the same glance the backs of the chauffeur and sergeant-major, the bonnet of the car and the dark, snake-like ribbon of road which ran towards and disappeared under the whirling wheels. His thoughts flew now forwards, now backwards, without break, like a flock of birds that have lost their way. Why did the general want him? Perhaps it had to do with Palagiesu's denouncement. . . . But then, why just now? And Ilona. . . . She had stood at the gate as if she were bidding him farewell for ever. Why did she bid him farewell?

The highroad ran through a wood of fir-trees. Just before they were through the wood Apostol heard a voice which scattered all his thoughts. He saw that the sergeant-major's face, now split across by a grin, was turned in his direction.

"Sir, we are just coming to the place where the spies have been hanged," he said, his strange grin remaining fixed, just as if he had not even moved his jaws in speaking. "It's worth while your having a look at them; you'll see they still hang there like . . ."

The car bumped over a hole and cut short the sergeant-major's words. Bologa, staring at the man, said nothing, but stretched his neck forward a little as if he wished to see better.

"There is still one more bend," added the sergeant-major, with pride in his voice.

"Two, two!" yelled the chauffeur without looking round.

"That's right, yes, it is two!" said the sergeant-major, rather crest-fallen, still staring at the lieutenant as if waiting for him to say something.

The sergeant-major's voice got on Bologa's nerves. He looked quickly away from the man's face and fixed his gaze straight ahead of him. His whole soul shrank in an anguished suspense. When they arrived at the second bend there suddenly flashed through his mind the name Klapka had used and which seemed to cling to his mind as closely as a loop round a button: The Forest of the Hanged. . . . And immediately the suspense became a horror, studded with thousands of thorns all pricking at his heart with increasing violence.

The bend was left behind. The highroad descended into a large hollow, all meadows and fields. In the middle of the hollow, like a tuft of hair on a bald head, a dark wood stained the greenness.

The car hardly seemed to touch the ground.

The sergeant-major looked round quickly, convinced that the lieutenant would order them to slow down. Apostol had eyes for nothing but the grey ribbon of the road and the trees in the wood.

The car took but a few moments to swallow the four hundred metres which was the length of the wood, and yet it seemed to Bologa that it had taken an eternity, so clearly had he seen everything. There were four on the right-hand side, each one on a separate tree, all bareheaded, the bodies swinging only slightly as if from the wind caused by the speed of the passing car. The two outside ones—right on the margin of the wood—had their backs to the road and wore *opinci*[1] on their feet. The one in the middle, who was wearing heavy boots covered with mud, stared out with eyes as black as the fir cones in the road, and from his swollen, purple face he put out his tongue at the passers-by. On the left hung three others, facing the road which ran on the right, indifferent and motionless, as if the tops of their heads had been glued to the branch above. Two were strung up on an old alder-tree, while the third dangled from a smaller tree and from so thin a branch that it made you wonder that it did not break. His hands were tied behind his back and his body was short and frail as a child's; his whole face was brown as if it had been smeared over with clay. On the same tree and at the same height there was another thicker branch, as yet untenanted.

Apostol Bologa had seen them all so clearly that he could have told you how many buttons each man had on his dirty and ragged clothing. And nevertheless in his eyes these seven

[1] The footgear worn by many peasants, a sort of leather sandals, strapped up the leg and with long toes, curling right over the instep.

multiplied incessantly and the wood became transformed gradually into a limitless forest, cut through by a road without end. And from each tree of this limitless forest, all along the unending highroad that ran through it, it seemed to him that other men were hanging and still others, all with their eyes fixed on him, asking him to justify himself.

The car was now rushing alongside the railway line on the right side of the highroad, straight and level as a ruler. The wood could no longer even be seen. In front, about two kilometres ahead, gleamed the spire of the church in Faget, and a little nearer could be distinguished the reddish roof of the station, which was actually on the border of the village. Apostol stared straight ahead, but in his eyes danced the hanging men, nothing but hanging men, more and more numerous and more and more reproachful. And then in their midst appeared again the face of the sergeant-major, with the nasty smile which showed all his yellow teeth and a black gap in his lower jaw, and the nerve-racking voice, now trying to be ingratiating, again broke on his ear:

"The two sentries you saw are there only during the day-time so that the ravens should not get at them, for there are lots of ravens hereabouts—lots. At night we withdraw them, for of course the ravens do not hunt in the dark. At first the order was they were to hang only three days, but later His Excellency, in view of the numerous cases occurring, decreed that all hanged should remain there until further orders."

Bologa had not noticed the sentries, and he now only noticed for the first time the gap in the man's mouth. The voice sounded to him totally unknown and seemed to be issuing from a damp underground hole. Every word was spoken clearly, and Bologa wondered how the fellow could speak so calmly, as if he were reading out of a book. All at once he felt an overpowering need to speak himself, and he stammered hoarsely:

"Horrible!"

The sergeant-major did not catch what he said, and stared with wide eyes at Apostol, who, furious now, yelled so piercingly that even the chauffeur looked round a moment:

"Horrible!"

"Horrible. . . . I understand!" answered the startled sergeant-major, his smile gone, as he quickly turned his head away.

As soon as he was left to himself the Forest of the Hanged again sprang up before Apostol's eyes. But now they seemed to be all the same man, and in the eyes of all blazed a strange courage which reminded him of the flame in the eyes of the men going over the top. Apostol shuddered. "The same man, hanged innumerable times as an endless protestation." And all at once he said to himself: "It's Svoboda . . . his eyes . . ." As he thought this, he remembered with torturing clearness how he had helped to condemn the Czech, he remembered his pride at being chosen for the honour of sitting on the court martial, he recalled how, from excess of zeal, he had mixed himself in what had not really been his job, and had given a hand at getting things ready for the execution—he had even tested the rope to see if it were strong enough—he could now feel in the palms of his hands the rough touch of the rope. . . . And this remembrance was now turned into a feeling of shame and regret, and he felt as poignantly remorseful as if he were standing before God on the day of the Last Judgment. The strange feeling lasted only a second, but it seemed to reveal unpenetrated depths, where seethed explanations of all the mysteries of life.

And then the ghostly vision of hanged men disappeared abruptly and a great peace descended upon Apostol. His eyes saw again the mountains and valleys and sky. Above the swish of the furious car he could hear clearly the rustling of the young beech leaves and the dry crackling of the fir needles in the distance. The brooding green of the forests blended harmoniously with the bluey-white of the ether.

§ IX

The car drew up sharply before a large courtyard with open gate. Bologa jumped out and waited for a moment for the sergeant-major, who was saying something to the chauffeur. They entered together and the car drove off.

Two large, old houses bordered the courtyard. The one on the right, white-washed recently, with a little flower garden in front of it, had about five rooms. Three of them were occupied by General Karg, and in the two remaining back ones lived the proprietor, the burgomaster of the village. The house on the left belonged to the schoolmaster, who had been killed the year before in Italy. He had been married to the burgomaster's sister. The widow, with her five children, had been obliged to move to the house of a relative because the headquarters offices had been installed in her house. Originally the courtyard had been partitioned by a wooden paling which the soldiers had used for fire-wood, so that now the well, with its sweep, stood out stark and alone like a menace. At the back newly erected buildings could be seen. A little nearer there was a garden, stretching as far as the slope of fir-trees, with plum-trees in flower. Before the coach-houses soldiers were busy washing down two motor-cars and a whole park full of motor-cycles. In the corridor and before the main entrance of the house on the left, soldiers of all units crowded round waiting for orders, and while they waited they pushed and jostled one another, laughing and talking in whispers, for the general allowed no noise whatever which might disturb his occupations.

Near the well with its sweep stood the military prosecutor of the division, talking with a civilian of about fifty or so, ruddy, well-built, kindly looking, dressed partly in peasant, partly in town garb. The corpulent, dark-moustached prosecutor approached Bologa, exclaiming in a relieved tone:

"Thank goodness, you've come, my dear fellow! At last! I am relieved of a terrible anxiety. . . . Imagine, a lieutenant on the court martial has fallen sick, and we could no longer function, although to-morrow we have a very grave matter to settle. His Excellency will not consent to our withdrawing officers from the front to complete the court. In fine, you can imagine what a terrible strain it has been for me!"

While shaking hands Apostol asked:

"Is that why the general wanted me?"

"Surely. Probably he wants to give you personal instructions, you know his way," said the prosecutor, and continued with a fanaticism which contrasted unpleasantly with his corpulence: "We must wipe out treachery by every means in our power, Bologa! What is happening here is simply unheard of! Every movement of ours is known to the enemy the next day. Even our most secret plans are known to the enemy. Well, this can't go on! Very important events are pending, and here we are surrounded by nothing but spies, as if we were in an enemy country. Of course my own conscience is clear! Long ago I did my duty and reported to His Excellency that there was no great ardour of patriotism round about here. His Excellency did not heed me. He trusted them. He said we were in our own country. Now here we are in our own country! No later than last night the gendarmes brought me twelve scoundrels collected from the forests behind the front. Twelve! What do you say to that? A nice number, eh? I was just telling the burgomaster how indignant I felt. An ant-heap of traitors!"

Apostol Bologa interrupted him irritably:

"Why can't you people leave me alone, captain? Why do you worry me?"

The burgomaster nodded approvingly, somewhat encouraged. But the prosecutor became angry and answered indignantly:

"Yes, of course, you all talk like that and hold back, as if the court martial were something . . . something disgraceful! You don't realize that at bottom all your bravery is dependent on us. The war is not won merely with guns and hate, sir! In olden times, perhaps! To-day the brain does more than the arm. It would not be at all bad for you others to grasp what immense services this department is rendering to the country, it would not be bad at all! Only the mentality of you others is responsible for the fact that this division has no permanent court martial, as is decreed by regulations, and that we are compelled to lasso members in order to form one each time there is a case to try! The scarcity of officers is no valid excuse. If every officer worked as I do, then there would not be a lack of officers for so necessary an institution as a court martial to a division. Why, I am the prosecutor, the examining magistrate, and the judge advocate of the court martial all in one! Naturally I have to work till my eyes drop out. Let the others do as I do! For let me tell you, boys, there can be no victory if there is no court martial!"

The prosecutor had been a captain in the regulars, and in order to escape having to go to the front had persuaded himself that his services were the decisive factor in the war. He was terrified of death, and the sound of guns frightened him so much that he had to stop up his ears. He always thought that headquarters were placed much too near the front, and he devised special subterranean holes in which he could hide from enemy aeroplanes. Nevertheless, he considered himself a hero, and had an almost daring contempt for the men in the trenches. Now, catching sight of the ashen-faced sergeant-major behind Bologa, and noticing that Bologa was examining attentively the houses and scenery with the obvious intention of not listening to him any longer, the prosecutor called out importantly and significantly:

"Now then, sergeant-major, to work! There is no rest for us! Such is our fate! There are still a few examinations we have to take down, and there are the briefs to be finished off, for to-morrow is an important day."

He glanced disdainfully at Bologa and went off hurriedly towards the house on the left, his paunch wobbling before him, and closely followed by the faithful sergeant-major.

Apostol gave a relieved sigh. Then after a moment he asked the burgomaster, who didn't quite know what to do:

"Is the general here? Perhaps you could . . ."

"He is asleep," answered the burgomaster quickly. "He always rests two or three hours after his midday meal. But I expect he'll soon wake, as it is getting late."

While Bologa was making up his mind to hunt for the adjutant, the grave-digger Vidor came in at the gate. Seeing Apostol, the grave-digger's face darkened.

"My goodness, sir, what are you doing here?"

"On duty," murmured Apostol. "They've summoned me to the court martial."

"You don't say so?" came from the horrified grave-digger. "You? But what for?"

"To act as a member of the court," said Bologa strangely.

Vidor crossed himself three times. But the burgomaster's face cleared when he heard that "this is the gentleman who intends to marry Ilona," and he said more heartily:

"Well, if that's the case, don't you worry, sir; you won't have a too bad time with us here! And if you have to stay longer, we shan't leave you without a roof over your head. Look over there, at the back . . ."

He pointed out with his finger a small wooden kiosk with a door and a window, a passage in front of it, and three steps connecting it with the house on the right.

"Do you think I would be able to get into that little cage?" asked Bologa, carefully examining the kiosk.

"Surely! When necessity demands it man can even fit himself into a snake-hole," continued the burgomaster pleasantly. "I built it myself about seven years ago as a joke, because my little granddaughter kept on begging me to do it—she is no longer here, she is grown up now—so that she should also have a doll's house. I'd put her off day after day, but the little thing would not let me forget, so one fine morning I said: 'Very well then, come on, I'll make you a doll's house,' for we have more than enough wood round about here. And look, that's how I built it with my own hands. She had inside a little bed, a little table, and a little chair: everything as for a doll. But a grown-up man can rest there too, if he sets about it cautiously. It is empty now. The authorities have set it aside to be used as a punishment cell for officers—that's why it's always deserted. It has only been occupied for one week, that was last autumn, when the Bosnians were here, by a quite young standard-bearer. God knows for what crime. Since then no one has set foot in it."

Apostol kept on staring with fixed eyes at the kiosk. The burgomaster, somewhat confused, stopped speaking, and the grave-digger stood there shifting his weight from one foot to the other, as if he wished to ask something and didn't quite know how to start.

"But those others, where are they?" abruptly asked the lieutenant.

"Over on the other side," whispered the burgomaster, understanding. "O Lord, the wrath of God. . . . They are Rumanians, poor fellows, and not one of them will get off, to judge from the captain's fury!"

Bologa followed the burgomaster's glance and saw a sentry with fixed bayonet standing before a stone barn.

"There?" he murmured still more faintly.

The burgomaster nodded. Then in a tone that seemed to wish to drive away some thought, he said:

"Maybe the general has finished his nap by now."

Apostol followed mechanically on the heels of the burgomaster. The grave-digger kept close to them both, brooding all the time. At the door of the house the burgomaster's wife appeared, her hair done in a bun on top of her head. Because she was rather deaf, the burgomaster, so as not to shout, because of the general, said to her, moving his lips exaggeratedly and pointing to Bologa:

"That gentleman is the officer who is going to marry Ilona."

The woman smiled widely, delightedly, at Bologa. Her husband put his hand on her arm and added:

"Now he is here in connection with those others!"

The woman's smile changed immediately into a grimace of fear, and her husband signed to her that Bologa had to speak to the general.

"She is a soft-hearted creature, my wife," explained the burgomaster, lest the lieutenant misconstrued the woman's look of fear. "She has been ill with horror since she saw the poor men being taken off in procession to the gallows. As a matter of fact, the general thinks a lot of her," he added rather proudly. "She cooks for him, looks after him . . ."

Then the grave-digger, sullen, as if someone had been preventing him from speaking until now, cut short the burgomaster's speech, saying:

"Half a minute, brother-in-law. The thing is, how is Ilona to stay over there all alone?"

"There's time to see about that," replied the other, rather annoyed at being interrupted. "Let her be now, no one will eat her. First we must find out what this gentleman has to do. Then, if it's necessary, we'll fetch her over also and be done with it! Well, are you satisfied now?"

The grave-digger said nothing more, but went into the room into which the burgomaster's wife had unobtrusively retired. The burgomaster accompanied Apostol to the general's door:

"In there!"

Apostol Bologa opened the door. The adjutant greeted him volubly:

"Have you been here long? You'd better tell me. His Excellency has asked three times after you."

He disappeared, slipping through a door, and three seconds later introduced him into the general's room, where the blinds were drawn and the lamp was lit.

General Karg was walking about feeling very complacent, with hands behind his back, and the Havana cigar between his teeth was releasing blue rings of smoke. His face was rather puffy, as after a long sleep with pleasant dreams. The adjutant slunk to the writing-table and began to turn over some documents. The general paced the room twice more, as if he were getting a speech ready, then removing the cigar out of his mouth between two fingers, he stopped in front of Apostol. He stared at a few minutes, knitted his brows, and declaimed, but without harshness, in the tone he had used not very long ago on the train:

"I have chosen you to sit on the court martial instead of a sick man—of course this is only provisionally—because I do not care to withdraw officers from the front for . . . on principle. To-day, however, the court martial has become as important as . . . the information bureau, for example. Perhaps even more important, for until we have done away with the danger which threatens them from the back, the fighters will have no confidence. I do not wish to give you instructions or to urge you to carry out sacredly the duties of your new office. I wanted to see you merely to draw your attention to the extraordinary importance which the meting out of military justice has just now, in connection with the progress of the war! Yes . . . unfortunately, and to our shame, many sad cases have occurred here recently among the civilians who surround us. These cases are much more fraught with danger than the foe with whom we fight honourably face to face. Through the spies and traitors in our midst the brave men in the trenches would be disarmed if the arm of military justice did not protect them. That is why we must prosecute without mercy the criminals within our gates! That is the sacred duty of every conscientious and disciplined soldier! We condemn! I hope, therefore, that you will do your duty here as you did it in face of the outside enemy, Bologa! You are intelligent and upright; I have great faith in you, and that, in fact, is why I chose you. You once had an aberration, but I have wiped that off the slate; I have forgotten it. Similarly, I have purposely taken no notice of the accusations regarding your unmilitary attitude when on leave. I judge the soldier from his behaviour at the front, and there you . . ." (he glanced at Bologa's breast)—"you should wear your decorations, you have won them with blood and gallantry. That's what I wanted to say to you before you took up your new duties. I am not in the habit of interfering in the proceedings of the court nor of guiding the arm of justice. All I ask for is stern justice without quarter! Just that and no more!"

The general coughed and stopped speaking. Apostol stared at him with phosphorescent eyes.

"You understand?" asked the general, instinctively avoiding his eyes.

Apostol Bologa, with set lips, bent his head.

"Then forward!" shouted the general.

His cigar had gone out. The adjutant, who never smoked but always carried matches in his pocket, rushed forward diplomatically, happy to be able to light the general's cigar.

§ IX

Out-of-doors darkness had descended. All around behind the black hills lazy clouds had climbed up, and from the forests a whitish mist had spread a sheet over Faget, through which the twinkle of the stars which shone in the still serene portion of the sky could barely be seen. The windows of the house shone yellow, and the bucket on the well-sweep floated in the mist as on a sheet of water.

Apostol Bologa closed the door carefully. The darkness outside seemed to him so bitter that fear gripped his heart.

273

He walked towards the gate, reached the street, and turned towards the village. The houses stared at him with yellow, astonished eyes. The road beckoned to him peremptorily. His mind was a perfect blank, but his heart urged constantly, "Forward! Forward!" like a commanding officer who brooks no hesitation. His feet stuck to the road as if he had been barefooted, his spurs clinked rhythmically, faintly and pleasantly, like little silver bells in a far-off distance. A few black silhouettes and two carts with wounded coming from the front, at a walk, passed him.

He increased his pace without noticing he did so, as if he had to reach some place at a fixed hour. He felt warm, and all the warmth seemed concentrated in his heart. He passed the station with the reddish roof and left the village.

Where the highroad crossed the railway line he remembered that coming back Klapka had avoided the Forest of the Hanged by riding along the railway line. He walked between the rails, which gleamed faintly like two unending sword-blades. Several times he looked towards the left, but the mist hid the view, and the darkness made one of sky and earth. He stumbled on the sleepers and caught his breath. The road here seemed more difficult. When he came out again on to the highroad the gurgling of the stream close by sounded to him like strange whisperings.

Before entering Lunca, at the beginning of the road leading to the front, he halted abruptly, as if something had hit him in the chest, and in his brain buzzed the question:

"Where, in point of fact, am I going? Where?"

And he felt a strange feeling of oppression and murmured painfully:

"I've left it at home. O God, what have I left at home?"

And for answer he went on towards Lunca.

The grave-digger's house could barely be distinguished in the courtyard. Apostol entered hurriedly, as if he were late. The door of the lobby was wide open and flat against the wall, as always now since the weather had become warmer. He entered his room, felt for the matches in the usual place, and found them. He struck one, and saw Ilona lying on the bed, fully dressed, with eyes wide open, as if she had been expecting him, certain that he would come. He was not surprised either. The match went out, but Apostol could see her eyes in the dark. Then Ilona got up, and Apostol drew her to him despairingly, kissing her mouth, her eyes, her hair. Then suddenly he released her, afraid, muttering:

"I have forgotten something, and I don't know . . . It's not possible any longer, it's not possible."

The sound of his own voice calmed him. He lit a candle and set it slowly on the table. Ilona was staring at him with frightened eyes, feeling that a terrible danger was lurking near.

"God, what is it that I have forgotten, what *is* it?" said Apostol, looking at her questioningly.

Then he realized that he was lying, that he had come because of Ilona. But he hadn't the strength to own that he had lied, and so he began to hunt round feverishly, turning over the books on the little chest and those on the shelf above his bed. Accidentally his hand encountered the map with the positions on the front, which he had completed one evening, and had forgotten there.

"Here it is! I have found it," he shouted triumphantly at Ilona, to excuse his lie.

He opened it, glanced at the red-pencil marks, folded it in half, and slipped it into his pocket. Then he raised his eyes to

Ilona and shivered. He said to himself, "I must explain to her," and the roof of his mouth went dry. He felt he *must*. Thousands of thoughts chased through his mind, but they all either got mixed up together or else melted away so that they could not be formed into an "explanation". But under the confusion of his thoughts a powerful torrent bore his soul far away, driving out all doubts and hesitations.

"Ilona . . ." he stammered, terrified because he could find no words to tell her.

"I know the mountains better," whispered Ilona all of a sudden, guessing his thoughts. "I know all the hollows, all the paths, all the streams. I will be your guide!"

"No, no!" Apostol stared up, dazed. "You must not . . ."

His voice trembled. He was silent. But a few moments later he said again quietly:

"I'll come back for you, Ilona—to marry you! Do you believe me?"

"I believe you!" she answered, looking wildly into his eyes.

Bologa put on his helmet and took a last look round. The room seemed to live and breathe out happy memories. Ilona threw herself into his arms and kissed him.

Then Apostol went out. In the lobby the thought crossed his mind that he ought to have put on warmer clothes and taken his revolver with him. In the middle of the courtyard he looked back. Ilona had blown out the candle. From the gate he could hear her quick and barefooted steps coming towards him, but he did not stop. In the street he heard her whispering voice, but caught only one word: "God!" He crossed himself fervently, raising his eyes towards the heavens. The sky was as black as the earth. But the sign of the cross had lit in his soul the light of faith, and reconciliation showed him the way.

§ XI

At the bridge of the stream which came from the front he had to wait to let the train pass. The bloodshot eye of the engine seemed to hurl itself at Bologa, who stood there calmly leaning against the railing, exactly as he had done a short while ago, while waiting with his mother for the arrival of the train from Bistritza.

"I didn't even look at the time," thought he, watching the dark carriages running past, and noting curiously the harsh grinding of the wheels and thinking they could not have been oiled for months. "It must be past nine . . . But what do I care? There's plenty of time. If only God will help me to . . ."

Then he turned to the left along the waterside. The murmur of the restless waters floated away through the mist. Here and there on the hills flickering lights—marking unseen houses—trembled like glow-worms. The road wound greyly in the darkness. Now and again a silver streak flashed through the stream.

Although he had only once before travelled that way, Apostol had the impression that he was walking on a road on which he had journeyed thousands of times. He did not grope at all. He walked on through the darkness, as if he were walking on a pavement at high noon. He was not tired. In his heart he felt like a pricking the longing to get there more quickly. But not once did the question "Where?" appear in his mind. It seemed either as if that point did not interest him, or as if he knew only too well the place he had to reach.

The road ascended continually. Now the stream was on his right. A few white stars trembled like a little garland of hope on one comer of the sky above the summit of a treeless mountain.

"What would Klapka do if he saw me now?" Apostol said to himself rather gleefully when he arrived on the height where the batteries were.

There was no mist here, but nevertheless the darkness seemed denser, thicker. Bologa tried to find Klapka's dug-out, but gave it up and did not stop. The map with the positions of the units began to unroll itself in his mind. He remembered that the principal road led right up to behind the regiment of dismounted cavalry which formed the left wing of the division. But about 500 metres along it another road branched off, towards the infantry sector; this was the road he must follow. While he was working this out Lieutenant Varga's face unexpectedly flashed into his mind, and he thought with a smile:

"Varga is expecting me all the time."

He went on serenely. The road descended into an arid crooked valley.

"I only hope I won't run into a patrol," said Apostol to himself, without fear, as if he were talking of someone else.

Then after a few steps he could hear the tramp of his boots on the bumpy road and the clinking of his spurs. The thought again passed through his mind that he ought to turn off to the right, towards the infantry regiment. But it wavered and did not seem to take root, and instead he found himself saying happily:

"Really I have been amazingly lucky not to meet a single soul. I think it really must be true that I was born under a lucky star!"

He wanted to laugh and to start running, in order to arrive more quickly, but the road began to ascend again, and the going became rough. Apostol had to stop twice to wipe the perspiration from his face. Finally, he arrived in a glade where the road disappeared.

"I believe there is a parting of the ways here," mused Bologa, trying in vain to find the road again.

The tops of the fir-trees were outlined black against the sullen sky, showing by a wavy line the margin of the glade. Apostol made his way towards the lowest point where another valley should start. And as he entered into the wood he felt, indeed, under his feet a beaten track. He stopped to rest a minute and to wipe the perspiration off his face and neck. Suddenly he held his breath and listened. Behind him in the glade he heard footsteps. He flattened himself against a thick tree-trunk. The steps seemed to come nearer, and he caught a few foreign words spoken in a smothered voice. Two shadows were moving along the outskirts of the wood; they were going away from him. Apostol waited a little while. His heart was beating violently. Again the map appeared before his mind. The infantry trenches were on two peaks, the Rumanian trenches were lower . . .

"Then perhaps I am on the other side already . . . perhaps I have crossed our lines!" he thought with a thrill of joy, forgetting his fatigue. "The Lord be praised! Now the worse danger is over. O Lord, do not abandon me!"

He crossed himself, thrilling with relief and gratitude, and his lips muttered fragments of prayers.

He went on, his heart aching with joy. After a few steps he caught his foot in a rotten tree-trunk put across the road as if on purpose. He skirted it. Ten metres further on, however, another tree barred the way. Then a little farther on he came upon some barbed wire stretched across and twisted round the trunks of the fir-trees. He tried to slip through the barbed wire fence, but found it impossible. Hoping to find a way in, he turned towards the left. He went on about thirty steps and found a gap. On the other side of the fence he turned to the right and went straight on in order to get back to the track. He couldn't find it again. He went straight on and once more found himself facing a wire fence.

"This is apparently a dead angle which they have shut off with several rows of obstacles to prevent surprises," Apostol said to himself patiently, with unshaken trust.

He again turned to the left and kept alongside the wire fence, reckoning there must be a small gap somewhere. After ascending for about ten minutes it occurred to him that he was probably straying too far away from the bottom of the valley, so he retraced his steps to try the other side. He now went right down into the valley and up another slope, a steeper one. The forest here seemed denser and younger. From time to time the low branches clutched at Apostol's clothes like hands trying to stop him. The ascent tired him. He kept on mopping his neck with his damp handkerchief, and the hot sweat rolled down incessantly from his hair into his collar and down his back.

At last the forest became less dense and the wire fence disappeared at the foot of a steep which rose towards the sky like a wall. Bologa halted a minute to get his breath and to cool himself a little. At the base of the steep he found another track. Relieved and rested, he started down the valley and descended for about five minutes. Then the track skirted a rock and narrowed into a corridor with the walls of the steep on one side and the trunks of the fir-trees on the other. For the first time Bologa began to feel really tired. His feet ached and his knees felt strange. He had got out of practice of long marches, and to-day he had walked a great deal. His hair was wet, and from under the hot helmet the perspiration oozed and trickled down his temples. He took his helmet off because it felt so tight that he simply couldn't bear it on any longer. He took hold of it by the chin-strap, and as he walked swung it rhythmically to and fro in his left hand. Suddenly the helmet struck against something with a metallic sound. Apostol stopped in surprise. He put out his hand. A fir-trunk so resinous that his fingers got sticky, and again the barbed wire—three rows with frequent entanglements. Bologa became uneasy. He had hit on the track used by the reconnoitring patrols in the valley between the two enemy lines. Suppose he ran into a reconnoitring patrol. For a moment he thought of turning back as far as the point where the barbed wire ended, and there going down into the valley to cover up his tracks. He could wait in the wood even until daylight if necessary, protected and sheltered. . . . Nevertheless he continued on his way, as if that thought of turning back had concerned someone else, not him.

The track again ran round the foot of a rock, and Apostol banged right into a tall man, who, jumping backwards, shouted in a hollow voice:

"Halt! Wer da?"[1]

The voice seemed familiar to Apostol. He answered:

"Offizier."

A short, suffocating silence followed. Bologa's eyes searched the darkness keenly. Then suddenly an electric pocket-torch shot out a streak of white light and the voice that had spoken sounded again, clearer this time, reflecting surprise and satisfaction:

"Ah! Bologa!"

Now Apostol recognized Varga's voice, and under the helmet, which gleamed in the reflection of the rays, he could see his round eyes, like two black glass beads. And all at once a

---

[1] "Halt! Who goes there?"

violent shudder ran through him, as if he were a sleep-walker who had awakened from sleep on the brink of a precipice.

Lieutenant Varga wavered a few seconds, mumbling. In his right hand trembled the barrel of a revolver, with its muzzle pointed straight at Bologa. Then he shouted in a voice like a knife-blade entering living flesh:

"Disarm him, corporal!"

A puny soldier stepped out from behind Varga.

Apostol murmured lazily:

"I am not armed."

The man stopped two paces away. Varga hissed impatiently, furiously:

"Corporal! Search him!"

Apostol said nothing more. The hands of the soldier ran over his pockets, quickly, nervously.

"May you live long, sir, he hasn't any."

"Four men to act as escort!" shouted Varga again curtly and icily. "The corporal to walk behind!"

Apostol Bologa flattened himself out against the rock to make way for the lieutenant. In passing him Varga turned his face towards Apostol, who felt his harsh, cutting, stinging breath.

Then the streak of light was swallowed up in the maze of darkness.

BOOK IV

§ I

A POSTOL Bologa walked serenely, as if all his troubles were at an end. The sweat had dried on his face and neck. It crossed his mind that he might catch cold, so he put on his helmet, carefully adjusting the strap under his chin. He remembered the barbed wire fence, and fearing he might scratch himself he kept his right arm motionless. He stared straight ahead of him, his head erect, his wide-open eyes drinking in nothing but darkness. Behind him he could hear tired pantings, and now and again the chink of arms. Before him walked an under-sized soldier, and above the soldier's helmet he could see Varga's silhouette, blacker than the darkness. He kept on treading on the heel of the soldier in front of him and continually wanted to apologize, but found himself totally unable to unclench his jaws in order to speak. In point of fact, no one uttered the slightest whisper; it was as if nothing had happened and as if nothing were about to happen. But every time Apostol distinguished the lieutenant's silhouette just one thought would leap into his mind:

"At last . . . at last . . ."

He felt a strange relief, exactly as if he had had a happy escape from a great danger. The road back, though ascending, seemed to him much easier going than it had seemed coming down. Only the time seemed not to move at all, as if a heavy hand had stopped the works of the divine timepiece.

Presently a few rifle-shots rang out somewhere nearby in front. The sound was repeated by echoes more and more faintly.

"We have arrived! Thank God!" said Bologa to himself, as if the crack of fire-arms had announced a great joy for him.

But his joy was soon swamped by a multitude of thoughts set free by the echoes of the shots. He realized that he had been caught trying to get across, and fear gripped him. He reproached himself for having gone off without considering what he was doing, and without a weapon, so that now . . . He suddenly felt so tired that all his thoughts merged into one torturing desire to rest. The roof of his mouth was hot and parched, and he was again wet with perspiration. It was on the tip of his tongue to ask if they still had far to go. Gnawing fear possessed him that they would never arrive, and again that they would arrive only too soon.

"At last, at last," buzzed again through his brain in answer to all his confused thoughts and feelings.

Then the convoy halted in a glade. Varga retained two soldiers to escort the prisoner, and he ordered the remainder of the patrol to return with the corporal to the squadron sector.

Apostol, a soldier on either side of him, followed Varga, who was now walking faster and with more confidence. In the wood the road was wide and easy going, and descended at a gentle incline. After a few minutes they skirted a hill. Among the sparse tree-trunks glimmered wavering spots of yellowish light. Here and there, like buffaloes at rest, were black huts half buried in the ground and camouflaged with dead branches and twigs. A sentinel with fixed bayonet demanded the pass-word, and Varga without halting threw him a word. From a dug-out situated on the very margin of the road issued a real concert of snores. They turned to the right, and suddenly Varga muttered, "Halt!" Bologa and the soldiers halted, and Varga entered a hut. After a few moments, however, he returned, and a voice from within could be heard clearly saying:

"Yes, that's it, Varga, you hand him over to the regiment naturally with the usual formal proceedings."

They went on for two minutes and arrived at the regimental command post, a large hut made of thick planks and surrounded by smaller huts. Varga descended into the large hut, where he stayed somewhat longer. He came out accompanied by a wizened, sleepy officer, who was grumbling crossly:

"The best would have been for you to keep him with you in your sector until the morning. If you are going to keep on rousing me from my sleep for every little unimportant matter . . ."

"If you'll take the responsibility I'll let him go!" said Varga irritably, more especially because the adjutant was saying this in front of Bologa. "I have done my duty."

"Duty, duty," murmured the officer sullenly. "Day and night . . . duty . . ."

About thirty paces farther on they all entered a large dug-out lighted by a large oil-lamp. In front of a telephone apparatus dozed a sergeant with the ear-phones on. On a plank-bed snored three other non-coms., all on their backs with mouths wide-open and faces shining with sweat. In the corner, on a table covered with documents, lay an open register. The telephone officer woke up with a start and turned an alarmed face towards the entrance.

"Call up the officer on duty at headquarters, my lad!" said the vexed adjutant, and immediately took up his grumbling again. He addressed Varga, but his eyes were on Bologa, who stood between the two soldiers with a bewildered expression on his white face, furrowed by sweat and making him look as if he had shed tears.

While the telephone officer bellowed into the apparatus the adjutant stopped his grumbling all at once, and laying his hand on Varga's arm muttered in a different tone, almost astonished:

"One can see he's been through barbed wire. His clothes are torn. . . . He may be injured?"

Varga glanced quickly at Bologa, knitting his brows; then with a shrug he said:

"He may."

At that minute Apostol, as if he had felt their eyes on him, raised his own and looked at them. Varga turned his head away and crossed over to the telephone officer.

"I am dead-beat," muttered Apostol in a strange, cracked voice, meeting the adjutant's eyes. "My legs cannot support me any longer. May I sit down over there for a little while?"

"Yes, yes; why not? Do!" stammered the adjutant, as if startled by his voice. Then he added in a firmer tone, addressing the soldiers on guard: "Just shove that man's feet on one side!"

"Sir, here is the division, the division is at the other end!" shouted the telephone officer, getting up and taking off the ear-phones.

Apostol Bologa, exhausted, sank down on the corner of the bed. His soul was full of gratitude, and his dry lips mumbled unconsciously:

"Thank you . . . very good . . ."

After a moment he felt better, and began to look round and to ask himself perplexedly: "What am I doing here?" He saw the adjutant standing at the telephone, and Varga next to him bending forward slightly from the waist, listening. Then he heard the adjutant speaking and listened carefully:

"A patrol—in charge of an officer—of course—has caught an artillery lieutenant who was trying to desert to the enemy. What was that? What's his name? Lieutenant Varga in command of Squadron III. . . . Oh, the prisoner? What's the prisoner's name, Varga?"

"Bologa, Apostol," whispered Varga.

"Lieutenant Bologa, Apostol—Bo-lo-ga, of the Artillery. . . . I don't know—yes, yes, of course. . . . Now what are we to do with him?—with the prisoner, I mean, of course. . . . What a question! . . . Naturally we must send him to you, but I want to know what we are to do now, *now*? . . . What? We are to send him along now? In the middle of the night? . . . Oh, yes! I see. . . . All right, all right, I understand. Varga is to write out a report explaining the circumstances in which he caught him, and to make a sketch of the place? That's it, isn't it? Naturally the report is to be handed to us and then we are to hand it on to you . . . Very well! . . . I beg your pardon? . . . Search? . . . Documents? . . . I don't know. Varga will do all that is necessary. All right, all right. . . . Good night!"

Handing the receiver to the telephone officer, the adjutant explained to Varga:

"You heard? I repeated on purpose so that you should hear. You are to have him searched in case he has documents or arms, or goodness knows what. . . . So you'd better sit down over there and write out your report! But make it short, without rigmaroles! I shan't wait because I feel absolutely dead. . . . The telephone officer will give me the report to-morrow morning to send on in the proper form. The prisoner remains here under the guard of your men, and you are responsible for him."

"As soon as I have finished my report I take no further responsibility," answered Varga shortly. "At most I can leave you my two men, but only until the morning, and only on the condition that you don't send them off somewhere on some errand or other."

"Oh, very well, I'll take the responsibility. You all run away from responsibility," grumbled the adjutant; then, looking at the prisoner, resumed: "He doesn't look as if he were likely to run away. . . . And, anyhow, where could he run to?"

Apostol smiled gratefully and wanted to tell him not to worry, for now it was all over. But the adjutant buttoned up the collar of his coat, saying again grumblingly:

"You woke me up for . . . You soulless creature! . . . Well, good night everybody!"

Lieutenant Varga was filled with a vague embarrassment. He felt he ought to ask the prisoner a few questions, to find out what had been his intentions. It even flashed across his mind that perhaps the man had not even intended to desert, but had lost his way, not knowing the ground. Otherwise why should he just choose to go through his own sector, more especially as he had once threatened him? He went to the table, cleared a space, got writing materials out, still wavering. Then suddenly he turned and said to Bologa, irritably and harshly:

"Turn out everything you have in your pockets!"

Apostol, with the remainder of the smile of a little while ago still on his face, got up and emptied his pockets. A soldier took the contents from him and put them on the table. Varga watched from under his eyebrows. The prisoner's calm annoyed him. He was on the point of telling the soldier to see if . . . Then he relieved his anger by muttering an oath under his breath and, sitting down, began to examine every article. When he saw the map with the positions he could no longer restrain himself. He jumped up and, waving it at Bologa, shouted:

"And what about this?"

His eyes flashed with contempt, hate, and triumph. Then he wrote out the report and made a sketch calmly, with easy conscience, while Apostol, sitting on the edge of the plank-bed, racked his brain in vain trying to guess what the sheet of paper which Varga had brandished at him could possibly be.

After he had wrapped up all the prisoner's belongings and handed them to the telephone officer Varga ordered the soldiers to be very careful of their prisoner and to take it in turns to watch, and afterwards not to waste their time there. While he talked to the soldiers he was busily doing up the buttons of his coat. He put on his helmet, drew on his lined gloves, and against his will looked at Bologa. He was thinking that he ought to say something to him, a word of reproach or contempt, in order to humiliate him. And instead he said softly:

"You see, Bologa? Do you remember when I warned you in the train, and after I . . . I am sorry that . . . I have done my duty—only my duty, as every man the world over should do, no matter where or in what circumstances."

His eyes encountered the other man's tired and troubled gaze, and his last words faltered with uneasiness. He took a step towards Bologa to put out his hand. But realizing abruptly what he had been on the point of doing, he passed on without another glance in the prisoner's direction. And on going out he coughed as if he wished to clear out from his heart all traces of emotion.

Apostol sat on the corner of the plank-bed like a block of stone. Behind him the heavy snoring, like rusty saws at work, began again. One of the soldiers squatted down in the angle by the door with his rifle across his knees, and immediately fell asleep. The other stood first on one leg and then on the other, his eyes fixed immovably on the nail from which the lamp hung. The telephone officer looked round frequently, burning to know more, but not daring to ask anything.

The tranquillity and light flowed into Apostol's soul as into an empty vessel. Fatigue had killed all his thoughts. He lifted his left hand to take off his helmet and heard a ticking sound. He caught sight of the watch on his wrist and murmured, pleased:

"Fancy, my watch is still . . ."

He looked at the white face.

"It is only one o'clock. . . . Only . . . which means it is seven hours since . . . seven . . . seven."

He forgot entirely what he had wanted to say. His arm fell limply on his knee. Then his lids closed, and his head, terribly heavy, sank on his chest.

§ II

At half-past six Apostol Bologa, escorted by four soldiers, in charge of a second-lieutenant, started for the headquarters of the division.

"If we could only come across a cart of some sort, perhaps round by the artillery, it would be a good thing," said the second-lieutenant with a backward glance as soon as they were on their way. "We'd get along more quickly and we would not tire ourselves out!"

And indeed, quite near Klapka's dug-out, they saw several carts ready to start, and the second-lieutenant immediately began to argue with a sergeant and to point out to him why it was imperative for him to give up one of his carts to them as far as Faget. The sergeant had belonged to Bologa's battery, and seeing his former commander between bayonets, lost his head, and could not follow a single word of the second-lieutenant's explanations, and kept on muttering:

"Please, with all submission, we . . . orders please—with all submission . . ."

The second-lieutenant lost his temper and began swearing and raving at him, saying he could not imagine that there existed a sergeant so stupid that he could not understand such a . . . At that point Captain Klapka approached the group, a sheet of paper in his hand. When he recognized Bologa he stood transfixed. The second-lieutenant hastened to get first innings and told the captain what a perfect idiot the sergeant was, and asked if he might have a cart, telling him what he knew about the prisoner. Klapka stood there a few moments, apparently listening to the lieutenant's prattle but not hearing a single word. His arms and legs shook as he stood there staring at Apostol with horror in his eyes.

Then, cutting short with a gesture the young officer's tale, he went quickly up to Bologa and said, his face distorted with fear:

"So you tried all the same? Ah me! My foreboding was only too true! I dreamt of you again last night."

Apostol looked at the ground and shrugged his shoulders. The captain stood wringing his hands and mumbling all sorts of disconnected words, words of pity and horror, waiting in between, as if he expected Bologa to answer him. Suddenly he remembered that this man was under arrest for a terrible crime and that by standing there talking to him he risked being compromised, as had happened to him once before. He wanted to go away, but he could not.

"I'm going to defend you, Bologa!" he murmured with a sudden resolve in which all his fears melted away. "I want to save you! Do you hear? You *must* be saved!"

Bologa shuddered and looked at Klapka incredulously with a curious interest, as if he were seeing him now for the first time in his life.

"Yes, yes . . . of course," he whispered with a voice like a long-drawn-out sigh.

"You poor unfortunate!" said the captain, again shaking his head, and then added: "Courage, courage, Bologa!"

And he walked away quickly towards the command post without another backward glance.

The cart arrived quickly, and at first they had to keep at a walk, for the descents were stiff and the slopes many. The second-lieutenant, very talkative, tried to converse with Bologa "to pass the time and forget our troubles". He told him he was a Transylvanian Saxon, son of a peasant from a village near Brasov, half Rumanian and half Saxon. He would have been fairly well off had not his father married three times and had a child by each wife, so that now everything would have to be divided into three when the old man died. His two half-brothers, older than he, had stuck to the plough. Now, of course, they were also fighting, but both were alive. He himself had liked study, and he was a graduate of the Commercial Academy in Vienna. He had had a job as accountant kept for him in a bank in Sibiu. He had barely started there when the war broke out and his career was ruined. If only there were something "doing" in the Army! A military career would not be so bad either. Having finished his biography, he tried to find out how and when Bologa had been caught, and why he had been trying to desert. Because Apostol was not very communicative the second-lieutenant began to tell him of various "cases of desertion".

"In fact, in our own regiment we had one, not very long ago, about four months ago, a standard-bearer of Polish origin—a good fellow. God knows what came over him; anyway, they caught him and he confessed honourably: 'Yes, I wanted to desert.' And all the same he was just shot! You see? Because simple desertion is punished by shooting, that is to say it is a quasi-honourable death—a military death. At bottom there is no difference between the bullets of the execution platoon and the enemy's bullets, except as regards calibre and quality, is there? Of course, when desertion is complicated by treason or some other capital crime, then the halter comes into play, and that without hope of escape. In such a case no court martial even debates the question, for the code is explicit: the halter! I know of a case in point—it was when I was with the IIth Division in Russia—a typical case, I might say . . ."

The road was level now, and the driver whipped up his horses. The cart began to rattle and jolt so much that the second-lieutenant in the excitement of telling his tale bit his tongue badly. His face turned crimson with the pain, and he cursed under his breath. He tried to continue his tale, but the jolts maimed his words, and he was forced to keep silent. At last, fearing that his tongue was bleeding, he began to spit out towards the river which flowed on the right side of the road, exactly as the soldiers spat when they had a chance of a peaceful smoke.

The noise of the wheels and the jolts of the cart cleared Apostol's mind.

"To-day at nine I was to condemn again. Now others will be condemning me!" he thought without fear, with almost a thrill of pleasure; and then: "I wonder who'll be taking my place?"

He tried to answer this, and thought of the various officers quartered there and of their rank, and of all sorts of unimportant things in connection with them. Then he forgot why he was worrying about the officers and remembered Ilona, and then the hanged men in the wood along the highroad. With a rather vague, not quite conscious, tinge of regret he thought: "We shall not be going past their houses now, and I don't expect I'll ever see Ilona again, but we have to pass the hanged men, and I'll never be free of them!"

The sun shone hotly from behind. The forests on the mountains quivered under the caresses of the rays. Along the stony road the little stream, with silver glintings, ran noisily down into the valley like a turbulent child. From the jolting cart the fixed bayonets rose threateningly towards the heavens.

Near the bridge over the river, when they turned into the main road, Apostol looked towards the right, trying to catch a glimpse of Ilona's house, but Lunca was hidden behind a hill.

And soon they approached the wood with the hanging men. Apostol did not want to look at it again. He bent his head low, and through a space between two of the planks forming the floor of the cart he watched the highroad running away under them. As soon as the tired horses reached the shade they slowed down until they were going at a walking pace. When the second- lieutenant saw the hanging bodies he could not hide his amazement, and even a certain delight, as if he had discovered some great novelty.

"Just look, just look! How interesting!" he shouted, looking attentively now to the right, now to the left. "Keep them at a walk, lad, so that we should see better, for it really is very interesting. We at the front live as under the earth; we have no idea what's going on in the world. They must all be spies, surely. Yes, spies of course, and traitors. Just fancy! Let's see how many are there? Wait a minute . . . three . . . seven. Bravo! Our general *is* going it! Well, well! There's no bunkum about *him*!"

He laughed noisily and widely, and turned to Bologa to ask what he thought about it, forgetting that he was under arrest. But seeing him with head bent low, his long, thin, white neck showing, he suddenly remembered, checked his mirth abruptly, and filled with shame shouted violently to the driver:

"Let them go, you fool! Do you want us to dawdle along here till noon? Or is it that you've never seen any hanged men before? You fool, you!"

Apostol, his eyes fixed on the floor of the cart, saw, through the space between the planks, lying on the highroad which was running away from under them, a crooked, dry twig, in shape exactly like the branch on that tree on the left on which one man only had been hanged. A sudden strange fear ran through him, and, as if he were uttering a prayer, he began to mutter, moving his lips:

"O Lord, O God . . ."

By repeating these words with feverish hope, confidence re-entered his soul, and he said to himself, raising his head towards the sunny blue of the heavens:

"Why should I die? I don't want to die! Life is beautiful. . . . Life!"

Now he felt an urgent need to talk, to come to life again, to show that he was alive. He looked at the dumb second-lieutenant, and said with smiling eyes and tense voice, as if he were announcing some incredible news:

"The weather is beautiful, isn't it? The whole world is always beautiful—the whole world."

The second-lieutenant kept silence, confused. Apostol took hold of his arm and went on hurriedly, afraid lest he might forget what he wanted to say:

"You were talking just now of various cases of desertion. . . . Well, comrade, you are still young and . . . Do you know that to-day at nine I was supposed to sit on the court martial?—to judge, of course . . . Does that not sound absurd now? I sat once before on a court martial—a very interesting case. A Czech second-lieutenant, a man called Svoboda. Do you understand? Svoboda . . . Czech . . . hanged!"

The cart jolted so terribly that Apostol's thoughts became muddled. He knew this, and yet persisted obstinately in continuing to tell the second-lieutenant about his "case", and to explain to him that his intention . . . The jolting became even worse, and Apostol began to feel unhappy because they would be reaching Faget before he would have time to explain things clearly, so that the second-lieutenant should understand the exact state of affairs, just as if the latter had been a judge on whom his fate depended.

§ III

Almost on the same spot where he had stood in talk last night with the prosecutor and the burgomaster, Apostol Bologa, now in the midst of four soldiers with fixed bayonets, waited for the return of the second-lieutenant, who had gone to announce the arrival of the prisoner. At the back of the courtyard the same two cars and motor-cycles, outside the barn with the prisoners stood what looked like the same sentinel, in the corridor and before the door on the left the same crowd of soldiers. And the trees in flower behind the outhouses, and the well with its sweep in the middle of the courtyard. Only the sun shone more brightly, and the people in the courtyard, at the windows, and even in the street, stopped to stare at the officer with dirty, torn clothes, with face haggard from fatigue and excitement, who stood between the bayonets.

All these staring eyes were like arrows shot straight into his heart, and once again he began to mumble: "Lord, Lord!"

as a protection against the terrible shame which sapped the strength of his whole being. He kept his eyes fixed on the plum-trees in flower which rose above the roofs at the farther end of the courtyard, and so did not see the grave-digger Vidor, who, coming out of the burgomaster's house, approached bareheaded, unable to believe the testimony of his own eyes, horrified.

"What has happened, sir?" stammered the gravedigger, halting a few paces away. "We thought you had gone home last night because of Ilona. And now . . . My God, what a misfortune!"

"Yes, because of Ilona," answered Bologa, starting and turning his eyes on Vidor with a flicker of joy. But at that very moment it flashed upon him that the paper which Varga had brandished in his face last night was the map of the front with the positions of all units, and he wondered what Varga had meant by brandishing it at him, and why had he mentioned the map especially?

"Back! It is not allowed!" growled a grumpy soldier at the grave-digger, who had tried to come nearer, and who recoiled at those words as if stung by an adder.

The second-lieutenant appeared amongst the soldiers grouped round the doorway, and signed to the escort to bring their prisoner over.

In a room full of writing-desks of all shapes the military prosecutor stood waiting impatiently. He had been informed during the night and had everything ready to speed things up. At last he had an exceptional "case"! He rubbed his hands and walked backwards and forwards, continually colliding with the corners of the desks. He looked pleased and excited. On one side, at a desk, sat the ashen-faced sergeant-major, twisting in his hands a pen-holder fitted with a new nib.

When Bologa entered the prosecutor took up his position behind one of the desks, listened gravely to the second-lieutenant's report, took over the parcel with the "objects found in the prisoner's pockets", and signed a formal receipt. But as soon as the second-lieutenant had departed the prosecutor's face again reflected such satisfaction that Apostol smiled at him trustfully and with relief.

"Well, sir," said the prosecutor blandly, exactly in the same voice as of yesterday when Bologa had arrived in the car, "we must proceed quickly and systematically and not lose any time, must we? Take it all down, sergeant-major! You, please sit down there, nearer!"

While the prosecutor was dictating to the sergeant-major the usual introductory phrases Apostol Bologa sat down on a chair between two writing-desks, feeling calm but dominated by an annoying feeling of shame. The prosecutor read twice Varga's report, nodding with satisfaction, then opened the parcel, examined every article with minute care, smiling to himself now and again like a man who sees his deductions confirmed, and so grows in his own estimation.

"And now please give me brief, soldier-like answers to the questions I am going to ask you," murmured the prosecutor, without looking at him, and continuing to examine the "exhibits".

Apostol, filled all at once with a violent desire to unburden his heart, answered hurriedly, barely keeping control of his tongue, trying at each question to explain to the prosecutor secret spiritual impulses. But the prosecutor cut him short continually with new bewildering questions, adding that clear, precise facts only were of interest to him, not explanations. As he talked Apostol became worked up, his face flushed, and a strange light flamed in his eyes. At last the interruptions got on his nerves to such an extent that he got up and in a shrill voice said:

"Captain, I do not wish to conceal anything—not a shadow—not a detail which can contribute to the clearing up of—the situation! On the contrary, I want to open out my heart to you as to a father confessor, so that you should be able to understand how my spiritual equilibrium was disturbed."

"Please remember that I am merely the judge who wishes to get at the truth and not a father confessor!" answered the prosecutor with a cold and slightly mocking smile. "So far we have one point gained, viz. the acknowledged attempt to desert, is that correct?"

Bologa, startled by the quality of his smile, was silent.

"As I was saying, confessed and acknowledged," resumed the prosecutor. "Motives? H'm! . . . I hope we'll discover the motives also in time. Please give me tangible things, not . . . spiritual equilibrium! In any case, being nominated to sit on a court martial, you must own, cannot be a motive for desertion to the enemy, can it? If your conscience had found that the accused were innocent, you were perfectly free to say so. To mete out justice or to punish the guilty is no crime but every man's duty. In this respect you, a man who had studied much, who would have been called upon to-day or to-morrow to play a leading part in society, you especially should have . . ."

"Sometimes it is more terrible to judge others than to be judged oneself!" said Apostol, as if the great light had been kindled in his soul.

"Yes, of course, if someone . . . But more of that later on!" said the prosecutor, again rubbing his hands. Then, picking up the open map and holding it under the prisoner's eyes, he added triumphantly: "And this, how does it fit in with the tale of spiritual equilibrium? Would you kindly explain that to me?"

Apostol paled. In a flash he remembered how he had lied last night, saying he had forgotten something, and how to substantiate his lie to Ilona he had taken the map, and yet now he realized that even as he was slipping it into his pocket he had felt that he must have that map, that he would most assuredly need it.

"That is the official sketch necessary to my work," he began, looking down at the map and seeking instinctively the road by which he had meant to cross over and the spot at which he had encountered Varga.

"I know, I also am a soldier," answered the prosecutor with scorn. "But how did it get into your pocket? And just when you were trying to desert to the enemy?"

"Because . . . because . . ." stammered Apostol confused, the blood mounting to his face; and then breaking off ashamed, for once again he had been on the point of lying.

"I'll tell you why," resumed the prosecutor, looking at him long and searchingly. "Because you did not want to go empty-handed! Isn't that it?"

Bologa made no answer, and did not even waste another glance on the prosecutor, who, after a short pause, continued, folding the map and throwing it on the desk:

"And now I am also going to explain to you the real motives which you are trying to hide under fairy-tales of spiritual equilibrium!"

Before Apostol had actually arrived the prosecutor had discovered "the real motives" and the cross-examination had merely confirmed his discovery. The seven hanged men, together with the twelve waiting out there in the outhouse, were members of a vast organisation of spies and traitors, nested in the very heart of the division, owing to the indolence of the general, who would not listen to his counsel. Naturally such a criminal body could not have worked so secretly except under particularly clever leadership. Those caught had refused to confess their guilt, even in face of the halter—a marvellous proof of the solidity of the organization. His secret ambition had been, right from the start, to get hold of the leader of the band. This might even win him a decoration, apart from the prestige it would assuredly give him. In fine, Bologa! The prosecutor only marvelled that the thought had not struck him before, so that he could have had him watched. Bologa, a Rumanian, on the Rumanian front— what could be clearer! If chance had not unexpectedly come to the help of justice the criminal might have continued to operate without interference! An officer with decorations, a hero—who was to suspect him? His nomination to sit as a member of the court had upset all his plans. How was he, the leader of the band, to condemn his accomplices? It would have meant running too great a risk; any of the accused, seeing him on the jury, might have revolted and torn off his mask. Rather than expose himself to so risky an eventuality Bologa had chosen the best way out, namely, flight to the enemy, whom he had served faithfully, and where no doubt rich rewards were awaiting him. For that reason he had also taken the map on which he had marked not only the positions of the troops but the exact locality of all the different services of the division, even this very house where the prosecutor's office was, in order that the enemy aeroplanes should be able some day to drop bombs on this very spot, and kill him—the prosecutor—also.

Apostol Bologa listened at first with amazement and bewilderment to the prosecutor's reasoning, but after a while he smiled incredulously, as if he were listening to a curious tale. But when at last it dawned on him that it was a serious matter, and that his life hung on this "reasoning", it seemed to him that he had been trailing his soul in the mud for the last hour, and a feeling of unutterable disgust for everybody swept over him. Henceforth, whatever the prosecutor said no longer interested him. He turned his head away and looked out of the window, and his eyes fell on the kiosk which the burgomaster had pointed out to him yesterday as a place where he could sleep. "Well, the doll's-house won't be empty any longer," he thought, seeing an armed soldier standing in the corridor of the kiosk, his head almost touching the roof.

The prosecutor tried to get something more out of him, but Bologa did not utter another word.

"Very well, you are not obliged to answer," said the prosecutor, unruffled, blinking rapidly. "We have sufficient proofs, and we'll have plenty more. That's all right. Now read the statement and sign it, please."

Apostol did not move. The prosecutor considered him awhile, controlling his irritation, and then said, his eyes like slits:

"Of course I can't force you to sign. But don't think that this will obstruct the course of justice! . . . That's all right! Don't think perhaps that . . ."

He broke off, and turning to the sergeant-major, added:

"You'll take the accused to his prison; for the time being I've finished with him. I hope you have made the necessary arrangements? Then you'll leave at once for Lunca, you'll carry out a minute search of the accused's quarters, and you'll bring back with you all his things, and more especially all documents and papers you find!"

Outside the soldiers crowding in the doorway made way for them. The May sunshine kissed the prisoner's cheeks. In the middle of the courtyard General Karg, gesticulating violently, was arguing with a colonel. The sergeant-major saluted very smartly. Apostol felt acutely the general's furious and indignant gaze, but he did not flinch. In going past the burgomaster's house he came face to face with the grave-digger Vidor and the burgomaster's wife. They looked at him with eyes full of fear and compassion. He answered with a confident smile, as if he meant to tell them that all this was of no importance whatever.

He walked up the steps of the little house and now saw at close quarters the petrified soldier in the corridor: tall, very thin, and lanky, his face wan and yellow, his clothes filthy and several sizes too large for him, he was doing his best to look martial. The sergeant-major threw open the door, allowing Apostol to enter first.

"If you desire anything will you please call me? I am sending you coffee immediately, or would you prefer tea?"

He waited a minute, but receiving no answer he went out, pulling the door to. He turned the key twice in the lock and then fastened a large padlock to the door. His instructions to the soldier were purposely given in a loud voice to enable the prisoner to hear: the soldier was not to budge from the corridor, was to look in through the window from time to time, and was to call him (the sergeant-major) if anything happened. The soldier had to repeat the instructions three times. Then the sergeant-major ran down the wooden steps.

§ IV

Apostol Bologa had remained stock-still in the middle of the little room, his eyes turned towards the tiny window near the

305

door. He started when he heard the key being turned in the lock, and he listened to the instructions given to the sentinel without moving, as if he had been glued to the spot. He then heard first the sergeant-major's departing footsteps on the wooden stairs, then heavy footsteps in the corridor, and finally he saw framed in the window a little square piece of the soldier's greenish tunic rucked into folds by the black cartridge-cases, and the rifle-strap clutched by a gnarled, chapped, and very dirty hand.

He took stock of his surroundings. His eyes wandered to the table fastened to the wall, to the bed in the corner with bedclothes turned down, to the stool at the foot of the bed, to the wash-stand in the other corner. Slowly, noiselessly, he took off his helmet and set it down with care on the stool. He smoothed back the hair on his temples with both palms, passing them over his temples again and again, as if he wished to alleviate a pain. Then he walked to the door, four paces, and came back to the table. It was obviously long since the walls had been whitewashed and the whitewash was peeling off. He rested his hands on the ledge of the table. The boards did not meet well, and the space in between was filled with black dirt, although it was obvious that the table had quite recently been scrubbed with lye and sand. On the edge nearest the wall, in letters carved with a pocket-knife was written: "Here I have suffered . . . days."

"The Bosnian standard-bearer," thought Apostol, remembering the burgomaster's words. "Why doesn't he say how many days?"

His brain felt so numb that his thought trailed off. He realized this, and moved backwards and forwards several times to bring back consciousness. The face of the prosecutor appeared before him. He sat down on the bed, swinging his legs from the knee. Now the window was a wooden cross in a white square.

"The outer wall of the prosecutor's office," thought he, and as the face reappeared before his eyes he muttered rhythmically: "The idiot! The idiot! The idiot!"

Then all the other events since his encounter with Varga came back to him one by one. The seconds filed past in his soul, each one teeming with life—like glass bubbles through which the contents were visible. But they went past with dazzling speed, like a film worked madly, and nevertheless each one was terrifyingly distinct. There were thousands, perhaps millions of them, and they flashed by in the twinkling of an eye, and returned the very next moment, unending, untiring. And he rummaged amongst them, and as he watched them murmured:

"A second more powerful than a man's life."

Presently he thought that what he had said was incorrect, and shaking his head he added:

"Man's life is not without but within—in the soul. What is without is unimportant—it has no being. Only the soul exists . . . When my soul will no longer be, all the remainder of me will cease to be—all the remainder . . ."

Through the window he saw two soldiers go through the courtyard holding hands. And the trend of his thoughts changed.

"And yet it is the remainder of me that decides the fate of my soul. And the remainder of me depends on something else. Everywhere dependence. A circle of interdependence in which each link prides itself on its absolute independence! Only God . . ."

The key turned twice in the lock, the door opened, and a soldier put a loaded tray on the table. The sergeant-major, before relocking the door, said respectfully:

"There is coffee or tea—for you to choose from."

With hands resting on the edge of the bed, with his feet hanging down motionless, Apostol stared hard at the tray on the table. He remembered that he had eaten nothing since yesterday midday. He got up and drank the tea greedily. Afterwards he was overcome by a heavy torpor. He no longer cared that he was locked up in a small room with a sentry standing outside the door. He stretched himself on his back and shut his eyes. He stayed like that, his mind empty, for a time that seemed to him an eternity. Then he glanced at the watch on his wrist.

"Eleven!" he thought disappointedly. "Hardly an hour since I am here. If the time is going to drag like this I'll go out of my mind!"

He jumped off the bed and began to walk backwards and forwards, trying to understand clearly just how he stood. The thoughts in his brain were disconnected and confused, but the fear and anxiety in his heart was strong and clear. He now knew that something horrible was in store for him, something that threatened the very foundations of his being. With his back to the door he stood staring into space, and all at once the thick branch of the tree which had held only one victim appeared before his eyes, like an arm pointing to a fixed goal in the future. He wanted to shriek, to protect himself, and with great difficulty he managed to keep on walking to and fro more and more rapidly, clenching the hands which were crossed behind his back. He tried to find a defence against the prosecutor, and found it in his past actions.

"A brave deed surely counts for more than a momentary lapse," he murmured with renewed confidence. "Every fighter knows that brave men have moments of weakness. But just one lapse cannot wipe out a whole life of deeds, no matter how hard the prosecutor tries to disparage me".

Gradually he grew calmer. Love of life found constant arguments and proofs in his favour. Afterwards a new life would begin from the very foundation, built on realities, not on chimeras. All his past life had grown from a diseased root which he must tear out from his soul at once. He needed a different soul, free from everlasting doubts and maxims capable of facing the world as it was, not as a morbid imagination pictured it. Meditations merely provoked conflicts with the world.

"A lot will depend on who will be the members of the court," he switched off, curbing his thoughts. "And also on the counsel! Who is going to defend me? Oh, yes—Klapka. Did I tell the prosecutor? It was his first question, and my first answer."

Klapka? Perhaps it would be better to have some brave soldier whose words would move and carry weight with those on the jury. Klapka? Perhaps it was due to Klapka himself that he was where he was. It was he who had come along with his Forest of the Hanged, and had trickled doubts into his heart. Life was a declivity with one end in heaven and the other in nothingness, and man had to make immense efforts to keep his footing, and if once he slipped no one could restore to him his equilibrium.

"I cheated myself with words, as if life could be guided by words!"

And then in thought Ilona appeared before him, and at once he felt a beneficent warmth, as if her face had filled his heart with a vivified love, like a giant light in which all men and the whole world were comprised. Cheered, his eyes aglow, he whispered unconsciously:

"Love lives for ever; it has no beginning and no end. Through love you get to know God and you ascend to the very heavens." He sank for a few moments into a deep peace over which his soul floated serenely like a leaf on the mirror of waveless waters.

Then he shook himself, and again began his perambulations through the little room, listening to his footsteps, which rang on the floor with the regularity of a pendulum.

"I have lost my balance," he said to himself bitterly. "The mind with its laws and discipline collapses like an engine into whose works a lump of rock has been hurled, as soon as it comes face to face with the wall which divides existence from non-existence! I'll sleep and let things go their own way!"

He threw himself again on the bed, trying to banish the thoughts which nevertheless would come to torture him like merciless foes. At intervals outside noises came to their help: the changing of the sentinel, the hooting of a motor, an angry shout. Then the midday meal . . . And again thoughts . . . thoughts all the time.

Towards evening he heard the footsteps of the sergeant-major: perhaps the prosecutor had sent for him. He would be glad. It would mean a little respite from the tyranny of his thoughts. The sergeant-major pushed the door open and remained in the corridor. On the threshold, carrying a wooden tray on which she was bringing his supper, Ilona appeared! Apostol sprang to his feet, transported as in face of an alluring apparition. Ilona went to the table, set out the plates and knives and forks, her eyes on him all the time. Her cheeks were wet with recent tears, but her eyes and lips smiled encouragingly, humbly and shyly, trying to hide their horrible fear. She emptied the tray and then stood there a moment immovable, murmuring several times in a soft undertone:

"God will . . . don't worry . . . God . . ."

Then she went out with eyes cast down. Apostol saw her descend the three steps. He rubbed his eyes bewildered. The sergeant-major entered and, lighting the lamp hanging from a beam, said in a low voice, so that the sentinel should not hear him:

"The burgomaster plagued me so much and the lassie cried so much that at last I gave in and allowed her to serve you. The girl swore she would kill herself if I didn't allow her to . . . We are but human, sir. Only I beg you to be careful. If the captain got to know it would be the end of me, for he is implacable."

Bologa stood there like a wooden post, his face illuminated by a great joy. He no longer felt alone, and his soul flamed with hope. He whispered in an ecstasy of prayer:

"O Lord . . ."

§ V

The next day, the very first thing in the morning, Klapka arrived, agitated and overwrought. The sergeant-major, watch in hand, remained outside with the sentry, near the closed door.

"We have at most one hour," began Klapka quickly, gripping his hand. "That much time the prosecutor has granted me, and it is exceptional at that. But I don't even need more, for I know everything . . . everything. I am here since last night, and I know all the details, not only from the 'dossier' compiled by our good magistrate . . . When it got about that I was your counsel I was besieged by the grave-digger, and the burgomaster, and the little lass—your betrothed. Poor girl! What a heart! Now I no longer wonder that you . . . Now I understand perfectly. They consulted with me as to what they could do to save you. The grave-digger, a big-hearted man, offered to knock down noiselessly the back wall of this little house so that you could run away. Childishness of an old man! The burgomaster's wife threw herself at the general's feet last night, wept, and begged him to forgive you. They say that the general thinks an awful lot of her, because the woman cooks him really royal meals. All she could get out of him was a promise that he would not act against you, but would allow the court to judge independently. Which means your fate and your life lie in the hands of the members of the court. With a vigorous and subtle defence I hope we shall avoid . . . But your statement is terrible and revolting! It is simply thrusting your head into the noose, Bologa, of your own free will! It is lucky that you had the presence of mind not to sign it. That is why I asked for a supplemental examination, and after tremendous efforts I succeeded in obtaining it. Now you have to do your share; you understand, don't you? First of all you'll repudiate your first statement, and strenuously, mind you; then you'll deny firmly that you intended to desert to the enemy. The remainder will be my business. I'll find plausible explanations for your losing your way at night on ground unknown to you. I hope even to be able to explain away in my speech the map, on which the prosecutor means to base his charge of espionage and treason. We must hope, Bologa! That's all we can do!"

While he had been talking Klapka had drawn the stool up to the table and had sat down. Apostol, calm, his back to the window, stood staring down at the carved inscription on the edge of the table boards: "Here I have suffered . . ." When the captain stopped speaking and waited expectantly, Apostol said shortly, looking him straight in the eyes:

"When shall I be tried?"

"In three hours' time. . . . Yes . . . at ten . . . without fail," stammered Klapka, surprised.

Bologa's eyes went back to the inscription; he spelt it out and resumed softly:

"Then why is there any need to . . ."

He broke off, but Klapka had understood, and he leapt to his feet, stung almost furious. He seized Bologa by the shoulder and shook him, hissing:

"Wake up, man! Are you mad? Don't you understand what is awaiting you?"

"Death," said Apostol, again looking straight at him with the ghost of a smile on his lips.

"The halter, Bologa! Do you hear? The halter!" whispered the captain, turning red and staring against his will at Bologa's neck encased in the high collar of the tunic. "Only a madman thrusts his head into the noose when life is full of promise for him. It is your duty to live!" he added more quietly after a pause, patting him on the back. "When you are offered an almost certain loophole of escape, you have no right to refuse it; you are not entitled to! I have also been in the same situation: perhaps mine was not quite so serious, not quite. I could see the gallows in my cell, yes . . . and I know that if you contemplate death too long and too profoundly it begins to look alluring. But you must tear yourself away from its allurement, Bologa, for any kind of life is better than death! I have told you so before. Life is real, whereas beyond death . . ."

"How do you know that beyond death there is no real life?" asked Apostol in drawling, lazy tones. "Had you come yesterday with your loophole perhaps I would have embraced you and you would have lifted a stone off my heart. For yesterday life tortured me horribly—with ghastly red-hot irons! But last night I saw Ilona, and I found myself again, I found love again. . . . Otherwise how could I have endured a whole night here, alone? Now my soul is at peace. Why should I begin torturing it again? I do not desire anything more. Love is enough for me, for love embraces alike men and God, life and death! The Great Love

313

is here in this little room. I breathe it in all the time. It is in me, and around me, in the whole of the infinite. He who does not feel it does not really love. He who does lives in eternity. With love in one's soul one can go through the portals of death, for love rules also beyond death, everywhere in all existent and non-existent worlds. Life may tempt me again, I may still have to suffer, but . . ."

Klapka listened to him impatiently, anxiously. Bologa's words seemed to him to be the result of the fear of death. At last he interrupted him.

"My dear fellow, you don't realize you are rambling! A man may indulge in such phantasmagoria when he is at home or in his office, at rest, or in moments of enthusiasm, or in a debate, but not in face of death!"

"A phantasm which reconciles the soul is all a man can achieve in life!" murmured Apostol with shining eyes.

"But, my good fellow, you are going to die as a deserter, a spy, and a traitor—in short, as a criminal, not as an apostle of love," raged the captain, adding: "And let me tell you if you continue in this way I am going to declare you insane in court, and shall save you all the same!"

"A criminal?" repeated Bologa gently. "Any grave is an abode of love, because . . ."

"That's enough! Shut up, Bologa!" exclaimed Klapka indignantly. "I am not going to listen to your nonsense any longer. You can tell me all this afterwards, when the danger is over!"

"Do you think a life tainted with lies would have any attraction or value?" asked Bologa in a different tone.

"The lie which can save a man's life is worth more than all the truths!" answered the captain with decision. "I shall do my duty to the end! I'll save you even against your will, and I am sure that later you'll thank me! For your sake I am braving all the suspicions that surround me. But I don't care! Only don't put a spoke in my wheel! That's all I ask of you! The prosecutor will be coming. . . . Help me! I implore you! Good-bye—may God make you see clearly!"

He pressed both his hands and gazed at him long, with encouragement and affection, as a father at a thoughtless child. From the door he again whispered:

"Courage, Bologa!"

The sergeant-major saluted, and as soon as Klapka had gone down the steps rushed into the little room and looked round searchingly. The prosecutor had ordered him, again and again, to keep a sharp look-out lest the prisoner should attempt to commit suicide. Now he trembled for fear the captain had left him some weapon. Though he could not see anything in the least suspicious, he said beseechingly:

"Do not ruin me, sir, I beseech you! I'll do all I can and more, only do not ruin me, sir!"

Apostol understood and smiled. He answered with a shrug, and being tired lay down on the bed. He rested for about ten minutes or so, and then began to walk up and down and across the little room. Thus the prosecutor found him when he arrived carrying a fat portfolio under his arm. He ordered the sergeant-major to close the door and to remain inside.

"Your counsel," said the prosecutor coldly, gravely putting his portfolio on the table, "has informed us that you have further very important statements to make, which could modify radically my conviction, even as regards the qualification of your action. Although I do not hide from you that I doubt this, nevertheless with the permission and by the order of His Excellency I am ready to put down anything you may still have to say . . ."

"I have changed my mind. I have nothing to add!" answered Apostol quickly, as if he were afraid of being too late.

The prosecutor, who had just signed to the sergeant-major to go to the table in order to write, turned sharply to Bologa, at first surprised and then with an expression of satisfied triumph.

"I was sure of it!" he exclaimed conceitedly. "I told Captain Klapka so . . . Don't I know the psychology of guilty men? In any case, it would not be dignified for an officer, even in your case, to have recourse to falsehood. A man should have the courage to bear the consequences of his actions!"

Apostol could not restrain a smile at the prosecutor's maxims, and more especially at the martial tone in which he uttered them. The prosecutor, however, delighted as he was, did not even look at him, and made his way to the door. He remembered that he had left his portfolio on the table.

"Oh yes, we must not forget," he said, hunting in the portfolio and drawing out a letter. "Here you are! This was found yesterday at your rooms; probably it only arrived yesterday. I could not give it to you until I had found someone to translate it, for it is written in Rumanian."

When he was left alone, Apostol drew out his mother's letter and read it slowly, carefully, as if he wished to understand it well or register it in his heart. He read it a second time and still could not understand a word. The words penetrated his brain without sense, like lifeless signs. While his eyes had slipped over the black lines, in his mind there was only one thought, dominating and perturbing:

"Now I am floating between life and death, between heaven and earth, like a man who, having cut the branch from under his feet, is waiting to fall, without even knowing where he will fall."

§ VI

"Bologa, I implore you, help me!" whispered Klapka in the prosecutor's office—transformed into a court of justice—just before the proceedings began.

Apostol's eyes, red-rimmed with dark circles under them, seemed more deeply set in their sockets, and his cheeks were of a transparent pallor. On the tip of his tongue lingered the salt taste of tears, the roof of his mouth had that parched feeling which follows sleep haunted by nightmares. But in his soul peace had settled down.

He looked round curiously, as if he had never been there before, although the room was as it had been yesterday, except that the desks had all been pushed to the back, in order to leave more space round one single long table covered with a green cloth and divided in the middle by a cross of white metal. Apostol examined all the officers who sat round the long table, stiff, straight, solemn, and almost frightened. He was glad when he saw that the president of the court was the colonel with the rugged face whom he had met in the general's compartment, that time in the train, and who had taken his part. Now he seemed paler, and in his eyes there was something . . . The others he did not know, not even by sight, except Lieutenant Gross, who kept his head down as if he were ashamed. Apostol stared at him hard, wishing to meet his eyes and to ask him how it happened that he had consented to judge a comrade, and to show him that he, in any case, was neither a charlatan nor mad, for rather than condemn again he had run away.

When he heard his name called out in a loud voice, he gave a surprised start. Why did they call out his name? He answered "Present!" and did not even grasp the situation when the colonel asked him unusual questions, as to a stranger. Nevertheless, without thinking of what he said, he answered correctly, looked the colonel straight in the eyes, realized that his life was in the balance, and seemed to hear a strange rustling of wings which wafted a cold wind through the room. But into his heart there trickled incessantly from somewhere drops of bitterness from which a creeping fear spread all over his body like some loathsome pulp. He tried to keep it off and could not, and because of this he felt that he would have to burst into sobs. It seemed to him that the president talked so drawlingly that a century passed ere he finished uttering a question to which he himself answered in three lightning words.

Then someone near the prosecutor's little table began to read something for some minutes, in an odd voice, pronouncing the words strangely.

"Now tell us the motives and circumstances of the desertion!" said the colonel, moving his lips stiffly, like an automaton.

The question fell on Bologa's ears discordantly, like a knife which falls on a bottle and breaks it. And this sound awoke all his thoughts and feelings, sharpening them like knives, ready to cut up his body and soul. He looked towards the window and encountered the head of the prosecutor, proud and self-satisfied, as if long since he had solved all the secrets of the world. So much self-satisfaction annoyed him, and so he turned his eyes in the opposite direction, where Klapka, the defending counsel, sat. Klapka, wishing to encourage him, tried to signal to him, but this resulted in such a strange grimace that Apostol shuddered and immediately felt abandoned and alone, as if he were on a limitless prairie full of poisonous weeds and thorns. And yet, simultaneously, all his anxieties disappeared and his soul was filled with an immense trust.

"Desertion?" he whispered, gazing with shining eyes at the white cross in front of the president.

Then he bent his head and in the bitter silence which followed his question floated for a few moments like a gentle reproach. And again came the voice of the colonel, shaking as if some unseen hand had gripped his throat:

"Answer my question, Lieutenant Bologa!"

And after a silence still more painful and threatening, the voice went on, still wavering:

"Guilt, of course, is inexcusable, but the court will listen with great care to your defence. Therefore speak!"

A soft rustling movement filled the short pause. Then, like a bullet, the voice of the prosecutor shot out indignant, mouthing his words, which echoed round the room, rose to the ceiling, then fell like blows on the heads of all those present. Then Klapka's voice, pathetic, protesting, insistent. And both voices worked their way into Apostol's heart, like the worms of two gimlets, and unable to bear them any longer he murmured, without raising his head:

"Hurry, hurry, for God's sake!"

Although his throat was dry and the echoes of the two voices that had been speaking still lingered in the air, his whisper buzzed long in the ears of all present, and drew all eyes on him, expectant and perplexed.

Other questions followed rapidly, the tone growing harsher and more peremptory. These dug themselves into his heart like sharp claws and pressed at his throat, stifling him. When he felt he was choking he started up terrified, yellow in the face. The collar of his tunic seemed to him an unbearable rope. With a desperate wrench he tore open his collar and shrieked hoarsely:

"Kill me! Kill me!"

His gesture and outburst caused amazement and indignation. The colonel sprang to his feet with flashing eyes, and banged with his fist on the table, while Apostol fell back in his chair in a heap, breathing heavily, his face the colour of slaked lime, his red-filmed gaze glued to the white cross.

Quietness was soon restored in the room and everybody regained his former grave composure. The incident was discussed for a few minutes, then the proceedings—which had been disturbed for a moment by the writhings of a human soul—went on. Apostol sat on his chair, quiet and motionless. In his ears buzzed words and phrases which did not interest him at all, for the cross on the table was pouring balm into his soul.

Then all at once the president called out sternly:

"Has the accused anything more to say?"

Bologa heard and understood the question; but he made no movement, as if the matter did not concern him at all.

"The discussions being ended, the court will now deliberate!" said the colonel angrily.

The president made a sign, and the sergeant-major approached Apostol.

"Is it over?" he asked, starting up from his chair so violently that the sergeant-major was alarmed. "Yes? Is it over?"

He bowed low to the court and went out hurriedly, briskly.

§ VII

"Well, sir, that's over too! Now you'll feel easier!" said the sergeant-major with a mysterious smile, when they had reached the little room. "There is your luncheon waiting; it has probably got cold."

Apostol looked hard at him and wanted to ask him something, but before he had framed the question in his mind the sergeant-major had gone.

"What was it the sergeant-major said?" thought Bologa, left alone. "Perhaps he knows something. He has been long at this job and has seen many cases."

When he realized what hope was connected with that thought, he put it away from him, mumbling:

"What nonsense! Just fancy what nonsense I am thinking now . . ."

He threw his helmet on the bed and gave a short, dry, hollow laugh, rubbing his chest with the palms of his hands, as if he were trying to stop the throbbing of his heart. In doing this he heard in the pocket of his tunic the rustle of paper, and stopped suddenly.

"Now, let's see mother's letter and understand it."

Doamna Bologa wrote just unimportant things about Parva, about people he knew and people he didn't know. That Palagiesu went about boasting that Apostol had apologized to him, that Marta constantly came to see her and still considered herself his fiancée, that Domsa still called her *cuscra*,[1] that she had made lots of good things for the Easter festivities, but that they would probably remain untouched, as she was alone and depressed, for she had dreamed a very horrid dream about him on Good Friday, and had had a special Mass said on Easter Sunday that the good God should protect him from danger.

---

[1] Name given to a woman related by marriage.

"Poor mother!" thought Apostol with a sickly smile. "If she only knew in what danger I am now! When she'll hear the news! She must hear it from me, so that she may at least know that it was she who soothed my heart during my last hours on earth, as she did during my first hours!"

He drew the stool to the table and while he ate some of the food, that had got quite cold by now, he read the letter several times over, stopping each time at the horrid dream and trying to guess what his mother could have dreamt about him.

When the sergeant-major arrived with a soldier to clear away, Apostol asked for paper and ink. A few minutes later the white sheet of paper on the table laughed up at him like a gleam of hope, but he was no longer in a hurry to write. He paced backwards and forwards, his hands behind his back, his thoughts in a whirl. Every time his eyes fell on the paper the thought flashed through his mind that he had always, before entering into action, when he had felt the fear of death in his soul, sat down and written long letters to his mother, bidding her farewell. He always wrote then in fear and anxiety, and yet while he wrote he always read hope in between the saddened words. Love of life was then stronger than fear of death. Then, after the danger was past, he would read over his "testament" and smile happily as he tore up into shreds the sheets covered with gloomy thoughts. How many such "testaments" he had torn up! But now he had to write a definitive testament. Now at any moment the prosecutor might come to read out a few paragraphs to him, informing him that at such and such an hour he would die without fail, without the tiniest hope of escape. And exactly at the fixed time a few men would force his young soul to part from his body for ever, at a fixed hour— now when he would have written the letter he would know for certain that the hands which had written it would never tear it up and his eyes would not see it again, because to-morrow at this time his body would be buried in the ground or would be hanging somewhere, and his mind, that realized all these things now, would to-morrow no longer give birth to a single thought, for it would be nothing but a small heap of dead brain covered with clotted blood.

And still the paper gleamed white on the table, as if there were still some hope somewhere. Apostol Bologa unearthed remembrances of novels and tales he had read in which, at the supreme moment, a messenger on a galloping horse arrived bringing a pardon and life. This cheered him for a few minutes, and then he exclaimed angrily:

"I'll die for certain in . . . in how many hours?"

And then terror gripped him, more and more fiercely and wildly, turning his blood to ice. And while this terror was upon him his mind tried to drive it away by telling him that death had to come to everyone, that this life was not worth anything, for had not he himself cast it away believing in the life to come, where his redeemed soul would be united unto God. But all the inventions of his mind tumbled down like castles built with playing-cards—only horror remained defiant, dominating, whispering into his soul one single word before which everything fell: Death. He felt like weeping, but could not. He looked at the time. It was four o'clock in the afternoon.

"And they haven't yet told me what my sentence is! Why doesn't the prosecutor come? At least I'd know for certain. But come to think of it, why should I know?"

The certainty would probably increase the tortures of terror. Better so. Any delay was a respite—even from suffering. Besides, the delay might mean something favourable. Why should not the court have grasped that he was innocent? Perhaps it would have been better if he had spoken, testified. But why should words be needed when his past spoke for him, if only through the four medals for valour? In such cases the court's duty was to send the imbecile prosecutor packing and to acquit unanimously; or at least by a majority of votes. The colonel had taken his part that time in the presence of the general. Gross could not vote for condemnation, then there would surely be someone else of the president's opinion—behold, the majority! That, then, was the meaning of the delay!

The sheet of notepaper under a dirty, rusty inkstand still gleamed white. Apostol, feeling cheered, went to the table, sat down on the stool, took up the penholder, and tried the nib. His fingers trembled frightfully, and he could not form a single clear thought.

"Later . . . there is still time!" he said to himself after a while quietly, and again began to walk backwards and forwards.

After a quarter of an hour he stopped dead near the foot of the bed, every drop of blood drained from his face, his eyes fixed on the door, in which the key was turned with a more grinding noise than usual.

"Now I shall know!" darted through his brain like a tongue of fire, and he almost felt the cells of his brain being destroyed.

It was the sergeant-major with a soldier carrying the supper tray.

"Have you finished writing?" he asked, without looking at Bologa.

"No, no, I haven't even beg . . ." said Apostol, all of a sudden very agitated, adding quickly with eyes starting out of their sockets: "Is there so great a hurry as all that? Has the sentence been decided, has . . . ?"

"Of course the sentence has long since been decided," answered the sergeant-major slowly, with an odd ring in his voice. "They are merely waiting for sanction from the top—from general headquarters. Such are the regulations for officers . . . But it won't be very much longer now. . . . No—no. . . . The answer is due to arrive any minute, for in war-time and in cases like this things move quickly. In war-time things happen quickly."

Apostol Bologa could see that this man knew his fate, he longed to question him but had not the courage. The soldier went out on tiptoe, as if he were in a house of mourning. Then the sergeant-major said in a lower voice:

"The little lass is weeping and carrying on fit to break her heart, poor soul! But I can't, sir. Please forgive me and don't be angry! I would have allowed her to come, as I did yesterday, but the captain keeps on hanging round the courtyard, and if we should be caught . . . God forbid it should happen! I'll light your lamp when the lad will come to fetch away the plates, for it isn't quite dark yet."

The sergeant-major's voice lingered in Apostol's soul like a source of luminous hope . . . even after the door had closed behind him. His heart beat with renewed strength. He was sorry he had not sent a kind message to Ilona, but consoled himself with the hope that perhaps very soon he would be able to give her his messages in person.

"Who knows?" he thought more cheerfully. "Only God knows what the hour may bring."

He looked hopefully at the window with the brown cross. The twilight was furtively putting up the shutters of night.

§ VIII

After midnight Apostol Bologa, utterly exhausted, stretched himself on the bed. An intense stillness surrounded him, as if the whole world had fallen into a sleep of death. The yellow light from the ceiling shone in his eyes and made them smart. He dozed.

All at once he woke up. Footsteps sounded suddenly outside on the stairs and in the corridor. He leapt into the middle of the little room and remained transfixed there with shrinking heart, murmuring with white lips:

"O Lord, my God . . . My God . . ."

The door opened wide, violently, and banged against the wall. Out of the darkness appeared the military prosecutor, holding a sheet of paper in his right hand. He wore field dress, and the eyes under the steel helmet looked lifeless. Behind him followed the sergeant-major, also wearing his helmet, and carrying something on his left arm and in his hand. He looked nervous, as if he expected the prosecutor to turn on him at any moment. In the darkness beyond the door many heads seemed to writhe with terrified eyes, like apparitions in a tragic ballet.

In the centre, motionless, his long hair slightly dishevelled, Apostol flashed quick glances without moving his eyes in their sockets, at the prosecutor's face, at the sheet in his hand, at the sergeant-major's helmet. And all the time millions of thoughts surged up and died in his brain as if all the atoms of the grey matter had caught fire and were burning with blazing flames.

The prosecutor approached the table, on which the white notepaper still gleamed white, held the sheet under the rays of the lamp, and without introduction began to read carefully, in a clear voice, turning his eyes on Bologa after words on which he laid special emphasis, as if they had been underlined. Apostol listened and kept his eyes on the prosecutor's red, wide, dry lips, over which he passed the tip of a pink tongue now and again. He understood clearly "in the name of the Emperor", "the attempted but unsuccessful crimes of treason and desertion to the enemy", "degradation and dismissal from the Army", "death by hanging".

"The sentence will be carried out immediately!" ended the prosecutor, folding the sheet and stealing a furtive glance at Bologa's face.

"Immediately . . . immediately," repeated Apostol very calmly, thinking: "But at what time? Why doesn't he mention the hour?"

Then he caught a movement of the prosecutor's and saw that the sergeant-major was approaching him so humbly that he seemed a stranger who in some way or other had strayed into this place by mistake.

"In accordance with the sentence—degradation—the military tunic—civilian garb must be worn." The prosecutor had begun to speak sternly, but Bologa's eyes fixed on him put him out of countenance, and he ended up pleadingly. Apostol did not understand, but without understanding he was slowly unbuttoning his tunic. He took off his collar and put it on the table over the rusty inkstand; then he slipped out of his coat, folded it with great care, laid it on the bed, and smoothed it out twice with the palms of his hands. His shirt was damp with sweat and bunched up at the back between the striped braces. He pulled it down and lifted up the braces, which had slipped from his shoulders. Then while he waited expectantly, he caught the prosecutor's eyes looking nervously at his long white neck, with the swollen arteries. He turned to the sergeant-major, who was holding out something towards him, and he noticed that the man was also staring at his neck. He became uneasy, and wondered why they were both staring at his neck.

"The coat and hat are from the burgomaster," stammered the trembling sergeant-major, holding them out with a rapid movement, as if he no longer dared to keep them.

Apostol took the coat and put it on quickly, shivering with cold, but he made no motion to take the hat. The sergeant-major, in a hurry to be done with the business, laid it down gently on the table over the collar, and so covered up entirely the white gleaming sheet of note-paper.

A silence followed in which panic-stricken eyes trembled. At last the prosecutor, steadying his voice a little, spoke, but he became confused, and stammered:

"If there is anything you wish for . . . I . . . we . . . in accordance with the regulations, any wish at the moment of . . ."

Apostol gave him a long, straight, compelling look and then abruptly turned his back on him, as if he had just remembered that on the bed there was something. The prosecutor made a movement of curiosity, as if to see what he would do, but he remembered himself in time and made a dignified exit, followed by the sergeant-major, who pulled the door to gently without locking it.

Used to the sound of the key turning in the lock, Apostol looked round bewildered and whispered:

"I wonder why they haven't locked the door and fastened the padlock? Is it perhaps . . ."

From all the corners of his mind dozens of answers rushed forward with enchanting news. Perhaps now that he was dressed in civilian clothes all he had to do was to put his hand on the door handle and to go away . . . far away . . . to live. Perhaps the sentinel was no longer there either. Perhaps outside Ilona and Klapka and Boteanu were waiting for him.

But even while he was imagining these wonderful things, the door reopened and on the threshold stood Constantin Boteanu, tall, thin, with the stole on his breast, a book under his arm, and a crucifix in his hand. He hovered there a moment mild, uncertain; then he entered, closed the door, and went straight up to Apostol, intoning in a deep voice:

"In the name of the Father, of the Son, and of the Holy Ghost, now and for evermore."

For a second Apostol believed that through a divine miracle his hopes were about to be fulfilled. Crushed by suffering, he fell to his knees, kissed the crucifix passionately, and hiding his face in the folds of the stole burst into loud, stifled weeping. His breast heaved from the violent thumping of his wounded heart, in which the blood raced round madly. The tears streamed on the golden flowers of the stole, which smelt of incense, like the waters of a river which has burst its banks through a violent storm. In between his heaving moans the gentle, consoling voice of the priest percolated timidly into his soul, and gradually from the simple, unprofessional words he uttered there formed in Bologa's soul a calm like a pall of crape, diaphanous, yet sufficiently thick to blacken and turn aside all worldly temptations and vanities.

When he regained his composure and looked up, Apostol's face was as white as the driven snow; although his eyes were red with dark rims under them, a calm light shone in them. He saw thick beads of perspiration clinging to Boteanu's temple, when the latter sat down on the stool by the table. Bologa had lost his hope of just now in a divine miracle, and fearing lest the phantoms he had fought for hours should reappear, he dragged himself on his knees to the priest's feet.

"I rushed over," spoke Boteanu faintly, wiping his forehead with a large handkerchief, "for in Lunca no one knew what had happened to you. And then last night Vidor's girl, your betrothed, came to me and begged me to come quickly and bless you. Ah me, the human heart! Ilona had come of her own accord. The gentlemen here had decided to send you a military chaplain, in truth also a servant of God. We all begged the captain to have pity and to let me come instead . . ."

"Father!" Apostol suddenly burst out anxiously, "I wanted to write to my mother, and look, there is the paper untouched. I could not—because . . . Let her know, Constantin, afterwards—after I'll be—after . . . Tell her how I . . . She is to look after my betrothed— she is to care for her. For the two of them have sown love in my heart—and out of their love I built up my faith, my guiding faith, and . . . and . . ."

He hid his face in the stole, in the faint clinging smell of incense, murmuring disconnected words. The priest stroked his damp hair murmuring:

"In the midst of life's temptations you remained your father's son, Apostol! You did not forget his teachings, but carried them ever in your fiery blood. Do you remember how he used to tell us, every time he came over to Nasaud, sternly and solemnly, as if he had been speaking to grown-up men, 'Never forget that you are Rumanians!' The storms of life sway the human soul, but they cannot eradicate from it imperishable roots! Pleasing in the sight of the Lord God is he who willingly sacrifices himself for the race of his fathers and for their faith for ever and ever!"

"For the race of his fathers," whispered Apostol, burying his face in the smell of incense and forgetting the words immediately, as if his mind could no longer hold anything for long.

Presently the door opened of itself, turned quietly on its hinges, and came to rest against the wall. In the blackness of the doorway stood the prosecutor—a dumb summons. Popa Constantin bent over Apostol's head, gentle as a father who awakens from sleep a beloved little child:

"Arise, my son, and be strong in the hour of the last trial, as was Our Lord and Saviour Jesus Christ."

Apostol Bologa shuddered, but rose at once and looked round with expectant eyes. Seeing the figure of the prosecutor in the doorway, he remembered, and stretched out his arm towards the table for the soft ribbonless hat with worn-out edges. Fie caught sight of the watch on his wrist and sharply drew back his arm. He carefully undid the strap and gave the watch to the priest without looking at the time, saying in a low voice:

"Constantin, don't forget me . . ."

The priest gripped the watch in the palm of his hand under the shaking crucifix. Then Apostol took up the hat, crumpled it between his fingers, and looked perplexedly first at Boteanu and then towards the prosecutor in the corridor.

"Bologa . . . the time has come. . . . Courage!" said the prosecutor, and disappeared immediately.

Apostol went towards the door, crossed the threshold, and at the top of the steps stopped dead, bewildered. The courtyard was full of soldiers with lighted torches and shining helmets, as at a torchlight procession on the eve of some great festival. The torches spluttered noisily with ruddy gleams and clouds of suffocating smoke. The house, with the offices of the division, stood out against the hill-side at the back, and the old poplar-trees which crowned the ridge rose up like black, imploring hands stretched out towards the purple sky sprinkled thickly with stars.

The sight awed Apostol, and all those eyes fixed on him oppressed him. The cold gripped him, he shivered, and with both hands he put on his hat, drawing it right over his eyes so that he should no longer be able to see anything. Then, very agitated, he turned up the collar of his coat to cover his bare neck.

"Forward!" the prosecutor's voice sounded all at once above the spluttering of the torches—somewhere—far away.

Apostol tried to start, but his legs would not move. The priest was at his side. He took his arm, thankful, that he had found a support, and descended the steps. They went on for a while. All around him he heard nothing but the spluttering of the torches and the noise of heavy boots being dragged along with difficulty. Then from the left came a burst of loud, long-drawn-out, shrill weeping, which covered the whole convoy and filled the air like a dirge. Apostol said to himself: "That's Ilona," and gripped the priest's arm harder, but he did not turn his head that way, nor did he raise his eyes.

They came out into the highroad. The torches no longer burned so brightly; it seemed as if their light had become scattered and only the smoke had been left. Behind, the sobs still moaned, but fainter and farther away. Apostol saw that they had turned off to the right; he was surprised, and whispered to the priest clearly and with a tinge of regret in his voice:

"Where are we going, Father?"

In his heart, side by side with the regret, he found a tiny thread of hope which whispered to him secretly, "Perhaps after all . . ." Soon, however, they left the highroad, passed under a brick-built viaduct, then over a tiny bridge of new planks.

"My God, where are we going?" Apostol now asked himself painfully, for he had never been this way before.

He could not feel his legs, and wondered how he could walk without legs, and it seemed to him he was floating in the air as in a dream. He turned again to the priest, who was holding the crucifix before him.

"Forgive me, Constantin, that through my fault you must tire yourself out so . . . tire yourself so . . ."

For answer Boteanu murmured fragments of prayers. Apostol could not understand a word, and wanted to ask him what he had said, but the unknown surroundings vexed him so much that he forgot what he wanted, and thought again, distressed:

"Where are we going?"

For a time they ascended a road which had been cut into the slope of a hill. The streamlet from under the little bridge of new planks now gurgled noisily on the right at the foot of the slope. Hearing people pant all round him, Apostol whispered into the priest's ear:

"I don't seem to have any legs—I seem to be floating." Boteanu uttered his prayer in a louder voice, alarmed at Apostol's words and at the weight which pressed more and more heavily on his numbed arm.

The ascent ended, the streamlet was murmuring again somnolently alongside. To Apostol it seemed that he had been walking for an eternity on an endless road, and once more the question sprang up in his mind:

"Where are we going?" And then the priest seemed to stumble and at once began to pray more fervently and more hurriedly.

"Have we arrived?" asked Bologa, not daring to lift his eyes.

"Be strong, my son, be strong!" mumbled Popa Constantin tearfully.

Then Apostol felt grass under his feet, and all at once his legs began to ache, as if he had been carrying a load beyond his strength.

"Make room! On the other side, Father!" called the prosecutor in a very hoarse voice.

Bologa, not recognizing the voice and wishing to find out who had shouted, looked up and saw barely ten paces away a white glossy post with an arm curving from the top. The halter swayed slightly, and this swaying reminded him how a short while back he had tried with his own hands the strength of the rope. Something strange was being made clear by the white gloss of the wood, and Apostol hastily bowed his head.

When he reopened his eyes he was quite close to the post. His right hand accidentally touched the wood, which was cold and slimy, like the skin of a snake. He felt sickened, and started to wipe off the sliminess on his trousers. Meanwhile he let his eyes rove calmly over the multitude of strange and unknown faces, which hardly looked human in the light of the smoky torches, and hid themselves under the wide-brimmed helmets. The smell of burnt resin tickled his nostrils, and the smoke irritated him because it obscured his vision. He bent his head slightly and saw that the ground at his feet had an ugly, yellowish open wound. The hole did not seem deep, and the clay had only been heaped up on the right-hand side, forming a mound on which the prosecutor stood, towering over everyone else, just as if he were going to . . . On the left, on the margin of the grave, stood a fir coffin, empty and uncovered. The lid, with a black cross in the middle, lay next to a large wooden cross on which was written in crooked letters: "Apostol Bologa". The name seemed strange to him, and he asked himself almost crossly:

"Who on earth is Apostol Bologa?"

"Ready? Ready!" shouted the prosecutor from his mound, waving a sheet of paper.

Apostol listened only to the beginning of the sentence, then he looked at the people nearest to him. The thought passed through his mind that the general had not come, that he was probably asleep. Near the prosecutor's mound he saw a doctor, watch in hand: "It isn't Doctor Meyer . . . no . . . no." At the foot of the grave he recognized Klapka, with swollen and panic-stricken eyes, which harassed him so much that he looked away. Two paces away, on the left, stood a peasant leaning on a hoe. He was bare-headed, and his hair, clammy with sweat, clung to his forehead; his cheeks were wet with tears. "Why, there's the grave-digger Vidor," he thought, pleased, and wanted to wave to him. But just then the prosecutor finished his reading in a shrill, strident voice, like the creaking of a door with rusty hinges, and Apostol, now attentive, asked himself fearfully what would happen next. A moment later he heard clearly behind him a faltering voice saying:

"Must . . . on the stool . . ."

Bologa understood that he was required to stand on the stool, which almost touched his knees but which he had not noticed until then. He was afraid that again he would be unable to move his legs. "I must . . . must . . . try," flashed through his brain. And then, suddenly, he felt someone's arms around him. He was terrified. The grave-digger kissed him heavily on the cheeks, with moist lips and damp moustaches.

"Back!" roared the startled prosecutor, raising both arms.

Apostol stood up on the stool, and his head knocked against the dangling halter. The hat was pushed right over his eyes. He took it off and threw it into the grave. At that moment a deep, desperate, wild sob burst out. "Who's weeping?" thought Bologa. Klapka was beating his breast with his fists.

Then a wave of love, as if issuing from the very bowels of the earth, encompassed Apostol. He raised his eyes towards the sky, in which a few belated stars still lingered. The peaks of the mountains stood out against the sky like a gigantic saw with worn-out teeth. Right opposite, the morning star gleamed mysteriously, announcing the rising of the sun. Apostol fixed the rope himself, his eyes athirst for the light from the east. The earth was snatched from under his feet. He felt his body hanging like a weight. But his gaze flew impatiently towards the heavenly brightness, while in his ears the voice of the priest was growing faint:

"Receive, O Lord, the soul of Thy servant Apostol . . . Apostol . . . Apostol . . ."